Destiny Dollars

Book 2

The Diana Diaries Series

Other Books by Cindi R. Maciolek

Destiny Drop – Book 1: The Diana Diaries Series

Divatiel: Reflections of a bird's companion

How to Screw Up a Good Idea

Tame Those Pesky Details

Java Jems: 5 Minute Inspirations for Busy People

Destiny Dollars

Book 2

The Diana Diaries Series

Cindi R. Maciolek

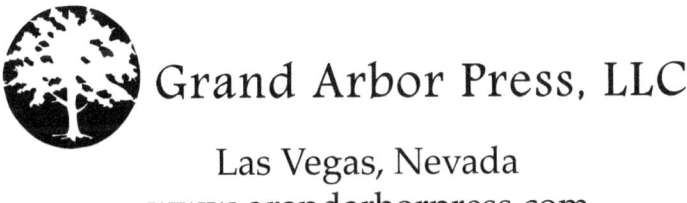 Grand Arbor Press, LLC

Las Vegas, Nevada
www.grandarborpress.com

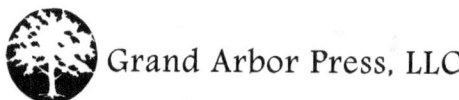 Grand Arbor Press, LLC

Grand Arbor Press, LLC
1930 Village Center Circle #3-388
Las Vegas, NV 89134

Visit our website for current contact information:
www.grandarborpress.com.

Grand Arbor Press, LLC books may be purchased for educational, business or sales promotional use. Please contact the company for more information.

Grand Arbor Press, LLC and the Grand Arbor Press logo are trademarks of Grand Arbor Press, LLC. All other trademarks are the property of their respective owners.

Printed in the United States of America.

First Print Release: July 2017

Credits:
Cover design: Charles H. Small

Print Edition:
ISBN13: 978-0-9647911-9-0
ISBN10: 0-9647911-9-6
Electronic Edition:
ISBN13: 978-1-946509-00-0
ISBN10: 1-946509-00-0

*To those in need of financial blessings –
may they come your way*

Table of Contents

Dear Diary,

Does anyone ever win the lottery? I mean, anyone you know? And, what would you do with all that money anyway? If it's anything substantial, I'd spend it on a house, a car, some travel, trust funds for family members, charitable donations – but that's only like a few million or so. What would I do if I won a hundred million dollars? I can't even imagine.

Sure, I have these daydreams since I'm part of the Lotto Ladies, as I still try to figure out who I'm supposed to become in my new life. I'm certain the world doesn't need me to be the nation's best retail store manager. I'd honestly rather interact with customers than do paperwork. Of course, if the pay was incentive enough…

So many things have changed. I got a new job, albeit in retail. I moved to a new rental – a house! Who knew it would make such a difference in how I felt about myself. And, I'm finally meeting some nice guys. Maybe there's a good man out there for me yet.

Still, I've faithfully contributed my share to the Lotto Ladies, buying tickets with the hopes of someday having the financial freedom to do what I really want – if I only knew what that was. It also means I'm still interacting with some of the staff at *Positano*. I usually like to keep moving forward but the Lotto Ladies has held part of me in the past. Curse you, Jazzy!

I'm studying up on all the feng shui/law of attraction/manifestation principles I can muster, but I'm still working in retail. Having family in town sure does make things better, but it doesn't pay the rent. Maybe there's a pot of gold at the end of this Lotto Ladies rainbow!

More tomorrow!

All my heart,

Diana

The Bod

Dear Diary,

I can't believe how living in a house again makes me feel. Sure, it's not my own. I don't have the money for a down payment yet, but just being in the rental has perked up my spirits.

I discovered that for about what I paid to rent the townhouse, I could live in a single family detached home, with a backyard and everything! There's even a small koi pond with a calming waterfall.

It's about the same size as the townhouse but in a very quiet neighborhood and with great neighbors! And, the floor plan of the house works much better for me. You could have two places the same size but configured completely differently. Some places just make much better use of their space.

I'm also much closer to Helen and Gabe. They're just a few miles up the street. It's been so much fun spending time together and playing with the kids. Now, if we could only get Mom and Dad to move out here, we'd never have to go back to the snow and cold of Michigan again!

Gabe introduced me to a co-worker of his, Tom, who I've been seeing quite casually. Tom is not the caliber of man I'm used to, but he's a really nice guy and treats me well. Unfortunately, he loves horror movies and I can't stand them! I'm a sucker for a happy ending. Of course, I'm still living in this fantasy world of being part of the one percent. Someday, I'll just have to accept I'm perfectly normal!

More tomorrow!

All my heart,

Diana

Hanging at The Bod

{ ONE }

I've seen more naked women's breasts than Wilt Chamberlain, and it's not a statistic I'm proud of.

I finally had my fill at *Positano*. I'd set myself a deadline – September 15 – to find a new job, a real job, and when that came and went with no new prospects in sight, I wasted no time, bit the bullet and opted to look at retail again.

My hope was to find something that utilized my business degree and years of marketing experience in consumer electronics, but given the state of the economy – which has been down in the dumps *forever* – my age and my lack of recent marketing experience, I found myself in the eddy of the underemployed. Unless I wanted to hawk cell phones, I wasn't sure what else I could do in this town in technology.

Once I updated my resume and filled out applications, I could see things from the hiring manager's perspective. I had three plus years of retail sales experience, most of that in lingerie. I sucked it up, gave in to my new reality and put in an application at *The*

Bod in the ever-energetic Runway Fashion Mall, located at the opposite end of where *Bergstrom* is.

While *Isabella's Intimates* is all about sex, *The Bod* is all about comfort and affordable luxury. The store has a slightly older demographic while still appealing to more practical younger women, indicative of their discretionary incomes, not a result of their tastes. No string thongs here but you will find – horrors! – Granny panties!

One appealing aspect to *The Bod* is its green approach to lingerie. All products are either 100 percent cotton (did you know they grow cotton in colors?) or other sustainable fabrics. The quality is exquisite for the price, and the nightshirts are to die for. Everything is soooo soft.

The company also takes a carbon-neutral stance to its business, utilizing solar energy, electric cars and natural gas powered trucks, doing corporate visits via video conference and recycling as much as possible. I thought California was crazy about being green! *The Bod* is over-the-top conscientious about the environment. Honestly, it's kind of a nice change.

Pay here was a bit of a hybrid, matching the company philosophy. I would get paid two dollars an hour more than minimum wage. Plus, there was a bonus program. For example, if I sold more than $150 in a single sale, I received an extra seven dollars in my paycheck. If I sold more than 50 bras in a week, that was worth an extra $10. There was a whole list of opportunities with the bonus structure, but I didn't memorize it. I would do as I always did – sell what the customer wants. See, that's why I shouldn't be in sales!

"Diana, can you help me clear the table?"

Helen got up from her seat, grabbed her plate as well as Gabe's, looked at me with one of those sisterly looks that said I needed to follow her, nodded her head toward the kitchen and started walking in that direction. I followed suit, taking both my plate and Tom's.

"Why don't you and Tom go sit in the family room, Gabe, and Diana and I will bring coffee and dessert."

"Sounds like a plan, honey," Gabe said and ushered Tom into the family room where they immediately set up a video game to play.

"May I please be excused, Mom?" Grace asked. "I want to practice a new dance routine in my room."

"Sure, go ahead, Grace. Do you want me to bring you some dessert?"

"What are we having?"

"Fresh fruit bowls with vanilla bean ice cream."

Both Grace and Justin let out a collective, "Yum!"

"OK, go on you two. Grace, I'll bring dessert to your room and Justin, you can have dessert with us in the family room."

"Cool!" Justin said as he ran off to join his dad on the sofa. Grace made a quick exit upstairs where in short time we could hear her spinning and jumping.

Helen placed the dishes in the sink, took the ones from my hands and placed them there as well. She grabbed dessert bowls from the cabinet and dessert from the refrigerator. We chatted as we filled the dishes.

"So, what do you think?" Helen asked.

"About what?"

"About Tom! What did you think I was referring to?"

"I don't know."

"You don't know about Tom?"

"No, no I don't. He's a little different than what I'm used to."

Helen put one hand on her hip and the other on the counter to pause for effect.

"He's a guy, Diana. Isn't that what you wanted?"

I took a quick look into the family room where the boys were snorting beer through their noses because of some idiotic zombie video game the two of them had bonded over. And, by boys I mean Gabe and Tom. Honestly, they were acting like 12-year-olds when even the 12-year-old on the sofa didn't find it that funny.

"Look at them, Helen! Could you honestly see me married to, to, that?"

The game was now up on the big screen and Gabe and Tom were entranced in zombie land.

"Look how well they get along, Diana. Tom is a very nice guy. He'd fit well into the family, not like some of those brainiac ego-tistical millionaires you date. Tom is just a regular guy with a normal job."

Wow. I didn't know Helen hated the guys I dated so much. To me, the brainiacs were normal, not the Toms of this world. Besides, how many of them had she met anyway?

"I don't even think he owns a suit, Helen."

"Such petty details, Diana. Gabe only owns *one*, for weddings and funerals and other important family events. Otherwise, he's in jeans and t-shirts all the time and overalls for work. What's so wrong with that? Gabe got a tux for our wedding. He knew as much to do that. Tom would do the same."

There was just something about the feel of a perfectly starched shirt wrapped around the broad muscular chest of a freshly showered businessman, monogrammed french cuffs at the wrists of his long, lean arms, beautifully tailored custom suits to complete the package, that held a major attraction to me.

I used to dress the female equivalent of that perfect man. While I was now into the leggings and t-shirt routine when I wasn't working, I could certainly jump back into my pre-downfall mode of designer clothing if I met the right man who could give me that fabulous wardrobe. Tom wasn't it, and I could no longer afford to purchase those sumptuous clothes for myself.

I wanted the perfect couple. *My vision* of the perfect couple. Not a perfectly normal couple. How boring.

"He owns his house outright, has a brand new truck and a steady job with a good salary."

Cheers and screams came from the family room as the boys continued to play their game.

"He bought a foreclosure during the bad economy in a part of town where I wouldn't live…"

"Seriously, Diana?"

"…which is the only way he was able to afford a new truck. Besides, all he talks about are zombie movies and video games. He's obsessed!"

Helen laughed.

"And you're not obsessed with designer clothing and how wonderful your life was in the past and how you are just in this position temporarily until you figure out what you want to do?"

I was a bit shocked at Helen's comment.

"I didn't know my problems were such a burden to you, Helen."

Helen came over and gave me a big hug.

"Diana, you're not a burden. Don't ever think that. I understand that you've been going through a lot since the divorce, but you seem to have been floundering for the last few years. It's not like you, or at least not like you've ever been. It might just mean you're at a different stage in your life and you need to consider someone who's just plain normal like the rest of us."

I looked up at Helen.

"But, he likes zombie movies!"

"So, Gabe loves westerns. Old, black and white westerns. When we have family movie night, once a month we know we'll be watching westerns. But, that's what a relationship is all about. You don't have to love what Tom does, just accept that's who he is and he'll do the same for you. It can work out. Just give it a chance."

Helen gave me those big sister eyes, grabbed two desserts and took them into the family room. I grabbed two more, sighed, and followed.

Maybe Gabe needed to have the same talk with Tom, at least the part about meeting me halfway. I could always close my eyes during zombie movies but he absolutely refused to watch a romantic comedy. I love romantic comedies! There are some I've seen 50 times!

It seems as if I'm just settling into so many aspects of my life. That's not who I am. Yes, Tom is a nice guy. Yes, he'd get along with the family. Well...at least with Gabe and Justin. Maybe Daddy. But I'm the one who has to live with him and if there isn't a connection, I can't create one.

He's an OK kisser – funny, Helen didn't ask me about that! Chris was such a dreamy kisser. I don't think there's a man better. If the kiss doesn't suck you in, the whole relationship will just suck.

"How's your new boy toy?"

"Oh, please, Giz. Tom is not my boy toy."

"Well, it must be nice to have a little male companionship. It's been ages, dearie."

"Ain't that the truth. Good men in Vegas exist but are just hard to find."

"They're hard to find everywhere, Diana. Even in Silicon Valley."

"Yes, but at least there it's easy to find the ones in executive positions. Here, everyone dresses really well or really sloppy. There's not much in between."

"Sounds like Silicon Valley to me!"

"OK, well, at least the really intense engineers are easy to pick out. They're quiet and shy and sit at their desks watching porn when they're not writing code or playing video games."

"I can't believe you said that, Diana! It's not just the engineers who watch porn, you know."

"I know, but I'll never forget that one kid that worked for me. He seemed like the nicest guy but after I fired him and we checked out his computer, it turned out all he did was watch porn all day in his cubicle. No wonder he never got his work done!"

We both laughed. Gizzi remembered when I had to fire my analyst. He was a really nice guy but he never could deliver reports on time. It was hard for me to fire anyone, but I was the boss and I had to do it. It tore me apart for days. I'm not sure I could ever be a CEO.

"But, you are sleeping with him, aren't you?"

"No, we haven't slept together. Don't think it's going to happen."

"Wow! A platonic relationship with a man. Have you lost your sex drive, too?"

"OK, seriously Giz, that's just mean!"

"I know. Sorry, sweetie. I couldn't resist."

"Let's just say that Tom is not up to my standards as a partner and while I have lowered my standards significantly in other parts of my life, I refuse to lower them where men are concerned. He and Gabe get along great but if I hear one more zombie reference…"

Gizzi burst out laughing.

"Sounds like a keeper, Diana!"

"Let's just say he's no Jean-Louis."

If Gizzi could, wherever she was at the moment, she would be rolling on the floor laughing.

"But, let's get serious now. How's work going? I know you were looking for a new job."

"Oh, yes. I forgot to tell you. I'm now at *The Bod*."

"You're working at *The Bod*? Well, I, just don't know what to say."

Thanks, Gizzi.

I could always count on my best friend for support, but as she was now enjoying her status as vice president of sales at the semiconductor company where she's worked for several years, my lowly lingerie job was a little hard for her to accept.

"I can get you a good discount!" was the best I could offer.

Like she needed it.

"No, sweetie, I'm glad you left that chaos at *Positano*, but I didn't think you'd find another retail position. *The Bod* is a great company, but if you want to move up, their corporate headquarters is in Mississippi. I can't imagine Diana MacKenzie moving to Mississippi, even for the best job in the world. Too many mosquitoes!"

"No worries, Giz. I'm not physically moving anywhere. I'm just moving forward in finding my future. I promised myself I'd find a new job and I did. Is this my final destination? I hope not. I'm only in my 30's. I should still have a few more rounds in me!"

"So, is it at least a management position?"

"Hmm…well, no, just sales. But it's a much calmer environment. This is the only store in the area and their management roster is full. I'll have to bide my time, although management here is not really what I'm after."

I took a deep breath, knowing what was to come.

"What exactly are you after, Ms. MacKenzie? I mean, if retail is it, then that's fine. Accept it and use your free time to better yourself, find a good man, join a tennis league – do something! I just want what's best for you, you know that. And, I've finally accepted the fact that you won't be moving back to Silicon Valley."

Well, hallelujah! I never thought I'd hear those words coming from Gizzi's mouth. Every single discussion we've had revolved around my returning to California. Maybe Gizzi's relationship with Jean-Louis was softening her a bit.

"Well, I've looked into all sorts of things. I thought being a mortgage broker might be a good option, but honestly, not until the market recovers. I checked into getting my real estate license which I think is handier than being a mortgage broker, but that's another one of those always-on-call careers like I had as a consultant. Not interested. So, while I'm here at *The Bod*, I thought I'd do some substitute teaching, kind of try it out and see how I like it. Plus, it will bring in much-needed extra cash."

"But, aren't you full time at *The Bod*? How will you manage it all?"

I could hear Gizzi take a long drag of her cigarette. She promised she'd quit smoking before she got engaged, an event we'd all been waiting to celebrate. Perhaps her love of nicotine was keeping her from walking down the aisle. Poor Jean-Louis.

"Actually, no one works more than 24 hours a week except for management. It's just the way they operate. I'm lucky I got the position. The competition to work for this company is tough. I'll just utilize my time well so I can do both. I'll have two or three weekdays free which will make it easy to substitute. There are always positions available."

"Only 24 hours a week? Even during the holidays?"

"I know, it seems strange but there are big periods of downtime and on the weekends we have cashiers who come in to ring our sales."

"And the pay for subbing?"

"Probably about as much as I make at retail on a daily basis. Just a different environment. And, I have to get up much earlier. Some of the schools around town start at 7 a.m.!"

Gizzi laughed.

"Oh, sweetie, you'll never make it. I know how you like to leisurely rise!"

Now I laughed.

"Trust me, I'm not looking forward to it but a girl's gotta do what a girl's gotta do."

"The students will love it. You'll be napping by noon!"

"Well, Ms. Boudrot, I'm glad I put a smile on your face. Now, get back to work. I have cleaning to do!"

"Chat with you soon, sweetie. Ta!"

"Ta."

"So, how do you like it here at *The Bod*?" Taneesha asked.

We were folding nightshirts on the front table, reminiscent of folding countless panties at *Isabella's*. While the quantity was much smaller here, the nightshirts were touched constantly by customers and the table had to be straightened on average once an hour. It stood right inside the store entrance so it could be seen by any mall walker who happened by. The company prided itself on an organized and inviting environment, so that particular table absolutely had to be in order at all times. Contents varied weekly, and this particular week it was nightshirts.

I wasn't quite sure how to respond to Taneesha. At least she wasn't interested in discussing sex like so many of those *Isabella* girls did. Yet, at 19-years-old, she was as young as they were. Her head was just screwed on differently. She was a college student studying accounting and hoped to work either in the fashion industry or one that was environmentally supportive, which made her a perfect fit for *The Bod*.

Taneesha was the store's key holder, an entry level management position that meant she had the keys, 'natch, and was the supervisor on duty when no other manager was working. It also meant that I could point any complaining customers in her direction, not that there were ever that many. As the older worker on the evening shift, most customers assumed I was the manager, but it gave me great pride to turn them over to Taneesha and walk away. The less stress in my life, the better.

Although I had been here two months and we were in the throes of the holiday shopping season, I still wasn't sure how I liked it. The space was small, so there wasn't that much room to even walk around. The staff was much more professional and actually worked as a team, which meant there was little if any drama. However, aside from straightening the front table, most everything else was set up in such a way that the merchandise was well-behaved and needed little attention. So, most of the time, I was actually bored.

The Bod had a very boutique-y feel to it which looked great but also meant that each and every customer needed a lot of attention. If you were in back helping a client with a bra fitting, it was nearly impossible to help another on the floor with anything else.

Just one or two sizes were on display of each item and everything else was under lock and key. A customer would point to the item they wanted, tell the associate what size they needed and the associate would get it for them. *The Bod's* management felt it went a long way to build customer rapport and literally forced one-on-one customer service while alleviating the dreaded nightly straightening session. Of course, there was stocking that needed to be done, but as we were all trained to fold and stock *The Bod Beautiful* way, everything was in order at all times.

The more I thought about it, the more I realized how much I actually hated working at *The Bod*. Some things can be too controlled and it's the imperfections that drum up the interest. I'd dated men before who led very controlled lives and dating them was like beating my head against the wall. At least at my other retail experiences – *Isabella's Intimates, Bergstrom* and *The Shop at Positano* – there was an energy and excitement that didn't even come close to walking through these doors.

The merchandise was fabulous, the décor was interesting and the corporate concern for the environment was admirable, but working here was a yawn with a capital Y. The one nice change? I could get out of those creepy old lady polyester uniforms at *Positano* and wear street clothes once again. Although...I had to buy a new wardrobe. Seems those free lunches in the employee dining room plus my late night beer and breakfast burrito snacks helped me pack on a few pounds. I'll definitely make some changes now that I'm working here and trying to 'get my life together' as my ex-husband, Chris, had suggested.

"Oh, it's great! I've learned so much about sustainable fabrics and non-toxic clothing manufacturing since I've been here. It's a valuable personal education and it's wonderful to be able to help our customers learn more as well."

"I know! And the way the company builds its message into the décor is absolutely ingenious!"

Taneesha had obviously bought into the whole concept and I'm sure once she graduates and becomes a CPA, she'll be heading to Mississippi to work in corporate. Good for her. But, I lied. I had to. I lied about liking to work here because if the manager knows you're not happy then you're not going to be around for very long, even if it's only the key holder you're talking to. I lied about the décor. It reminded me of a mountain cabin with images of fresh water streams and forests and clear blue skies with an occasional cloud that just happened to form the words, *The Bod*.

The wide-plank wood floor could have come from Santa Monica Pier, again giving it that outdoorsy natural feel. And when we weren't playing Christmas music, we alternated the sounds of nature – mountain streams, ocean waves, forest birds and even varying forces of wind. There were times I could feel my head bobbing, and I forced myself to stay awake. I could swear I had those sounds on my sleep machine at home.

"Ingenious doesn't even begin to describe it," I replied. Politically correct without expressing my inner angst.

Taneesha looked up and a smile grew across her face.

"Looks like your customer is ready. Should be a great sale. Her arms are full!"

I looked back toward the fitting rooms and my client was overflowing with all our top-selling merchandise. I met her at the cash wrap in the middle of the store.

"My, you had a lot of success in there," I said. "I'm so glad you were able to find some things you like."

The customer dumped everything onto the counter, pulled a lace hanky from her pocket and wiped her brow, responding in a strong Virginia accent.

"It almost seemed like work in there, but y'all just don't have a store nearby so when I travel I like to stock up for myself and for presents. I love what y'all sell and I much prefer to touch and try on than just order online. I know, I know, I'm one of those people!"

The customer let out a raucous chuckle that even made me laugh. Hell, she was the most excitement we'd had all day.

"I'm a member of the *BodLiving* rewards club, dear. Can you please look up my number and see what coupons I have available?"

Ugh! Those dreaded coupons!

Once a *BodLiving* rewards club member spent $1,000 in a calendar year, their account was loaded with coupons on a regular basis. As items in the store were a bit more costly due to their environmentally-friendly nature, the coupons were a reward for those shoppers who supported the corporate mission and they felt $1,000 was a good baseline threshold. Anyone who spent $5,000 would receive one new free item per month for six months. Not a bad deal, but these natural fabrics tend to last longer than normal so unless you buy a lot of gifts, I'd rather see the company partner with another environmentally-conscious company and reward the client that way. But hey, what do I know?

"Sure, let me look. OK, Mrs. Grantholt, you have three coupons, each $10 off a $100 purchase of regular priced merchandise. Oh, and I see one of them is for your birthday, so Happy Birthday!"

"Why, thank you, Diana! I try to think of this as the 29th time I'm celebrating 29! Well, anyway, can y'all separate this into three purchases so I can use all my coupons? I'm sure there's enough here to handle all the minimum requirements."

I glanced up at Taneesha and she smiled. We'd all been there. That was the way the company operated and its customers were trained well. They knew how to work the system. It also meant that while a large single transaction like this could have resulted in an extra $20 bonus in my paycheck, instead I'll get nothing because not one of the three would at least reach $150. While I applauded the company's environmental stance, *The Bod* still had flaws in its structure. The coupons took money out of their employees' pockets, which was nothing to celebrate.

"Certainly, Mrs. Grantholt. I'll take care of you. We appreciate your coming to see us today and giving us the opportunity to help you."

"Why, Diana, y'all are so sweet! I can see why they hired you. If they ever open a store in Virginia, I do hope y'all will consider transferring. Y'all would do well there, I promise. I'd send y'all all my friends!"

The Bod only had 57 stores nationwide, which meant there were some major shopping areas that lacked a location. The company had only been in business a few years and was intent on growing only if and when they could afford it and demand required it. While a large quantity of their revenue was generated online, many shoppers like Mrs. Grantholt preferred the in-store experience and sought out the stores when they could. While many people came to Las Vegas to gamble, fans of *The Bod* felt visiting this store was the highlight of their vacation

"Thank you, Mrs. Grantholt. I appreciate your thoughts and I'll definitely keep that in mind should the opportunity arise."

I finished her third transaction and took a quick look at her rewards account.

"Wow! I see you're just $400 from the golden $5,000 tier. Care to do a bit more shopping?"

"Oh, my Diana, y'all are quite the charmer, but I fear I can only sneak so much up the back staircase to my closet without my hubby finding out. It will have to wait until my next trip. I think I'm going to Austin next."

Well, what can I say? I tried. I brought the bags from around the counter and handed her purchases to Mrs. Grantholt, just as we were taught to do at *Bergstrom*. She grabbed her bags and double air kissed me before she turned to leave.

"Thank you, Miss Diana! You are quite the superb sales lady. See y'all next time!"

Taneesha approached me at the cash wrap after Mrs. Grantholt's departure.

"Great job, Diana! That sale put us up for the day. You *are* a superb sales lady!"

Taneesha knew her compliment was appreciated but wouldn't help to replace the lost bonus money. At least I could hope we meet our stretch sales goal for the quarter and we would all receive a $250 bonus in February. I didn't know if I would stick around that long so I might not see it anyway. Somehow, no matter who develops the corporate structure, someone gets screwed. At least we get to buy one item at 50 percent off as our Christmas reward.

"Thanks, Taneesha," I said. "Now, let's dust!"

"Lovey, there you are!"

Ugh. Jazzy greeted me as I walked into *The Shop at Positano*, my old stomping ground. It was time for me to make my weekly Lotto Ladies payment and to find out who was going to make the trek to buy tickets. At one point we opted for monthly buys but everyone just got too anxious – or disinterested – and we went back to purchasing them weekly.

"Yep, here's my five bucks," I said as I handed Jazzy the money.

"Great, lovey. Now, there's been a bit of a change. Will you be able to get the tickets this week?"

Hmm…there's been a change. Those words coming from Jazzy's mouth didn't bode well.

"What kind of change?"

I was almost afraid to ask.

"Well, Diana, our group is shrinking. You'll soon be receiving certified letters notifying you that some members have decided to no longer participate."

In our Lotto Ladies contract that I drafted and that each Lady had to sign, there were instructions as to how a member could disengage from the group, relinquishing her claims to any future winnings. A certified notarized letter was to be sent to my business mailing address, something I maintained after my divorce even though it was no longer a Chris requirement. I found that I liked having all my mail go to one location, and I never had to worry about being home should a package or, in this case, certified letters arrive. The employees at Tall Tree Post took care of all that for me.

But, this was troubling. Who could be dropping out of the group? Less money means fewer tickets and fewer chances of winning. Is it worth it to continue?

"Who's withdrawing now? I just received a letter from Lynn. She said now that she's on to her new job she doesn't want to be tangled up with old memories."

"Oh, my, lovey. Lynn dropped out, too? Well, that certainly will make for a much smaller group of winners. Oh, well. More money for us!"

Jazzy was rubbing her hands together with a sinister look on her face. Her actions, coupled with her horrible fake British accent were enough to send me over the edge. Maybe Lynn is right. Why should I continue to subject myself to the likes of Jazzy? Maybe it's time for me to withdraw, also.

"What do you mean 'too'? Who else is leaving?"

Jazzy looked over to the *Genesis* counter before she answered.

"Well, it seems we've had a bit of a falling out with the *Genesis* Girls and they're all withdrawing. And, Polly is stepping aside as well."

Polly is withdrawing? That surprises me. I could understand Tracey, Katrina and Emily stepping away from the group. They're just a different breed than the *Positano* ladies. But, Polly?

"Wow, that's a shocker! Why is Polly pulling out?"

"Polly's been getting cold feet. Now, you know as well as I that Polly sure could use a substantial cash infusion as much as the rest of us, but she's concerned about how management will view her participation with the employee group. She just doesn't feel comfortable with it. I mean, she's not even allowed to eat lunch with us, remember?"

Yes, yes I sure do. But, once we win, I'm certain Polly wouldn't stick around. She should have retired a long time ago anyway. Why would she care what management thought? She'd no longer be an employee, subject to their whims.

"So, that leaves just the three of us – you, Pamela and me. Do we want to continue?"

Jazzy let out one of her shrieky laughs.

"Oh, lovey, it just means less we have to share. Of course we'll continue. I still plan to win, don't you?"

Considering it was my only hope for a secure financial future at this point in my life, I really had no choice.

"Sure, I'd love to win, but how should we handle this? Do you want to increase our weekly contributions? Fifteen tickets a week isn't that many chances. We've been buying 40 a week for several months and haven't won more than about $20. What does Pamela think?"

"We spoke about it but decided to just maintain as we are. Slow and steady wins the race, mate. Slow and steady wins the race."

So, it will cost more in gas to buy the tickets than the actual tickets cost, but, what the hey? You only live once, right?

"Fine. Just the three of us. I'm really not interested in adding anyone else to the group. If we decide to dissolve it, that's okay, but let's just maintain it for now."

"Excellent! I knew you'd come to the same conclusion as we did. Now, since Polly is no longer part of the group, can you take her turn to pick up our winners?"

Sure, why not. From the sound of things, I'll probably end up making the trip weekly. That's me. Everyone's patsy.

"Hand over the envelope. I'll go tomorrow."

"Diana, lovey, when we win, be sure to take out extra for your troubles."

Jazzy handed me the envelope with a mere $15 inside. I spun on my heels and high tailed it out of the store. When we win, I hope it's a big jackpot because I don't ever want to have to see that woman's face again, especially after what she did to me when I waited on slut wife. I can't believe I'm even civil to her. Why does the warrior inside me remain silent instead of telling her off? I'll have to find out Pamela's schedule and pick up the envelope when she works. The less Jazzy in my life, the better.

Dear Diary,

Sometimes my day starts out really well. Then, there are days like today.

I read in the paper that Chris's dream finally came true. His restaurant opened at *UpTown*. He's calling it *Christopheles*. Nope – no ego there! It's supposed to be an Asian/French/Swedish/Greek fusion concept, a nod to all his favorite vacation spots. I'm confused about the menu already but it opened to great reviews and he landed a chef from one of those reality TV shows. Good for him.

The article even identified slut wife as his business partner and developer. Wow! That's a huge change from the type of relationship we had. And, it seems, he's been with her longer than any other woman now, including me. I don't know if I should be happy he finally found the right one or pissed that it wasn't me.

I'm a bit disappointed that I wasn't invited to the grand opening; that I had to read about it in the paper. I mean, after all, we were wed at one point.

Why do I even dwell on it?

It seems Chris is on to a successful Career 2.0 but what about me? Am I still searching for it, or has retail become version 2.0 and I'm already on to the next update – 3.0? I read somewhere that with the portability of retirement accounts and lack of companies offering pension plans, the average worker nowadays will have as many as six different careers over a lifetime. I'm exhausted just thinking about it.

I'm good at nearly everything I try, so how do I decide?
What will really make me happy for years to come?
My brain hurts just thinking about it. Time to do more
self-evaluation. I can't manifest something if I don't
know what I want. Right now, I want a beer. Oh, look.
Here it is!

More tomorrow!

All my heart,

Diana

Holiday Fun

{ TWO }

"Love your new wheels!" Gabe said as he walked around my car, checking it out.

Naturally, once I scored a new automobile, I had to drive over to my sister's house to show it off. Well, it wasn't exactly new – it was another used one – but I bought it from a real dealership, got an actual car loan and it was at least manufactured in this millennium. It was kind of a Christmas gift to myself, finally kissing the old Buick goodbye and embracing a nice, white 2009 Ford Focus which, according to the ad was pre-owned, not used.

My payment was just slightly more than I wanted, but I got the car at a great price. I thought the salesman would cry when I told him my budget was $150 a month and I only had $1,000 as a down payment, plus my lovely Buick as a trade-in. Once he scraped himself off the floor, I showed him the special I saw on the Internet. He worked his magic and got it financed at just $167 per month, something I could live with, although the length of payments might just exceed the life of the car.

I was so glad I waited to buy my sweet, sweet Ford. If I had purchased it while I was working at *Positano* where I had a higher salary, I probably would have gotten a more expensive car with a bigger payment. But, now that I'm at *The Bod* working part-time, I have a monthly payment that nearly anyone could afford – even me!

The fact that I'd been employed at a W-2 job for the last few years instead of my 1099 consultancy helped me to qualify for a loan easily in spite of the fact that the car was already past its prime. In the old days, I could have paid cash for such a miniscule amount, but those days were long gone. And, had I been able to pay in cash, I would never have settled for such a vehicle. Alas, you learn to lower your standards when circumstances change so drastically as mine have. At least I'll have air conditioning come summer!

"I'll bet it even has a CD player."

Gabe loved to razz me about stuff, and my well-maintained but older vehicle was definitely something that amused him. He was the type of guy who had to have a new car every three years. He loved technology so much he just couldn't stand to not have the latest and greatest. If he could afford to do it yearly, he would, although I'm sure Helen would have words with him. She was perfectly content waiting until the odometer hit 100,000 miles or more. Her cars did. Gabe's never made it that far.

"Oh, leave her alone, Gabe," Helen said, coming towards us from the front walkway. "It'll get great gas mileage. It's exactly what she needs right now."

We all hugged hello.

"Oh, c'mon!" I interjected. "It has an engine. It has heat and air conditioning. And, I can flip down the rear seat and haul stuff. It's awesome!"

"It is great, sis. I'm so glad you got rid of that, shall we say, vintage vehicle. I feel so much better with you driving around in a newer car, one that has air bags."

"The best part is I can afford the payments. I never thought I'd be so grateful to do that in my life. When I worked in high tech, no amount seemed too big. Now, everything is huge. It's all so overwhelming."

"But, you're surviving and doing a great job, Diana," Helen said, rubbing my shoulder.

I felt like I was going to cry, all these years of stress and lack of money adding up, but I held my composure. I am a survivor and I will be a success again someday. I'm just hoping to get there soon.

"So, now that you have room to haul things, think you can fit some kids' Christmas presents back there?"

Gabe was laughing. Keeping gifts from the kids was hard for any parent. You eventually run out of hiding places they don't know about.

"I'd be happy to take some with me, but I have to go straight to work from here so they'll be sitting in the car all day. If that's not a problem, load 'em up!"

Just as I finished saying those words, Grace and Justin came running out to see me. I gave them both a big hug and a kiss. I didn't have any children yet and I cherished every moment I could spend with Helen and Gabe's two precious offspring.

"Aunti Di, I love your car!" Justin exclaimed. "I want one just like it when I get older."

"Thanks, Justin. It's pretty cool. Today's my first day with it so I'll tell you all about it on Christmas Eve."

"Awesome, Aunti Di! And it's white, the perfect color for the desert."

"How astute of you, Grace! I prefer red, but I got a great deal on the car, so sometimes you just have to take what's available."

These kids were young but they were both intelligent. Helen had them reading practically out of the womb and in addition to being a techno-nerd, Gabe was a big music fan and played a wide variety of tunes all day long, so the kids got exposed to music and literature from the day they were conceived. I was smart but

I was certain these two would far surpass my own intelligence in an even tougher world.

"Aunti Di, come inside and look at Mommy's decorations!" Grace said, pulling my hand.

I looked up at Helen and Gabe, trying to let them know I was short on time. It was Saturday, one week before Christmas and *The Bod* was calling.

"Aunti Di has to get to work, honey," Helen said, trying to help out.

Grace and Justin made pouty faces.

"Just for a minute, Aunti Di?" Justin asked.

How could I refuse?

"OK, let's go, but just for a minute. I have to get to all those crazy Christmas shoppers at the mall!"

We ran inside to see the most magnificent and wonderfully decorated home for the holidays. I felt like I had stepped onto a movie set. The freshly cut tree practically touched the tip of the vaulted ceiling, creating a real presence in the room. It was adorned with an assortment of lights as well as ornaments from the kids and for the kids and just ones they liked. No two were alike. It lent a real hominess to the room.

The mantel was stacked with opalescent garland, gold candles, silver deer and mirrors reflecting the twinkling lights. Stockings hung from the mantel – Gabe, Helen, Justin and Grace – all awaiting Santa's visit in just a few days.

All throughout the great room, Helen had vignettes of Christmas and snow scenes, drawing you in to each corner, wondering what the people in these settings might be thinking if they were real.

But, it didn't stop there. Each bedroom and bathroom had a touch of the holidays. I couldn't imagine how much time it took Helen to set things up. Although she decorated throughout the year, December was definitely her most elaborate display. She said she just used it as a time to clean all those little places you never get to and by putting something happy there, it made her time worthwhile.

I still hadn't decorated my tiny house for the holidays so seeing Helen's fantastic job made me feel a little jealous and incompetent. As a school teacher, she had a theme every month and she carried that through to her house. December was Christmas but January was penguins and snowmen, two of my favorites. I don't know where Helen learned all of this as Mom never sucked up to decorating in such a way, but Helen certainly thrived on it. Yep, it sure was great having family living here in town!

I left Helen and Gabe's house and zipped down the freeway, nearly forgetting I had to take a different route to work. You know how it is. You get in the car and zone out and it's as if the car knows exactly where to go. But, for the month of December, right through the 28th, Runway Fashion Mall employees had to utilize a different parking arrangement so customers had as many spaces available to them as possible. We lowly sorts had to park in Timbuktu, better known as a shuttered casino parking lot, and take a shuttle bus that ran about every 10 minutes. It was an inconvenience, for sure, and I hated leaving my new wheels so far away, but duty called.

Once inside, the mall was a zoo! I had to dip and dodge between holiday shoppers, carolers supplied by the mall during this last week before Christmas and regular, plain old tourists who were just shopping for themselves. I normally could park on the top floor of the parking garage across from the entrance nearest to *The Bod* but with this shuttle bus situation, I was dropped at the opposite end of the mall and had to sprint to the store.

Weary shoppers were the worst! I wish they would just recognize they need a break, something to eat and drink and to drop off their purchases either at the concierge desk or back at the hotel. The mall was so big, throughout the year it was not unusual to see shoppers overloaded with bags, dragging them – and themselves – across the marble floor to make one or two last stops. I could sympathize as I'd done the drag myself. But, as a sales associate, I just want to take them by the shoulders and shake a bit of reality into them. Oh, wait. This is Las Vegas. What reality?

"Oh, thank goodness you're here, Diana," Taneesha said as I blew through the entrance. "Lysette went home sick and we've just been swamped. 'Tis the holiday season!"

I barely had time to catch my breath, drop my stuff in back, clock in and hit the floor before I was accosted by three customers needing help. Lysette must be pretty darn sick if the store manager goes home early the Saturday before Christmas.

Taneesha was frantically running from one end of the store to the other. Temporary help was set up at the cash wrap to ring our sales as Taneesha and I bounced around doing bra fittings – six days before Christmas!?! – and selecting gifts for our customers.

Thankfully, we didn't have to wrap purchases like we did at *Bergstrom*. Oh, those days of fancy boxes and expensive tulle! Here, everything was recycled. No boxes, just basic brown gift bags with paper ribbon, as distinctive as the *Bergstrom* copper and gold box. There was no mistaking a gift from *The Bod* and it was just as well received.

Once the rush was over and we could catch our breath, it was 10 p.m., time to go home. We had a bit of stocking and straightening to do as the front table of nightshirts was nearly empty, but in general, the design of the store made it easy to keep clean.

"So, did you have any bonus transactions today?" Taneesha asked. "It seemed like you were really packing in some big sales."

Oh, Taneesha, you're a really nice person but I'm not about to discuss my pay with you. At least here, the company kept bonus sales private versus *Bergstrom* who posted each associate's sales every day.

"Oh, who knows what the final numbers will be," I said, trying to sidestep the issue. "The cashiers rang most of my sales so I really have no idea how many *BodLiving* coupons were used. I'll find out when I get my check."

Taneesha seemed a bit miffed that I wasn't sharing but honestly, I was so exhausted I didn't care. We finished cleaning up, locked the door and went our separate ways. As a manager, albeit a keyholder, Taneesha was able to park in the underground parking lot while I trudged my way the length of the mall back to the shuttle bus.

It was freezing outside waiting for my ride, but the brisk air did wake me up a bit. I sucked down a bottle of water just as the bus pulled up, and decided I was going to treat myself to breakfast at my favorite drive-thru. Surely I must have gotten one or two bonus sales tonight, but even if I didn't, my three dollar meal wouldn't break the bank. It was nearly Christmas and I deserved a little treat after all my hard work.

"Hey Giz!"

"Hey Diana! How's everything going?"

"Well, you know. It's nearly Christmas. I'm frazzled. Still working retail. Still trying to make ends meet. Pretty much same old same old."

Gizzi laughed, a somewhat nervous laugh. I didn't hear her taking a drag of a cigarette, but sometimes she called me from Jean-Louis's house and since he didn't smoke, he didn't allow her to do so on his property either.

"I understand, sweetie. These years just keep going by faster and faster. Before you know it, we'll be like the *Golden Girls*, looking for a couple of old lady friends for roommates because all our spouses have gone on before us."

"At least you've accomplished something with your life!" I teased, although I think I was looking for a bit of sympathy.

"You have, too, missy. You've traveled the world. You helped several companies reach their goals for product launches, mergers, buyouts, press coverage, trade show attendance – do I have to keep reminding you?"

"Yes, please madam, you must because the only thing I can remember is folding panties and fitting bras!"

"Don't forget buying lottery tickets!"

"Oh, don't remind me. My divorce from Chris was 10 times easier than having to deal with Jazzy. She makes my skin crawl."

"Well, you could leave the group."

"And have them win without me? Are you crazy?"

We both let out a roaring laugh, just what we needed at this stressful time of the year.

"So, I'm coming out for CES."

CES, the Consumer Electronics Show, was the largest trade show of the year in Las Vegas. It always took place right after the New Year. Since Gizzi specialized in semiconductors, she didn't always make the trek to CES but she was coming to town in just a couple of weeks and that made my day.

"That's awesome! I wasn't sure if you were attending this year."

"Yeah, well, I'm following up on a couple of contacts and I've been told the best place to lock in a meeting is at the show. So, my company is covering the cost and I'll be on the nerd bird down to Vegas."

"Just let me know your availability and I'll be at the ready. Unless I'm working, of course."

"Maybe I could buy some of that cotton lingerie you're selling, sweetie!"

"No way! You need sexy stuff so JL will propose. You are only allowed to shop at *Isabella's* or *Bergstrom* until you seal the deal. Then, once you get pregnant, you can wear the stuff we sell at *The Bod*."

"Cotton can be sexy."

Silence, then extreme laughter on both ends of the call.

"Speaking of cotton, I have to get ready for work. I'm so glad you're coming out in January. If I don't talk to you, have a wonderful Christmas!"

"You too, sweetie. Enjoy your time with your family."

"At least I get to enjoy the whole day. The mall opens at 6 a.m. on the 26th but I don't have to be there until 3 p.m."

"Oh, that's so unfair for everyone! Who the hell is out shopping at 6 a.m. the day after Christmas?"

"Tourists who never got to bed the night before? Who knows? I don't have to deal with them. Now, really, I have to go. Have a good one and say hi to Jean-Louis."

"Will do, doll. Stay safe."

Dear Diary,

The Bod certainly has a higher class clientele than *Isabella's*. In fact, I prefer these folks even to the ones I serviced at *Bergstrom*.

Take, for instance, the gentleman who came into the store yesterday. He's a military husband and his wife, a captain in the army, will be returning home during the holidays from her second tour in the desert. He wanted to make sure she felt feminine upon her return, so he purchased several bra and panty sets as well as some lovely nightgowns. What a gem of a guy! How many men would think about their military wives' return to that level?

I've been ever-so impressed with the gentlemen who have all their wives' statistics on their cell phones so they can buy the perfect color and size as a gift. There's an app for everything nowadays! I'm sure it reduces those awkward moments when the woman opens a gift and finds out it's the size he thinks she is, not reality. Most men don't care about size as long as you make them happy.

We see very few men in *The Bod* compared to *Isabella's* or *Bergstrom*, but the ones that do grace us with their presence are a joy to serve, even that attorney that comes in every other week from Kansas and buys all our XXL panties and pays cash…

More tomorrow!

All my heart,

Diana

Happy Holidays

{ THREE }

"Merry Christmas Eve!"

"Merry Christmas Eve!"

No snow outside, but Christmas is here nonetheless. And, what a glorious Christmas it is!

I hadn't celebrated a normal Christmas in a couple of years. When I worked in high tech, I had plenty of money to fly back to Michigan to celebrate with the family. But, as my funds dwindled and my employment shifted, it became harder and harder to jet home for the holidays. Thank goodness for video calling!

But, this year would be different. Helen and Gabe and Grace and Justin were here in town, and Helen was keeping up the family tradition of a big open house on Christmas Eve. All day long, family and friends – well, out here it was basically friends – would stop by for a quick bite and a fun chat to wish each other the best of the season.

Since Mom and Dad opted to stay in Michigan this year even though both of their kids were in Las Vegas, it was a bit melancholy to celebrate, but still quite nice to have family around. Mom and Dad did say they'd visit once the weather warmed up back home. I was grateful I didn't have to make the trek to Michigan for some time. I don't even know if I own a pair of winter boots anymore!

I had to work until 6 p.m. when the store closed, all those last minute shoppers – mostly men after 3 p.m. for some reason – and fight the traffic to get here. But, once inside this holiday palace, I could feel a happy transformation come over me. How wonderful to have my sister!

Shortly after I arrived, we set up a video call on the big screen and spent some time with Mom and Dad and whatever stragglers were still at *their* open house. With the time difference, it was already after 10 p.m. back in Detroit, almost time for Santa to make his appearance.

"Where's your boyfriend, Diana? We'd like to meet him."

"He's not my boyfriend, Mom. More a friend of Gabe's I happen to hang out with. He's with his family for the holidays."

"Are you sleeping with him, dear?"

"Daddy! I can't believe you asked that!"

"Well, it can't be that serious if they're not spending the holidays together, Ralph."

"He's a good catch, Diana," Gabe interjected in support of his friend. "He's very loyal and he'll have a good retirement. If you don't snatch him up, another eligible lady will!"

"Thanks, Gabe. I'll keep that in mind."

"Oh, all this lovely banter is so much fun. We miss you kids," Mom said.

"We miss you, too," I replied. "Sure would be nice to have you out here with us."

"Well, you know, all the cold and all those people! I can't imagine fighting the crowds at the airport. Maybe once it warms up a bit," Dad said. He was never good with crowds. Ask him how many Tigers games we went to.

"No, I mean, it sure would be nice if the two of you moved here!"

Mom and Dad laughed.

"What's so funny about that?" I asked.

"Oh, dear, we still are a couple of years from retirement. We can't even consider it until then. Don't want to mess with our pensions, you know," Mom replied.

"Maybe when you get married and have some kids, Diana, it will be incentive for us to relocate. Otherwise, we have all our social activities in town and we'd hate to give that all up."

Dad really liked to play cards with his buddies, and everyone golfed. But, I didn't want to bring up the fact that some of his friends were now wintering in Florida, snowbirds as we call them. As long as Helen and Gabe stayed in town, I probably would as well, so it was just a matter of time before the whole family was here.

"Did you get our gifts?" Mom asked.

"Yes, and thank you very much. From all of us," Helen replied.

Mom and Dad always gave us money for Christmas. Well, actually, for any occasion. Dad wanted us to put it into savings or retirement, but we usually spent it on something we planned all year to buy but knew we wouldn't have the money until that Christmas envelope was in our grubby little hands. Yes, even Helen, angelic Helen who handled her money with far more discipline than I ever did, would spend her Christmas bonus from Mom and Dad.

"OK, you be good, kids. We'll talk with you soon. Have a Merry Christmas!"

"Thanks, Dad. You, too."

"Love you!"

"Love you!"

After the call, I helped Helen clean up while Gabe quieted the kids and put them to bed. For sure, they would be awake in just a few hours hoping to catch a glimpse of Santa depositing gifts under the enormous tree!

Helen fixed me a plate with hors d'oeuvres and cookies. I grabbed a beer and plopped down in the recliner. By the time

Gabe took out the trash, I was fast asleep. Santa finally woke me up about 1 a.m. to go home and enjoy the day to sleep in.

Christmas was fun day in the family! Helen, Gabe and the kids had their own little celebration with gifts from Santa, then we all met to go to noon Mass. Afterwards, we headed back to Helen's house, put on fresh, new, Christmas pajamas and sat around watching Christmas movies all day.

The kids and I exchanged gifts, too. Helen knew I just couldn't afford anything for her and Gabe, but unbeknownst to me, she snuck a gift card into my purse for a massage at a local spa. I couldn't remember the last time I had a massage and after the craziness of the holiday season, it would feel good!

At least I didn't have to head home early. My shift tomorrow started at 3 p.m., plenty of time to catch one more movie and a little extra shut-eye before the mall madness.

The week between Christmas and New Year's was one big blur. While the crowds in town are a bit smaller just before Christmas, the post-Christmas/pre-New Year crowd is enormous! Daily traffic was a nightmare and parking in the boondocks until December 28th didn't ease my frustration a bit.

Any normal business near the Strip closed about 6 p.m. on New Year's Eve so employees could get home before streets were blocked off for the celebration. As low woman on the totem pole, I got to work New Year's Eve – and New Year's Day, thank you very much – and had the pleasure of battling the nearly 400,000 people who came into town while trying to snake out of the insanity and into the neighborhood calm.

Once again, Helen and Gabe stepped up to the plate and held an open house. There was no way I could reciprocate their kindness, not only from a time perspective but from a financial one. With any luck, next year would be better but this year I was down to my last penny.

Gabe started a new tradition that I really enjoyed and hoped that it would remain a family tradition for years to come. We each took a strip of paper, wrote down our wish for the coming year, stood in a circle around the fire pit in the backyard and read it aloud. When we were done, we threw the papers into the fire and toasted to our wishes.

Gabe began, "I'm thankful for the health and happiness of my family and my wish for next year is to have continued health and happiness and may the Tigers win the World Series."

We all laughed and clapped. It was our wish, too, but we're glad Gabe led the charge.

Next came Helen, "I, too, am very grateful for many things, but most importantly that we were able to make a fresh start in a wonderful community and make some dear, dear friends. My wish for the New Year is for continued health, wealth and love for family and friends, and that Mom and Dad will finally move to Las Vegas so we can all be together."

Woot! Woot! That was another big winner in the wish department.

Grace wished, "I get to take ballet this year and win our dance competition in May."

Helen gave Grace one of those Mom looks that said, "Wish all you want but ballet will have to wait until next year."

Justin's wish was, "to learn all the old Beatles songs on guitar so I can play along to the music when Mom listens to them in the house."

I was impressed that Justin even knew who The Beatles were, but as they were one of Helen's favorite bands, she must blast them through the speakers on weekends or when she's cleaning. I think Grace said she plays the tunes in the car as well and that everyone knew all the words to all the songs.

Now it was my turn. I really had lost my wishing ability with all my struggles over the last several years. I was just grateful to be alive and to have my family here with me. I really didn't know what to write, so I just went for it.

"I, too, am very grateful to have my happy, healthy family here with me. For the New Year, I wish that the Lotto Ladies win the Super Duper Millions!"

Everyone cheered and laughed. We all knew how impossible it was to win even a mere pittance of that jackpot, but it was a wish nonetheless.

Gabe came up and gave me a hug.

"You and me both, sister. You and me both!"

We threw our wishes into the fire, clinked our glasses and drank to our hopes and wishes.

"Hurry up! It's nearly midnight!" Gabe called.

We put our glasses down and ran for the garage. Helen and Gabe had a unique house with a rooftop deck atop the garage, the perfect perch for fireworks all around the valley. It was way too hot for us to use in the summer heat, but bundled up in the middle of winter, it was perfect, at least for the 15-20 minutes we'd be exposed to the elements.

Helen found the radio station with the musical simulcast and, once the show began, we oohed and aahed at every blast. It was the most fun I'd had since I moved to town, and I got to spend it with some very special people.

I dried my tears and cheered the finale. At that very moment, I felt it was going to be my best year ever.

Ouch!

One look at my income versus bills and I knew there was no way *The Bod* would solely keep me afloat, and it didn't look like anything better was on the horizon. *The Bod* was fine but definitely not financially rewarding. However, it did offer scheduling flexibility that would allow me to sub two or three days a week to bring in some extra money. (Read: work more than one job) Hey, who doesn't enjoy working seven days a week just to pay the rent? I put it off for as long as I could but, reluctantly, I applied to be a substitute teacher.

I know I kept telling everyone I was going to do it but, honestly, I just wasn't in the mood. Am I at that point in my life where I need to find a job that I can stay with for 30 years to guarantee a comfortable retirement? How could I live without the excitement of risk? Am I fiercely independent as my old boss described me, or just a risk-taking adrenaline junkie?

OK, so my life may have been a bit too risky in the past and I should have been paying more attention to the details. And, instead of whining I should be breaking out of my comfort zone and taking those risks again. You know the kind – the ones where instead of making excuses you seek a solution.

The problem is, I have to be passionate about what I'm doing and ever since my consulting business took a dive – fine, closed up shop – I haven't found anything I'm passionate about. Sure, I have some skills that are transferable, but being my own boss makes me giddy.

I keep trying to fool my brain into thinking of each job as a different client, but frankly, for the pittance they pay, it's more a matter of having to have multiple jobs just to put gas in my new little car. With multiple clients, I had the option of shopping at *Bergstrom* or some little designer boutique. Yes, I know. Had I paid attention to Daddy I would have saved that money and I wouldn't be in the position I'm in now.

But, enough dwelling on the past. I'm not a morning person. We've well established that. I'm not looking forward to being awake and perky so early in the morning for a roomful of hyperactive students. However, maybe this is something I'll be really good at and I will jump out of bed with a spring in my step. Subbing will certainly open my eyes to that possibility. Or, shut them for good.

Helen loves teaching. If I can get into a school on the same cycle as hers, we would have the same time off to explore and travel and who knows what! Maybe we'd even have time to start our own business of some sort. There I go, thinking about business again.

I sat down at my desk and clicked on the links that finally took me to the secure sign-up page. I didn't think the process was a big deal until I actually got into the system. The pages and pages-long application asked for everything but my blood type, which I was certain would be determined during one of the many pre-screening tests I'd have to endure prior to actually being accepted into the program. Oh, yeah, then there's orientation!

I hadn't seen such an extensive process since working for *Positano* – but this was much more detailed. I guess when kids' lives are at stake, the county wants to make sure as much as possible that you're OK to be around their students – as well as other teachers and district employees.

Funny thing. Seems every teacher I've ever met had a teaching gene. There's just something that's similar in every single one of them, no matter how different they are. I don't know if it's a way of thinking or acting or looking. I haven't figured that out. I know Helen has it. I can see it in her. Even as her sister, I'm not sure if it's present in me. Maybe it's latent and will show its face once I enter the hallowed world of the school district. I wonder if any geneticist has studied this. I can't have been the first to notice.

With any luck, I can be in next week's orientation class. Once my application is reviewed, I need to attend an interview session and clear a background check, all of which should move pretty quickly. I hope. I heard on the news the district is in need of 300 substitutes and I'm certainly qualified.

Look out, kids. Here I come!

Dear Diary,

Sometimes, the most amazing things happen right out-side your window.

When I moved into this house, I loved that it had a small pond with a waterfall in the backyard. The landlord had stocked it with 18 large goldfish, each about eight inches long, all of varying beautiful colors. It seemed like a lot of fish for such a little pond, but I loved to go out in the morning and feed them, a nice calming way to start my day.

One morning it seemed there were a few less fish. I counted. There were only 13! They couldn't have jumped over the rocks to their death, and the pond was too deep for even a sneaky cat to climb down and capture them. I had no idea where my fish had gone.

Saturday morning, I found a big silver fish lying up against the rocks. I had no idea where it came from. It certainly wasn't from my pond. I wrapped it in newspaper and put it in the trash, not realizing its owner would come looking for it.

A couple of hours later as I was doing dishes, I happened to look out the window to see a beautiful white egret snatching a fish from my pond! I was in so much shock I didn't know what to do. In seconds, it had bounded across my small yard and with one jump made it to the top of the five-foot mason-block fence, then one more jump and a flap of the wings and off it went. I'd never seen such incredibly powerful legs before. Those little pencil egret legs are much stronger than they seem!

I learned there was a manmade lake in the community about a mile from my house, stocked with fish for the blue herons and egrets that came to visit. What I didn't realize is that they discovered my pond and nibbled on my little goldfish as an appetizer. The silver fish I found against the rocks must have fallen out of his beak as the egret flew over, or he left it as the entrée to the goldfish starter.

I tried to pay more attention to my backyard and found that not only did the herons and egrets eat my fish, they would bring their catch from the lake, fly to my backyard and eat it there or from the rooftop of my neighbor's house. It was all so very surreal.

I'll have to see if I can capture some of this on camera. I'll be substitute teaching soon and I can regale the kids with stories of my backyard activities. Kids always love animal stories. Maybe I can turn it into a children's book someday.

More tomorrow!

All my heart,

Diana

Gizzi's Surprises

{ FOUR }

"Hello, lovey."

"Hello, Jazzy. What's up?"

I'd been avoiding Jazzy's calls. Who wants to ruin their holidays by talking to her?

"I'm just checking to see if you purchased our tickets for this week."

"No, I haven't. I've been a bit busy, Jazzy."

I had stopped by to pick up the ticket money from Pamela while Jazzy was in the fitting room with a customer. But, it was just the holidays for chrissake! Can't we take a week off?

"That's no excuse, lovey. Every week. Just like my vision showed."

"I thought in your vision you saw one of those big checks. It never said anything about buying tickets every week. Did the check happen to have a date on it?"

"Laugh all you want, lovey, but my visions come true. In order to get the check, we have to buy tickets every week. The drawing is tomorrow. When are you going?"

"You know, you and Pamela could drive down and buy the tickets. It doesn't always have to be me."

Jazzy let out one of her snorty laughs.

"Diana, if you don't want to be part of the group, then you can withdraw just like all the others, but you'll be sorry when we win."

Not as sorry as I am right now, Jazzy. And, how are you going to win when I seem to be the only one driving down to get tickets?

The jackpot this week was expected to top $300 million. That would be a cool $60 million or so apiece as a cash equivalent after taxes, not a bad haul to get those two off my back.

"Fine. I'll go tomorrow."

"Happy New Year, lovey!"

"Right back atcha."

I made the drive to Primm and back just in time to get together with my best friend. We met at a café on the Strip, near her hotel, as I was certain she'd need to rush off to a meeting. It was our habit to drink martinis at these heart-to-hearts, but to my surprise, Gizzi ordered a bourbon on the rocks!

"What's up with that, Giz?"

"Oh, I don't know. Martinis just don't seem to taste the same without a cigarette."

I knew it! I knew she was cutting back. That Jean-Louis must be one helluva catch!

Once our drinks were delivered and we drank to each other's good fortune, Gizzi swallowed hard and shook off the taste. Then she put nose in the air, trying to inhale the cigarette smoke from a neighboring booth, all the while drumming her fingers on the table.

"Really, if there's a non-smoking section, why do they put it directly next to smokers? Shouldn't there be a barrier or something?"

I'd never seen Gizzi like this. Must be the nicotine withdrawal. But I knew, once she passed through this phase, she would be her fantastic self again, albeit without the scent of nicotine. It was kind of a nice change. She *was* human after all!

"Well, you know, nothing's perfect," I said, accepting that those words were meaningless and Gizzi's ears would never absorb them.

Gizzi took another swig of the bourbon, closed her eyes, took a deep breath as if in a moment of meditation, turned to me and smiled.

"I know I told you I'd text a photo, but I had to come to town anyway for the conference so I thought you might like to find out in person."

Ohmigod! Ohmigod! Ohmigod! Gizzi is engaged! I never thought I'd say those words but there they are and they are awesome!!! I'm so happy for her – and so proud, too. Not only is she getting married, it also means she finally *quit* smoking! No wonder she's so edgy!

While I had hoped Jean-Louis might use Christmas or New Year's to make an honest woman out of Gizzi, I knew how she was struggling with giving up smoking, a habit she'd had since a teenager when her family lived in France for a couple of years. It was her refuge, her way to relax and think things through. Plus, she worked so many big international sales accounts, smoking was part of the culture of several of those client countries.

She wanted to quit, she had for years, but she felt she needed the right incentive. When Jean-Louis came into her life, she'd found her motivation. Sure, she wanted to do it for herself and her own health, but once she was married and wanted to have children, it would be harder to quit. So, out of love, JL made it a requirement for her to quit smoking before they got engaged. He was willing to wait, but being the wise woman that she was, she didn't take very long.

But, let's get to the important part of this visit. Omigod! You should see the ring! It was an eight carat cushion cut E-color, perfect clarity stone, flanked by blue diamond trillions, all set in platinum. Gizzi had the tiniest of fingers but the huge ring was the most gorgeous I had ever seen.

"So, what do you think?"

"What do I think?!? It's amazing, Giz! But the ring isn't important, it's the fact that you and JL found each other. I'm so very thrilled for the two of you!!!"

"I know, sweetie! I thought you'd be married long before me. Oh, wait – you were!"

I gave Gizzi a friendly glare, then we both chuckled.

"Sorry, Diana, this is all so new to me. But, it seems right. It's the start of many changes in my life, I'm sure."

"Changes? What kind of changes? What else is there besides quitting smoking, drinking bourbon and getting married? You're not moving to France, are you? I'd never see you and I hardly see you as it is!"

"No, no, don't read anything into it, Diana. It's just that as I look down at my ring every day – a ring Jean-Louis designed by the way…"

"Ooohhh…"

"…first we'll be married, then we'll find a new place to live, then we'll probably have a child or two…"

"Yes! I want to be an Aunti again!!!"

"…and who knows what I'll do regarding work? I love my job but I've always expected I would stay home with the kids until they were in school."

"But you would go nuts if you didn't do *anything*!"

"I know, sweetie. Once we get past the wedding and decide where we want to live, I need to come up with a game plan, start a company that I can manage from home."

"As always, Giz, you're on top of things, getting all your ducks in order. I wish I planned as well as you."

"Oh, don't cut yourself down, sweetie. You did a great job for your clients. You just have to learn to put as much planning effort into your own life as you did theirs. *You* are more important than any of your clients or their businesses ever were."

That's my Giz, cutting right to the core.

"OK, OK, this is not a Diana pep talk meeting. We're here to celebrate your engagement! And your future! I love your idea of starting a home-based company before you quit your current job. At least you won't have to worry about money. Between you and Jean-Louis, you guys have a great financial foundation. Have you thought about what you might do?"

Gizzi had made a very good salary in semiconductor sales, actively managed her money and did an excellent job of it. If I were smart, I would have had her manage my investments from the start, but I was in a different place mentally and didn't have much available for investment. Mom and Dad provided for us as best they could, but no one in the family ever made the type of money I made in high tech. While Mom and Dad were *very* frugal with their paychecks, I felt the need to purchase every material thing I ever wanted, just because I could, never thinking far into the future when I might need to have some extra money like, as Dad reminds me so often, retirement.

Jean-Louis was an intelligent businessman and had been through two IPO's as an executive, either as vice-president or CEO, plus he had family money. This third venture was one he founded and with any luck could be sold off or merged in a year or two for a tidy sum. After that, Gizzi and JL could do anything they wanted. They'd pretty much have unlimited funds, probably close to $100 million dollars, if not more.

"I'm not quite sure, but JL has mentioned venture capital, which is something I could definitely do from home. But, it will have to wait a bit as they just made me CEO."

I nearly choked on my olive. This was certainly a Gizzi visit full of surprises.

"They made you CEO? What? When?"

"Early December. I guess you don't keep up with the industry news much anymore now that you're not in it. We sent out a press release just before Christmas but since I didn't hear from you, I figured you didn't know and I'd just tell you in person."

"You got that right, girlfriend. I stopped reading the industry updates back at *Bergstrom*. I felt the chances for getting a new client were between slim and none so I just unsubscribed from everything. I know so many people, I really should keep up. But, what happened? How did you get the job? Not that you're not deserving. On the contrary. I couldn't think of anyone better to head the company. It's just interesting timing."

"Agreed. I considered declining the offer but JL said it would look good on my resume, adding to my credibility. Of course, he's right. I would have eventually told myself the same thing. It had always been my goal to head a semiconductor company but I didn't think it would happen so quickly.

"Everything's been changing in the valley. There aren't that many of us, but women are becoming CEO's more often. I wasn't in the board meeting when I was selected but I'm sure it was quite a lively discussion. They had a lot to think about.

"The market's been down for a couple of years. As vice president of sales, I'd brought a lot of new major accounts and partnerships to the company. They couldn't deny that. Our current CEO had to feel at a disadvantage. Plus, I think he was just getting tired. He made plenty of money in this industry, and he and his wife recently purchased a plush motor home. They plan to travel the country on their own schedule. He was already 67 and he told me he was ready to retire a long time ago."

Wow. I couldn't believe everything that was going on in Gizzi's life! I always knew she'd be over-the-top successful but I also had hoped to be right there alongside her, both of us enjoying the spoils of what Silicon Valley could offer to intelligent women willing to work hard. Sure, I was a bit jealous but I was also very proud that at least one of us would enjoy the fruits of her labor. Me, the only fruits I had were the olives in my martini. Olives are a fruit, are they not?

"So, let's get down to some wedding details. Of course, Diana, I do want you to be my maid of honor."

"Oh, Gizzi, it *would* be an honor! But, I don't know when and where and how much it will cost. You know my current situation, but I'll skip lunch and ride the bus to work just so I can do it."

"No worries, sweetie. Jean-Louis and I will take care of it. Total cost will be a few thousand dollars and I know you're tight on cash."

"But, Giz, that's not how this works. I can't have you do that. The maid of honor *honors* the bride, hence the title. I'll find a way to make it happen. You just let me know where I need to be and how much it will cost."

"Nonsense, Diana. It's done. I would feel very uncomfortable at my wedding if I knew you suffered for months just to pay for things. We're friends. This is what friends do. It's not about the money. It's about you being there for me. That means more to me than anything."

Hmm...she has the money to pay for me to be her maid of honor but when she so badly wanted me to move back to California to find work, she didn't offer a penny. Water under the bridge. Gizzi is good people and I know she's always looking out for me. This is her wedding, after all, and she has the right to make it special her way.

As for my contributing to my portion of the wedding costs, I knew there was no winning this argument with Gizzi, so I just let it ride. Truth is, I couldn't afford another dime let alone thousands of dollars for clothing, gifts, travel and so on. I had a true friend in Gizzi, someone who understood what friendship meant. I wouldn't bring it up again, and neither would she. At least for a while...

"Thank you, Giz. I'm grateful to have you as a friend, too. But, let's talk more details. Have you set a date? Colors? Theme? Don't leave me in the dark! Divulge, please."

"Well, JL and I are pretty open to when we marry so a lot is dependent upon venue availability. I'm so busy I'm doing everything I hadn't intended to do, like hire a wedding planner."

"Ohmigod! A wedding planner? I can't believe that, Giz. You're the one in control. How will you relinquish that?"

Gizzi looked at me slyly, and smiled.

"Let's just say I've been in touch with Colin Bailey's office and he has an opening in early December."

My mouth hit the floor. Colin Bailey! He was the ultimate in party planners. Even A-list stars had trouble securing him with their unlimited checkbooks. I knew he didn't take on a project for less than two million dollars, so this was sure to be the most extravagant event of the decade in Silicon Valley. And, I was going to be part of it!

"Wow, Giz, that's amazing! Colin Bailey? Wow!"

I was dumbstruck. I thought it would be a nice wedding but I really had no idea what type of money I was dealing with here. Gizzi must have done much better with her investments than I thought. I didn't realize her coffers were quite so full, although Jean-Louis might be paying for it and he had a sizable bank account, one that could easily handle Colin Bailey's fees. I'm sure glad I won't be driving my old Buick to the wedding.

"I really didn't want to go that route, but when Jean-Louis and I started discussing the wedding plans and he mentioned that long ago he designed Colin's logo and they still kept in touch, how could I refuse? Of course, there will be no special favors for us, we'll have to pay the standard fees but given the enormity of the event and the chance to work with such a creative force, it will be a pleasure."

Gizzi took a sip of her bourbon, cringed at the taste as she swallowed – she did so much better on martinis and cigarettes but I'm glad that's part of her past – took a deep breath and spoke.

"I know I've done well for myself in semiconductors, far better than most of my friends," she began, "but Jean-Louis is a whole different kind of money. He grew up in it. His family has had it for generations. They've been producing champagne for over a hundred years. He has a country home that would rival many royal estates. I'd read about all this prior to our meeting for the first time, but I thought it was all fiction. I had no idea it was reality. Between what he's earned through IPO's and his family funds, I know I've always dreamed of – no, planned to – reach those numbers but to have gotten there even through marriage is quite overwhelming."

I couldn't believe it. Gizzi almost seemed to lack confidence. Not the Gizzi I know! She was always so strong. She had three brothers, so she had a competitive side one doesn't always get with just a sister. She's the one *I* go to for a pep talk. Maybe it's just part of her nicotine withdrawal. I certainly hope she quits tapping the table before the reception. It's driving me nuts!

"Giz, Jean-Louis and his family are very lucky to have you. You are any great man's dream! It takes a very special man to win your heart and you found him! You have an amazing life, Giz, which will only improve once you marry JL. And, just think, free champagne for the wedding!"

Gizzi started laughing, as did I. Her moment of weakness past, it was time to get down to more details.

"So, as you know, my favorite color is green and JL's is blue, so I think we're going to go with orange."

"Orange! Wow! That color wasn't even on my radar!"

"Oh, Diana, it will be perfect for a late autumn wedding. I don't want to get all caught up in the red and green holiday wedding thing. I'd rather focus on the colors of post-Halloween and Thanksgiving. And, if anyone can do orange with class, it's Colin Bailey."

No truer words were ever spoken.

"Any other surprises? What do you want to do for a theme?"

"Honestly, we're just in the initial planning stages, sweetie. I'm sure there will be a bit of Silicon Valley for me and a bit of France for him, but that's about as far as we've gotten. I have a feeling we won't even know all the details until the wedding. Colin Bailey does have a bit of an ego, well, ok, quite the ego, and he likes to surprise his clients. So, we'll probably have a couple of meetings, tell him our preferences and requirements and let him run with it. Honestly, we're both swamped and while I do like to control things, the thought of letting Colin run amok with our wedding plans is kind of exciting."

Wow! This was a new Gizzi, changing before my very eyes. I always looked up to her because she was like a rock, always moving forward but with a solid foundation and feet on the ground. It was exciting to see her edge out of her comfort zone far more than normal. I used to be like that. I think.

"The only other thing I know for sure is we'll be taking our vows at St. Anne's. We're both Catholic and it's a tradition we want to maintain. In fact, I think one of the priests from JL's home town will come in for the ceremony, once we lock in a date."

Gizzi looked at me, let out a deep breath and smiled.

"I've never been happier, sweetie. We're just so right for each other. And, I'm so glad you're here to share it with me."

"Oh, Giz, I'm so happy for you! I could tell early on that you were smitten. It's a far more mature relationship than Chris and I ever had. I'm certainly learning just by observing. But let's talk important stuff. Who's designing the bridesmaids' dresses?"

Gizzi and I both let out a deep, belly laugh, a total stress reliever. Although the news was exceptional, we all know how nerve-wracking weddings can be. And Gizzi and JL's wedding was certain to be a major event lasting several days. But, I knew Gizzi at the core and she was the happiest I'd ever seen her, even when she landed a major Friends & Family stock purchase when one of her friend's companies went public. We raised our glasses and drank to the future Mrs. Ricard. At least I had almost a year to diet and tone up before the big event. I may not be contributing financially to this wedding but I want to look smashing in those photos!

Dear Diary,

Whew! I'm exhausted! All of Gizzi's good news has set my limbic system on overdrive.

First of all – Yay!!! Gizzi is getting married! And, she honored me by asking me to be her maid of honor. There are five other bridesmaids, too, although I have no idea who they could be. Gizzi only has brothers so I suspect the others are either friends or cousins, or someone from JL's family. There's so much to do – it's less than 11 months to the wedding! And, with Colin Bailey planning the event, it's sure to be amazing!!!

Secondly – Yay!!! Gizzi is now the CEO of her company! I can't believe it! Well, OK, I do. Gizzi is amazing but it's still such a surprise to find out my best friend is a CEO! OMG! I'm still hawking underwear and she's running a friggin' company!

It's hard for me to imagine what life would be like with all that Gizzi/Jean-Louis money. I know that Gizzi and I started out on more of a level playing field. Maybe she was a bit better off than me when we met, but the difference now is significant. Can someone who has ascended to such a completely different income level still be want to stay friends with me? I guess only time will tell.

I think it's great that Gizzi is thinking ahead to family life and working from home once the happy couple has children. I wonder what sort of company she intends to launch? Maybe there's room for me at the inn.

I know I've said this a thousand times before, but it's time to start making plans for myself. I've already made one major change. I broke up with Tom. There was no way I could sit through one more zombie movie while he refused to watch any rom coms. We'd never last, but it was nice to have a man around the house. He did fix my ceiling fan!

More tomorrow!

All my heart,

Diana

Substitute Teaching

Substitute Income

{ FIVE }

"Congratulations! You've just completed your substitute teacher orientation. Now, once you've been fingerprinted and had a TB test, you can begin work. Let's start the line here for ID badges."

I finally made it through all the paperwork and was accepted into the substitute teacher orientation class. I was ever so grateful as post-holiday hours at *The Bod* slipped to a maximum of 20 per week, and although the store had a faithful clientele, there just weren't that many shoppers after Christmas.

My goal was to sub three days a week. That would put me at 44 hours or so a week, a respectable number of hours, leaving enough time to better myself as Gizzi had suggested, and still be able to pay my bills.

I would probably focus on substituting at elementary schools. The school district staggered the starting times to maximize the use of the school buses, so high school started at 7 a.m., middle school at 8 a.m. and elementary school at 9 a.m. That meant that

I'd get to sleep in longer with the lower grades. I'd get out later in the afternoon but honestly, 3:30 p.m. still allowed plenty of nap time!

The school district was in need of a large number of substitutes, which I really didn't understand. I mean, they have a full slate of teachers on staff, right? I looked around the sparsely-attended orientation class and wondered why each of these people was here. I decided I'd do a quick survey while waiting in line to be photographed for our badges.

The woman standing in front of me looked to be about 65 years old, well dressed and well organized.

"So, what brings you to the world of substitute teaching?" I asked.

"Oh, all my friends do it. You only have to sub two days per pay period to stay on the roster, so I'll have plenty of free time and earn a bit of play money while my husband golfs."

Well, that's interesting. They didn't say anything about minimum number of days. So, technically, I just have to work two days every two weeks. I think I can handle that. I'll probably put in more time so I should be good.

"Two days? Heck, I plan to do this full time," said the man standing behind me.

"You do?" I commented.

"Yes, of course. I was forced to retire early but I don't want to look for a new job. I can go to a different school every day and take a day off when I'm in the mood. It's pretty sweet."

I didn't think there were enough open positions to be able to do this full time. Again, more interesting information.

"Yeah, a lot of people drop out after their first couple of assignments," Mr. Full Time said. "Going through orientation is easy compared to keeping a classroom full of wily kids in order for nearly eight hours. Plus, you have to deal with all the administration."

"I would think it would be a great opportunity to be able to substitute. I'm surprised people drop out," I said.

"Oh, they sure do," said Mrs. Two Days. "I have a lot of friends who substitute and it seems you either have it or you don't."

Hmm…I looked around again and noticed that illustrious teacher gene in many of the attendees. There were a few who seemed out of place – me included – and I wondered if I would become a dropout statistic. I'd handled many a lively boardroom. Surely, I could tame a roomful of energetic kids.

"There you go, Ms. MacKenzie," the photographer said as she handed me my shiny new badge. "Be sure to finish the rest of your requirements before you attempt to access the system. You won't be allowed to login until your file is complete."

I took a quick glance at my phone. It was nearly 5:30 p.m. I could race down the street to the police station to get fingerprint-ed by 6 p.m., and if they weren't busy, I'd still have time to get the TB test at the health district by 7 p.m. I could complete all my requirements today, grab a turkey burger at the drive-thru on the way home and spend the rest of the night attempting to read through all the policies and procedures of the school dis-trict. Knowing my precarious financial position, I couldn't risk screwing this up.

I was on the schedule at *The Bod* for the next couple of days, so I opted to wait until the following week to get my feet wet as a sub. The system seemed rather simple. I just had to logon and se-lect the area of town where I wanted to work. The system would generate a list of schools in that area that had open positions. I had to review school by school to see exactly what was available. If I didn't like what I saw, I could expand my options to another area of the county but I could only review one area at a time.

If I saw a position I liked, I could click on it and review the opening in more details which varied depending on the teacher who completed the request. The system would only allow you to review one opening at a time which you could accept, reject or pass. If you passed on a position, it would stay on the list unless someone else accepted it. If you rejected it, you'd never see it again. Given the fact that you might change your mind, we were advised never to reject a posting unless we were absolutely certain we would never ever want it.

Multiple people could view the position simultaneously, so if I saw something that was somewhat decent, I had to take it right away because if I continued to look at other options, the first one would be gone by the time I returned and I'd have to search for another opening. The system was worse than buying concert tickets! All the good ones got snatched up early.

Over time, the system learned your preferences and ordered the openings with what it considered your best possible position first, followed by those less likely to interest you. It didn't prevent you from looking at everything; it just wanted to ease the process not only for you but to assure that all positions were filled prior to the first bell.

Teachers could start posting requests at 6 p.m. the night before, but you never could tell when something good might come up. A position might be listed as much as two weeks in advance so if you were savvy, you could lock in assignments far ahead of time and not stress about it.

Of course, there were postings that didn't appear until early morning just before school started. These would be teachers who called in sick for some reason or other. I didn't realize just how grateful I would be to have a regular job with a complete schedule for the week – or month – until I started substitute teaching.

The first three days – days I was off from *The Bod* and readily available to substitute – there were absolutely no openings in my area. It was the start of the New Year, so teachers were pretty much obligated to be in class after having a couple of weeks off for the holidays. I did check other areas of the county but the openings were snatched up quickly and I stared at a blank screen for hours.

This wasn't going as I had expected. I thought, if the school district needed that many new substitutes, there must be mountains of positions available. Unfortunately, I was wrong once again.

I continued to check every day, knowing teachers could post openings days in advance. I soon locked in a position for the following Monday – a third grade class at a local elementary school. Third grade. How hard could *that* be?

"Miss M! Miss M! I have to go to the bathroom!"

The little girl with the cute pig tails was waving her hand frantically from the back of the room. The entire class was snickering.

"She always does this when we have a substitute," one boy offered.

"Yeah, I don't think she has to pee. She probably needs to use the crapper!" added a second boy, who sent the entire class into rolling laughter.

"Class, quiet," I said with as much restraint as I could muster. This wasn't an E-staff meeting. These were little kids. I had to keep that in perspective.

I walked up to the little girl and handed her the bathroom pass.

"Here you go. Be back in five."

She grabbed the pass, smiled coyly at the boy who made the crapper comment and practically skipped out of the classroom.

"You know she's playing you," said crapper boy. "She just needs attention."

And there you have it. An eight-year-old who was smarter than me.

Once bathroom girl came back to class, things settled down a bit. The teacher had left lesson plans, which was very helpful, especially to someone subbing for the first time. The students started the day writing one page in their journals; then we read and analyzed quite an interesting story about a man who lived in a remote part of Alaska without electricity and running water. Not something on my bucket list, but very interesting nonetheless and definitely a contrast to the glitz and glamour of Las Vegas.

That brought us to our morning bathroom break. At this age, it was important to have scheduled potty breaks. These kids were still growing and their bladders needed to be emptied regularly. By the time we lined up, walked to the bathroom, everyone took a turn, lined back up and returned to the classroom, it was nearly 25 minutes! We had one quick math lesson to complete before I got some downtime while the kids went to art class.

Just as I was getting the students ready to head down the hall and over to the art teacher's care, the fire alarm sounded. I didn't know if this was a drill or an actual fire. No announcement was made and I hadn't received notice from the front office when I checked in. The kids went wild, grabbing their coats and scurrying down the hall and out the door.

I followed along. I had no idea where my class was supposed to line up. I was in such shock, I forgot to take the class roll with me. I'd been told I'd need to do that during orientation, but it slipped my mind. I didn't even take my purse. I just gathered the kids, closed the classroom door and lined up with them.

Once outside, a counselor came up to me and asked me if all my students were accounted for.

"Uh, I don't know," I replied.

"You don't know? Is that what you said?"

"Unfortunately, yes, that's what I said."

"You did learn during orientation that the first item you grab during any drill is the class roll. Do you remember hearing that?"

Of course I did. I'm not deaf, I'm just out of sorts.

"Yes, I did. It won't happen again."

"OK, fine. Now, how many students did you have in the classroom?"

I tried to remember. Today was such a blur, and being up early to teach threw my brain on autopilot.

"I believe there were 26. No, wait. 25."

"Is it 26 or 25?"

Honestly, you're not talking to an eight-year-old here.

"Let me think. OK, it's both."

"Both?"

"Yes. We had 26 this morning but one girl left with her father for a dental appointment. So, we currently have 25."

The counselor turned to the line-up of students.

"Fine. How many do you have here?"

I quickly counted.

"25."

"Great. Now, are all of these yours?"

How the hell should I know? I quickly looked up and down the row of students, all their impatient faces. From what I could tell, they all looked somewhat familiar.

"I'm going to say, yes, they are all mine."

The counselor looked at me, looked at the students, then turned back to me.

"You were lucky this time. Don't ever forget that roll again."

We were given the all clear and made our way back into the school. The students had missed most of art class, but I took them to the art room anyway. After what I'd been through, *I* needed a bathroom break.

I checked my phone for messages as I approached my car in the parking lot after school. I'd made it through the day, all in one piece although I'm sure I lost a few years of my life during the fire drill. That counselor was tougher than many a CEO I'd met, but after all, we are talking about human lives here and not consumer electronics.

I scrolled through the unimportant ones like traffic and weather updates, and much to my chagrin was a message from Jazzy and Pamela.

I opened the message to see a photo of a Lotto Ladies money envelope, with the message:

Ready when you are.

It was time to do my weekly pickup. I had planned to drive to Primm tomorrow to purchase the Super Duper Millions tickets but that meant I had to get the money from Jazzy and Pamela tonight. They worked nights tomorrow and I wanted to make the drive earlier in the day. I could just buy the tickets with my own money then pick up the envelope at another time, but it didn't seem right. In order for us to win, the money had to come from the three of us. For better or worse, we were in this together.

I texted my fellow Lotto Ladies that I was on my way, got in my car and sat in rush hour traffic on the 15 down to *Positano*. I shouldn't have ignored those traffic updates.

"That's so great that you decided to pursue a teaching career, dear," Mom said when I told her and Dad about my new adventure. "Now you and Helen can have the same time off."

"And in 30 years, you'll have a great retirement," added Dad.

"Slow down, slow down," I said. "I'm only substitute teaching. I'm not really sure about the whole career thing, but at least this way I can try it out. I know I've done training before in high tech but I'm just not sure how I'll be as a teacher."

"Nonsense," Dad said. "I think you'd be a great teacher. You're very patient, Diana."

"Patient? Me? Hmm...I don't know about patient. Tolerant maybe, but not patient."

"No, Diana, your father is right. I've see you with Grace and Justin. You're always so patient with them. Maybe you should try the primary grades first, just like Helen teaches. If her kids could learn from you when they were younger, that may be your best introduction to teaching. Plus, I'm sure Helen can give you some guidance there."

"Well, I have tried third grade..."

"Excellent choice, Diana!" Mom interjected.

"...but it wasn't as easy as I thought it would be. It's difficult to hold a conversation with an eight-year-old, plus keep to the schedule and the lesson plans and all the shenanigans that happen when you have a roomful of kids."

Mom and Dad laughed.

"Well, I'm so glad you find this funny!"

"We only find it funny because you've never had children of your own, Diana," Dad said. "Taking care of several small children for a day can be a challenge, I'll grant you that, but I never got paid extra for it!"

"Oh, Ralph, I'm the one who did all the big events with the kids!"

"But I was there, too, Georgia. What a mess they made, but boy did we have fun!"

"OK, enough reminiscing. We're not talking about a birthday party here. We're talking about public school teaching. I was exhausted! I've planned major events around the world and I never worried as much as I did one day in a third grade classroom."

"Oh, dear, of course you were exhausted! You *will* worry about taking care of those kids. Anything can happen on a given day and they're your responsibility. It's different when you're dealing with adults who can act and think for themselves."

"But the fire drill was a mess!"

"But, how was the rest of the day, dear?"

"Oh, Mom, it was OK I guess. I survived. It wasn't fun. I thought it might be fun, but it was actually nerve wracking. I don't know if I'm cut out for this."

"Diana, it was your first day. How long does it typically take you to get used to a new job?"

"I'd say six months to feel comfortable and about 18 months to know it pretty well."

"Well, there you have it! One day and you're already throwing in the towel. You have to give it time. Like you said, substituting is an opportunity to try teaching while getting paid for it. It won't be exactly the same as running your own classroom, but you'll learn a lot about the schools, the administration and classroom management. I think it's an excellent approach."

"Thanks, Dad. I've just been so lost lately it's good to know I have your support."

"Of course you do, dear. Your father and I are always there for you. Now, maybe next time you sub, you could try a different grade level, perhaps something in high school."

"Oh, I don't know if I'm ready for high school. Maybe middle school."

"Middle school is a tough time, Diana. High school might be better."

"Yeah, but in middle school the kids still look up to you as if you know something. In high school, I'm not so sure. Anyway, I'll try them both and see what pans out."

"Sounds good, dear. Let us know how you do."

"So, when are you and Dad coming out for a visit?"

"We're still shoveling snow here, so it will be a while," Dad said. "By the time it warms up here, it will be a scorcher over there."

In unison, we all said, "But it's a dry heat!"

We laughed. It was always good to connect with Mom and Dad, especially since video calling was so easy. Hearing their voices was great but actually seeing them was such a blessing. I tip my hat to whoever invented the video call. And, having worked in high tech, I should know who that is.

"OK, dear, it's nearly bedtime over here. Time for us to relax a bit before we turn out the lights."

"It was good talking to you. We'll talk again soon."

"Love you!"

"Love you, too!"

Dear Diary!

If my home is an outward reflection of who I am inside, then I'm just one big jumbled mess!

I'm living a pained financial existence in a rather ordinary middle class house filled with furniture and art that I purchased for Chris's million dollar mansion. They're still in relatively good condition, though a bit ragged around the edges after a couple of moves and a few years of wear. Is that me?

It made no sense to part with everything after the divorce. I needed to furnish my new residence. But, looking around the room now, most of it just doesn't fit. Maybe I've changed and that's the reason, but what have I changed into?

My closet is as much an amalgamation of income levels as my furniture. I have some designer clothing left, though very little with no place to wear it and a body that doesn't fit into it regardless. There are other assorted clothes I purchased for random retail positions and now something conservative for teaching in the public school district.

I've been reading my inspirational books but I can't remember which comes first, the chicken or the egg. Meaning, if I organize my home to reflect who I want to be, my interior will pick up on it. Or, if, once I get myself together on the inside I'll quickly and easily be able to get my house in order. I'm sure there are two schools of thought on the subject, as there are on almost any topic under the sun.

Right now, I'm eating my 99 cent turkey taco special on exquisite bone china and sipping my beer from fabulous French crystal. One place setting of my silverware cost more than what I currently make in a week!

Do I think of Chris when I look around at all this stuff? I want to lie and say I don't but honestly, how can I not? Is he what's really holding me back? It was he, after all, that told me I needed to get my life together.

And, I will. Right after I finish my tacos.

More tomorrow!

All my heart,

Diana

Goodbye Hello

{ SIX }

"Good morning, everyone."

"Good morning, Lysette."

"Thank you all for being here today."

Lysette, the store manager at *The Bod*, called an emergency meeting yesterday. I got the news just as I was logging on to look for a sub position. Today was supposed to be my day off but because I had to attend Lysette's meeting, I lost out on the opportunity to make some money teaching. Meetings at *The Bod* were always on the weekend, so I was surprised that we were called in on a Tuesday morning.

"Gather 'round. We have a message from our CEO. He'll be giving you some big news. Go ahead, Jerome."

Ohmigod! The CEO is at our meeting? This must be some pretty important news. Maybe the company got bought out.

Lysette held up her tablet to the small group gathered here and we could see Jerome Olsen appear.

"Good morning, ladies."

"Morning, Jerome."

"I want to thank y'all for being here so early on a Tuesday morning. I know your lives are rather hectic and I really appreciate y'all making the effort to join in."

OK, Jerome, get to the news already!

"I know how hard y'all work to make *The Bod* a success in Las Vegas. Your numbers for the holiday season just made stretch goal. So, I'm happy to say you'll be receiving your $250 bonus in your next check."

The entire room cheered. A $250 bonus was such a blessing with the post-holiday slowness that we experienced. But, the CEO doesn't show up at a company meeting to tell us about our measly $250 bonuses which, hmm…, are coming one paycheck early. I wasn't prepared for the real news.

"Now, y'all know that we opened the Las Vegas store two years ago and we had great expectations for that location. However, after further analysis and review of our history at Runway Fashion Mall, we've decided to close the Las Vegas location and relocate to Scottsdale. We feel we can reach more of a regular clientele there and not face the ups and downs of tourist traffic."

After a combined, "What?" the room fell silent. We couldn't believe that after such a short period of time, *The Bod* Las Vegas was closing its doors.

"Of course, those of y'all willing to relocate we would welcome with open arms. It's always great to have a new location with current staff. Y'all are great members of the team but I do understand if y'all choose not to follow with us."

I was in shock, as was everyone else in the room. Everyone except for Lysette. Hmm…and Taneesha. As store manager, of course Lysette was informed as to the urgency of the meeting agenda. She'd been with the company since the beginning and was sure to go on to Scottsdale to manage that store. Jerome considered her a valuable commodity. I wasn't sure what Taneesha's deal was. I'd have to find out.

"Now, Lysette will answer any questions y'all may have. Once again, I thank you for your service to our company and our loyal clientele. If you choose to move on, I wish y'all the best of luck and we'll gladly give y'all a glowing reference."

Well, there was certainly no way I was relocating to Arizona, even if they offered me a management position, which I knew would never happen.

Lysette turned off her tablet and gave us her undivided attention.

"I'm really sorry that *The Bod* is closing here in town. I fought to keep our location open, but outside of the holidays, for two years now, our sales have not met expectations. I think we have a great team and it's a shame we have to break it up. Unless...any of you are thinking you might join me in Scottsdale?"

Aha! I knew she'd be opening the new store.

Not a hand went up. These were diehard Las Vegans. There was plenty of retail in town and eventually each and every one of us would find a new job.

"Oh, and one more thing. Our target close will be Valentine's Day, if not sooner. Today we'll begin marking everything down 25 percent. If we sell faster than anticipated, we'll close earlier and pay you your average weekly pay for the remaining days until February 14th. Since I'm the only one moving on to Scottsdale, I realize you may find a new position sooner than our closing date. If it's possible for you to stay till the end, I'd greatly appreciate it but I do understand if you want to move on."

Lysette paused while she looked out at the sea of shocked faces. I'd never worked anywhere that closed its doors, so this was a first, even for me.

"OK then. I'll put up the liquidation signage. No need to mark the items individually. The computer will handle the discount automatically. We won't be receiving any new shipments, so if a customer needs a size we don't have in stock, they'll have to pay regular price to have it sent to them. However, we won't charge them shipping."

Lysette got a little choked up as she continued.

"I'm really very sorry that we couldn't make a go of it here in Vegas. It was a pleasure to work with each and every one of you. I'm just glad we made our numbers for the holidays so we can part on a high note with your bonus."

Everyone jumped up and group hugged. I stayed to the outside of the circle. It definitely was a sad day but I wasn't that emotionally tied to anyone here.

The circle broke up and I pulled Taneesha to the side to chat.

"So, what are your plans, Taneesha?"

She was such an evangelist for the company I'd be surprised if they let her go.

"Well, nothing is finalized at the moment. I'm a year and a half away from graduation. I have two choices. I can transfer to Scottsdale and finish my schooling in Tempe, which will probably extend the time it takes for me to graduate which seems silly. Or, I can stay here and graduate, then move to the corporate headquarters. I'd have to find another job in the meantime, but my heart is with *The Bod*."

"I can see how that's a tough decision for you. Are they offering any incentive to move?"

Taneesha gave me one of those 'I don't share such financial information with you' looks. Funny, coming from Miss Noseypants.

"It's an on-going discussion. I'll just have to see what works best for me. What about you, Diana?"

"Well, luckily I started substitute teaching, as you know, so I'll probably do that for a while until I figure out my next move."

"That's so smart, Diana. I was surprised you didn't offer to move to Scottsdale as I think that would be great for you, but as long as you have income here, it makes total sense to stay."

Well, obviously, Taneesha bought into my whole politically-correct crap that I offered her. I hated working at *The Bod* but at least it paid the rent.

"Yeah, well, I have family here so I don't anticipate I'll be moving for a very long time."

Lysette stepped in to interrupt us.

"Taneesha, can you please help put up the signs in front?"

"Oh, sure, Lysette. See you later, Diana."

I thought it odd that Lysette dismissed Taneesha so quickly. Either they had some big plans in the works for Taneesha that Lysette didn't want her to share with me, or Lysette wanted to speak with me privately.

"Diana, it really has been a pleasure working with you. I know you'll find a new position in town. Just let me know if there's anything I can do to help. I have contacts at many of the stores in the mall."

Well, la di da. Lysette is practically kicking me to the curb.

"Thanks, Lysette, but I'll be fine. I always am."

"Great, Diana. That's the spirit!"

Lysette knew I wouldn't stand for a hug from her, so she rubbed my shoulder and walked away.

I was still reeling from this morning's announcement when I got home. I wasn't quite sure what to do. I could call Mom and Dad or Helen, but actually, they were all working, so I couldn't really bother them. Gizzi was more easily reachable – oh, wait, no she's not, she's traveling out of the country. I'd already broken up with Tom. I went through my phone contacts and realized I had no one to talk to about my dumb luck of having to look for still another job. Maybe the Universe was telling me I needed to solve this one on my own.

I wasn't quite prepared to have to spend all my time substitute teaching. I wanted to ease into it while I was still in retail in the event I decided I really didn't like it after all. Now I had no choice unless I was incredibly lucky and got hired at another retail store.

But, that could have its downside as well. If I were hired full time, I wouldn't have the flexibility to try out the teaching gig, unless I was guaranteed to have my weekend so to speak on weekdays. But, working full time in retail is exhausting and I'm not sure I'd have the stamina to sub on my days off, knowing how energetic some of those youngsters can be.

This certainly was a dilemma but I just had to work through it myself. The only other people I really kept in touch with were Jazzy and Pamela and I wasn't about to share one minutia about my personal life with either of them. We were simply the Lotto Ladies. That was it. No more.

I decided I was given this time for a reason – boy, all those spiritual books must be melting into my psyche – and spent the rest of the day journaling, cleaning through my office and checking out my finances. It was ugly. There's no other way to describe it.

Once 6 p.m. came, I logged on to the school district site to see what positions were available for tomorrow. I didn't have to be at *The Bod* until 6 p.m. so I had plenty of time to sub during the day. A quick scan found nothing in my area or adjoining areas. There were a few positions across town but I didn't know those sections of town that well and I didn't want to screw up so early in my substitute teaching career.

I promised myself I'd look again later in the evening, but instead I fell fast asleep while watching old episodes of *The Nanny*. How I love that Fran Fine. I'd have to check again in the morning and rush off to the school if something became available. Otherwise, my daytime was my own and I had a lot of thinking to do.

I woke up at the ungodly hour of 5 a.m. after an incredibly restful sleep. I checked for openings and sure enough, there was a sub position at the high school right around the corner from my house! I wasn't sure I wanted to attack high school yet after my experience with third grade, but the opening was for an instructor in the fashion program. How perfect! I didn't even know any of the schools had a fashion program. I quickly snatched the opening, made myself some coffee and hopped in the shower.

As I entered the school building on my way to the front office, I looked around and realized many – if not most – of these students were bigger and taller than me! How was I supposed to keep these students in line when any one of them could probably knock me to the ground with a single punch. Not that that happens in school. I just didn't have my feet grounded enough yet in teaching to feel comfortable at any grade level.

I walked into the classroom to find the teacher there! Turns out, she was just finishing up the lesson plans. Her child was sick and she had to take her to the doctor. She handed me a couple of pages of notes and a DVD, wished me luck and ran out the door.

I looked at the lesson plans. They were very simple. Show the DVD to each class period and have them write up three questions for open discussion following the DVD, which lasted approximately 35 minutes. The movie took the viewer behind the scenes of the creative process for a major fashion design house. I thought that would be extremely interesting. Unfortunately, these were mostly 12th graders who were pretty much focused on graduation and graduation alone.

But, my job as a substitute is not to impart extreme knowledge; it's simply to keep the kids safe and sane for the day. If they learn anything, that's bonus. As I watched the film for the seventh time, I wondered how even the teacher could keep her sanity through the day, and with the lights off and the lack of windows, my biggest problem was staying awake.

One thirty p.m. came soon enough, and I went through the drive-thru on my way home to catch a nap before heading to *The Bod*. The day was far more uneventful than third grade had been, but I still didn't feel like I found a comfortable fit in substitute teaching. I'll try again tomorrow.

Dear Diary,

Contrary to what Jerome and Lysette said during our urgent meeting, my hours have been cut drastically at *The Bod*. I'm on the schedule only two days a week now for a grand total of just 10 hours!

It's so stressful trying to find a new sub position every single day. If I'm lucky enough to find something the night before, I can plan how my day will be and go to bed at a decent time, knowing I'm going to make money tomorrow. If there's nothing available, I have to get up extra early to check the new postings and get ready in a flash, not knowing if I'll be subbing nearby or across town. And, sometimes I'm up and dressed and the only openings are in very challenging neighborhoods. I'm still not confident enough as a sub to attempt those positions although they do pay $15 more per day.

I added up how much I'd make if I were to sub full time. I would gross less than $20,000 for the year. And, I'd still have to find work during the summer. There are several schools like Helen's that are year round so there may be some positions, but not enough to pay the rent.

I was watching *The Secret* again last night. Somewhere in there was the comment that I create my own problems. Really? Like, I willed myself to live a poor and destitute life when I know how wonderful a successful life can be? I don't understand it.

Maybe I'll start listening to country music. Those lyrics always ring true.

More tomorrow!

All my heart,

Diana

The Unruly Mob

{ SEVEN }

"Welcome to Buffalo Bill Cody Middle School. You must be our long term."

"Yep, that's me. Just show me to my room."

"Ahem, yes, well, you understand this is just for a few weeks. We have been trying to hire someone and I think we'll have a new staff teacher in place by the middle of next month. The students have struggled all year. Their original teacher had to leave town unexpectedly to care for an ill parent, and it's been difficult ever since. It's hard to find someone who can take on a long term position and is willing to do so. We were ready to break up the class but everyone is so overcrowded already we really wanted to keep these students together."

The principal looked me up and down, then looked at her assistant principal before continuing.

"OK, I think you may have the strength to deal with this class. I'll walk you over."

Cindi R. Maciolek

I was a bit perplexed by her comment. Sure, I'd only been subbing for a couple of weeks, but I'd been in business management for a long time prior. I'd dealt with the toughest of the tough. Of course I'd have the strength to deal with this class.

The principal led me through the administration building, out into the courtyard and over to what should be my classroom for the next few weeks. I'd seen the posting a couple of times for this position, but it had an LT next to it, so I thought that meant limited time, like a half day, so I ignored it in favor of something day-long. I guess I should have paid more attention during orientation.

Last night I was desperate for something close to home so I decided to click on the listing. Lo and behold, LT meant long term. It was for seventh grade English. I figured, I could handle that. Plus, long term positions paid an extra $10/day after the first two weeks and I'd always know where I was going the next morning. No more hunting for positions every night. It would also give me my closest experience to full time teaching in the public school. With *The Bod* fading behind me, I needed all the extra bucks I could get.

The principal opened the door to the classroom, where the noise level was at a higher decibel than a Las Vegas nightclub. However, the minute she walked in, the class settled down. It was like recruits coming to attention at basic training.

"Class, here is your new long term substitute, Miss MacKenzie."

"Hello, Miss MacKenzie."

"Now, I know we've had this discussion several times in the past, but Miss MacKenzie assures me she'll be with you until your official teacher arrives in a few weeks."

Groans from the students.

"Miss MacKenzie will be responsible for maintaining the lesson plans provided by the other teachers and grading you according to their policy. If there are any issues, she is to call myself or security immediately. I will not have you treat Miss MacKenzie disrespectfully."

Security?

Already, two of the students in the back row were planning something. I could see it in their eyes. Plus, they power bumped which could only mean one thing: trouble for me.

"Miss MacKenzie?"

"Thank you…"

I didn't even know the principal's name. I'm sure I'll learn it quickly given the demeanor of this crowd.

"I'm very happy to be here. We have a lot of work to do, and I'm sure with the support of the entire team, I'll be able to do a fine job until your teacher arrives."

"Chica, why should we believe that you'll stay? None of the other subs did."

I looked to the principal for support, who just put her head down then looked the other way.

"I prefer to be called Miss MacKenzie. However, in answer to your question, I promise, I'm not going anywhere. I'll be here every single day until your new teacher arrives. We need to work together to be in the best shape possible when he or she comes into the classroom. You haven't had a regular teacher all year and that's not your fault, but we'll do our best and make a go of it."

The classroom started to get noisy and I could feel myself shake. I'd never been in front of such an angry mob before. But, I made a promise to these students and I planned to keep it. My only other choice was to go back to the daily grind of looking for other open positions and I much preferred this long term opportunity. Plus, in spite of their cold reception, I could tell these were students I could communicate with. Maybe I found my calling in middle school as I suspected.

The principal walked up to me and whispered in my ear, "I'll give you three days."

I looked at her as she walked out the door while the noise level in the classroom continued to grow.

Immediately after her departure, one of the other seventh grade English teachers came in and provided me with a stack of lesson plans and teaching manuals. She smiled, grateful that she wouldn't be adding a number of this unruly crowd to her already overflowing classroom.

She left then security walked in. Once again, the class became quiet. This security guard was female, large and obviously strong. She gave a few specific students a look that said she was watching them, then she said to me, "Just call if you need anything, Miss."

She turned around and walked out the door.

That was it for the moment. No more visitors. It was already halfway through first period. The one good thing about middle school is that the students change class every 50 minutes or so as they rotate through their schedules. I was to teach three regular English classes, two advanced placement and one journalism class.

With my background in PR, I felt pretty good about that one – well, honestly, I should be able to handle all of them with some ease, once I get the class under control. I would only have my homeroom class first thing in the morning and last class before they went home. One period was for English and the second was study hall. I wasn't sure how much I'd accomplish at either, but the classes in the middle were well behaved and under control.

Now that I was acting like a full-time teacher, I really had to pay attention to the school policies. With the long term position came more responsibilities, not only regarding caring for the students but doing lesson plans, grading papers and actually teaching them something!

One important school policy was that students were not allowed to have their cell phones out or even turned on during class time. They could only use them during lunch or before and after school. To a generation of texters, keeping their hands idle for such a long time proved a major challenge.

One morning, I was writing the day's assignment on the board as the students were arriving for first period. Something caught the corner of my eye. I noticed two students moving their fingers in unusual ways. As I stopped to watch what they were doing, they noticed me and stopped their actions. It was then that I realized they were using sign language!

Now, some people might say that's pretty commendable, that at some point in their lives they will put that skill to use. Others will say it's pretty ingenious that these students who won't do their English homework would become adept at a language that typically is not taught in middle school. The planners they receive at the beginning of the school year even have a complete sign language alphabet section, taunting them to learn a practical skill without any prodding from a teacher or parent.

But, to a teacher, sign language is a threat to classroom attention and organization. As passing notes in the old day was bothersome, this is the modern-day secret communication code.

On some level, I was proud of everyone who embraced it and used it. My biggest annoyance was the fact that I didn't know sign language myself! I felt as if I were in a foreign country, sitting at a table for dinner, not understanding a word of the conversation.

There was no real way to ban their use of sign language. Cell phones were an easier thing to control. These students were savvy. We locked eyes. They knew I knew what they were up to and they knew I couldn't do a darn thing about it. Well, at least they're learning something worthwhile in school. And, I continued to learn something new every day.

"Do you really think you could be a public school teacher, sweetie?"

"Helen does it."

"Yes, and Helen is very good at it. She has a passion for it. You're a different breed than she is. Seriously. How much did you decorate your house for the holidays?"

Ooh, Gizzi was cutting to the core.

"Uh, not at all."

"There! If you can't even decorate your own house for one month-long holiday season, how are you going to keep a classroom interesting for your students?"

Perhaps Gizzi knew me better than I knew myself, but it was still worth a shot.

"It's my personality that will engage them, not my decorating skills."

"Not listening, Diana."

"But, they have a great pension plan!"

I could hear Gizzi let out an exasperating sigh.

"Diana, you're only in your early 30's. You're a businesswoman, not a teacher. You have a long *business* life ahead of you. You just need to focus and build a career that you love."

"And, I need to pay the rent and put gas in my car and food in my stomach!"

"Look, doll, teaching is a noble profession but at least at the public school level, it's not for you. Trust me. Go ahead and try it. See how you're able to engage students. It takes a very special person to be able to teach K-12. You're very special, but a different ilk. It's not for you."

Well, at least Gizzi still cared enough to give me the truth about myself. I kept trying to fit into everyone else's world instead of creating my own. It was truly a struggle as I was very different from the rest of my immediate family. I was more of a risk taker, an adventurer. They preferred to enjoy life and know there was a weekly paycheck in their accounts. Both sides had their positive points. What was so wrong with me trying the other way for once?

'Thanks, Giz. I'll work it out. You have enough on your mind."

"Oh, don't go that route with me, Ms. MacKenzie! I am your friend – your forever friend. I am here through thick and thin. I always have time for you."

"You're so sweet, Gizzi Boudrot! Thanks for always being there."

"Any time, sweetie. Any time. Now, go back to your room and put a plan together!"

Sometimes when I need to clear my mind, I head to the Strip to do a little communing with the neon gods to see if they have any answers for me. I guess they're not neon anymore but digital LED. Perhaps I'll have to go downtown if I want a bit of vintage Vegas!

So often, Las Vegas residents run as far away from the lights as possible, forgetting the very reason millions of people visit our fair city on an annual basis. There's something inspiring and rejuvenating about a stroll down Las Vegas Boulevard. In just a short drive from my house, I'm transported to another planet. Amidst the margaritas by the yard and drunken revelers, I can't help but find some spiritual guidance. Walking among the crowds was my way of quieting my inner voice so I could listen to my angels. One of those inspirational books I read told me to commune with my angels. Could they be found here in Sin City?

Looking around at all the over-the-top architecture and attractions, I couldn't help but respect the amount of work that went into creating each and every one of these projects. I wonder if someday I'd be responsible for my own legacy contribution to this world.

When I look back, I have to admit, I've had my ups and downs but somehow, I've always been able to pay my bills. Some new opportunity arises just when one disappears. Naturally, I wish the new opportunity provided a significant salary increase from what I'm currently earning, but I also have to admit that I'm still not sure what I want to do, and Gizzi wants me to go to my room and put together a plan.

I've lost touch with high tech – at least behind the scenes as I knew it. I've gone through various stages of retail. I'm now substitute teaching. None of these were ever on my bucket list. Running a company, traveling the world, marrying my soul mate and having two children – a boy and a girl – those are at the top. I always thought I'd get my career started whereupon I'd meet my soul mate. Then I could take time off to care for our children until they started school, somewhat similar to Gizzi's plan, only she's actually living it!

I've heard time and time again you accomplish more goals if you write them down, and even if you only get halfway to your goal, you're farther along than most people will ever be. I understand that, but I'm not happy going halfway. I want to go to the top! I have the ability to go to the top. Why am I holding myself back? Oh, yeah, I don't know what I want to do.

Sometimes, in a world in which we have so many options, choosing one is difficult. Have you seen those 20 page restaurant menus? How in the world can you decide what to eat? You just pick something and hope there wasn't another item you wanted more that you missed on page 18.

A lot of people live their lives that way, me included. I can pretty much do anything and I've just fallen into my future, one job at a time. Some people are perfectly content spending 40 hours a week doing *whatever* so they could spend their free time doing what they love. Good for them because, honestly, I don't know what I want to do with my free time either.

I once had a boss who was really tough on me. He always picked on my work and it upset me. I finally confronted him about it because he didn't seem to do the same to others on staff. He told me he paid more attention to me because he felt I would do great things with my life and I'd appreciate the lessons in details in the future. It worked for a while. Now I'm waiting to put that into practice once again.

I'm really good at – and quite enjoy, in fact – identifying opportunities and weaknesses in a business. But who would take the advice of a substitute teacher/retail sales associate? No one would take me seriously. Not anymore, regardless of what my experience has been.

It's a hard pill to swallow. I'm only in my 30's and I feel so – disposable! No one needs me! I used to be in such demand but I feel as if I surpassed my Use By date.

Some folks move to Las Vegas with high expectations and soon relocate. Others are able to make a success of themselves. Then there's me, who currently is still working on survival.

Someday I'll really appreciate all I've gone through and look back on it as a blessing. At the very least, I hope I'm better with my money!

Dear Diary,

I've been through so much financial hardship these last few years, I'm always interested in ways that people are making a go of their lives.

Case in point. There's a male teacher at Cody Middle School who is hell bent on retirement, but in a good way – I think. No matter how you look at it, he's definitely motivated.

He started teaching immediately after college, after which he got his Master's degree and took any additional classes he could to put him at the top of his pay grade. Once he finished his schooling, he took a job delivering pizzas at night, which he does six nights a week. His goal is to save all the money he can so when he turns the ripe old age of 52 with 30 years of teaching, he can retire.

I admire his hutzpah, for sure. Not many people will make that sort of commitment. He has given up other things like starting a family until he retires. He wants to focus strictly on his finances for now. Of course, he also has to be healthy and able to commit to this schedule for such a long term.

He's currently 42 and has just 10 years till retirement. He looks a little rough around the edges, but considering how long he's been maintaining this crazy schedule, he actually looks pretty good! More power to him!

I'd normally be attracted to a guy who is that motivated, but I'm still looking for the custom suits and laundered shirts, not blue jeans and a Toyota with 200,000 miles on it. This man wants to retire but lives very frugally. I've done it. Trust me, it's not for me. Mom and Dad are that way. I can't do it. I want money!

I could never go about my retirement plan the way he does. I need a job – no, a career – that offers creativity and leadership and travel plus a life! – but once he turns 52, he'll be able to do anything he wants as long as his health holds up. That's still a very young age to be free financially, but my heart needs to be free when it comes to my work, and to treat myself to something materialistic every now and then. I just hope in the end I'll still be able to have a very comfortable retirement with complete financial freedom as well.

Here's to a happy retirement!

More tomorrow!

All my heart,

Diana

Shape Up and Ship Out

{ EIGHT }

"Miss MacKenzie?"

I heard a voice call my name as I flew through the administration building on my way to pick up the class roll for the day. I had been enjoying my long term sub position for a week and a half and I could breathe more easily, knowing I'd have a regular gig for at least a few more weeks. Next week I would start to earn that extra $10/day until the end of my assignment. Not a lot of extra money, but every dollar counts.

I turned to see who was calling my name. It was the assistant principal. She motioned me to come back to the principal's office. Had I done something wrong? Was I wearing something inappropriate? I mean, why else do you get called to the principal's office?

"This way, please," she said as she let me into her boss's office.

I sat down and put my messenger bag on the floor. I felt extremely uncomfortable and something in my gut told me this was not going to be a good day.

Principal Masala came breezing in with a smile on her face.

"Morning, Miss MacKenzie. How are you doing today?"

I wanted to say that as soon as she told me why I was here I would be able to answer that question, but I was polite.

"Fine, thank you."

"Great!" she said as she sat down. She put her arms on her desk and clasped her hands before she spoke again. I felt like a 10-year-old in Miss Wilson's class.

"Well, I have some good news and some bad news and some good news," she said.

Oy! Get to it already!

"The good news is that we were able to secure a full time teacher for your class and he starts today," she said.

Now, how exactly is that good news? Oh, wait, that's good news for her.

"The bad news is that your long term sub position has ended."

And she couldn't let me know yesterday so I could find a place to work today?

"We weren't sure if he would be able to get to town today so I didn't say anything. However, since you're here, we'll use you in the administration building so that you don't lose any income for the day."

So, is that the second good news? Doesn't sound like good news to me. I still have to get back on the computer tonight and look for something for tomorrow.

"Now, the other good news. One of the science teachers is having unexpected knee surgery on Monday and will be out for three weeks. You've proven yourself to us and other teachers at your grade level, so we've decided to offer that position to you first before we post it online. Would you be willing to accept that? It's sixth grade science."

Wow! OK, that was nice of the principal to find a new position for me so quickly at her school. I wasn't keen on science but I'd certainly pick that over some of the other options.

"Sure, that would be great. Thank you."

"Fabulous! I'll have Mrs. Gordon meet with you after class today so you can get a complete understanding of what she needs you to cover over the next few weeks, as well as introduce you to her tenants. Good day."

Principal Masala got up and breezed out of the office to greet the new seventh grade English teacher that just arrived. I was still trying to wrap my head around everything we just discussed, especially that whole tenants thing, but I was quickly led to the mail room to work among some of the students I had just been teaching. It was a bit humiliating as I had no idea what I was doing and had to rely on them to train me. It definitely made me look powerless and gave them all something to talk about in their sign language.

Luckily, 15 minutes into the whole episode, I was taken to the music room to sub for a sub who called off the assignment. Reminiscent of the fashion class, I would watch the exact same music documentary for seven classes. As informative as it was, musicians want to play. I wish I had more musical knowledge but a sub knows to do as they are told, so I popped in the DVD right after I took attendance and perched myself in the back of the room where I could watch the students be bored.

"Diana, I'm so happy you're here!" Gizzi said as she gave me the biggest hug of her life. She was positively glowing, Jean-Louis by her side, who followed Gizzi's bear hug with a friendly one. JL and I were friends, mostly through Gizzi, and this was the first personal social event where we'd seen each other although we'd met at many a business networking event. In just a few short months, he'd practically be family.

Destiny Dollars

I was summoned to San Jose for the start of my friend's wedding season. When Gizzi and Jean-Louis compared schedules, they realized the only time they would have a Saturday night together for a couple of months was this Saturday. If they waited to hold the engagement party, it would start to conflict with wedding plans. So, on a spur of the moment, I was asked to fly into town to mix and mingle and celebrate the lovely couple's engagement.

I held back my tears. This was the most emotional day of my recent memory. Helen and Gabe were married 15 years ago and although the birth of their kids touched me tremendously, that was several years ago as well. My own wedding to Chris was such a spontaneous event, I didn't really have time to get emotional about it. But this! This was true love.

"I wouldn't have missed it for anything!"

Well, that's not exactly true. Ok, maybe it is. I was lucky that I was working as a substitute teacher because I now had my weekends off. If I was still working retail, I'd probably be closing on a Saturday night and this event was planned on such short notice I would have had to call in sick in order to attend. Which, I'm sure I would have done. I am the maid of honor, after all.

I had hoped I'd be able to spend some time with Gizzi, maybe even stay at her house for a night or two, but that was not to be. I tried never to miss a family event now that I had family in town, and Justin and Grace both had recitals – Justin on Friday night and Grace Saturday morning – so I wasn't able to even leave until Saturday afternoon, arriving just before cocktail hour. I'd be flying back after dinner. Gizzi and JL were both heading out of town on redeyes for business, so there was no real reason to stay.

I stressed over what to wear; Lord knows I don't have the expansive wardrobe I once owned nor a penny to spend on something new. Plus, I still had my *Positano* poundage going on. I looked fine for a Midwestern lass but I wasn't my svelte California self. I searched through the remnants of my closet for a cocktail frock that would be forgiving but fashionable and go with my lone pair of stilettos. I found a wrap dress buried deep among all my too-small favorites, a dress that would hide my tummy while still show off my great legs.

I was picked up at the airport in a town car and driven straight to the country club where the intimate affair was to unfold. Gizzi emphasized this would be in definite contrast to the wedding. The only people attending the engagement party were her parents, her brothers, his sister, the remaining bridesmaids, the ushers and any of their significant others. I had no plus one so I went alone, but even this small group numbered around 30 for dinner.

Colin Bailey obviously put his touches on the event, but it really was very low key, just a cocktail hour and dinner. The clubhouse was beautifully decorated, with fragrant flowers everywhere, and tiny lights twinkling like stars across the ceiling. Other than that, the only significant indication of the special event was the engagement cake in the shape of France, their honeymoon destination. Colin was a class act but I could never forget whose money was actually paying for this.

I looked around the room, inhaling the sweet smell of abundance, knowing that this was just the start of a most amazing year for this happy couple. I was anxious to have my own special time, but I had to step back and allow this to be Gizzi and Jean-Louis's moment. Still I planned to keep my eyes open to the possibility that the man I was to marry might be right in front of me. Or, be introduced by someone in front of me.

I was so close with Gizzi that marrying into this happy crowd would be like completing the circle. I never thought about marrying for money. I was certain I could provide amply for my future, but I seem to have lost the ability to do so. If ever I had the chance to meet someone of financial value, this wedding would be my ticket.

Unfortunately for me, Gizzi's brothers were all successful – and married. JL's friends and family were mostly in France, a place I would surely love but had no intention of relocating to, leaving no one at this particular party potentially available but the waiters who, like me, walked among the wealthy but weren't part of them. However, I hadn't seen the guest list for the wedding, so I was still holding out hope.

"C'mon, sweetie," Gizzi said as she grabbed my hand and led me to the other side of the room, "I'll introduce you to everyone."

Once the small crowd cleared, I was faced with the buffest, most gorgeous bridal party I'd ever seen. No need to Photoshop these bodies. I don't think there's an ounce of fat on them! I'd be the only one to go under the cursor unless I stepped up my game and got into fighting shape by December.

As I suspected, four of the five bridesmaids were Gizzi's cousins. The fifth was Jean-Louis's sister. The ushers included Gizzi's three brothers, two of Jean-Louis's cousins, and the best man who was a childhood friend of JL and just happened to be in town. He was visiting with his girlfriend and his child from a previous relationship. Pierre was a Frenchman with a wandering eye and an even worse wandering hand which squeezed my butt the moment we were introduced.

"Giselle. It's time," Jean-Louis said as he stepped up to take Gizzi's hand. JL never called Gizzi by her nickname. He only called her Giselle or some other pet name he had for her. I'd called her Gizzi for so long I'd nearly forgotten what her given name was!

The DJ announced the engaged couple who took the stage to give their thanks for all of us sharing in this special time in their lives. They were both beaming, eyes twinkling, so tender, so touching – it was so obvious they were madly in love.

We took our seats at various tables around the room. I, unfortunately, had the seat next to Pierre who repeatedly put his hand on my thigh.

"I like some meat on my women," he whispered in my ear. If it weren't for Gizzi, I would have stabbed this man's hand with my fork and stormed out of the place. I simply put my hand on top of his and poked one of my nails into his thumb. He jumped a bit, blamed it on a chill, and went on with his dinner.

After an exquisite French meal, we spent the next hour taking turns toasting the happy couple. Luckily, none of us had to drive after imbibing as cars were provided for even the locals.

By 9 p.m., Gizzi and Jean-Louis were heading out the door, air kissing the crowd. I managed to sneak in a good-bye hug before they left for the airport.

"I'm so happy for you, Giz," I said. "You deserve the best."

"Thanks, sweetie," Gizzi replied as Jean-Louis pulled her toward the car. "Thanks for always being there for me, Diana. You'll find your prince. I can feel it in my bones!"

We both laughed as she sat in the back seat of the car, next to her betrothed. This was all like such a fairy tale, only in this story, the woman is just as strong and confident as the man. She doesn't need to be rescued. She simply needs to find someone special to share her life with. Once she does, she doesn't let go. Now, that's the kind of fairy tales we should be reading to young girls!

I grabbed my handbag, said good-bye to Mr. and Mrs. Boudrot as well as Gizzi's brothers, waved a quick farewell to the other members of the bridal party then headed for my car to catch the last flight of the night to Las Vegas. On my way to the car I was accosted by Pierre who planted a wet one down my throat. When I finally wrangled myself loose from his grip, I slapped him strong and hard across his face. He smiled and grabbed my ass, then turned and went inside the clubhouse to collect his belongings – his girlfriend and child.

"Such an idiot," I muttered to myself.

The flight home, thankfully, was uneventful although it was full of people excited to visit Las Vegas. I was going home so my perspective was slightly different. I just wanted to climb into bed and let the good memories of the night lull me to sleep. Pierre would have to be dealt with, but he was out of my hair at least until the rehearsal dinner which was months away. I put him in the Jazzy compartment of my brain and instead concentrated on the beauty of true love between Gizzi and Jean-Louis.

I woke up Sunday morning with a bit of a hangover and a lot of incentive to get back in shape. Having met the other members of the bridal party, my Las Vegas curves were not going to cut it. I needed to be buff for this wedding.

Everyone says you want to look good on that special day. Well, it's not my special day but I still want to look as if I belong. This was a joining of two major forces in technology and as the happy couple, they were the darlings of the industry. Not only would that special day be exceptional, the photos would live on forever. Granted, the whole world is only interested in Gizzi and Jean-Louis, but photos of the entire bridal party were sure to surface in both national and international media and I wasn't about to stand out as the dowdy one. I want to look hot!

It was an eye-opening experience to see how far down the hole I'd gone. I used to be right there, side by side with Gizzi. Now, she was at the top of her game and I was barely treading water. It showed in every aspect of my life, not only my slightly-plump body but also my complexion, my hair color and style and important things like my manicure and pedicure, which I now did myself. Money may not buy happiness but it certainly can make you look good.

While I enjoyed renting a home I did miss the days when I had access to the free community exercise equipment at the townhome. I sucked it up and signed a two-year contract with a local gym to prepare for Gizzi's wedding. I'd have to find something else to give up – food, perhaps? – to balance my budget because looking good for this wedding was a top priority. I was not going to risk being the ugly maid of honor. It'll be tough but I'll force myself to go to the gym on a daily basis.

I know I have to focus on my own career, but this wedding will be at the forefront of my day until December. All I can hope is that my personal life gets a boost from my laser focus on Gizzi's wedding, as the high tide lifts all boats. Still, December was a long way off and anything could happen in the meantime.

Dear Diary,

Oh, how I wish I could afford a personal trainer!

I want to look awesome at Gizzi and Jean-Louis's wedding. I've met the other members of the bridal party and they're all in magnificent shape! I'm the dowdiest – and I'm the maid of honor! I've kind of let myself go living in Vegas for these last few years. But, a perfect body doesn't just appear overnight. It takes time, effort, commitment – money!

Sure, I joined a gym and they have personal trainers but even at a discount, it's still like $40/hour! That's nearly three times what I make! There's no way I could do multiple weekly sessions. The funds just aren't there. I'm having a hard enough time figuring out how to pay the gym membership!

I may be able to scrounge up just enough funds to pay for one session and have the trainer map out a schedule for me. Then, the onus will be on me to perform. I'll have to make the effort to get in the car and actually drive to my workout. I know I can do it. I did it in San Jose. Of course, I was years younger then, too, but a woman can look good at any age, right?

I know Gizzi would want me to look and feel my best at her wedding, and if I mentioned it to her, she would pay for my trainer without blinking an eye. But, she's already covering so many of my costs, I couldn't possibly add another to it. Plus, I would just become a needy scumbag instead of being a friend.

I couldn't do that to her. I'll look good no matter what. There must be some videos online of how to get a great body without a gym membership – even though I now have one! Hmm…I should have thought of that in the first place.

Oh well!

More tomorrow!

All my heart,

Diana

Spider Lady

{ NINE }

Teaching science class was a definite shift from English. First of all, there are no desks in the room, only tables, which allowed to more easily conduct experiments and projects. The tables in this room were set up in a U shape, with the opening at the front of the classroom to allow me to lecture from the center of the U, with the teacher's desk at the front. Students sat on both the inside and outside of this configuration which meant some of their backs were to me if I were in the center of it all.

I had already been introduced to the class by Mrs. Gordon before her departure for surgery, who informed them she would be out for four weeks – three weeks of class and one week of winter break – and they should obey my every word. She told us all that she would be in touch to make sure everything was under control. Mrs. Gordon was especially passionate about her class and took great pride in teaching them all things science.

Mrs. Gordon was also passionate about teaching the students the responsibility of taking care of pets. However, since the school district didn't allow dogs or cats in the classroom, an entire section of the room was dedicated to unusual tenants, each having their own student owner responsible for taking care of them and taking them home during break.

To my chagrin, I was introduced to an iguana, a hamster, a small snake and – horror of horrors – a tarantula! I informed Mrs. Gordon I would not handle any of them, and if they got loose, they were on their own. She laughed.

Sixth graders are a little bit quieter than seventh or eighth graders. They still have some of that elementary school innocence. They also tend to follow instructions as long as they are given clearly. So, I followed what I was taught during orientation, writing today's agenda on one side of the white board, the homework on the other, and my own added twist of what crazy holiday it was in the middle. This little tidbit helped me to bond with the class and let them know I had a sense of humor. It's amazing how many crazy holidays exist!

Just three days into my science long term assignment and all seemed to be going well. It was early morning and the students were arriving and went directly to their seats. As the bell rang, I was finishing up my assignment on the white board. The first 15 minutes of each morning were dedicated to free reading, so the students were quiet in their seats. As I shuffled though some papers on my desk, I started to hear a rumbling in the classroom and one girl let out a shriek which she tried to muffle.

I looked up. When the students realized they had my attention, they all pointed at one boy on the inner circle who was quietly reading his book. I was a bit confused but walked around my desk to stand behind him. And there, I saw it.

Comfortably perched on this boy's back was a spider, the largest I had ever seen. It must have been at least three inches long with thin, long legs. I momentarily froze, trying to figure out what to do. I wanted to scream and run away but I couldn't for the sake of the students. I also had to make sure this wasn't the tarantula that might have gotten loose and chose this boy's back for a playground.

I took another, closer look and it didn't have hairy legs. Confirmed. Not the tarantula. At that moment, the student realized something was going on. He looked up and the class screamed. I told him not to move, there was a spider on his back and I would take care of it. He started to cry.

I couldn't hit the poor student with a newspaper to kill the spider. Even if I didn't miss, I'd probably be hauled into the office for brutality. I needed to be wise about this. I'd never even been camping before so I really had no clue what to do.

I went to my desk, emptied a manila folder then walked back to the boy and stood behind him. I realized I only had one good chance to get this right. I didn't know if the spider was poisonous or how quickly it could move. I just knew I had to send it off to that big web in the sky.

"Lean back," I said.

He leaned forward.

"No, lean back," I said again.

He leaned farther forward. Honestly, they know everything they possibly can about technology but they don't know the difference between forward and backward. I tried again.

"No, bring your back closer to the back of the chair, but don't touch it."

The boy began to move in the right direction. The spider started to prowl as well. I only had a few seconds to become a hero or a loser.

"Stop!"

Thankfully, the spider stopped, too.

I took the manila folder and slid it across the student's back, under the spider's legs and slowly dropped the spider to the floor whereupon I squished it to smithereens. The class exploded in cheers!

"Wow! You're the best, Miss M!"

While I enjoyed the jubilation, my attention turned to the boy.

"Are you OK?" I asked. "Would you like to go to the nurse?"

He wiped the snot from his nose and the tears from his eyes.

"No, I'm fine. My dad parked the truck under the tree last night and left the windows open. I'd better tell him not to do that again."

"That sounds like a smart decision," I said.

I turned to the class who, lucky for me, had not thought to take out their cell phones and either photograph or film the event. I would not be immortalized online as the Spider Lady.

"OK, now that the fun is over for the day, let's get started on Chapter 6."

Word spread fast in this little school and I was the talk of the campus during lunch. The administration was pleased that I handled things so smoothly but other teachers felt I should not have killed the spider, or killed it in front of the entire class. No matter what you do in life, you just can't win. I had to keep reminding myself I did the best I could given the circumstances.

First period after lunch, the female students were still glamming up, taking out their highly-scented *Isabella's Intimates* hand lotion and slathering it all over their hands and arms. Within minutes, one of the male students nearly dropped to the ground. I rushed over to him and helped him back up onto his chair. I had no idea what was going on. A few of the students mentioned he was having an asthma attack.

I quickly called the nurse who came rushing to class with a wheelchair. The moment she walked in, she knew the culprit.

"Hand it over," she said, and all the girls who had just used their scented lotion dug into their purses and gave the containers to the nurse.

"You know we do not allow any scented lotions on campus. We have students who are affected by it. Do you want to send one of your classmates to the hospital just so you can have hands that smell like wildberry?"

"It's not wildberry, it's Lovegods," one of the smartass students replied.

"You. To the dean's office. Now!"

The student had obviously had previous experience with the dean's office, packed up her books and sauntered out of the room with a smirk on her face.

While we were tied up trying to help the student with the asthma attack, other students made their way to the pen and began to play with the pets. The iguana was soon in someone's hands and out of the tank.

"Put that away!" I scolded.

"Mrs. Gordon lets us play with him!" they replied.

"I'm not Mrs. Gordon. Put that away. Now!"

Reluctantly, they placed the iguana back in his tank, stuffed in a few lettuce leaves as a treat, and went back to their seats.

"Who told him to bend over?" the nurse asked me as she tended to the student suffering from the asthma attack.

"I did. I thought it might calm him," I said.

"You should never do that with someone having an asthma attack. They need to get as much air into their lungs as possible. Tell them to sit up straight and take deep, slow breaths until help arrives."

"Thank you. I will."

Wow! I had no idea that being a teacher – even a substitute – required that I have zoology *and* nursing skills.

I know I thought about teaching so I could be in a more professional environment, but honestly, folding panties required a lot less responsibility for human life. What people did with their panties when they got home was their business. Here, I oversee over 200 students in a seven-hour day, all of whom depend on me to keep them safe during the time I have them. That's a big order for anyone.

I'd had enough excitement for the day and when that final bell rang, I grabbed my belongings, turned in my attendance book and headed straight to the store. I needed a drink today. Whipped cream vodka, here I come.

Dear Diary,

I've never been the type of person to have a lot of friends, but as I get older I'm really beginning to realize what a deficit I have in that category. I never really thought about it much; I always felt like I had all the emotional support I needed. But, sometimes you just need a good friend to turn to and she's not there.

When I lived in California, I always had someone I could turn to, to talk through my troubles – and theirs! – or meet and gossip over lunch or tea or happy hour. I know, most of the time I spoke with Gizzi, but there were other more casual friends I could connect with. Of course, we were all single or married without children so it made those get-togethers much easier.

Here in Vegas, I practically know no one, let alone have a good friend. Yes, of course, I have Helen but she's family so she was there when I was born. And I still have Gizzi who is a super great friend but she's very busy as CEO and she's planning her future with JL. I hate to interrupt her with my troubles although I do miss those long talks we had when we were both single and living in the same town!

No one else in Silicon Valley will even speak to the *Isabella's* lady. You really find out who your true friends are in times of trouble. Gizzi has stuck with me through thick and thin but if I don't get my shit together pretty soon, who knows if she'll still hang around when she can be off leading her fabulous life!

It's so much easier to make friends when you're younger. You see each other at school or you live down the street from one another. Maybe you're in the same clubs after school or your parents are friends.

As you get older, unless you have children where you can connect with other moms at dance and swim or clubs, most people are already set in their ways, or have crazy schedules or have close friends and they don't have the time or the mindshare to add another. And, we all carry so much baggage that connecting with an adult friend is nearly as difficult as it is to finding a boyfriend.

And, don't even get me started on dating! Finding a good man in this town is a near impossibility. I'm not a size 0 with 36DD implants. I don't wear skin tight mini-skirts and six inch heels. In the old days, they would call those women hookers. Nowadays, they're just normal.

One would think that being a young divorcee in Las Vegas would have its advantages, but how can I date when I can't even make a friend?

I've never been a joiner – one who joins clubs or organizations. My networking skills are pretty bad. I did participate in a number of networking events when I was in high tech, but it was like a small social club. Everyone knew everyone so it was just one big party. Outside of that, my joining skills have been limited. Remember the worthlessness of my joining the local country club?

I don't even have money to socialize now, so how exactly am I supposed to have the possibility of friendship? And, as a substitute teacher, no one cares to even learn your name unless you did a good job for them and they want to use you the next time they need a day off.

Even Jazzy and Pamela don't have time for me, except to pick up the Lotto Ladies money and update them on our winnings – or, more likely, our losings. Not that I'd want to associate with them. I'm just trying to make the point that even people I don't like don't want to hang out with me!

Whatever happened to that happy, confident twenty-something that seemed to be queen of the world? Maybe she was really on the Titanic!

More tomorrow!

All my heart,

Diana

Thanks but no thanks

{ TEN }

The rest of my three weeks as a long term sixth grade science substitute were rather non-eventful, although it seemed as if nearly every other day we had some sort of drill – fire, shelter in place, earthquake, flood – it was overwhelming! I learned so much about safety but I just couldn't imagine having all these kids depend on me in the event of an emergency! It really taught me how impressive teachers were and I had so much more respect for them.

"Miss MacKenzie?"

I knew that voice. It was Principal Masala. What good-bad-good news was she bringing me today?

"Yes?"

"Well, as you know, your long term position with Mrs. Gordon's class will end Friday, then we have one week winter's break."

Yes, I do know that because I won't earn any money that week.

"You've done a very good job here and we'd like to keep you on our preferred sub list, if that's all right with you."

"Sure, that would be great. Thank you."

"Now, if you'd like another long term assignment, one of our sixth grade math teachers is pregnant and due in early May. If you're interested, we could slot you for that assignment. It would go through the end of the school year so there will be a number of additional requirements, including grading, that are part of that assignment."

Hmm…May was such a long way off. Sixth grade math. I should be able to handle that, right? So much can change in a person's life in three months, I'm not even sure if I'll still be substituting then!

"Great! Sounds like a plan," I said. Might as well lock in the known until the unknown rears its head.

"Fantastic! Have a great break!"

Well, I'll do the best I can. I've heard assignments after winter break are very hard to come by. Then, around April or so, they're abundant as teachers want to use their personal days. Then, closer to the end of the school year, they dry up again, but I've already been spoken for, so at least I won't have to worry about that.

I checked my mail slot on my way out for the week-long break and found a note from the principal. It said, "Thank you for agreeing to take on the long term math assignment in May, but we've found a former math teacher who is currently subbing that we're considering hiring full time, and he's agreed to take on the assignment. Thank you for all your hard work and we wish you the best!"

"What are you having?"

"Oh, I don't know. Maybe the lemon chicken?"

"It's delicious here, but I think I'll go for the chopped chicken salad."

It was winter break from school which meant I had a lot of free time on my hands. Helen always scheduled projects during her breaks but she was kind enough to sneak me in for a girls' day out. The kids were on play dates for a few hours and we decided to go to lunch and just talk.

It was such a treat to be in a real restaurant with tablecloths and servers and multiple everything on the table. But, what I missed most about eating in restaurants was the bread. No matter where you buy it, you can never get delicious bread like the bread basket of a good restaurant. I know, it's carb heavy and I have Gizzi's wedding to think of, but I just can't control myself around it. I'll just have to work out a few extra hours this week to compensate.

"How do you do it, Helen?" I asked as I stuffed the butter-slathered slice of olive bread into my mouth.

"Do what?"

"Everything! I mean, literally, everything. You work fulltime teaching second graders. You're married with two children who have incredibly busy schedules. You clean, decorate the house, cook meals daily, entertain, have weekly movie nights – you do it all. I'm by myself and I can hardly get out of bed to substitute. Seriously, how do you do it?"

Helen took a sip of her diet cola and thought about it for a bit before she answered.

"Well, there are a few differences between you and me. First of all, I'm very structured and while you can juggle and organize your life on a grand scale, I'm good at the day-to-day stuff."

I could see what she was saying. I enjoyed the exploration, not the maintenance. But, Helen is the first born child so she would have those sorts of natural tendencies, right?

"I never thought about it that way, but I have always recognized that we were two completely different types of people."

Helen nodded and sipped again.

"And, Gabe and I fell in love at a young age. We've been together forever. We work on our relationship all the time but because we're so much a part of each other, we don't waste a lot of energy on the things that bother so many couples."

Again, I agree. Helen and Gabe are like one. They truly belong together. And, although they occasionally fight, they are in it for the long haul with each other.

"I know, I'm so jealous about you and Gabe. I had always hoped to have that sort of relationship but I'm already in my mid-30's and there's nothing on the horizon."

"You could have had Tom."

"Don't go there, Helen."

"Fine. I'm just saying…"

I gave Helen a dirty look and she backed off.

"But, your schedule is insane, Helen. How do you do it?"

Helen laughed.

"My schedule is insane? Who was on planes all around the world for so many years? Who was planning product launches and press tours on multiple continents at the same time? It's all perspective, Diana."

And, once again, I needed someone to remind me of what I'd accomplished so far in my life. I might not be doing those things now, but at one time I did and I never thought twice about how I got it done. I'm just in a different place right now and I'm searching for answers.

Helen could see that I needed a little more than what she was offering. She grabbed some bread for sustenance and continued.

"I think that if you're doing things that you love, the time just makes itself available. I love teaching. I love being married to Gabe. I love my children and they each have their passions. I don't mind driving them around to their classes because I support what they love. And, I make the best of every moment while allowing myself some down time."

Something Helen said hit a nerve and I started to get choked up. Then the tears fell fast and furious down my cheeks. Helen did what any mother would do and reached into her over stuffed magical tote bag which held a solution to any emergency, and handed me a tissue.

"What's wrong, sis? What did I say?"

I dabbed my eyes and blew my nose. I felt so embarrassed to have such a public display of emotions especially since I hardly ever brought mine to the surface. The last time I cried like this was when Chris broke up with me a few months before we got married. Funny, I don't remember crying as much after our divorce.

"You mentioned how you support your children."

"Yeah, so?"

"I don't ever remember Mom and Dad offering us such support. They were so frugal with their paychecks there was no play money left for us. We had to pretty much fend for ourselves when it came to experiences."

"Mom and Dad grew up in a different time, Diana. They did what they felt was right. You and I both turned out OK, didn't we?"

"Yes, in general, but I feel you're way ahead of me in so many ways. I mean, sure, I did a lot in Silicon Valley but was it – was I – just a fluke? We were never taught to think big, just to work hard, and once I experienced the good life, both financially and in business, I always felt it would be there. But, it didn't last. Neither did my marriage. We weren't taught how to make the good things last. It's been years since I felt like I knew what I was doing."

Helen took a deep breath, the way she always did when she got ready to lecture me. It wasn't like a fatherly lecture, although Helen often sounded like a young female version of our Dad. It was a kind, sisterly lecture based in love that was similar to when Gizzi would slap me with words. Right now, I felt so weak

I wasn't sure I could handle it although I'm positive I needed to hear it.

"First of all, young lady, your marriage was a sham. You know it. I know it. Everyone who knew you tried to talk you out of it, but you pressed on. So, that was your first mistake. When you succumbed to being Chris's wife, your life changed, and not in a good way.

"Secondly, you have been going through a rough patch financially, I'll grant you that, but much of it was your own doing."

My own doing? Has Helen been watching *The Secret*?

"So, you just need to suck it up and log some hours until you discover what you are passionate about and pursue it. You know what that is. You just won't allow yourself to follow your dream."

I would follow it, if I only knew what it was!

"You've lost confidence in yourself, and now you're like a spoiled child who keeps whining because they can't afford all the toys and gadgets they want. Most people in this world operate on a budget. You never did. So, take this time to learn to manage your money and that will help to build your confidence."

Ugh! A budget? I'm nauseous already.

"I highly doubt you'll ever be happy working for anyone else again unless you have a lot of flexibility in your schedule and control over your work. That's where you thrive, calling the shots. Again, very few people in this world are blessed with such a great work environment and are able to flourish. Silicon Valley wasn't a fluke. It brought out the best in you. Maybe teaching college will be a better option. I don't really know the answer to that but you won't have great flexibility or control in the public schools."

Helen's right. Silicon Valley did bring out the best in me – at least the 'me' I was then.

"If you plan to stay in Vegas so we can be together and hopefully, have Mom and Dad move out, you need to come to terms with your financial side. You should have had a million dollars in savings, all that money you earned, but you blew it on who knows what and sat on the sidelines while you could have been bringing in a paycheck. While I admire you for going way beyond *my* comfort zone, I'm disappointed that you won't just stand up and take responsibility for what you've done and create a situation you can now live with. Or, better yet, one that makes you happy."

Yes, that whole million dollars in savings is true. I had the money – even more – but I blew it. I do like to shop.

"You need to believe in yourself again, Diana. You have to feel it on the inside before anything happens on the outside. We were starved as children, yes, Diana, we were, for attention, for money, for opportunities, but don't wallow in it. Embrace it and create that life that you so crave!"

And there you have it. A sisterly smack down. Right here in the middle of a fine dining establishment. I was so shocked, I didn't quite know how to respond. First of all, I'm glad at least Helen knows how that whole inside/outside thing works. I have to work on my inner Diana, although I will continue my workouts. There is no way I'm going to explain to Gizzi that I looked like crap in her wedding photos because I was working on the inner me.

Second, I had no idea my sister thought about how to solve my life issues more than I did! I mean, she certainly seemed to have so many aspects of my life figured out. She must be friends with crapper boy who could also call the shots.

Third, I had to agree, a lot of what she said had merit. That honestly didn't surprise me coming from Helen. She usually made sense when she talked but it was very rare that she was so forthright with me about my life. She wanted to allow me to make my own mistakes. She told me that in a past smack down. Although, there was that whole Tom discussion…Maybe Helen is just getting more vocal as she ages. I've heard that happens to women, right around menopause. If I calculate correctly, Helen is about 10 years away and is getting an early start.

"Are you okay, Diana?" Helen asked as she touched my hand.

I guess I hadn't moved since she began her little soliloquy. I nodded.

"Diana, I don't mean to seem rude and uncaring but the fact is, *you* need to create your life, a life that will make *you* happy. No one can do that for you. I created mine. You had yours for a while but it must have needed tweaking or else you would still be living it."

I just stared at Helen. I didn't know how to respond. Why does everyone seem to know how I should live my life but me?

I finally summoned the courage to speak.

"Is there going to be a test on all this?" I asked.

Helen laughed.

"Yes. The rest of your life. One big test!"

I finally relaxed and laughed, too. No, this was no laughing matter but we both needed a release. I dried my eyes one more time, thanks to the fresh tissue from Helen, and we had quite an enjoyable rest of lunch, talking and laughing about the things we two sisters normally did.

Once I got home, I cracked open a beer and cranked the tunes. Helen was right. I just wish I could get motivated again. I felt like I was being dragged down by a ton of bricks.

I decided to do some searching online for potential jobs. I stayed clear of retail positions this time, focusing on those in more professional environments. I also checked out some of the technology companies that were moving to downtown Las Vegas. I wasn't sure I wanted to be involved in high tech again. I'd been away so long it almost made my head hurt just to think about it. But, there were other types of companies moving to downtown as well, and one of them might have an interesting opening.

And, per Helen's suggestion, I also checked into teaching positions at local colleges. There were a number of openings, which really surprised me but in a transient town like Las Vegas, there always seemed to be jobs no matter what type of work you were looking for.

After an hour of searching, my head was spinning, not only from the job hunt but also from lunch with Helen. I turned off my tablet, slugged down the last of the beer and went to bed. It was the first time in ages I actually slept. I didn't wake up until 8 a.m. the next morning. Thank goodness it was winter break!

Dear Diary,

I took Helen's words to heart and took a good, hard look at my budget and spending habits.

I can't believe that I seem to be going downhill again, at least financially. My last good income was at *Positano*, but there was no way I could live in that drama any longer. Part-time at *The Bod* really screwed with my budget, even when I added my income from substitute teaching. With the store closed, it's even worse! I keep reminding myself – I'm an intelligent, college graduate with extensive business experience. There has to be some place that will respect me for what I have to offer. Helen thinks so. Gizzi thinks so. I should, too.

I did notice an ad online for instructors at a local college. It didn't list the name of the school but I always enjoyed sharing my knowledge with clients, so perhaps sharing it with students, the budding entrepreneurs of tomorrow, might be a good place for my talents. I already have some experience substitute teaching and like Helen said, I won't have the control or flexibility I want in the public school district. So, we'll see what happens. Maybe teaching college is the career for me.

In my lowest moments, I do think about Chris. I know he's very happy – well, he appears to be from this vast distance – and I'm happy for him. You know why? Because on some level, I still love him. I always will. I don't know why. He's scumbag royale – OK, a business-savvy scumbag, I'll grant you that – but we have this connection that will never go away. I don't ever mention it to Helen because she will give me another sisterly lecture and I'm just not up for one at this time.

I do hope I'll find a new man someday who will treat me as I always thought Chris would and that I'll love with all my heart – even the part that still seems to link to Chris. I wonder if he ever thinks of me. Hopefully, in a good way, not as the sales GIRL from *Positano*.

More tomorrow!

All my heart,

Diana

MFILV

Orientation

{ ELEVEN }

"So, what do you know about MFILV?"

"Well...not too much."

I can't believe I just said that! Honestly, I didn't know anything at all about them. I'd never even heard of the school until yesterday.

To be fair, I was so shocked that I got an interview at the Media and Fashion Institute of Las Vegas I never even investigated them. At that moment, I was every interviewer's worst nightmare – someone applying for a job with no clue about the company that was going to hire them.

I saw the ad online and submitted my resume. It was a blind submission so I didn't know the name of the school until they called. I'd been busy substitute teaching and running around with Helen – so much fun! – that when I got the response that they wanted to see me in the next morning, I didn't even pause to think that I should do a bit of research. Now, here I sit, embarrassing myself in front of my potential future employer. Yikes!

"Well then, let me tell you a bit about us. We're not very well known in the West, but we have several campuses east of the Mississippi. Our emphasis is on creativity – students who would struggle at a traditional university but want to pursue respectable careers such as fashion, graphics, art, film making, gaming, culinary, audio production, animation – these are the students we want and who do best under our training. We're a for-profit college, we've been around for over 50 years and we're eager to build a strong community connection in Las Vegas, hiring the brightest and most talented instructors."

Oh, and hopefully instructors who know who the heck you are, right?

"For our lower-level course instructors, we require a minimum of a bachelor's degree in either business or the area of study in which you'll be teaching, as well as three years of practical application in your field. You far surpass both of those, in addition to your substitute teaching and training experience. You've also traveled extensively, and we have students and instructors from around the globe. Once you've been with us for two quarters, you can enroll in one of our online university programs to secure your master's degree or even your doctorate at our cost, provided you stay with the school a minimum number of years upon graduation. Otherwise, you'll have to pay back your tuition."

Wow! A free master's degree? Like an MBA? I didn't see that coming. I really must check this place out. They are accredited, right?

"Since you've never taught at the college level before, we would start you out with just one subject. With your level of experience, the pay is $2,000 per class per quarter. How does that sound?"

"That sounds great!"

Those words just flew out of my mouth, but I guess I really should investigate the school before I get any more excited and start doing the happy dance. Still, the one class here could be my foot in the door to a career that's more in line with who I am. Plus, I get a free master's degree!

I'd still have to have a second job somewhere else initially – probably substitute teaching, but we'll see – it's a start. If they like me, maybe they'll give me more classes. If I can lock in three classes a quarter, I wouldn't have to do anything else; I've cut my expenses so low. Or, I could use my free time to create my own wonderful future, knowing all my expenses were covered. After all, how hard can it be to teach three college-level classes?

"Fine. That's good to hear. Now, we have two other candidates we're considering, so we'll let you know the early part of next week as there's an orientation class for new instructors on Thursday and Friday. Would you be able to attend?"

"Absolutely!" I said, without even consulting my calendar. Honestly, what kind of plans could I have with my boring life?

"OK, well, thank you for your time, and we'll be in touch either way."

"Thanks so much. I really appreciate the opportunity."

Well, I did, didn't I? I mean, it totally seemed like a more professional environment than I'd been exposed to the last several years. Plus, I wouldn't need to be on campus more than the time of my class – one four hour class per week – plus a half hour on either side.

There would be occasional meetings but from what I understood, they only took place the week before each quarter began and were wrapped up in two or three days, including departmental meetings. With any luck, my class would be scheduled for 6-10 p.m. so I could sleep in on those days or still have time to substitute.

The 35 mile drive would be a doozy during rush hour, but one day a week wouldn't kill me. Fingers crossed, they'll bring me on board and I'll be on my way to an upgrade in my career! The stress of substitute teaching was getting to me, so a more stable environment would certainly help. Teaching college was definitely a reputable career. And, I get a free master's degree!

If I had toothpicks to hold up my eyelids, I don't think even that would help right now.

Sure, I got the call. I got the job. No one told me orientation was two solid days starting at seven in the morning! To be more precise, 7-7:30 a.m. was registration, coffee, juice and bagels; 7:30-7:45 a.m. was time to mingle and by 8 a.m. we were in our seats, ready to absorb all the knowledge of our school and campus that one could. We really didn't need all that pre-show time but this school operated by schedules.

By 10 a.m. I was ready to crawl back into bed; by noon, I felt as if I were in a deep slumber. If Dean Wilcox hadn't had such a booming voice, I was certain to snooze in my seat for the entire two days. Just like econ class in college. Front row seat. Eight a.m. class. Slept through the entire two semesters. I'm just not a morning person.

I'd been interviewed and hired by Dean Anderson, but still hadn't met my direct supervisor, Glori Bonhoffer. Seems Glori was the only one who didn't walk around with a title attached to her name. Otherwise, I felt like I was walking amidst royalty, all present calling each other by their regal titles. They really thrived on hierarchy here.

I also discovered that the fashion program was new to this campus – surprising since that's part of their title – and several of the teachers in the orientation class were part of the founding team that would see to its success. I'd worked with start-ups before in high tech, so I wasn't much concerned but I would soon learn the speed – or the lack thereof – of a college versus a technology startup when it came to implementing changes and acting upon opportunities, or even providing the support the instructors and students needed.

These two days of orientation were meant to allow us to get to know the school policies and procedures, adherence to federal law, the history of the school, employee benefits and, of course, a chance to mix and mingle with the brass that ran this campus. I felt the most important parts of the discussion were the federal law requirements. It seemed as if keeping someone's grades secret were akin to not divulging their medical histories. Yet, there were other parts that were far more interesting.

"Although you're not involved in enrolling students," Dean Wilcox said, "you will all be chartered with Open House duties monthly, on Saturday mornings. The finance department will handle direct inquiries from prospective students regarding tuition, but for your information only, culinary runs $120,000 for the two and a half year program, and all other four-year degree programs we offer are $100,000. Most students will be able to achieve that through our private student loan initiative."

Twenty-five thousand dollars a year? For a school I'd never heard of? With me teaching? Wow! That's a shocker. None of that information was available on the school's website, and now I understood why. I mean, we're not talking Harvard or Yale here. We're at the Media and Fashion Institute of Las Vegas, for chrissake. These students might be better off taking classes at bartender or dealer school for just a few thousand dollars and make far more than they ever would in fashion. No wonder the school could afford to pay for my master's degree.

I took a deep breath. Maybe I was drawing conclusions too early in the process. Maybe this was one of those hidden educational gems that would prove to have not only the most amazing instructors but the administration would overwhelm me with their scholastic intelligence and care for the student population.

After a catered lunch – wait, don't we have a culinary school here? Why aren't they serving us? – it was time to meet the people who ran this joint.

"Now, you've all met Dean Anderson," Dean Wilcox said as he pointed to her coming through the door, "but many of you will be working directly for Glori Bonhoffer who heads the fashion and interior design departments."

As Glori walked through the door, I nearly threw up. I now understood why Dean Anderson did all the interviews and hiring. Glori obviously liked a liquid lunch – and I'm not talking protein shakes, here. I could see that today she added an Italian dish, perhaps lasagna, as evidenced by the stains running down the front of her ivory silk dress. Her hair was a bit disheveled and her lipstick didn't quite make it entirely onto her lips. This looks like it may be another disaster of a company. When it comes to career choices, I just can't catch a break.

"Thank you, Glori, Dean Anderson," Dean Wilcox said, ushering them out the door. "You'll have a chance to meet with your staff tomorrow afternoon when we break off into department groups."

Dean Wilcox was not expecting to see Glori in her finest, but he handled the situation so smoothly it was obvious that he'd been through this before.

"OK, now, let's break up into teams of two to work through the next three pages in your packets."

I turned to my left to see a happy, smiling face, the face of someone who belonged here, someone who understood this crap and could deliver it well to anyone who would listen. Someone with the teaching gene.

"Hi, my name is Celine, Celine Waters. What's yours?"

"Uh, hi Celine. I'm Diana."

"Oh, hi Diana! Want to work together?"

Anyone with that much energy after sitting in these chairs for nearly seven hours deserved to bottle it and make millions.

"Sure, why not?"

"So, are you teaching in the new fashion program here?"

"Yes, as a matter of fact, I am. You?"

"Yes, yes of course! I was so grateful I could rearrange my schedule to be here for these two days. It was quite short notice but I couldn't teach without going through orientation and what better way to represent my company than by being one of the founding teachers in this program. Aren't you excited?"

"Uh, sure. Who do you work for?"

"I'm a manager for *Buttons and Bows*, a children's store. They have 276 locations throughout the country. I transferred here from Kansas and although they're in a bit of a rough patch right now, I've been with them for over 10 years and it's been a real blessing. What's your background?"

"I've worked at some of the best – *Isabella's Intimates*, *Bergstrom* and *Positano*, but I also have several years' experience in high tech marketing."

"Oh, my, that's so wonderful! No one could compete with that background in this program. I bow to you."

Celine attempted a fake bow from her seat.

"So, what's the scoop on our boss?"

"You mean Glori? It's very interesting. I had a long talk with Gray, one of the gaming instructors."

"You've already met one of the instructors at the school?"

"Oh, yes! I hung out after my interview and spoke with several. It was between classes so I said 'Hi!' They were all a bit curious who I was and were very forthcoming in their comments."

"And you decided to stay?"

"Oh, absolutely! This is a dream come true! I have several friends on the east coast who are familiar with the school and highly recommended that I take the position. After all, I can't be a store manager forever!"

"Understood. So, what's the deal with Glori?"

"Oh, yes, well, I guess she's in the midst of a nasty divorce from some hoity-toity Mr. Moneybags from L.A. whose family has buildings named after them. Supposedly, she had a hard time fitting in and eventually the family suggested to her husband that it was time to part ways and to take full custody of the children who bore the family moniker. She wanted to keep her last name for the sake of her kids but her husband's family would have none of it. I guess the divorce has dug her deep into a hole where alcohol is her only refuge."

Well, that explains a whole lot. It certainly is a sad situation for anyone, but Glori was obviously taking the divorce very hard. And who wouldn't? Her ex-husband was taking her kids away from her, moving them to California. That would be hard for anyone to cope.

"Couldn't they give her a leave of absence or something?"

"I guess that won't work. She needs the money and benefits to keep her head above water and the interior design program is getting ready for certification. If she isn't on staff, the school will have to wait two more years for another opportunity, and she was hired specifically to lead them through to certification. They understand her situation but insist that she stay on target."

"Then why give her the fashion program on top of it? Since it's just starting out, wouldn't it be better to have someone like Dean Anderson with a level head on her shoulders at the helm?"

"I totally agree, and not one of them has fashion background, by the way, but each administrator is only allowed to have so many students under them, and the one with the least was Glori. So, it's you and me, girlfriend, along with some of our fellow teachers who will need to keep the ship afloat and headed in the right direction until Glori pulls herself through the muck. It's such a great opportunity to prove ourselves and what we have to offer!"

Celine needed some downers. I'm not a drug advocate by any means, but anyone who was excited to work for the wreck that headed our shiny new fashion department needed to either have her head examined or run the department herself. Maybe that was her goal, who knows? Her perkiness alone would lead her to great heights within this organization, I could tell already.

"Ladies, how are you progressing?" Dean Wilcox interrupted. Celine put on her perky face and lit up her eyes before she answered.

"Oh, Dean Wilcox. Part of the orientation is an opportunity to get to know our fellow instructors. Please don't let that dissuade you from allowing us a bit more time to complete our project?"

"Oh, Celine, don't worry. I have you covered. You're good. I just wanted to say hello."

As Dean Wilcox walked away, I wondered how she could charm such a man, someone who had already retired from one university and should be out golfing but instead was here leading the charge. From the sound of their conversation, they had already met and become friends. This girl works fast!

"Come on, Diana. Let's get this done. We can talk more after class."

The rest of orientation went well, and we were finally in our department group meetings. Here we had a chance to spend more time getting to know Glori who, from the looks of things, had Chinese today. I could tell by the bits of water chestnut stuck to her skirt.

There were five of us on staff: Celine, whose classes would focus on retail management; George, who would run the finance and business law classes; Touffée, who taught merchandising and design basics; Bo, who taught psychology of dress and history of designers and me, who was assigned the general introductory course. Celine and I were the only two females but I could tell we would all bond.

Name cards were placed on tented cardboard around the table so we knew where to sit, and beside each name was a copy of our meeting agenda, a sample syllabus and the text for our class. I was impressed that Glori was able to organize all of this, given her delicate state.

I hadn't taken any college classes in quite some time, and the 500 page text for the class I would teach seemed daunting. As this was all new to me, I felt I needed to read the entire book prior to creating the syllabus, then re-read it along with my class so I could remember what we were supposed to talk about that week. Generally, instructors were able to select the text for their classes but as we were a new program, all of us would be using texts for the first year or two that were popular on other campuses. Oy! This was going to require a lot of beer.

"Now, you'll find that the syllabi are already written for you," said Glori, in all her drunken stupor. "We've made it as easy as possible. You'll need to access the file online and input your contact information and any specific requirements you are making for your class, but you can follow the plan of other instructors this first go-round before making any changes. I need to have your course syllabi in by tomorrow morning."

What? Tomorrow morning? Is she crazy? I'd like to customize my syllabus a bit but the deadline didn't allow enough time to even familiarize ourselves with the text. Using the proffered syllabi sounded like the only good option as I'm sure none of us had ever taught our classes. Glori's game plan was helpful but not preferred.

"The one thing that's missing is links to graphics. This younger generation is all about graphics – videos, photos – you know. Some of the syllabi have more details than others, but you'll have to research any graphics on your own. Plus, you'll be responsible for determining the one major project for the quarter for your class. It should be equivalent to 50 percent of the student's grade. They'll be able to work on it during their labs and it should require at least another 2-4 hours outside of class to complete."

Yes, this was not the traditional school I went to. We had no labs. We rarely had a class project that was worth half our grade. It was mostly book work, research and exams. I almost felt like *I* was the student here!

Ten minutes later Glori left the meeting, never to return. Well, at least to that meeting. Seems she went to the restroom and back to her office, completely forgetting she was leading a staff meeting. Luckily, we were a spritely, intelligent group and worked together to guide each other through the syllabus development process though it seemed I was on the giving team rather than receiving.

As Glori had noted, the syllabi samples offered differing amounts of information for us to reference. Mine, of course, was the worst! Not only did it state a general topic per week, it was based on an entirely different text. The school changed texts as often as they could to remain current, and the sample syllabus I had referred to a four-year-old text. So, I was basically starting from scratch, as were all the other instructors of this intro class. The syllabus most well received company-wide would become the new sample for this text next quarter and beyond. The other instructors in the room were luckier than I and were able to mock up their syllabi in short order.

I tried to view this like taking on a new client. If I regarded every company I worked for as a client, maybe I could eventually bring on new clients that actually appreciated me for my knowledge, not use me to do their dirty work. In the meantime, the ramp up was steep and I only had a few days to get my first week's lesson plan completed before class started. No more television for me! I'll be searching for applicable videos to use in class.

Celine and I stopped for some coffee after our group meeting before heading home.

"I can't believe it!"

"What's that, Diana?"

"It's great that I'm teaching an introductory course so I can get my feet wet, but the fact that I'm the one with the new text and the worthless syllabus sucks. How can I possibly create something worthwhile by tomorrow morning?"

"Oh, Diana, don't worry."

"Don't worry? I've faced some major deadlines in high tech but never a 500 page text and syllabus in 12 hours."

"Where's your text?"

I pulled the weighty tome from my bag and plopped it on the small table. Celine swiftly located a yellow highlighter her tote bag.

"No worries, girlfriend. We'll do this together. Just watch."

Celine opened to the table of contents, highlighted 10 sections, one for each week of the quarter, along with some important subsections, flipped to the back of the book which had teacher tools, highlighted five possible major projects, flipped to another section and highlighted the sample tests for midterm and final, put her highlighter down and smiled.

"There. Done."

I just stared at her. No real thought. No heavy analysis or evaluation. Just a few swipes of her highlighter and we were good to go.

"How did you do that?"

I was dumbfounded.

"Have you forgotten? You can't have been out of college that long! The syllabus is like a big outline. It's easy. As long as the main topics are identified, along with page numbers, you're covered. Add in the highlights of the major class project, a grade breakdown of 50 percent project and 25 percent each for midterm and final, or maybe 20 percent for each plus 10 percent attendance and quizzes or they'll never show, and you're done. You'll probably add your school email and phone, but that's it. Syllabus complete!"

I couldn't believe my ears! Just like Pamela saved me from slut wife, Celine rescued me from the dreaded syllabus deadline.

"Of course," she added, "this is just the syllabus. Weekly lesson plans will take far more time. You'll actually have to do work for that!" Celine laughed.

"I don't know how to thank you, Celine. I never would have thought to do what you did. I'm impressed. Have you taught before?"

Celine laughed again.

"Oh, heavens no. This is my first time. But, I have been taking a lot of post-graduate courses, just for my own amusement, and I've noticed a trend recently regarding the syllabi. It's exactly as I showed you and it makes a lot of sense. Students have such a hard time following along if you change the order of information in the book, and the text was written in a particular way to guide you through the course anyway, so, why fight it?"

Why fight it exactly!

We quickly finished our coffee, picked up our things and headed out the door.

"It was really nice to meet you, Celine. I look forward to teaching with you."

"It was nice to meet you, too, Diana, but with our schedules, we'll probably never see each other. Text or email me if you have any questions or want to get together to gossip!"

Celine practically skipped to her car while I felt like I was hauling a set of dumbbells, the weight of the text and all the handouts from orientation causing a dent to form in my shoulder.

I was only two days into my new job – just barely surviving orientation – and I was already having doubts about my ability to perform. Once I got into the classroom, I would be in control, so certainly things would improve, right? As long as I follow company policy, I had quite a bit of freedom in the classroom. Oh, and the students had to like me and learn from me. Yikes!

However, the time commitment seemed significantly more than I bargained for. The hourly rate for each class was starting to look like a miniscule amount. The school calculated that I would get paid four hours a week for teaching and one hour for prep. Yet, with grading various assignments like weekly quizzes, major projects, lab work or exams, plus writing detailed weekly lesson plans and reading that ominous text – twice! – I could see I was already up to 10-12 hours a week for just one class. This was way more work than I anticipated. Maybe some of Celine's perkiness will rub off on me cos I sure needed the energy boost.

Dear Diary,

I could smell her coming.

I got to school early to set up for my first class. Well, not too early. My intro class was scheduled from 1-5 p.m. on Wednesdays, so I was able to sleep in just a bit and avoid rush hour traffic at least in one direction. I arrived about 12:15 p.m. and attempted to bond with my new classroom.

I decided to maintain the format I did in public school where I posted the homework on one side of the whiteboard and the day's agenda on the other, adding an inspirational quote from a fashion icon in the middle. I was just finishing my inspirational quote and getting revved up for my first class when Glori stumbled her way into my classroom.

Turns out, she wants me to start a fashion club. Well, rather, to help the students start one. Seems each department has a student club and being the new kids on the block, we needed one, too. The students were keen to get one going, to become a bigger part of the institute, but the club couldn't get started without a faculty advisor.

We didn't have a full-time instructor on the roster yet, so Glori was free to select whomever she pleased. To my horror, it was me. I asked why she didn't pick Celine, who I think is so perfect for everything having to do with the fashion department here, and she said it was just a matter of schedules. Celine worked full-time as well as taught, and I had flexibility in my schedule. So...lucky me!

I hadn't even met any of the students yet, and already I was being summoned to organize them into a club to help them interact with the community and gain hands-on knowledge of what all of us teach in class. That meant it was up to me to call on local businesses and organizations to see how we could lend our skills to facilitate any of their events. Oh, and I don't get paid an extra dime for the time.

The students have more than paid for it with their outrageous tuition, but as a for-profit college, the money went into the owners' coffers rather than to pay people what they deserved, contrary to my experience in high tech. Yet, they were willing to keep the drunk one on board just to get certification for the ID department. Surely, there must be someone more capable than her to fill that spot – who could also lead the fashion club! Oy!

More tomorrow!

All my heart,

Diana

Who's teaching whom?

{ TWELVE }

"OK, class, let's get started with a little game. We'll go around the room and introduce ourselves. Then we'll describe ourselves using a word that begins with the first letter of our first name. For example, I'm Diana and I'm dynamic. OK, let's start here."

For my first class, I thought I'd open with an ice breaker. We used those for sales meetings all the time in high tech and since these students were adults, it would be a fun way to get to know one another.

I pointed to a blonde girl with very long hair and breasts the size of cantaloupes. She seemed a bit aloof, so I was curious how she would describe herself.

"Hi, I'm Cassandra and I'm cool."

Snickers from the peanut gallery.

"Crazy is more like it," someone said, supposedly under their breath.

More snickers.

"Hi Cassandra. Very nice to meet you. Who's next?"

"Yo, yo, yo, y'all, I'm DJ Daze and I'm dyn-o-mite!"

Woot! Woot! "Hey, DJ Daze! Great show Saturday!" Woot! Woot!

Obviously, DJ Daze was someone well-known in town. I've been a bit of a hermit lately, lacking funds to hit those amazing nightclubs on the Strip, but obviously the students who were paying outrageous tuition used some of their student loans to support a fellow classmate.

As we went around the room, I realized that the ice breaker exercise was being conducted solely for my benefit. Seems these students had already met, exchanged contact and social media info and made judgments of their classmates. I was the odd man out, the older generation – just a mere 10 years or so older – who was to attempt to impart my higher wisdom on a class that seemed to know everything better than I. This was going to be a bigger challenge than I thought.

"That was great. Now that we know each other, I'd like to hear a bit about your plans for your career in the fashion industry. This is an introductory course that covers several potential opportunities, so by knowing your preferences, I could highlight important details when we come to those sections. So, DJ, what are your hopes and dreams for the future?"

"Yo, dude, it's DJ Daze."

Oh, I get it. He's a deejay. It's his stage name, not his initials. I'll have to remember that.

"Sorry, DJ Daze. So, what do you hope to do in the fashion world?"

"Yo, Lady Di, I'm already livin' my future. I started a graphic t-shirt business with my character sketches. I call it 'Poop' cos my shit don't stink. It's great shit. It's payin' for my college education."

"Yeah, Diana, you should see his shit. He draws some great shit, man," said T'Rina, who was tragically ignored by her family, according to her ice breaker description.

"Oh, you've seen his work? Thanks for sharing, Trina."

"It's T'Rina, not Trina. Honestly, I don't understand why the teachers here can't get it right. Shit, it's my name."

"Sorry about that, T'Rina."

I wasn't sure that swearing was allowed in class, but since it seemed to be so casually expressed, I would let it ride until I clarified it with my boss. Well, maybe my boss's boss. Well, no, Celine could probably tell me. I just want to make sure I don't slip into those habits myself – at least while I'm teaching. As for T'Rina's name, well…everyone has such unusual names nowadays I'll have to be more careful.

"So…graphic tees. You've already started your business. That's awesome! What brings you here, DJ Daze?"

"Yo, well, I'm only sellin' on my website and at my shows and I want to expand my distribution, you know what I mean, Lady Di?"

"I do, indeed. You ultimately want to be like Russell Simmons or Jay-Z. I hope that you'll find some inspiration from this class but there are other classes that will give you better insight into your specific needs. I'm glad you're here."

DJ Daze smiled.

"You cool, Lady Di. I can tell. I gonna put you on a shirt. It will be a Poop Deluxe!"

The whole class laughed. DJ Daze started sketching. I had to smile even though I honestly didn't know how to respond. I mean, don't I have rights to my own image? Do I get final approval? Was it an honor to be a Poop Deluxe? Or, did that mean I was a Poophead? He did say I was cool, so I'll take that as a compliment and move on.

I really couldn't get over his company name – Poop. Who would name their company Poop? There must be some interesting backstory. I'll have to find out during one of our breaks. As for distribution, with a company name of Poop, he should look into a joint marketing agreement with a laxative or diaper company. I'm sure a lot of his buyers are young fathers who would enjoy wearing a little Poop graphic-tee while cleaning up their baby's poopy mess.

After we went around the room a second time so I could get to know the class better, I realized that only 20 minutes had passed. It was a four hour class. Reviewing the syllabus would take another 10 minutes. We had two 15-minute breaks and an hour to work in lab. How was I to fill those two empty hours?

Luckily for me, the discussion was lively for the most part. As time went on, everyone seemed to relax, well, probably mostly me as these were people who had been students all their lives and I was just heading back. I had them do research on current events in fashion, and we looked at a number of videos of fashion shows and clothing manufacturing. We just kind of went with the flow which tied into my first week's syllabus topic – from fashion shows to Fifth Avenue: overview.

I did notice a couple of students constantly looking at their tablets or cell phones during class. This was not only a graphics-oriented generation, but one that multi-tasked constantly. Or, at least they thought they were doing a good job multi-tasking. Some of the students would never understand the beauty of focus. I'll have to see how other teachers handle the whole "device at the ready" situation.

During lab, the students broke into groups and I popped in my playlist with my portable speaker. I was playing all my favorites – mostly classic rock and country – until one of the students covered his ears and yelled out, "I can't stand it anymore! I feel like I'm at my grandmother's house!"

I'm not *that* old! I turned off my music.

"OK, then, what shall we listen to?"

I was pleasantly surprised when the students offered their own playlists – everything from jazz to pop to punk rock to rap. I had assumed that everyone in the room would listen to the same sort of music since they were all about the same age, but just as we are all individuals on this planet, so is each and every one of *them*. The only music the class would agree on was classical, so I found a Mozart station and off to work we went.

I wasn't sure what the class learned that first night, but I sure learned a lot.

"How are the wedding plans coming along?"

It was so nice to be able to catch up with Gizzi. Her work schedule was insane since she became CEO and emails and texts just don't do our conversations justice. Gizzi was back in California for a couple of days and, good friend that she was, she set aside time for me.

"Absolutely fabulous, I must say. Working with Colin is a dream. He just tells me when and where to show up and I'm there. Or, he texts me things for my opinion. Honestly, I don't know how I'd be planning such a lifetime event without him."

"That's wonderful, Giz!"

Gizzi could sense I felt a little left out of the planning process, but the Gizzi-JL wedding really was a lifetime event and I had to sit back. I'd never been so closely involved with people who had so much money. It was a whole new experience for me. Maybe I'll meet an awesome millionaire at the wedding who just happens to be my soul mate. Then, everything I learn from Gizzi's wedding planning process could be adapted for my own.

Oh, shit – *everyone* will be at the wedding. How will I ever show my face there? I hadn't seen the guest list but Silicon Valley was very incestuous. I'd probably know or know of everyone at the wedding. Certainly, my *Isabella's* story has circulated in the valley given the way I've been ostracized from the high tech community. I hadn't heard from a soul except for Gizzi pretty much since I moved to Vegas.

Plus, I look a mess! I can't even remember the last time I had a pedicure, although I'll be sure to have one for the wedding. Knowing Colin, a spa day will be provided for all and I won't have to worry about that. I'll just have to put my own fears aside for the sake of my best friend. But, could I?

"Not to worry. Your time is coming. Everyone will be fit for their bridesmaids dresses next week. Colin has made arrangements with a local salon in Las Vegas so you won't have to travel for your fittings."

"Wow! Colin thinks of everything! Who's designing the dresses?"

Gizzi cleared her throat and took a deep breath. In the old days, it would have been a drag from her cigarette but now it was just clean, fresh air.

"I'm not quite sure myself. You'll see them later in the year. We're still deciding on styles, but once Colin has everyone's measurements, he'll make suggestions. He wants to review body types, hair and eye color, even shoe sizes! He can analyze anything!"

"It's a major designer, isn't it?"

"I can't really say at this time, sweetie."

"Giz, I'm your best friend, your maid of honor."

"I know, Diana, but nothing has been finalized and I don't want to get your hopes up. Just know it will be fabulous!"

"OK, OK, I understand. This is like a product launch where only the E-team knows the details. I'll wait until you can release the info."

"Honestly, doll, I don't know who the designer is. A couple of big names have been bandied about, but nothing has been finalized. Colin needs to do his analysis first. I'm just in shock that we would even have access to some of these people."

"Tuxes?"

"Don't ask."

"And, what about your dress?"

Gizzi laughed.

"That I'm keeping a secret from everyone! Not even my mother knows!"

I laughed too. That was just like Gizzi. Once she set her sights on something, she didn't share. She didn't want anyone to influence her decision. She kept it to herself and you only found out about it once she reached her goal. Like the time she decided she wanted a luxury car but she wouldn't buy it until she hit a certain dollar figure in her retirement account. The day she drove up in her new car I was so very proud of her. Gizzi didn't purchase things just for the extravagance. She rewarded herself for accomplishment.

'So, how's the teaching going so far?"

Ugh. It was so much more fun talking about her wedding.

"I'm learning. It's a totally different environment than public school. These are kids that really want to be there and it's up to me to make their time worthwhile."

"Well, for what they're paying, it had better be!"

We laughed, but Gizzi's words rang true.

"I know. That kind of bothers me."

"Don't let it. You are there to do your job. You have experience these kids could only dream of. Your background is priceless."

"Thanks, Giz, but I have to say, I suddenly feel very old. I know there's only about 10 years' difference between the students and myself, but they grew up in a totally different world. From what I've seen in public school and how these students are at MFILV, I don't know if I'll ever connect with them."

"Geez, Diana, it's only been a week!"

"I know, I know. But, if you think Colin analyzes everything, I do, too, and I'm trying to figure out the best way to reach them, especially since Glori now wants me to start a fashion club."

"Oh, fun. At least you'll get some extra pay. That will help you out right now."

"Well...not exactly. I'm expected to do it out of the goodness of my heart."

"What? Who do these people think they are? You get paid for one class and you're expected to volunteer the rest of your free time? If you were a full-time instructor I could understand their pressuring you to be on campus 40 hours a week. But, you're teaching one class. Don't be their sucker. Do what you have to do and walk away from the rest. You're too quick to agree. You always have been, taking on more than anyone should."

Ouch. I guess that's what best friends are for, to tell you what you don't want to hear. Gizzi was great at cutting to the core and telling me the truth. She was not in sales mode right now. She was in friend mode and that required a bitch slap.

"You're going to tell Glori no, correct?"

"Yes, I will tell Glori I don't have the time. If I could get a long-term substitute position, then I really wouldn't have the time and I'd feel better about it. I mean, these students want to get a good education and we want the program to succeed. Otherwise, I won't have a job at all."

I could feel Gizzi rolling her eyes. What is she going to do with me?

"Diana, just say no. You don't need an excuse; you don't need a sub position just so you don't feel guilty. You need to build up your own business profile again and honestly, I don't see you at MFILV long term. Just my opinion. If you think BODs are hard to deal with, just try the administration at a for-profit college. I guarantee, in a matter of months, you'll be telling me you're living a nightmare and you will be shopping for your next job. Job, Diana, not career."

Whew! I guess Jean-Louis hasn't softened Gizzi at all. Maybe being CEO has made her stronger than ever. I held back my tears. Gizzi didn't hurt me. The pain was from realizing the truth, that I was just job hopping. MFILV is just a stop on the paycheck highway. My old boss used to call me fiercely independent. Where is that Diana? Is it age, exhaustion or something else that caused me to back off from my life and spend so much time trying to please others? Where is my passion for *me*?

Meditate. Focus. Release. I'm sure I read that in one of my New Age books.

"I'm sorry, sweetie. You're my best friend and I know you're better than MFILV. Tons better. I miss how much fun we had when you were confident in yourself. I can't bring that strength out in you again. You have to find it yourself. It's there. And when it surfaces, we'll all know."

"Thanks, Giz. I know you say these words out of love. I can't believe with everything going on right now that you would even have time to consider my life."

"Sweetie, you are part of my life. A very important part. I always have time for you. Understood?"

"Understood. Now, I need to make time for my sister who is having dinner tonight."

"Oh, fun! Tell Helen I said 'Hi.' JL and I are going to my parents tonight as well. Must be family dinner night!"

"Talk soon."

"You bet, doll. Anytime."

"I'm so glad you could fit us in for dinner, Diana. Your schedule is so crazy it seems like we never get together anymore."

Helen was right. We'd hardly seen each other since our winter break lunch.

Between substitute teaching and the work required for my class at MFILV, I had minimal breathing room for family fun. Then, there were the kids' extracurricular activities that kept Helen and Gabe on the run. We lived just a few miles away but we hardly even saw each other. That's not how I wanted it to be. Having my sister and her family here in town meant everything to me. It's just a shame that life gets in the way of living.

"I know, isn't it weird? It's like we're still 2,000 miles apart! I remember when I lived in California, my next-door neighbor and I would text each other rather than get together for a glass of wine or talk over the fence. We definitely have to plan to do this at least once a month."

"OK, we'll try but you know how crazy it gets around here."

"Understood. At least it's fun stuff!"

"Oh, yeah, right. Like digging up weeds and tiling the patio!"

Gabe might make fun, but he really did enjoy doing those manly things.

"So, how are things at MFILV?"

It was nice to see Gabe show an interest in my life. Most of my conversations were with Helen, even at the dinner table.

"Well, so far so good, although I'm still adjusting. It's only been a week. It's requiring a bit more time than I anticipated but I'll get used to it."

"Do you think you'll stay with the college?"

"I've made a commitment to myself to stay for two years. After that, I'll see how I feel. I'd like to help get the program off the ground and see that it's running smoothly. Glori is a total waste of space so the burden is on the staff to make it happen."

"That Glori sounds like a winner. I'm amazed they keep her on the payroll," Gabe interjected between bites of food.

"She must have some connection or good blackmail material on someone at the school that's allowing her to stay. I was shocked to hear she had designed some of the hottest nightclubs on the Strip. She's a total mess."

"Sometimes through chaos comes genius creation," added Gabe.

"Yes, we see it in music and art all the time but not in a management position at a school where students are paying a ton of money to be taught by the best."

"Amen to that, sister," slurred Gabe through his mashed potatoes.

"I know you made this commitment to yourself but is teaching what you really want to do?"

Now it was Helen's turn. She'd been pretty quiet so far and that was never good as far as I was concerned. It meant she was planning to make me think hard about my decision.

"What? I can't believe you're asking me that! You're the one who has been pushing me into it."

Seems today is the day everyone picks on me about teaching as a career choice.

"Well, I wouldn't exactly say pushing you into it. More of a nudge to try it out. I love teaching and one of the best parts about the public school system is I get large chunks of time off. It used to be the whole summer but now that we go year round, it's still several weeks at a time. That gives me an opportunity to relax, regroup, pursue some things that I might not be able to do otherwise. But, I'm not sure it's for you."

I was flabbergasted! All this time I thought I had Helen's support, and I guess I did in a way, but now I'm not so sure any more.

"Teaching at the college level is different."

"Agreed. Do they offer a pension?"

"What? No, I don't think so. I'm not even thinking in those terms yet."

"Well, you should keep it in mind wherever you work. It's very important."

Yes, Daddy.

"Look, teaching at MFILV gives me an opportunity to grow with my students, to learn new things. I always loved fashion but buying clothing and understanding how it's made and where it comes from is a totally different perspective."

"Agreed as well. But, while you're educating yourself, and your students are learning, are you growing in a way that works for your future?"

Oh, Helen has so many questions. Sometimes the older sister is just like Dad.

The kids – and Gabe – sat quietly around the table eating while Helen and I had our little discussion.

"Helen, I just started. Let me give it a chance. I have a lot of business knowledge I can share with my students that will be valuable to their future. As for me, I will get my master's degree. In business, as I wanted. An MBA! I've wanted that for a long time. I won't have to pay for it either."

"You could get your master's through the school district's special initiative and they would pay for it."

"But it would have to relate to education. Unless I'm willing to commit to 30 years of public school teaching, why would I want to have that degree?"

"Precisely. And there you have it. You're not committed to teaching. It's a pass-through career for you, just like retail. Getting your MBA is a bonus but I'm not sure you'll even stay in it long enough to meet your payback commitment. And, it will be from a school you wouldn't have attended if you chose on your own."

Helen was right. I was becoming stronger personally as a college instructor, keeping up my quick thinking and speaking skills. Organizing data and presenting it in a way others could learn. That part was really no different than what I did as a marketing consultant.

But, there were other big differences. I wasn't working for myself – which I loved. I hadn't made the type of money I was worth in years. And, quite honestly, I missed working in business. However, I had to accept that the world was not the same as it was when I was in high tech. Things have changed dramatically. The economy's been in the tank for so long I'm not sure it knows how to climb out of the hole it's in.

Tears started flowing. I hated when I cried, particularly during a meal! How appetizing could that be for the kids? I'm sure they didn't appreciate their aunt falling apart before their very eyes. I was a hero to them. But, I just couldn't help it at the moment. Gabe handed me a box of tissues so I could dry my eyes and blow my nose.

"Mom and Dad and even you have been very lucky in that you found work that satisfies you, that you could stay in for a long time. I'm too restless. I want to make a name for myself, and I had when I worked in high tech. But now, I'm just a nobody trying to pay the rent. It hurts. It hurts so badly…"

Before I could finish my thought, we were interrupted by a message on my phone.

"You know I don't allow cell phones at the table, Diana."

"Yes, sorry sis, but it's a text from Jazzy and Pamela."

"The Lotto Ladies? What do they want now?"

"It's a photo of the two of them holding a mock check made out to us as the winners of the Super Duper Millions."

Helen took the phone from my hand to look, then gave it back, a disgusted look on her face.

"I'm sorry, Diana, but you really need to get away from them and spend your time on important things."

"Like teaching?"

"Teaching. Dating. Whatever. You spend too much good energy on the two of them."

Once again, Helen knew how to live my life better than I did. I put my phone in my pocket, trying to block out the image that was now in my head, an image that I would love to come true. But, reality was staring me in the face by the name of Helen.

Having a teaching job that resulted in regular pay, good exposure to the fashion industry and an MBA might just lead me to new heights in a totally different field than my past. Fashion didn't pay as well but it was certainly more fun than high tech. I had to give it a chance. It's all I had at the moment.

"I believe I'm in the right place for me right now. I'm still getting through my opening night jitters and learning the lay of the land, but in due time, I think it will work out. It's a good career choice that still allows me some scheduling freedom. It will be OK for the time being."

I felt my comment was as politically correct as I could get over dinner. I wasn't in the mood for another lecture from Helen, who just looked at me and smiled. Now she reminded me of Mom. Helen always looked out for her little sister, but sometimes I just needed a friend and not a parent. Although, Gizzi and I just had a similar discussion a few hours ago!

Justin eyed us back and forth, waiting for an opportune moment.

"OK, enough about school. Can I tell you about the new song I'm learning on guitar?"

Dear Diary,

My, what a week it has been!

I survived orientation and created my first syllabus, with Celine's help, of course. I read through the first few chapters of the text so I could sound knowledgeable in class and created a format that I felt would work for me for this first quarter. In between all the work at MFILV, I'm still substitute teaching, but I have to admit, now that I'm at the college level, public school just doesn't interest me.

However, there are bills to be paid. I am somewhat proud of myself, though, from the financial front. I finally have a thousand dollars saved in an emergency fund! It's been years since I had more than about $25 in a savings account. It would make Dad proud. I actual banked my Christmas bonus last year as he always hopes and that helped to build my savings.

Helen and Gizzi were really hard on me this week. Neither believes teaching is my calling. They could be right, but it's where I am right now. I've committed to two years at MFILV but as the famous saying goes, people plan and God laughs. So, let's see how my plans change as time goes on.

I could look into public speaking. It's like teaching without all the administrative and testing crap. I'd have flexibility, earn a good income if I marketed myself well, but I have no idea what I'd speak about. I don't think anything I've learned over these last few years is something anyone would care to listen to. It's been my journey to discover my true destiny and each and every person needs to walk their own path. Can you tell I've been watching *The Secret* again!

Next week I host my first open house at the school. Each of the instructors is expected to take turns and somehow I was selected to host the first one of the quarter. All the different disciplines are represented to give presentations in classrooms to those attendees seriously interested in that major. My problem? I have to tell these prospective students how great it is to be here when I'm not even certain that's true.

I need to keep reminding myself that when a company pays you, you speak the party line to the outside world and it's up to me to convince a roomful of potential students that MFILV is the place to be. I hope they don't hate me when they find out the truth in due time.

More tomorrow!

All my heart,

Diana

Mexican Moonshine

{ THIRTEEN }

"OK, class. Welcome back!"

The students just stared at me. I felt like a stand-up comedian without any new material.

"Now, last week we discussed an overview of the entire fashion industry, from forecasting to design to manufacturing, buying and selling. Starting today, we'll look at key steps in the process in more depth."

As I was talking, I noticed Glori enter into the back of the room. She must have had Mexican for lunch today because, although she walked with confidence, rice and beans cascaded down the front of her blouse. I thought I saw a hint of guacamole as well.

I'd been forewarned about this. As per her job description, Glori audits each instructor once per quarter, to make sure we're of MFILV caliber. How she could make that judgment call in her current state, I have no idea, but at least she did manage to complete some of her duties as department director. Unfortunately, my future was in the hands of this, this, *person.*

"Oh, don't mind me. I'm just here to learn from Diana, just like you," Glori slurred as she took a seat toward the end of one row. "She's great, isn't she?"

The class gave me stronger acknowledgement than I expected. Perhaps they'd been around enough drunks to know that emotions needed to be exaggerated to be recognized.

For just a moment, Glori threw me off my game, but I quickly recovered and continued on with my lesson. I glanced in her direction a couple of times and saw her taking notes. I wasn't sure if it was regarding my teaching methods or her shopping list for the liquor store.

I hadn't seen Glori that many times, but she never seemed to be without her bottle of water, with the ice cylinder in the center. Now, living in Vegas, I'm never without my water either, but considering Glori's constant inebriated state, I had my suspicions that there was more than just water in her bottle. There may have been water in there at one point, perhaps in the morning, fresh from the freezer, the first few licks to combat sunrise cotton mouth, but gin or vodka were certain to fill the void as the H2O was either sucked down or poured out.

Glori graced us with her presence for about an hour, writing, drinking and occasionally chuckling or voicing comments. As she got up to leave, she slurred in my direction, "Diana, be sure to stop by my office during break."

And, away she went.

It was as if the entire classroom heaved a great sigh of relief when Glori left. To all those people who think one person can't make a difference, here was proof of how badly one individual could bring down the energy of a room full of young, vibrant students.

I waited until mid-point in the class, just before lab started, before I made my way to Glori's office. Whatever she had to tell me probably wasn't good, so I wanted to wait as long as possible before she spit it at me.

Once inside her office which, surprisingly, was an organized mess rather than complete disarray, I took a seat next to her desk. She initially ignored me, or so I thought because she started to talk to me while she read through her emails. Her office reeked, offering the excuse that she was taste testing liqueurs for Chef for future recipes, an excuse I quickly dismissed.

The smell of alcohol on her breath meant she wasn't thinking clearly, so I was a bit concerned with what she had to say. Did my audit go that badly? Honestly, I always got the highest marks when I taught a training class in high tech. Just because the topic was different and perhaps it had been a number of years since I was in front of a crowd like this, I was certain my presentation skills were still strong. Besides, if Glori gave me anything but a five-star review, I'd have words with her boss.

"Is there something you wanted to tell me, Glori?"

She finally turned and gave me her full attention. She was a wreck. I tried to just listen and not watch as she stumbled through our little chat. Surely, someone at this school had addressed her drinking and was offering her help. I'd check with Celine for updates once I got out of this uncomfortable meeting.

"Yes, as a matter of fact I do have something to tell you, Diana. First of all, I want to thank you for teaching the introductory class for our program. You appear to be doing a good job and the students like you. I haven't heard one complaint so far."

I wasn't sure if a compliment from Glori was something to get excited about, but it certainly beats bad news.

"In fact," Glori continued, "you're doing such a great job the department heads have decided that whoever teaches the introductory class would automatically become the faculty advisor for the fashion club."

So there is bad news after all.

Was I hearing right? I'm doing such a great job that all future instructors of the intro class will be required to be the faculty

Cindi R. Maciolek

advisor? Or, will that requirement change as I move up and teach higher level classes. Will the assignment follow me or will I be able to leave it behind? Regardless, this was not good. As part of my job description, I couldn't fight it. And, holding a logical conversation with Glori was a near impossibility, but I still gave it a go.

"That's interesting news, Glori, as that wasn't in my job description when I was hired."

"Well, you know, we're a very fluid organization at the moment, trying to decide the best way to lay the foundation for this program."

Wow! She actually was capable of spouting out a multi-syllabic party line for the school.

"I'm flattered, Glori, but have you talked to Celine about this? I know I mentioned it before but now that the quarter has started and schedules have shaken out, it might be worth another try. I think Celine would be fantastic as the faculty advisor. She's right in the thick of things. I'm just a bit removed."

The look on Glori's face was almost of a parent when her child has disobeyed her one too many times. I was waiting to be sent to my room without my cell phone.

"Let me be clear, Diana. This isn't open to discussion. This is part of your job. It wasn't there before but it is now. Things change. You can take it or leave it. I don't care. But, if you stay, you will organize the fashion club and do a bang up job. Understood?"

I looked long and hard at Glori, pissed beyond words. Here was my *boss*, drunk as a skunk, totally unprofessional in any normal academic or business environment. Her clothing was soiled from assorted meals that accompanied her liquid lunches. Plus, she was basically getting a free pass at the college just because, for some reason, management had deemed her their golden ticket to achieve certification for the interior design program.

But the biggest reason she bugged me was there but for the grace of God go I. Had Chris and I stayed together, who knows how my future would have looked. I suspect we would have

{ 158 }

parted ways eventually, even if we did have children, simply because his family didn't deem me worthy enough.

I was luckier than Glori in many respects regarding my marriage to Chris. I'd never even met his family! Nor, he mine. Glori had it rubbed in her face every time she went to L.A. She couldn't miss their names on the buildings. Even though she designed the interiors of some famous properties here in town – albeit several years ago, before she had children – she was still deemed a loser by her ex's family. There's only so much you can tolerate before your self-esteem takes a major hit.

My situation with Chris was not very different from Glori's except for the fact that she stuck it out longer than I did. I had no choice. If Chris hadn't filed for divorce, I'm sure I would have hung in there, being insulted and demeaned constantly for not having royal blood or whatever their exclusion clause of the day was. It didn't matter that Chris and I supposedly loved each other. I had to pass some sort of acid test by his family that was never to be.

I'm not sure I'd be hitting the bottle as hard as Glori was but just consider how troublesome my own life had been the last few years since my divorce! I suspect she had to sign some sort of iron-clad pre-nup, too, which left her in such dire financial straits that she felt the only satisfaction she could get was at the bottom of a bottle.

I understood where Glori was coming from. I didn't understand how management was handling the situation and, although I've worked with some extremely unreasonable people in the past, reporting directly to an alcoholic is an impossible situation. No one wins here.

And, it's the worst possible role model for the students. They aren't dumb. They don't know the circumstances but they can see what's going on and that makes it even worse! I know what Glori is recouping from and I'm still having a hard time dealing with her.

If I refuse to do her bidding, she'll turn into a belligerent drunk, maybe even fire me. If I do take on the challenge of faculty advisor to the fashion club and I do it well, I'll have basically completed my charitable service for the year. There's no money in it. It's a matter of giving, giving, giving of myself with no respectful compensation – and it doesn't have to be monetary.

Here I was, in another impossible career situation. It was only the beginning of the quarter and without this class, I wouldn't be able to pay my own bills. I hated my life.

"Understood. I'll get right on it."

"Thank, you Miss MacKenzie. Those are all the measurements Mr. Bailey requires."

"Diana, please."

"Miss MacKenzie. Now, what is your heel height tolerance?"

"My what?"

"Your heel height tolerance. How high of a heel can you wear comfortably? Mr. Bailey will select a shoe that is deemed comfortable to all six bridesmaids. I'm not certain if they will be sandals or pumps, but heel height will be a consideration."

I laughed.

"Forget the heel height! Who's designing the dresses?"

Jolie, the sales consultant at Haute Couture Bride in Las Vegas, looked at me as a mother to a young child.

"I'm sorry, but I'm not at liberty to disclose that information. Quite honestly, I'm not privy to those details at this point. I can say that they are expected to be in the orange family, but I don't know if they will be tangerine or rust."

Boy, trying to pry juicy tidbits from Jolie was even harder than getting snippets of information from Gizzi.

"Uh, well, I guess I could handle up to about four inches. If we need to go higher, I prefer a platform or a thicker heel."

The consultant flashed me a look of displeasure, knowing that in her world, it was inappropriate to wear a thick heel in a wedding party. Stilettos were the winners here.

I hadn't had much reason to wear heels of any sort in recent years, given my current lifestyle. I did have those fabulous stilettos in my closet that I refused to part with. I'll have to practice walking around the house with them so I don't make a fool of myself at Gizzi's wedding. The only time I wore them in recent memory was to the engagement party.

"Perfect. Medium width?"

"Yes."

"OK, I think I have everything I need at this time, Miss MacKenzie. The wedding is in December so your dress should be here late October. We'll be able to do a final fitting before shipping the dress to California."

Yikes! October! That just shaved two months off my schedule for my bridesmaid's diet. I hadn't thought about the dress fittings being so early. However, I was thrilled the salon would ship the dress to the wedding. One less thing for me to worry about.

"Thanks for the warning! I'll be in rock star shape by then."

"Yes, of course you will," Jolie sneered. "Will you be maintaining your hair color as well?"

Oh, you mean the bits of gray I can't afford to color?

"I'm sure Mr. Bailey will see to it that we all look our best at Gizzi's wedding."

Jolie smiled.

"Yes, that is his specialty."

"Well then, I guess we'll see each other again in October. Just call if you need anything else."

"I'll be sure to do so. Good day, Miss MacKenzie."

"Good day."

I walked out of the salon, back to my car, emotionally confused. I was happy I could get all my fittings done here in town, but sad that I wasn't partaking of all the fun back in Silicon Valley. Certainly, Gizzi would plan a fitting party for the other five bridesmaids, and I wouldn't be part of it. Although…given the fact that I still carried around some *Positano* poundage, I'm not sure I'd want to be seen in my undies with the girls who were all as gorgeous as Gizzi.

And, as maid of honor, how would my dress differ from the others? Colin Bailey tended to dress all the bridesmaids alike, but I wanted everyone to know just how special I was to Gizzi and I hoped that my position as maid of honor was positively reflected in some way.

I enjoyed the lux glamour of Haute Couture Bride, but the uppity consultant was a little much. Is that what all people are like in the moneyed world? I mean, we're all just people here, right? I truly felt like an outsider, not referring to Gizzi's wedding in particular, but from a class standpoint. I'd been wallowing in the muck for so long now I'd forgotten just how snotty designer sales people could be. It's as if they were trained to believe that individuals with money wanted to be treated that way. Well, I certainly would prefer to interact with people who are real and not so uppity. Oh yeah, but I'm not one of those with money so how would I know.

I took a deep breath, sped home as quickly as I could, and rushed into my closet. I had work to do! It was my day off so I could play in my stilettos for hours. Sure, I had vacuuming and laundry on my list. Why couldn't I do chores in my gorgeous heels?

And do chores in heels I did. I vowed I would enjoy my stilettos every week until December. I blasted my music, put on my pumps and pranced around the house, prepping for the most perfect wedding. Wearing stilettos while cleaning burns more calories, doesn't it?

Dear Diary,

Oh, I hate myself so much right now.

It's bad enough that Glori has pressured me into organizing the fashion club. It's unsettling that I feel there is no recourse for me at MFILV, that a trip to the dean's office will only result in an emotional confrontation between the two of us, with nothing but hurt feelings as a result.

Now, I've decided, at least for the rest of this quarter, I would leave a little extra treat in Glori's mail slot. I know she's hurting financially and once all the divorce negotiations are finalized she'll be fine, but in the meantime she has kids to care for. I overheard her borrowing gas money from Dean Anderson. Naturally, if Glori didn't spend so much on booze her budget would be in better shape, and with her drinking she shouldn't be driving, but she needs an outlet and alcohol was her current demon of choice. I'm sure all her bottles of booze at home had photos of her ex-husband on them as a reminder of who she hates so much.

I have my own precarious financial position, but I figured 20 bucks a week in an envelope, anonymously left in her mail slot, might help her trust in people once again. Maybe she'd realize that not everyone is out to get her or use her, but that someone cared enough to think of her.

I also worry about her kids and how they felt about her drinking. She only has them every other weekend; the rest of the time they're with their father in California, but those weekends should be special.

Glori needs a friend right now and I'm not talking about Johnny or Jack.

More tomorrow!

All my heart,

Diana

His Hotness

{ FOURTEEN }

"Do you have time for coffee?"

My class had just finished and I went to the teacher workroom to check my mail slot like I always did before I went home. Gray, the hot gaming instructor, caught my attention before I flew out the door. We'd never met but I knew his name from Celine who chatted with him after her interview, and because I privately lusted after him. I mean, I had no one else to dream of at the moment.

"Uh, sure, Gray. What do you have in mind?"

Just looking at Gray, I had a lot in mind. He was hot! Hot for a guy with the teaching gene. Yes, even here on this campus of creative misfits, the teaching gene was apparent. I'd better take a closer look in the mirror when I get home to see if something is surfacing on me. Teaching genes are usually not latent, but who knows? There's a first time for everything.

Gray also was gifted with the nerd gene, but in his case, he wore it well. No one rocked a plaid shirt like Gray. No, he didn't wear those laundered, starched shirts I so desired, but maybe it was time for me to find a new kind of guy. And, oh, the way he styled his hair, tousled and lifted on one side, like sexy bed head. Hmm…maybe on closer inspection, he didn't style it. It *was* sexy bed head! He simply left it that way when he woke up. Either way, it was his look and he wore it well.

"Well, I wanted to discuss a joint class project with you for next quarter."

That was the latest directive from the administration. Since MFILV was a creative college, the powers that be felt a lot of benefit could be had by having cross-departmental class projects. We were the first of the many MFI campuses to try it. Our success would determine whether this idea would go corporate-wide.

"As you may know, I teach gaming. Now, I don't know how much you know about gaming development…"

"Honestly, not much at all. I don't even play video games!"

The look of disappointment on his face was almost heartbreaking. I wanted to give him a hug. Now! Come here, into my arms…

"Well, yes, I see. Anyway, the students are quite talented in creating the stories and scenes for the games but their one downfall is outfitting the characters. They really don't know very much about fashion."

"Yes, I have seen the gaming students. They remind me of the engineers I used to work with back in Silicon Valley."

These were students who were extremely talented and could play or code for hours without a break. They didn't see the sun much, let alone worry about what they wore, especially those who walked around in tails and ears. What's up with that, anyway? But, I could see Gray put some thought into his wardrobe. Or, was that the same shirt I saw him in last week? Perhaps he wears it the same day every week. I've known people to have organized wardrobes like that.

"Oh, good. So you should be able to communicate with them. Anyway, the project I'm proposing is that we team your students with mine to develop a fashion story board for the gamers. They'd be like wardrobe mistresses for a movie."

"You mean costume designers."

"Sure, whatevs. They would basically help define the characters through their clothing."

This could be an interesting project. Who knows? Maybe one of these games will make it big and my students will have designed the costumes! It's not really our focus in this program, but so many students are interested in design it would still be a lot of fun. Plus, I'd get to spend all that extra time with Gray. I won't get paid for it but sometimes you just can't put a price on lust.

"What do you think? Are you interested?"

Am I interested? Absolutely! Your place or mine? Oh, wait, I think he wants to know if I want to team up for next quarter. Hell, why would I turn down such a hot guy? He could have chosen from any instructor in the entire school and he picked me. Me!

"Sounds great, Gray. We can meet now if you like."

"Fantastic! Let me just grab my things."

"So, Gray, tell me why you selected me to be your cross-department project partner?"

I had to know. I mean, I'd never spent any time talking with Gray. I hardly ever saw him on campus even though he practically lived there from what I heard. Didn't matter. He picked me!

"Oh, I had asked Celine but she was already committed to one of the ID instructors. They're going to do some sort of fashion/home fusion project, showing how your home needs to be refreshed every season just like your closet. Whatevs. Celine suggested you. I'd never met you but I have seen you and you always seem to be nicely dressed so I thought, why not?"

Gee, thanks, Gray. Suddenly, His Hotness didn't seem so hot anymore. I don't like playing second fiddle to anyone, even if it is the woman I suggested would make the best fashion club advisor at the school.

Maybe I'm taking this a bit too harshly. After all, I will get to spend several weeks with His Hotness. That's not such a bad consolation prize.

But, that Celine. She must be kissing someone's ass to be partnering with the interior design department. Maybe she got suckered into that one by Glori like I got suckered into the fashion club. Glori may be alcohol's greatest friend but her ability to blindside people was legendary. I've done *some* research. Maybe that's how she snagged her ex in the first place. Was she pregnant when she got married? I'll have to investigate.

And the way he says, "whatevs." It's so annoying! How could someone so hot use such a throw-away word. Now I know how my old boss at *Bergstrom* felt. She said it was very disrespectful. I don't think he means to impart that feeling, but I feel it nonetheless. He certainly has other redeeming qualities that would help me to overlook his terminology. Surely, there are things about me he must dislike. Or, am I perfect?

"Well, I'm sure we'll do a great job together."

Even if our cross-department project doesn't work out, we could still do a bang up job during the off hours. I wonder if there are any places on campus without security cameras.

"Great! We won't know exactly how many students we'll have until the next quarter starts, but we should probably have a couple of meetings ourselves in the next few weeks to fully define the project. Sound good?"

"Sure. I could cook dinner. You're welcome to come to my place."

Ooh, was that too soon? I mean, we just met. Am I being a little too assertive? Aggressive? I could never use those two properly. Anyway, men today like strong women, right?

"Uh, where do you live? I don't have a car."

His Hotness doesn't own a car? Wow! This may be scraping the bottom of the barrel for a little spring fling. I do like a strong man. One who owns a car!

"I'm over in the northwest part of town, about 35 miles from here. Where do you live?"

"I live in the apartments across the street. Have for years. I can walk here, walk to the grocery, walk to the local restaurants. It's very convenient. If it's a little further, I ride my bike or take the bus. And, I can always find a ride with someone when I need to."

Sorry, but I am not going to pick him up, have dinner, bring him back and drive home, no matter how much I want him. I'd feel like his mother. Unless, of course, he wanted to spend the night. Then I could accept bringing him back the next morning. There is some good shopping on this side of town. I can't afford anything, but I could always window shop.

"Don't you feel lost without a car, especially in this town? I mean, it's not New York."

"Nope. Better for the environment. I lead a very simple life. If you want to make dinner at my place, that's fine. Or, we could just meet here to go over notes."

Is he shy? Is he involved? Is he clueless? I mean, I don't look my pre-marriage self but I certainly am attractive, aren't I? Pierre liked me! If I can't catch the eye of a gamer, who can I get? Maybe he just needs more time to warm up to me.

"Coffee will work. Every week after my class?"

"Like now?"

"Yes."

"Cool. This works."

"Should we exchange contact information?"

"No, you're in the staff directory. I'll just pull it from there. You can do the same for me."

How romantic...

"Perfect! See you next week. Same time. Same channel."

As he got up to leave, he looked at me with his twinkling eyes, shot a finger in my direction and said, "Later."

Sweet dreams, Your Hotness…

"Hi. Thank you for taking my call. My name is Diana MacKenzie, and I'm an instructor in the fashion program at MFILV and faculty advisor to the fashion club. I wonder if you might be willing to host a club visit and have someone available who could speak to our students about the process of designing for your brand and managing your boutiques."

"I'm sorry, Miss, but we really don't have time for that here. You'll have to contact our corporate office to see if that's something they'd like us to support."

And so it goes. Call after call. I was trying to plan some field trips for the club, thinking that might interest the students, but in actuality, it probably is something they'd do anyway in their higher level classes.

Didn't matter. Only one of the high end designer boutiques agreed to have the club tour their store and give background information on the company and I'm still not sure if the students are interested. Of course, I didn't contact any of the places where I used to shop or work. Why embarrass myself once again? However, there's so much turnover in sales staff at these places I'm bound to run into one of my old contacts or colleagues at some point.

After near continuous rejection, I came up with a different plan. I'd offer some suggestions to the students then follow up on the ones they liked rather than try to plan something without their input. Brewing up interest at the boutiques seemed almost like class work. Maybe there's something else they'd like to do. I don't want to waste any more of my precious time.

I can't believe how much work the fashion club is. First, I had to market to the students on campus, through email and text messages. The graphics department created posters but I had to go to every bulletin board on campus and post them, hoping someone else didn't pin an announcement on top of mine.

I spoke about the club in class; all the other fashion instructors did the same. It was a small group of students but everyone had such different schedules, we wanted to make sure everyone heard about it. We didn't want a fashion student left out. As it was, by the time everything got organized, the first meeting wouldn't be held until after mid-terms.

The powers that be wanted to get the overall fashion program off to a good start so we weren't even allowed to convene the new fashion club during those first crucial weeks. Once the students were oriented into the program, the launch of the fashion club would, hopefully, not interfere with their studies. Our first club meeting would take place week six of the quarter, then we could meet weekly until finals, and start this whole circus again after break.

Picking a time to hold the first club meeting has been a challenge. We had a full slate of classes this quarter, so finding an available space to meet was a near impossibility. The room availability defined the meeting time for the club for now but it would change from quarter to quarter as class schedules changed.

Once that was locked down, a new flyer was printed with time and location and I made the rounds once again, taking down the old flyer and posting the new. And, this all had to be done in the evenings because I was still substituting during the daytime. It was exhausting! Plus, I'd been making all those calls to local businesses. I seem a little parched. Perhaps I need a pale ale to whet my whistle.

I am only the faculty advisor. I suspect I'm supposed to let them run the show while I offer suggestions or do their bidding since most of them are working full time and carrying a full load at school as well. I, on the other hand, as far as everyone is concerned, have all the free time in the world.

"You are so out of there!"

Gizzi practically jumped through the phone when I told her I was, in the end, faculty advisor to the fashion club.

"We spoke about this. Have you forgotten?"

"She made it part of my job description. What was I to do?"

"She can't just helter-skelter add items to your job description that you don't get compensated for. If that's how that organization is run, then you need to find another."

Gizzi was right, but after years in the career cesspool, I wasn't sure if an organization existed that didn't stink. Besides, I needed to make a go of something in my life. Teaching college sounded like a good compromise. That's what life is all about, isn't it? Compromise?

Well, that's not what my New Age books would say, but I'm looking at reality here. Then again, I don't think I've ever heard a country song titled, *Compromise*. Something's definitely wrong with my life.

"I know it sucks but I'm staying put for the time being. I've already invested a ton of time. There aren't that many fashion students. The club shouldn't be a big deal, once we get it going. You know how it is. The setup requires more time than the execution."

"I'm frustrated for you, sweetie. But, you do what you must."

"OK, enough about work. Let's talk wedding."

"Yes, because I never get a chance to talk about that!"

We both laughed. I'm sure Gizzi was on the wedding channel 24/7.

"How did your fitting go?"

Hmm...should I tell Giz just what a bitch Jolie was? Or, that I wanted to lose about 20 pounds before her big day?

"It was fine. I'm just anxious to see the design – and the designer!"

"I am, too, sweetie, but some aspects of the wedding will be secret right up until our wedding day. I've been trying to wrangle it out of Colin but he won't budge, not yet. We'll start on my gown next week so at least I'll know the details on one of the dresses!"

"And, will you share?"

"Diana! I told you that one was definitely secret. I've had an idea of my dream dress for years. I know it won't look like that but it will have elements of it. I've never shared those ideas with anyone so it will surprise even my family!"

Now, this was definitely interesting news. Gizzi dreaming of her wedding dress – for years? I couldn't imagine. That seemed so unlike her. I could see her being very specific as she tried on gowns but having already forged the design in her mind was news to me.

"That's awesome, Giz! I can't wait to see it! I promise, I won't pressure you. I'm sure the whole world will be asking."

"Thanks, Diana. And, you're right. Literally, the whole world is speculating on what I'll be wearing. I'm just a simple gal from San Jose. I don't understand what all this interest is about."

"You're a superstar!"

"Yeah, right. Keep that up and you'll be demoted to poetry reader."

Dear Diary,

I'd forgotten how creative people are when they are younger. I remember when I was a child, even a teenager, how many crazy, off-the-wall but potentially plausible ideas I had. As you get older, many people lose that ability to grasp those seeds of creativity and harvest them.

Many of the students in my intro class also have a business planning class with George. They chat about their projects while they wait for our class to start. I pretend I'm working but instead I'm listening to their discussions – and I'm fascinated!

Of course, DJ Daze is working on his Poop business, Brittnee and Alfonso are thinking through their business concepts and even Cassandra has her sights set on developing a very cool fashion brand, although to do it right, it would take far more work than she's anticipating.

I think back to my high tech days, and I have to admit, the types of companies these students want to launch are far more interesting. If I had the money, I'd back some of them. It will be interesting to see how many follow through on their plans and whether or not they're successful.

Maybe I should take that business planning course. George might have a unique way of inspiring ideas, considering the interesting ones I hear bandied about. That might spur me on to start my own company. But, wait – who's going to back *me*?

In this world, everything revolves around money. If I could only get my hands on some...

More tomorrow!

All my heart,

Diana

A Change is in the Air

{ FIFTEEN }

The drive across town was always a challenge, and having to be at MFILV in the midst of rush hour didn't help.

Today was the first fashion club meeting. Yay!!! I guess. I'd already spent way too many hours on this thing. If it was a flop, my ass was on the line. If by chance it was deemed a success, chances are, I'd be expected to spend even more time with the students. I wouldn't complain about any of this – if they could just pay me a little bit extra!

Don't get me wrong. I really enjoyed spending time with the students. Prepping for class has been quite intense as I'm basically learning the course along with them. However, we've had some very interesting discussions and at times I'm amazed at just how much fashion knowledge these students had acquired at such a young age.

Some of them watch every single runway show online over and over to study each collection from the different designers, to be able to identify designer traits as well as collection characteristics. Sometimes they play a game where one student pulls up a photo on her phone and another has to guess designer, year and season. It's really quite admirable. I'd shopped at designer stores for years and never studied the inventory to that level.

So, as I approached my first fashion club meeting, I was torn between giving so much of myself to this program that may or may not get off the ground and quite enjoying the whole process. A different part of my brain was coming alive. Where will all this lead? Who knows! If I had those answers, I probably would be there already. Maybe I should ask Helen her opinion.

As I entered the classroom where the meeting was to be held, I was shocked to see over 50 students in attendance! Now, we barely had that many in the fashion program and I was positive they couldn't all attend this first meeting due to scheduling conflicts and other commitments. These were students, definitely, but in the other majors! I had no idea I'd be advising them as well. I didn't think fashion students were allowed to join the other department clubs so I found it interesting that they welcomed their fellow students so warmly.

But, fashion students are an all-inclusive breed and I had to give them credit. They wanted this club to be successful so they asked all their friends who had an interest in fashion to join in.

"Welcome to our first fashion club meeting," I began.

Cheers went up all around. I had no idea there was such pent up demand for this.

"I recognize many of you from my class, but most of you I don't know. I'd like to hear why you're here and what your vision is for the club."

The first student raised her hand. It was T'Rina.

"I'd like to learn how to organize fashion shows for designers. I think that would be great to put on my resume."

Hmm…thinking back on the program overview I received from Dean Anderson, I don't recall a class that actually taught fashion show management. Sounded like a fun project.

"Great, T'Rina. We'll add that to the list of potential projects. Who's next?"

A male student raised his hand. He was surrounded by cameras which I suspect meant that he was in the photography program.

"Fashion editorial is my dream," he said. "And runway would be good, too. We do a lot of stills and some headshots in the program, a lot of landscapes and architectural shots and we learn about the cameras and exposure and lighting, but we don't have any fashion angle. If the club is willing, I'd like to organize some photo shoots so we could get experience."

"I can shoot, too," another student chimed in.

"And I can do hair and makeup," a female student said.

"Me, too," said another.

"And, the three of us can style the models," said a blonde that I believe was in Celine's class.

"So, I guess we have the first club activity to organize, but let's do some more basic things like naming the club and confirming a good time and place to meet."

There was a smattering of students acknowledging that this was the perfect time and place for meetings. That was good. One problem solved, although it meant I had to spend an extra day battling traffic to get here.

One student piped in with, "I think the name of the club should be an assignment for next week," to which students agreed wholeheartedly.

"I can do some logo designs once we have a name," another said.

Sounds like we have a graphics student or two here.

"And I promise to whip up some treats for sustenance," a gentleman added.

"Culinary?" I asked.

"Yes, ma'am. I want to learn how to cater celebrity events. Might was well start with budding celebs!"

I was a bit floored at how quickly the students themselves were pulling the club together. I didn't have to worry about what they wanted to do. They already knew. My function was simply to facilitate the group to help them achieve their objectives, as long as it complemented the program and adhered to school policies. The students actually seemed more alive planning the club activities than they were doing course work. Who could blame them?

By the time the meeting was over, we knew which students would model, what they would wear, how their hair and make-up would be done, which studio they would use to shoot, what snacks we would eat and who would photograph it all. Two students signed up to handle the social media aspect of the club, another to blog about the club on a school website and still one more who would build a website for the group. I'd never seen such cooperation with such a diverse group of people. I was used to arguing in the war room or the board room. These students knew what they wanted to accomplish, set a goal and were aiming towards it or identifying ways to gain experience in something they were interested in. Kudos to them.

I'd organized numerous photo shoots in my high tech marketing days, so I actually had some experience I could contribute here. However, the way the students organized themselves was a lesson in life for all of us.

On my way home from the fashion club meeting, I struggled with what to do. I could go straight home which sounded luscious but it was still kind of early so I'd probably just sit around and watch TV. I could have stopped by the gym but I just wasn't in a workout mood. Sorry, Gizzi. I promise, I will look hot for your wedding. However, there was one thing I had to take care of.

I decided to stop and pick up the weekly Lotto Ladies funds. I was on such a high from the great meeting that I almost chose not to, but I passed the Strip on my way home and it made total sense. Besides, it was later in the evening and chances were Polly would be in the office doing paperwork while Jazzy and Pamela were selling on the floor.

I really hated going to *The Shop at Positano*. I mean, even when I worked there I hated it but especially because four ladies who backed out of our little lottery group still worked there, I felt extremely uncomfortable. I usually texted ahead of time and Pamela would meet me near the store entrance to hand me the envelope. Then I'd quickly melt into the crowd of tourists in the casino, snaking my way back to my car.

Pamela texted me that she was ready and waiting, so I walked as briskly as I could to the store, hoping to avoid any unwanted encounters.

"Here you go, Miss Diana," Pamela said as she handed me the envelope with the Lotto Ladies money for her and Jazzy.

"Thanks, Pamela. I'll let you know how we do after the drawing."

I tried to walk away but she grabbed my arm.

"Don't you want to come inside?"

No, honestly, I don't. I had a great day going and I didn't want to blow it.

"I don't think so, Pamela. It's getting late and I haven't had dinner yet."

Pamela got a sneaky look on her face, something I'd rarely seen before. She must be working too much with Jazzy.

"Your necklace is on sale."

I stopped in my tracks.

"You mean…"

"Yes. It's 90 percent off. Just $26.50."

I couldn't believe it! I fell in love with a necklace nearly a year ago, while I still worked at *Positano*. It was an amber stone with a darling bird etched on top, dropped from a white beaded choker. It was absolutely beautiful and I drooled over it every shift. It cost nearly $300 and I wasn't in the mood to pay that for a necklace, knowing that I was still in such a precarious financial position. But $26.50. I could afford that! OK, well, maybe I shouldn't purchase it but I lusted for it for so long, I felt I deserved it.

"You're sure, Pamela?"

"Absolutely. I already have it at the register. Just give me your card and I'll ring it for you."

I'd forgotten how liberal the purchase policy was at the casino. It didn't matter where the customer was located. The sales associates were allowed to leave the store to close a sale with a customer, whether it was in a restaurant, in a lounge or in a hotel room. The only place off limits was the gaming floor.

There was a small grouping of sofas just outside the store. I gave Pamela my credit card and took a seat. Moments later, she emerged with my treat and my receipt.

I gave Pamela a hug.

"You are wonderful, lady. Thank you!"

"You are very welcome, Miss Diana. Would you like me to help you with it?"

"Oh, that would be perfect!"

Pamela took the necklace out of its box as I lifted my hair. She gently hooked my new prized possession at the nape of my neck. I touched the amber and a chill went through me. This wasn't a bad day after all. The necklace I pined for pined for me as well. Now it was mine!

"Thanks again, Pamela. I really appreciate it."

I gave Pamela another hug.

"Now, go buy us some winning tickets!" she exclaimed.

"I'll do my best," I called back over my shoulder as I stepped happily down the long hallway and back to my car.

I didn't look at the store as I left. Jazzy had been busy with a customer in the fitting room so she couldn't break away to say, Hi. Gosh darn it! However, the *Genesis* Girls and Polly stared out the window watching both transactions taking place – the proffering of the Lotto Ladies funds and the necklace purchase.

If they had second thoughts about dropping out of the group, I wasn't aware of it. Neither Jazzy nor Pamela made mention. If they wanted to cause trouble, they would first have to expose their involvement in the group which could cause them to lose their jobs. As for the necklace, it was a legitimate transaction. I checked the tag and verified the several markdowns that had been taken. I didn't know what the four of them had in mind, but aside from jealousy at my current inexplicable happiness, they could have no game plan of merit.

I touched my necklace all the way home, smiling for a change. Even if this bit of euphoria lasted just a few hours, it was nice to be out of the darkness. I'd forgotten what that was like. I was in such a good mood I celebrated with my favorite drive-thru meal and a beer.

My happy streak continued the next day after class when I was once again graced with the presence of His Hotness to discuss our cross-department project. We met at our usual place – the coffee shop across the street from the campus and next door to Gray's apartment building.

No plaid shirt today. His Hotness wore a graphic t-shirt bearing an image from a wildly popular video game he co-created called PodRockers, a game with a strong eco-friendly stance.

From what I'd heard, it was about a group of aliens who lived in pods in the desert outside Las Vegas. They posed as a rock band and traveled the world playing for their legions of fans while they sought to rid the world of Evil Earthlings who were wasting the planet's resources. Each level taught different lessons about caring for the environment.

Evil Earthlings were eliminated through such challenges as guitar-riff battles, drum solo competitions and sing-offs. Competitions could be performed live, with scores of bands battling each other in this virtual universe. Since it was selling like hotcakes on all the new gaming platforms that could mean His Hotness was receiving sizeable royalties, yet he chose to spend his life walking and teaching at MFILV.

While I found Gray to be very attractive, I still wasn't sure he was my type, given the lack of motor vehicle and all. I wondered how he would feel if I flirted with him. I was tempted to ask him my favorite dating question – Star Trek or Star Wars – but given his involvement in gaming I was certain I'd be drawn into a philosophical or technical discussion I wouldn't win. I decided to postpone the question to a future meeting.

"So, I hear the first fashion club meeting went well," Gray said as we sat at our usual table. "Everyone is talking about it."

"Wow! I had no idea. That's great to hear. I mean, I'm just the faculty advisor. It's the kids who are running the show."

"Well, of course they are!"

What the hell does that mean? I did market the club all around campus, didn't I? All those hours must be worth something.

"I was a bit surprised that so many students from other departments attended."

Gray took a sip of his coffee.

Oh, those luscious lips. I wonder if he's a good kisser. He looks like a good kisser. I wonder how long I'll have to wait to find out.

"I guess I'm not. Although the fashion club could stand on its own, the post-graduation employment would most likely incorporate liaising with others such as the different departments of the school. Just like we're working on cross-departmental projects, the fashion club encompasses the college en masse."

Wow! He's hot and he uses big words. Maybe he does crossword puzzles. I hadn't had a discussion like this with a guy since Chris.

"I never thought of it that way, Gray, but I see your point. And, it's a great way to build community on campus among the students."

"Bingo! That's precisely the goal. You'll pick up on the culture eventually. You've only been here a few weeks. It takes time."

Did he just dis me?

"So, PodRockers, huh?"

"Yep. I try to get out a positive environmental message anyway I can and the game has been a great forum. I never thought it would be the hit it is and I'm very grateful. I donate the bulk of my royalties to environmental organizations. We already have the sequel mapped out and probably another one or two after that. Since we have such a large fan base, we might as well capitalize on it. We're also going to develop a PodRockers branded merchandise line. Maybe that could be a project for the fashion department."

Man, this dude is way more business savvy than I expected.

"You should take it up with Glori. It sounds like a great idea! Maybe ID could get involved as well and develop some home products to expand the line."

Gray looked at me and smiled. We'd been meeting for a couple of weeks now and this was the first time I felt that we actually communicated. I could see it in his eyes.

"Now, we both know that's not a viable option. However, you could certainly head up the program."

Oh, sure, because I have absolutely nothing else to do. I'm not against it. If I were getting paid to do so, not a problem. Perhaps I'm rushing to judgment. Maybe he does have money. Although, he did suggest the students help develop the line. I don't know if he offered that idea as a great way for the students to work on a real world project, or if he's a bit cash-poor after donating his royalties to saving the planet.

"Do you have funding for everything?"

"No, not yet. We're working on the sequel on our own time and we'll just have to figure out the correct merchandise line and launch plan. Once we have all that in place, we'll know how much we'll need."

"Can't you use some of the royalties from the game?"

"I've already made commitments. Those environmental groups need that money. I'll find a way to make the rest of it happen. I've done it before and I can do it again."

I took a deep breath. I applauded Gray's attitude. He knew who he was deep inside and lived his life accordingly. I also admired his belief that he could recreate his success and in fact, make it even bigger. And, he was hot! What more could I ask for? Why was I not sleeping with him already?

"I'd love to explore all those ideas with you in more detail, but finals are coming up. Since this is my first end-of-quarter, I'd really like to concentrate on making sure I do everything right. And, we still have to kick-off our cross-departmental project."

I had to say those words. If I didn't, I might sound too excited and blow any possible relationship with Gray in the future. Much as I wanted to jump across the table and plant a wet one on him, I opted to pace myself and see if he truly is the one for me. After all, Tom liked video games, too, although he didn't create them like Gray does.

"That's precisely the way I would have hoped you'd prioritize. I can see this could be a good working relationship. Now, let's review the project details."

We can work this any way you want, Your Hotness. You just say the word. I'll drive.

Dear Diary,

Today was so much fun! I spent the day at Helen's house where she and I were teaching the kids how to cook. We have some favorite recipes from Mom and although nothing will ever taste exactly the way it does when she makes it, it's still fun to think of passing the recipes down to a future generation.

Justin and Grace were really quite good at cooking and thoroughly enjoyed it! We even took a quick trip to the local Gilcrease Orchards so we could pick our own fruit and vegetables for a very reasonable fee and the kids can learn that fresh food does not come from the grocery store.

The zucchini were the size of clown shoes – just one and I'll eat every day for two weeks! And, the apple cider is the best I've ever had. Picking my own vegetables was so cool. I didn't know you could grow so many different varieties in Las Vegas. I wonder if my landlord would let me start a garden in the backyard. His Hotness would be so proud!

The kids had a blast. Well, actually, we all did. We also found out that there's a Gilcrease nature sanctuary near-by. We'll have to check that out on a future trip. Maybe Gray can direct some of his royalties to such a good local cause, if he doesn't already.

These last few days I've really been happy, as if some-thing came over me to chase all my blues away. Maybe my planets are finally aligning. First the fashion club meeting went well. Then I got my necklace at a steal.

And, of course, my weekly meeting with Gray. Now I had my family time and although we made a complete mess of Helen's kitchen, we also made a lot of memories. – and good food!

I hope these good feelings last forever. It's such a pleasure to be happy again.

More tomorrow!

All my heart,

Diana

The Photo Shoot

{ SIXTEEN }

"That's it. Work it. Work it. Lift your chin. Nice. Watch the jazz hands. Good. Now give me some pouty lips. You're rockin' it! Let's put some wind on it. You look amazing! Blow me a kiss. Great! I think we have it."

The fashion club had access to the studio earlier than I could get there, so they started without me. I was impressed. They'd created a backdrop, styled the three models, added hair and makeup and were just finishing the first look of the first model. I'd never been on the set of a professional fashion shoot but I'm sure it was similar to this, only 100 times better. Not that the students were bad at this. It was their first time. In three or four sessions, they were sure to improve.

I looked around the studio and I was also a bit disappointed. Once the models were ready, the stylists were off in the corner texting and gossiping rather than watching what was going on and seeing that everything was working as expected. I didn't see one of them look at a test shot or adjust hair or accessories.

The models-in-waiting were paying attention because they didn't want to do the same moves as the previous models. These were just students, not professionals, and they had zero experience in front of a camera other than selfies. Still, the school had some students with the looks to pay their way through college through catalog work or casino ads.

The lead photographer was the same student who had mentioned it was his dream to do editorial shots. He seemed so natural at it that I wondered how he practiced. Did he have friends who were willing to be guinea pigs so he could get some experience? Or, was he just emulating what he had seen in videos? I didn't know what the photos looked like but the motions and words seemed right.

The club's culinary student came in bearing treats and headed for the back table to set up an amazing display. He was another seemingly natural talent although I had yet to taste anything.

"You know, celebs and models don't eat anything until they're done working," I teased.

"That's OK," he said. "There's always the crew. I could be part of craft services although I'd like to work my way up to private events."

Amazingly, so many of these students were very clear with their goals. There was no hesitation; they declared their intentions and expected them to be delivered. They must all watch *The Secret*, too.

I nibbled on some finger food and quickly licked my fingers. It was delicious! This student was talented. I'd have to get his card for future reference. At some point, my life might need someone like him, right?

Ah, who was I kidding. These students were miles ahead of me in their careers. This entire quarter, I was learning far more than I was sharing, the complete opposite of my goal. Now, there's nothing wrong with learning. It really should be a life-long thing, but with all the varied business experience I had I would think they'd look up to me in some way. Quite the contrary. They seemed to like me as a person but didn't view me as a mentor. But, who was my mentor?

Moments later, Glori came strolling in. She was usually leaving for the day about this time but today of all days, she opted to check in on the club. The minute she entered the studio the students disappeared against the walls, into the shadows to avoid her, everyone except for the model and the photographer who were relatively unaware of her presence.

The yellow stain on her skirt indicated either mustard or curry, I wasn't sure. It didn't matter. Everything was going so well today that I didn't want her to ruin the rhythm, but her visit alone already had.

"So, this is what a fashion shoot looks like, Diana?" she asked.

"Well, it's obviously their very first so it's a learning experience, but it's not bad," I replied, hoping that would be enough to end the conversation.

"Diana, you're the faculty advisor. If something is wrong, you need to correct it. What would you change?"

Jeepers, Glori, this is my first fashion shoot, too! Other than executive photos, there rarely was a human in any of the shoots I'd done in the past. I looked around and noticed a few things that I thought could change although I'd rather the students go through the process first, then evaluate and make changes for the next time. However, Glori was right in a way. I hadn't asked the students to pay attention to anything. They just set it up and away they went.

I cleared my throat.

"Well, I think everyone should have their eyes on the action, not only to observe what's happening but to see if something needs to be adjusted. See how that one model's hair is standing up in a weird way when the fan hits? That should be fixed. The photographer probably can't see it."

"Go on."

"I think the lighting's off, too. They could use some reflectors on the face. Some of those students standing around texting could help with that."

"Uh huh, uh huh."

"Some music would help. I've never heard of a fashion shoot that didn't have music."

"I see. Anything else?"

"I think the makeup could be bolder. It's too natural, more for a catalog shoot than editorial."

Glori looked at me and headed for the front of the studio so she could be seen in the light.

"Listen up everyone," she slurred.

All action stopped and eyes went to me, not Glori. I had no idea what she planned to do so I didn't know how to guide the students.

"Now, you think you're doing a good job, right?"

The students cautiously shook their heads in agreement.

"Well, I'm here to inform you that Diana feels you need help. Go on, Diana. Tell them what they're doing wrong."

I turned beet red, so embarrassed. This was Lily all over again. Why can't we all just work together? Plus, ever since I left my power position in high tech I felt uncomfortable with confrontation. I had planned to let the students work on the first shoot themselves then regroup before the next one and give them some pointers.

But, maybe Glori was right – hard to admit it – but I guess better to correct them at that moment than wait until the following week when they don't recollect a nanosecond.

I made my way to the front of the room while Glori stepped aside to let me take center stage.

"Uh, well, there are just a few things I would suggest."

I looked hesitantly at the sea of confused faces in front of me.

"First of all, I want to say that in general, for your first shoot, I think you're doing a good job."

Glori snorted then lost her balance and nearly fell when her arm missed the edge of the chair behind her.

"Go on, Diana. Tell them the truth."

The students now seemed really unhappy but didn't say anything.

"Uh, yes, well, there are just a few changes I would suggest. First of all, I think everyone should pay attention to the action. You might have to wear multiple hats on location and being aware of what others need, particularly the model and the photographer, are critical to the success of the shoot."

The students nodded but still remained silent.

"As for the models, I think the makeup is too safe. So is the hair. It's a very nice job but it's more for everyday than making an editorial statement."

The students who did hair and makeup shifted on their feet.

"And, the models' faces aren't bright enough. The lighting isn't right. They need reflectors on their faces unless you adjust the lights themselves. There's a hot spot in the center of the background that I don't think you mean to have. I know you may not have studied this yet but I'm just bringing it to your attention. It will make the photos much better."

Now the photographer seemed to have lost his confidence. Or, maybe he was just annoyed.

"And the last thing I would suggest, at least right now, is music! We need some music in here."

"We didn't play any music because we wanted to hear everything that was going on so we could learn," one of the stylists said.

Oh, I hadn't thought about that. Kids today learn so differently than I did just a decade or so ago.

"And, yesterday we decided we were going to practice this like a catalog shoot rather than editorial, so we adjusted the hair and makeup," the makeup student said.

Would have been nice if they clued me in.

"If you would look at the photos, you would see that there is no hot spot. That's how it looks from where you're standing but up here it's actually providing just the right light," the photographer said.

Well, he was correct. I hadn't looked at the photos. In fact, I was way in the back observing so my perspective could be off, just like my game had been for pretty much every single day for the last few years except for my happy day last week.

"Diana, you're just our faculty advisor, correct?" T'Rina asked.

I shook my head.

"This is our club. You're just around to make sure we don't damage anything or do stuff against school policy. Other than that, we can run the club on our own. We're having a debrief tomorrow to discuss what we learned and what we'd like to change for our shoot next week."

"That's right," the photographer said. "I'll have the photos up tonight on our private club page on the school website so we can all critique the shoot, even if someone can't make the debrief. They can leave their comments under the photos."

"I had no idea you had all this planned. If you could be sure to copy me on future correspondence that would really help," I said.

"We did," the culinary student said. "It was sent to your school email."

Oh, that explains things. I never looked at my school email. My personal email address was on everyone's list so I rarely felt compelled to look at the one assigned to me by the college. I mean, I'm just teaching one class a week. There are so many emails that don't pertain to me that I feel I'm wasting time reading them. I usually checked my account while the students were doing their lab work in my class and that won't be until tomorrow.

"Oh, OK, sorry for the misunderstanding," I said. "I'll be sure to check it regularly."

Glori stumbled as she headed for the door, regained her balance and looked back at me.

"Good work, Diana. Yep, keep up the good work."

Then she left.

Glori was obviously mocking me. Perhaps she was copied on the emails, too, and actually read them. She came in with an agenda and it looked like she accomplished it – she made me look bad in front of the students.

I'd gotten pretty positive reviews from everyone since I arrived and Glori hated me for that. Celine was respected as well but Glori didn't pick on her. I don't know why I was the target of her aggression. Could she possibly know that I was the one leaving her money and she resented me for it?

"Let's wrap it up," T'Rina said.

The other students agreed and in short time they struck the set and headed out the door, appetizers in hand.

I felt miserable. I thought I was doing the right thing but even Glori in her drunken state knew that I was just skating through my job, doing the least amount of work possible. It was still a lot of work, but I wasn't committed, not from the heart.

To be perfectly honest, I don't know a single employer who would want someone working for them if they didn't want to be there. Yes, I was putting in the time. Yes, I was learning – a lot! But, what was I contributing? That's what I had to figure out.

"Hey!"

"Hey, sis. How's it goin'?"

I was subbing at Helen's school today and stopped by her classroom before I headed home.

"OK, I guess. I can't believe how fast the quarter is flying by. Semesters always seemed to drag when I was in college, but quarters are over before you can get caught up."

"Well, at least you know every 10 weeks you'll have new students. I have to wait an entire year to get rid of my brood! How often are you subbing?"

"Oh, that's another problem. I'm trying to sub four days a week but there aren't always positions available. I need Wednesdays off because I teach at MFILV and that's the easiest day to get a sub position. Between the stress of subbing, prepping for my class and advising the fashion club, I'm exhausted."

"Just think how busy you'll be when you add your MBA program on top of everything else."

"I can't imagine. I have no idea how people can do all of this and have a home life. It's impossible!"

"So, I take it you're not dating anyone right now."

"Don't go there, Helen."

"Fine. "

Helen gave me a quick once-over.

"Have you lost weight?"

"You noticed? I've been working out, cleaning house in my stilettos. Hitting the gym. You know."

"You're cleaning house in your what?"

I laughed. Helen could care less about fashion.

"Never mind. I'm just glad you noticed. I'm trying to shape up for Gizzi's wedding."

"That's a great goal. You still have a few months so if you keep it up, you should look positively smashing!"

Oh, no. Helen must be watching one of those British comedies again. Either that or she's secretly in communication with Jazzy.

"Yep. Smashing. That's what I'm aiming for."

We both laughed.

"So, how are things with Mr. Hotness?"

"His Hotness."

"Sorry."

"That's OK. Um, well, I'm not so sure about a personal relationship, although I'd jump his bones in a minute, but he has some great business ideas he's working on and he might turn out to be a viable business partner."

Helen rolled her eyes.

"Diana, when are you going to look at men from a relationship perspective instead of from their IQ and earning potential?"

That was a new comment from Helen. I didn't think I kept men at a distance, viewing the relationship as totally business. Maybe Helen touched on a nerve here. I'd never been much of a social person when it came to cocktail parties or dinners. Sure, if it had a business focus or if I was the organizer, no problem. But, looking at my social life since my divorce, I'd have to give some credence to Helen's comment.

"I guess I feel when I find the one then the business aspect will disappear and I'll focus on the man himself."

"Oh, Diana, you'll never drop the business aspect. It's who you are. You just need to have that softer girlie side that you don't show very often. Has His Hotness seen it?"

"Um, no, but did you know he created PodRockers?"

Helen stopped breathing for a minute.

"PodRockers? The video game? We love that game! It's so much fun and it has a lot of good lessons about the environment for the kids. Gray created that?"

I smiled. Finally, I knew someone that Helen approved of on some level.

"Yes. And, there are going to be a couple of sequels as well as a merchandise line. He mentioned that he might want me to get involved."

"Are you sure he meant involved in the business and not his life?"

"Helen, he doesn't even own a car! Now, that might be endearing to some women but to me, it's a deal breaker. If we had kids, he'd probably want us to use cloth diapers because they're better for the environment."

"They're better for the kids as well. It's just not convenient carrying around dirty diapers when you're out and about with the baby. He sounds like a potential date."

"Look, I admit, I do lust after him but if there's any chance of me working with him on his business, I'd hate to ruin that opportunity by sleeping with him."

"Oh, Diana, you have so much to learn. I hope for your sake Mr. Right comes into your life soon so you can quit doing all this analyzing and just enjoy the relationship."

Helen gave me one of her big sister smiles.

"And make me an auntie!"

Helen never mentioned that before. Since she was already a mother I just assumed having a niece or nephew wouldn't be as exciting. It was for me because I didn't have any kids of my own.

"Come on, let's get out of here and celebrate your weight loss with a nice cupcake."

Dear Diary,

The end of the first quarter is near and I survived! I can't believe how much work one little class can be. Oh, yeah, I forgot. I'm also heading up the fashion club and sub-stitute teaching to pay the bills. But, I had His Hotness to brighten my Wednesdays every week since about mid-quarter. Hopefully, we can forge a life-long business relationship and I can drool over him on a regular basis.

Overall, the students are great although I finally under-stand what Dean Anderson said about them not being able to survive at a traditional university. They have such creative personalities that I could never see them study-ing physics or English. These are passionate people fo-cused on their careers 24/7. In many respects, they could teach students at a traditional university a thing or two about pursuing their dreams.

I've been asked to go full time. I think Celine would make a much better full time instructor and I've brought it up time and time again, but Glori assures me I'm the school's pick. Actually, it's not like I have a choice in the matter. I've been offered the position and I'm expected to accept. There is no thinking about it or offering an alter-native. If I don't accept, I'm out of a job. They won't let me remain part time.

I'll begin my master's program in the fall, after which I'll be expected to stay in MFILV employ for five additional years upon graduation. I struggled to make it through this first quarter, but what are the alternatives? Unless I'm self-employed, I can't see that I'll be happy no matter where I work. At least here the environment is somewhat professional.

As a full time instructor, I'll teach five classes. Yikes! My schedule will still be somewhat flexible due to the times my classes are held. I would only be required to be on campus 30 hours a week, allowing for two hours of prep for each class that I could do at home. Whoopee!

I attended my first graduation ceremony which was held on the runway at Runway Fashion Mall. Unique, to be sure, but it made me cry. I was proud of all of those kids who stuck to it and were heading off to their futures and I don't even know them. It will be four more years before the first fashion students graduate.

I was happy like that once. Then life hit. It's time for me to grow up and face the music. I've been offered a great chance and a master's degree from an online school I've never heard of. Maybe one day I can even take over the program from Glori, if we can get enough graduates to keep it alive.

Yep. Things are looking up.

More tomorrow!

All my heart,

Diana

Full Time Misery

{ SEVENTEEN }

"OK, everyone, that's the agenda for the week. Any questions?"

Whew! As the newest full time instructor at MFILV, I was still in recovery mode from spring quarter. I was looking forward to several days of sleep and relaxation, but that dream was quickly squashed when I received a memo in my mail slot on Friday afternoon reminding me of our week-long *Spring into Summer* session. I guess I'll have to start reading my email regularly so I'm not blindsided by these commitments.

Finals for spring quarter ended on Friday and here it was, Monday morning, 7 a.m., and we were already in meetings. The three weeks between quarters were free for the students but for us, we were forced to give back one of our weeks to our humble employer. As I was going full time, these were my last days of freedom, so to speak, before being overwhelmed by course work. Now, I realized, I had to give up even more of my precious time.

All full time instructors would spend three days in staff development and two days in departmental meetings. Dean Wilcox led the charge for the first three days, then took leave to helm another new teacher orientation on Thursday and Friday while we were off meeting with our department heads. I thought *I* was busy. He did all this week's planning and organization on top of teaching five courses – and he was in his 70's!

I was here reluctantly, having accepted the full time instructor position and grudgingly parted ways with my substitute teacher I.D. badge. There weren't any substitute teaching positions during the summer anyway. Teaching full time at a school where I was already employed would prevent that crazy job-hunting scramble I'd been doing off and on the last several years. I felt like I'd actually been promoted!

Unfortunately, I wasn't quite ready to commit in my heart to anyone or anything just yet, no matter how good it looked on paper, especially when I could see that someone else – namely, Celine – was the perfect fit and the school wasn't doing anything to lure her to the position. Yet, here I was.

As a plus, I will be the willing recipient of a regular paycheck based on a livable salary with full benefits. The last time I was even close to that I was hawking designer duds at *Positano* at full commission. This was at least a salaried position so I could budget more easily.

The one benefit I most enjoyed was my flexible schedule. I had to teach five classes – yuck! – but I didn't have to come to campus every day. I taught Monday mornings – pure torture – followed by the Fashion Club meetings. Then Wednesdays and Thursdays I had two classes each day back-to-back. I'd be on campus from noon till 10 p.m. those days but then I could work from home the rest of the time if I so desired. I lucked out.

Although I had to teach a Monday morning class which is like a gift from the devil himself, I was saved from teaching on Saturday. Saturday – yes, I know! I would still have to participate in Open House presentations, but those didn't occur every weekend. With this schedule, I could potentially sneak away on Friday mornings and not return until Sunday nights, once I have a little play money.

Fall quarter, along with teaching my full class load here, I'll begin my MBA program at one of the company's online universities. Not necessarily my cup of tea or chosen academic institution, but free nonetheless. By the time I finish my degree and pay back my time to MFILV, I'll be nearly 40 years old. Yikes!

In spite of all the positives, I was surprised to learn I was only allowed to take vacation between the spring and summer quarters after our staff development week or over the Christmas holidays. The students had time to recoup and regroup each quarter but not the ones leading the charge. I wasn't happy about this lack of freedom but I guess I should ask more questions before I agree to things. Oh, who am I fooling? I have no place to go anyway.

I looked around the room at my fellow full time instructors, this creative bunch that all possessed the illustrious teaching gene. Hmm. Either mine wore a disguise or I was blind to seeing it. Most of these people had had amazing careers but gave it all up to teach here. Rarely does a creative position come with a regular paycheck and benefits, and while the risk is tolerable and exciting at a young age, the marathon of job hunts can wear down even the heartiest and most gifted individuals. Hence, they teach.

I didn't feel I was as creative as these folks, but I was talented in other ways, particularly when it came to business. Whether I could translate that talent to this environment was another question. When I best operated in business, I was in total control. Here, I wasn't allowed to pick my classes or class times and I had limited knowledge about each topic which put me at a disadvantage. Certainly, some students had greater understanding than me in some areas.

However, as their instructor I was expected to perform as an expert. That meant a lot of preparation for each class, far more than the two hour prep time allocated. So, next quarter and several thereafter, I would be studying for my MBA along with learning this BS program, and by BS I mean Bachelor of Science, not bull shit. Or, do I? With all the new classes I'll be teaching, the school should confer a degree on me in four years, just like the students!

I noticed His Hotness was here, sitting among his fellow gaming instructors. He waved an acknowledgement but I didn't feel an invite to sit nearby. It seemed each department sat together, teachers from graphics, film, audio production, animation, interior design and culinary. I was the lone soul from fashion as the only full timer. Which group would I join?

I recognized some faces but I really didn't know anyone else. Unlike Celine who charms her way with every person she meets, I have to admit, I didn't reach out to connect with the other teachers at all. That was my downfall. Aside from teaching my intro class and advising the fashion club, I only passed these folks in the hall or in the teacher work room. As a result, people were cordial but everyone had their own little cliques and I hadn't been asked to join as of yet.

I didn't have a lot of love for this place even though I had committed myself to working here for several years. Hopefully, at some point, I'll connect with my fellow MFIers and feel at home and welcome. It would probably be to my benefit to make some friends here. However, it would have to be later in the day and after a lunchtime nap.

"Hi, I'm Diana. I teach in the fashion program."

"Yes, we know, dear," said Martha, an interior design instructor who, like Dean Wilcox, had a lifetime under her belt. "Glori let us know she hired you full time. Welcome aboard."

Wow, Glori had enough wits about her to let people know about me? Or, was it just Martha because she was in ID?

"I'm Kevin from animation. Diana, I believe the Universe brought you into our group for a reason. Let's all hold hands, close our eyes and breathe deeply, inhaling the energy the Universe shares with us today."

Right after morning break in which I gulped down as much caffeine as 10 minutes would allow, we were broken into random groups to share our favorite teaching activity from the last quarter. Finally, this was a great way for me to meet some people although I'll be sure to be more careful where I sit tomorrow.

Today I was surrounded by Martha, Kevin and Denora, a graphics instructor. Seems I sat amongst the New Agers as evidenced by Kevin's opening lines. He may feel I was brought to the group for a particular reason, but perhaps it was the other way around. Maybe not. Kevin was doing more than gently holding my hand. I felt like we were on a date at the movies.

"I'll start," I said as I pulled my hand out of Kevin's grip. "One of my favorite class assignments was for the students to share a bit of fashion news at the beginning of class, sort of like the old current events we had in school ourselves. "

Martha smiled.

"Do you find the students actually do the work? I mean, with all the information available on the Internet, I would think they'd be informed already."

Really, Martha? Did you not just ask me what my favorite activity was last quarter? I just told you and now you doubt?

Martha pulled out her crocheting and began to work on an afghan while our group discussion continued.

"I can feel your frustration, Martha, but Diana clearly has had some success with this," said Denora. "Now, Diana, did you find your students came prepared or were they given time at the beginning of class to do their research?"

So many questions! I'm not awake for this in spite of my caffeine drip.

"To be honest, they often researched just before class but I didn't mind it. At least it was current and surprisingly, we learned a lot from the exercise. I know I did."

Everyone in the group laughed.

"Of course you did, dear. These students are all smarter than we are."

Well, if that's true, then the school either needs new teachers or I'm in the wrong place.

I was glad when the other instructors took over and started sharing their activities, all of which were far more creative than mine. Kevin developed his own memory game program to slam home the key lessons for that week. As students took turns to match the tiles which each bore a different concept, Kevin would share the lesson associated with it. Once all the tiles were turned over, students could guess the meaning of the image revealed for extra credit.

Martha focused on a group of custom electronic flash cards she developed over the years. For a few minutes each class, she would show an image and students would have to identify the interior design style associated with it. From furniture to accessories, from draperies to carpets, students enjoyed the game and learned a lot from it. It seemed similar to what my students did on their phones with pieces from designer collections.

Denora would start each class with an incomplete image, perhaps just two or three lines. Students were then given 10 minutes to create a graphic. Even though each student had the same starting point, the end points were completely different.

"Wow! This was really informative. I've never taught at the college level so I really admire the amount of effort you put into your lesson plans," I said.

While somewhat true, it was more a matter of buttering up these few new friends than planning how I could implement something similar in my classes. I was exhausted just thinking about all the work I had already. These were instructors who had established classes and needed minimal prep time.

Kevin touched my hand again, giving me the creeps.

"See, Diana. The Universe did send you to our group for a reason. We are all very passionate about our careers and grateful we have this forum to share our knowledge with the students."

Then Kevin looked deep into my eyes.

"We're here for you, Diana. Any time. Any place. Just call and I'll be there."

I couldn't decide whether to knee him in the balls or laugh in his face, but I didn't want to get fired my first official day on the job.

I looked around my little group who now, I realized, all had a sort of Stepford quality to them. Their facial expressions were sweet but detached. These were people who had given up on themselves and settled for a paycheck. Would that be me in 10 years?

I didn't have time to dwell on it. Not at the moment. Dean Wilcox's alarm went off, signaling the end of our group sessions. I had just enough time to run to the restroom and wash Kevin off my hands before our pre-lunch discussion with the MFILV president.

I stayed an extra minute in the bathroom drying my hands, staring in the mirror, connecting with my inner truth. From what I've seen and heard, if this is what it's like to be a full timer, I have short timer's attitude.

Dear Diary,

Now that I'm full time at MFILV, I'm concerned about being able to fully participate in Gizzi and Jean-Louis's wedding.

All their festivities take place the first weekend in December following Thanksgiving and three weeks before the end of the quarter. As a full time instructor, that's a crucial time for me to be in the classroom and as a new addition to the staff, I feel a bit uncomfortable already asking for time off.

I'm sure I'll get the lecture from Glori about how I'm only allowed to vacation two times a year and definitely not in the middle of a quarter, but the wedding was planned long before I signed on. People's lives don't operate on the MFILV schedule. Besides, it's not like I suddenly booked a cruise to Hawaii or something.

Gizzi's wedding is the most important event of the year for me. She might be stressed, traveling the world for her job and leaving the bulk of the planning to Colin Bailey, but I want to be relaxed and happy and truly be in the moment for the two of them. I can't imagine flying in on Friday night then returning early Sunday morning just to accommodate my school schedule.

It's just not fair. I need at least Thursday through Monday to truly appreciate the enormity of their wedding. Oh, and I can't forget the time off for her bachelorette weekend! The last thing I want to do is look back on this time and regret not having fully participated. I'd never be able to forgive myself and there's no chance for a do-over.

I hate not having money. I hate being at the mercy of others. I want my life back.

More tomorrow!

All my heart,

Diana

Lotto Ladies

The Drive to Win

{ EIGHTEEN }

"So, do you think we're ever going to win?" I asked my car mates as I pointed my Ford Focus south down the I-15 toward Primm, Nevada and the California state line, on my weekly pilgrimage to purchase lottery tickets. Jazzy and Pamela decided to accompany me this week for some reason, and why I had to be the one driving, I don't know. Couldn't someone else use some wear and tear on their car?

"Why, of course we'll win, lovey! That money is destined to be ours. How could you think otherwise?"

Jazzy, a notorious back seat driver, was absolutely hell bent on us Lotto Ladies winning and winning big. We'd been buying tickets now for over a year and still hadn't won much more than $100, money we put right back into losing tickets. But, she says she had a vision that we were holding one of those big cardboard checks with a huge dollar amount on it, and her visions always came true, so how could we doubt her.

"I don't know," I responded. "I've been wondering just how long we should do this. Let's say, perhaps, we set a deadline like the end of the year. If we don't win by the end of the year, we dissolve the group and go on with our lives."

"Oh, lovey, we have no group without you!" Jazzy retorted.

Of course not. The word patsy comes to mind again. Why am I always her patsy? I don't even work with her anymore!

"You're awfully quiet, Pamela," I said. "What are your thoughts?"

Pamela shifted in the front passenger seat, obviously uncomfortable. She'd been friends with Jazzy for years and rarely went against the grain when it came to Jazzy's ideas. However, she was a practical soul and aside from her friendship with Jazzy, appeared to have a good head on her shoulders.

"Well…," she began uncertainly, "I know it's been unfruitful for us so far…"

Pamela paused and Jazzy and I both glanced at her and caught our breath. As the third person in the group, her vote could swing our future.

"But, I still think five dollars a week is an inexpensive investment in our future. I side with Jazzy and say we stay the course."

I could feel the air rushing out of my hopeful balloon.

Sure, I could withdraw and leave it up to Pamela and Jazzy to maintain their own group, but I would be horrendously pissed if they won without me, after basically running the Lotto Ladies for so long. I bit my tongue, took a deep breath and accepted my fate.

"OK, fine, we'll keep the group together for now," I said, "but I want to readdress this issue in another six months if we don't win. Understood?"

Jazzy let out one of her signature squeals, and Pamela beamed ear to ear like a Cheshire cat.

"Fabulous, lovey! Now, where are we stopping for lunch?"

I closed the garage door, walked into the house, put my purse on the counter, grabbed a beer and plopped down on the sofa.

What a day, I thought. What a totally wasted day. I expected it to be a nice, calm, accomplishing day but instead I spent hours with people I despise. Well, technically, one person I despise and one person who is OK but not someone I really choose to hang out with.

Once we arrived in Primm, we waited in line for nearly two hours to purchase our 15 tries at the jackpot, which was anticipated to be one of the largest in history at over $600 million. Everyone wanted in on the action and even though the drawing wasn't until tomorrow night, the lines were already snaking around stores nationwide. As we hadn't won anything worthwhile since the formation of the Lotto Ladies, the additional two hours of standing in line with Pamela and Jazzy were a bit more than I could bear. A beer was really a necessary evil at this point.

Pamela brought with her the infamous white business sized envelope with $10 and I added my five. According to the rules of our contract, each of us could play our own numbers for one try and the rest would be computer generated. So, we would have three pre-selected groups of numbers and 12 we trusted to the system.

Should our numbers be the lucky ones, the person who selected them would be entitled to one additional percent of winnings from each of the other group members, kind of a thank you gift. Otherwise, the winnings would be split evenly and regardless, we would take the cash prize rather than the 30-year payout.

Once we purchased the tickets which Pamela quickly placed in her purse for safe keeping, we dodged the traffic and made our way to one of the casino restaurants which was experiencing an extremely high volume of business due to the lotto frenzy. An hour's wait for a table, two hours for lunch, an hour's drive back and the entire day was shot. All I could think to do was crawl into bed and face the new day with a smile and a good night's sleep.

Instead, I decided to waste more time, grabbed another beer and caught up on the latest reality show marathon on TV. Might as well waste the *whole* day. No sense trying to salvage anything productive after hours with Jazzy and her fake British accent. "Oh, lovey, just think how mahvelous it will be when we all win!" she'd say. Or, "Diana, you must remain hopeful! My visions always come true. It's a family trait. Believe and ye shall receive." And, time and time again, "Lovey, just think how your life will change once we win! The money will impact our lives forever!"

Yep, it sure will, Jazzy. It will hopefully mean I don't have to spend another living breathing moment in your presence. Except to collect the check, of course.

I was certain that if we ever actually won, there would be no living with Jazzy. She would spend to the hilt, the ostentatious side of her screaming to come out and make true all those lies she'd told in the past. Maybe she would actually live in a house in a guard gated neighborhood with a swimming pool and a tennis court after all. She would remind everyone, every day, that it was her idea to start the group and her vision that kept us motivated and on track. Oh, and that we won one of the largest jackpots of all time.

Pamela, on the other hand, would probably use a big chunk of her winnings to create something grand and charitable back home in the Philippines. Or, in the U.S. for Filipinos. Her family ties were strong and her heart was made of gold, which always made me wonder why she hung with Jazzy. Maybe she's one of Pamela's charity cases, and if she can turn her around to being a useful human being, she'll feel she's accomplished something great with her life.

And me. What would I do with the money? I'd thought about it off and on over the several months we'd been buying tickets, but as time has marched on and our winnings have been miniscule to say the least, I haven't really wasted much energy on it. The money would allow me a certain sense of freedom in that I would no longer have to worry about my next career move or a future idiot boss. I could call my own shots. What those shots would be was still buried deep in my imagination. No sense wasting even more of my precious time on this earth. If we ever won, then and only then would I think about what to do with my winnings.

By the third episode of the marathon, I was sound asleep on the sofa, knowing that tomorrow would be just another day in the life of Diana MacKenzie.

"OK, class. That's it for today. By next week, I want to see the first draft of your merchandise plan for your favorite designer boutique. Email with any questions."

"Thanks, Diana. Have a good week!"

"Yes, enjoy your week as well."

The students filed out of the classroom, some stopping by for a quick chat, others running for the door as quickly as possible. The most popular stop before departure was the cell phone table. I now had a strict policy in my classrooms about cell phones. They had to be turned off and left on the table at the beginning of class so as not to distract from the incredible learning that was taking place.

I struggled with what to do with technology and teaching. Sure, surfing the web was important for some projects, so when the students had lab, they were allowed to have their phones back. But, to have access to them throughout class was a major distraction. I didn't even want students to use laptops or tablets. Some would say they typed their notes as I talked, but I could guarantee not one of them could type as fast as they could write. So, banning such devices during lecture seemed the most practical solution.

I adhered to the rule myself, turning off my phone the minute I entered the classroom. No sense any of us being tempted to text, no matter how bored one might be. I had access to a computer throughout class, so online searching was easy. And, most friends and family knew when I was teaching, so they tried not to bother me during those times.

"Say, Diana, want to pick up a quick snack?"

Kevin, head of the animation department, was at the door. He was a popular instructor on campus, going through a divorce, but he rubbed me the wrong way and the thought of him actually rubbing me made me ill. Besides, I had already emotionally supported one man through divorce and we all know where that got me – divorced!

"Thanks, Kevin, but I'm exhausted," I said.

It was already 10 p.m., certainly time to relax. I'd had two crazy days in a row – yesterday with Jazzy and Pamela – and today with my students. I had one more hectic day before a break. Teaching full time was going to be a challenge.

"I'm teaching back-to-backs today and tomorrow. I think I'm just going to head home and get some sleep."

"Oh, Diana, the body still needs nourishment. Don't neglect yourself for your students."

Kevin had a very Zen approach to life, maybe a little too much for my comfort level. I wasn't about to abandon my own nourishment because I was tired. I just wasn't in the mood to waste more time with someone I knew was not going to be a part of my future.

"No worries, Kevin. I have some leftover stir fry at home. I'll have something to eat before I hit the hay."

Kevin came into the room, a little closer to me, before he spoke.

"Well, perhaps I can keep you company. Man – and woman – was not meant to eat alone."

I got the creeps whenever Kevin started coming onto me. I just wasn't attracted to him. If this is how he was to his soon-to-be ex-wife, I could understand the pending divorce. Now, if His Hotness were acting this way...

"I appreciate the heads up, Kevin, but really, I'm good. Maybe Denora is still around."

Kevin's eyes lit up and he stepped back with a big smile.

"Ah, Denora. Good idea. I'll check in on her. Have a good evening."

"You, too, Kevin. Enjoy!"

Kevin and Denora seemed made for each other. She was the graphics instructor who was a little New Age-y, but not in a good way, much the same as Kevin. Denora didn't give me the creeps but she wasn't chasing after me either. I could see the two of them very happy in Zenland.

I packed up my stuff, took the elevator down to the first floor, shoved my teaching supplies into my trunk and headed home. I generally hated the long, 35 mile drive, but at night, after teaching for eight hours with an hour's lunch, it was almost a pleasure. Traffic was light and the skyline of the Strip was mesmerizing. I'd have the same schedule tomorrow followed by a couple of free days to do my lesson plans for next week and critique student work from the past. I don't know how teachers do it. It's a seven-day-a-week job.

I had lied about the stir fry, though, and made my way through the Taco Heaven drive-thru. No fears about running into drive-thru guy. He seemed to have disappeared about a year ago and I was free to eat whatever I wanted from my favorite fast food establishment.

I got home, turned on some music, plugged my cell phone into the charger without bothering to turn it on, ate and went straight to bed. It was nearly midnight. I'd have to be up no later than 8 a.m. to shower and prep for another long day of teaching. And, I wanted to get in a workout if I could. It was a beautiful night and my bed felt great. I fell sound asleep in no time.

My alarm went off at 8 a.m. I was surprisingly well rested. I hopped out of bed and right into the shower. Within 45 minutes I was fully dressed with makeup and hair complete. I felt so good I opted to forgo the workout and treat myself to another day of rest and relaxation – at least until I had to fight the freeway traffic on the way to school.

I popped in a cup of coffee, unplugged my cell phone and finally turned it on. It started beeping and flashing and I immediately received a call. It was Kathy from Tall Tree Post where I kept my business mailbox. I must have a package if she's calling so early.

"Diana?" she asked.

"Yes, Kathy. What's up? Do I have a package?"

Kathy was always so good about letting me know when something needed to be picked up. That way, I could stop on my way into work.

"Well, not exactly. You have two people here who are insistent they know you and need to see you right away."

Really? Who could that be? I didn't owe anyone money. Chris was off to his new life. My family knew where to find me. Could Kevin have stalked me over night with Denora?

"Who is it, Kath? I can't imagine anyone looking for me."

"They said their names are Jazzy and Pamela and they've been trying to find you all night. Is everything OK?"

Good Lord. Did Jazzy have a vision we needed to drive to Primm today to purchase more lottery tickets because the big one was coming our way? Why didn't they just call me? Oh, wait. I had my cell phone off for hours.

I pulled the phone away from my ear and saw there were a number of text messages, missed calls and voicemails, all from the dynamic duo. The first one came about 11:30 p.m., about the time I went to bed. It was from Pamela. It read:

OMG! OMG! OMG! I just watched the news. We won!!!

It couldn't be. It just wasn't possible. There is no way we could have won. The jackpot was expected to hit $648 million. We'd been trying forever, buying our tickets weekly but with no luck. These things just don't happen to normal people like us, do they? We must have won a smaller amount, maybe we matched five numbers. It could still get us a few thousand, and that would be a fine treat and Pamela was easily excited. Yes, that must be it.

"Everything is fine, Kath. Tell them I turned my phone on and they can call me at home. But don't, under any circumstances, tell them where I live."

"No worries, Diana. It's against the law for me to divulge that information. I'll have them give you a jingle. Have a good one!"

"You, too, Kath. Thanks for calling."

Moments later, my cell phone rang again. It was Pamela.

"Miss Diana, did you not get my message? We won, lady. We won!"

Pamela had a joy in her voice I'd never heard before. It was comforting to know Pamela was calling, not Jazzy, but I could hear her breathing over Pamela's shoulder. She must have me on speaker phone.

"Sorry, I had my phone turned off. I just got your message. How much did we win?"

Jazzy squealed her signature squeal at an ear-shattering decibel level.

"Oh, lovey, we won it all!" she said.

I plopped down, nearly missing the recliner, and took a deep breath.

This isn't possible. People don't win the lottery. Not the Super-Duper Millions! Not us! Can't be.

"Are you sure?"

"Oh, yes Miss Diana, I am sure. We checked and rechecked our ticket. Now we don't know what to do so we called you."

Hmm…I don't know what to do either. I was just grateful honest Pamela had the tickets and not that shyster, Jazzy.

"OK, for now, send me a photo and make a copy of the ticket. Keep the ticket and the copy in a very safe place, but separate. I'll get in touch with my attorney. I suspect for such a large amount we'll have to go to one of the regional lottery offices in California, but we don't have to claim the money right away. We can wait a couple of months, you know. Kind of adjust to the idea of it all and make some plans."

I was in shock and not certain how to deal with the fact that I was now a Super Duper Millionaire! Besides, I hadn't even confirmed that we had won.

"What! Wait? No way! It's our money and we want it! We're not going to wait a couple of months."

And, reality sets in. If in fact we did win, Jazzy would hound me until I led us to the district office to stake our claim. Or, worse, she would hound Pamela and I would read about it in the paper. Not going to happen.

"Fine. I'm off tomorrow so we can go then if you like."

Well, technically I wasn't off, but I wasn't teaching any classes nor did I have any meetings scheduled. I could "prep" for my classes at home rather than sit in my office on campus.

"Tomorrow!!! Lovey, you must be kidding! We want to go now!"

Jazzy would be the hard one to tame, and I wasn't looking forward to spending several hours in the car with her again. But, if what they were saying was true, it would be worth it.

"Yes, Jazzy, tomorrow. Live your life like normal until we get everything verified. I'll believe it when the lottery commissioner gives us a check."

"It's true, Miss Diana. You needn't worry. We really won! Jazzy double checked as did my husband and hers. We won. We really won!"

"OK, ladies. Keep it amongst yourselves. Don't start blabbing it to the world yet. I'll call you in a bit."

I hung up the phone, collapsed back into the recliner and cried. I felt it, too. It was real. We won.

Dear Diary,

I'm still in shock! I never in a million years – well, 648 million to be exact – expected that we'd win!

I tried to remain calm when Pamela and Jazzy were talking to me, but I confirmed the win once Pamela sent me a photo of the ticket and I verified the numbers on the Super Duper Millions website. Of course, she also sent me a pic of the two of them with mile-wide smiles holding the winning ticket.

We lucked out! OK, well just winning is luck enough, but there was only one winning ticket so we don't have to share the jackpot with anyone but us Lotto Ladies. Split three ways, we should each be set for life! And to think, it was the computer that blessed us with this great fortune. Even having worked in high tech, I never considered that a computer could be so caring and generous.

It will be really hard to concentrate at class all day, but I know the best thing to do is just keep things as normal as possible. Anything can happen between now and the time we actually have the lottery commission confirm that we are, in fact, the sole winners of this huge jackpot. I've heard so many broken promises during my lifetime that until the money is in my bank account, I can't let myself feel the joy that Jazzy and Pamela obviously are.

It's only the third week of the quarter at MFILV, so chances are, I'll be teaching a few more weeks regardless of our winnings. It's not fair to the students to drop them like a hot potato just because I'm suddenly a multi-millionaire. It's different than Jazzy and Pamela quitting *The Shop at*

Positano. There are people's futures at stake here. I don't want the students to think they're less valuable than money.

Speaking of money…what shall I do with my windfall? No, no – I'm not going to make any plans until we come back from the lottery commission office tomorrow. I just can't let myself go there until I know it's official. But once it is…

More tomorrow!

All my heart,

Diana

Check in Hand

{ NINETEEN }

"So, the Super Duper Millions, huh?"

"Yep, that's right."

"And you believe that you actually won."

"Well, from what I can tell, we have, in fact, won but I won't truly accept it until the lottery commission confirms it."

"And you're the only winning ticket, you say?"

"Yes, it appears so. Again, until I confirm with the commission, I can't say with absolute certainty, but I'd give a probability in the high 90's."

I managed to sneak in a call to my new Las Vegas attorney, Kourtney Wells, between her appointments and before I had to leave for school. I still kept in touch with my California attorney, Brian Garcia, but since I had now been a resident of Nevada for a number of years, I thought it best to have someone local. Kourtney was amazing and very kind although I'd heard she's a tiger in the courtroom, the best combination anyone could ask for.

It was hard for me to talk to Kourtney, having just hung up from that life-changing call from the Boopsey Twins. I was more overcome with emotion than I thought, and I still had a full day of work ahead of me. Still, I wanted to chat with my attorney to clarify a few things before the Lotto Ladies drove to California tomorrow to claim our winnings.

"So, what are your questions?"

"Well, I just wonder how I should handle receipt of such a large sum."

"Last we discussed, you were happy with your estate plan, so I would be sure to have the money deposited into your trust account. You can manage it from there."

"And if I wanted to start a new business?"

"I would definitely set up a separate business entity, probably an LLC, and fund it with an amount you choose from your trust."

"OK, good."

There was a bit of an awkward pause.

"Anything else, Diana?"

"Yes, well, there were initially eight members of the Lotto Ladies."

"What happened to the other five?"

"They each submitted their withdrawal via registered letter, their signatures notarized."

"How long ago was that?"

"Oh, my, it's been a few months."

"Then they should have no case against you. They're not contributing in any way nor have they since they withdrew?"

"Correct."

"Were they under duress when they signed and sent the letters?"

"To my knowledge, no. They sent them all at the same time, so I suspect they decided as a group."

"Well, we don't know for certain, but since a period of time has passed whereby they no longer contributed and willingly withdrew from the group forfeiting claims to any future winnings – "

"Yes."

"Then I think you're in good shape. Of course, anyone can attempt to sue anyone at any time for any reason, so you have no idea what may occur in the future. As for the others, do you feel confident the remaining two members will act according to the agreement and the three of you will split the winnings evenly?"

"So far, so good. We'll be heading to California tomorrow to file our claim."

"Tomorrow! Doesn't that seem a little too soon? Shouldn't you wait a bit? You have a few months before you have to claim your winnings."

"Understood but one of the members – Jazzy – is hell bent on getting her winnings now. I'm afraid if I try to delay it she'll grab the ticket from Pamela and claim it all for herself. I've convinced her to wait until morning. She's not happy but she will do it."

"Great! Well, it sounds like you have everything under control. Congratulations and be wise with your money!"

"Thanks, Kourtney. We'll be in touch soon. I'll have a number of legal items I'll need you to address once I have the money in hand."

With that conversation under my belt, I felt more comfortable claiming the winnings. I still wouldn't relax until I absolutely positively knew that we won, but from a legal perspective, it sounded like we were in good shape. Now, if only I could survive teaching back to back classes today – and the ride back to California with Jazzy.

"So, lovey, how are you going to spend your cash?" Jazzy asked from the back seat as we drove to the San Bernardino district office of the Super Duper Millions lottery.

"I don't know, Jazzy," I replied, trying to concentrate on the road which was riddled with construction. "What about you?"

Jazzy let out one of her signature squeals before she replied.

"The first thing I'm going to do is buy a Bentley. I think they are the most luxurious cars ever and now that I can afford one, I shall have one!"

Jazzy looked around the interior of my aging Ford and added, "If fact, you could stand to purchase a new auto, too, lovey!"

"Sure, I'll probably get something, but definitely not a Bentley, gorgeous as they are," I replied. "And, Pamela?" I asked.

"Well, I'm certainly going to treat myself. I'll probably pay off the mortgage first thing. Then, I'll make sure my husband and I are set for retirement. Once we've done all of that, I'll take some time to think about it. I'm sure I'll pay off my mama's house, but I haven't made any other decisions."

As always, Pamela had a good head on her shoulder. Jazzy, on the other hand, I was certain, will soon be covered in furs and diamonds from Rodeo Drive. As long as I didn't have to chauffeur her there, I didn't care. Once we have the money I really don't want to see either of them again. I just want to live my life, albeit a financially comfortable one.

"So, when do the two of you plan to quit *Positano*?"

Certainly, they had to have discussed it. I was sure they would do it together.

"The minute that check is in my account, I'm walking in to tell Lily I have better things to do with my time than be her servant," said Jazzy, exactly what I had predicted. "But, Pamela has other thoughts."

Pamela shifted in the front passenger seat, a common occurrence on these Lotto Ladies jaunts.

"I thought about doing that as well," she said, "but we already have 15 years with the company. If we stay just five more years, we get a pension. I'll need to keep myself busy somehow, so I haven't decided yet when I'll quit."

Jazzy snorted.

"Pamela, lovey, who needs a pension? You'll have over one hundred million dollars! You won't have to work another day in your life!"

"I know, but I just want to feel that all the time I put in with *Positano* was worth it. What if something goes wrong and I lose all my money? I'd rather know that I have a pension to fall back on."

Good thinking, Pamela. Although, with your smart chops, I highly doubt you'll run out of money in this lifetime. Jazzy, on the other hand, could be asking for handouts next year.

"I think that's smart, Pamela, at least for a while. I'll probably still be teaching for a couple of months. Then I think I'll take some time off and go visit my parents. Now that Helen and Gabe live here, and I have the money to help, maybe I can convince Mom and Dad to move to Las Vegas. Then we can all be together.

"It's always been my dream to have a family compound of sorts, a large plot of land with separate houses for each of us with a common area, like a swimming pool, garden, tennis court, hot tub – those sorts of things. If Mom and Dad are interested in moving, I think we may just make it happen."

"Oh, Diana, that sounds perfect!" said Pamela. "I'll bet I could do the same with my family. Then we could all be close but live separate lives. You're so smart, Diana. That's why I'm so glad you stayed with the group."

"As long as it's lavish and guard gated," Jazzy added from her throne in the back seat. Honestly, did she think I was her chauffeur? "With this kind of money, people need to know you have it. No sense hiding it from anyone, lovey."

And, that's where we differed significantly. From my perspective, having the money and flying below the radar was perfectly fine. Jazzy, on the other hand, wanted it all in your face. Maybe she should spend a chunk of her winnings on therapy. She definitely has some self-esteem issues.

Pamela and I thought more alike, and while we both anticipated celebrating our good fortune, we didn't intend to throw a $100 million party. Not even a million dollar one. I suspected we'd all have a nice family dinner at a really exclusive restaurant and call it a day, although, Jazzy would probably see to alerting the media. Someone she deems important has to see her in her furs and diamonds!

Upon arrival at the district office, I quietly informed the receptionist that we held the winning ticket to this week's jackpot. Her eyes lit up like a Christmas tree and we were quickly ushered into a conference room for privacy and protection.

She handed each of us a form to complete for our share of the winnings, provided identification and indicated how we would like to receive our money. When we purchased the tickets, we had already selected the cash payout, but we still had to tell the state where to deposit our funds – or request a check.

We could hear a lot of commotion in the background as the media opportunity was prepped. One team was in charge of generating the giant check we were to ceremoniously receive; another team was responsible for contacting the press. A congratulatory lunch was brought in since we hadn't eaten a bite during our long drive, after which we simply sat back in our chairs and waited.

An hour or so later, the head of the district office came in to congratulate us and to let us know how the rest of the scenario would play out. Yes, he had verified our ticket was legitimate and yes, it was the only winning ticket in the $648 million jackpot.

And, just like that, we were now Super Duper Millions super jackpot winners!

Having received confirmation, we hooted and hollered, and I could finally relax into the knowing that all the agony of driving to buy tickets and dealing with Jazzy for all those months had finally paid off.

We were informed that we would each receive a payout of approximately $120 million, not bad after taxes. Of course, we would be expected to participate in the announcement which was now scheduled for just 15 minutes away, and the money would be in our accounts in six to eight weeks, quicker if they could arrange it. In the meantime, he warned us that we would be deluged with media requests and advised us to find a good financial planner to help us through it all.

"Oh, we don't need a financial planner," Jazzy snorted. "We have Diana. She'll take care of us."

What???

Pamela nodded her head.

"That's right. No one could watch over us like Diana. She'll guide us to invest the money properly."

I was stunned. We had never spoken about this.

"Jazzy, Pamela, I'm flattered, but…"

"OK, ladies, you figure it out amongst yourselves," the district manager said. "But right now, we're heading out front for your big announcement. Congratulations again, and we thank you for bringing such great publicity to the fair state of California."

With that, we were led out to the front of the building where throngs of photographers and news crews had gathered. Since the state had identified the winning ticket as being purchased at Primm, the press was ready and waiting for the winners to reveal themselves at the closest lottery commission office. And, here we were!

After a few minutes, we were escorted back inside for a quick break, but then it was time to make that long trek back to Las Vegas. It had been such an emotion-filled day and I was a wreck. My preference was to take a nap at a local hotel, but Jazzy and Pamela were too excited to get home. Besides, I had a school open house to host tomorrow morning. And, I still hadn't told anyone we won.

"Mom, Dad, Helen," I began once I conferenced them all in on my cell phone, "I have something very important to tell you."

"You're getting married!" Mom blurted out.

"No, she wouldn't tell us on a conference call, Georgia," Dad said.

"Oh, Ralph, you know, with technology today she might just as well post a photo online. Of course, we'd never see it then, but…"

"Mom, Dad – puhleeze!!!" Helen begged. "I want to hear the news. Go on, Diana."

I took a deep breath before I continued. The news hadn't even sunk in for me yet, so how was I to tell them?

"OK, here it is. You're going to see it on the news tonight anyway."

"Oh, my, are you okay dear? What happened that you'll be on the news?" Mom asked.

"Mother!" both Helen and Ralph admonished.

"Well, it's nothing bad. Quite the contrary. I won the Super Duper Millions! Well, not just me, but me and two former co-workers. The Lotto Ladies."

Complete silence.

"Hello. Anybody there?"

"So, ahem, you're saying that you're now a millionaire?" Ralph asked.

"Yep, that's right. About a hundred and twenty million, to be exact."

Screams all around, so loud I had to hold my phone at arm's length lest I blast out my eardrums.

"That's fantastic, sis! I'm so happy it finally worked out, in spite of the fact that I told you to dump those two!" Helen shared her enthusiasm.

"Yes, dear, that is fantastic! After all you've been through, I'm so glad everything had such a positive outcome," Georgia said. "Now, maybe you'll be able to find a nice, young man, get married and give me more grandbabies!"

"OK, Mom, one thing at a time!" I replied.

"Well, Diana, you know we had you both later in life so no sense wasting your valuable youth working when you could be a mommy," Georgia continued.

"Georgia, really, let Diana enjoy herself," Ralph said. "I'm so happy for you, sweetie. "Now, just be smart with all that money. Retirement will be here before you know it. You want to make sure you have a good income stream in those later years."

"Yes, Dad," I said.

Of course, Dad would advise me to look out for my retirement at the same time Mom wants me to have babies!

"OK, well, I have to go. We still need to drive back to Vegas and it's been a long day. I'll be in touch soon. But, don't forget to watch the news tonight. You'll be sure to see us on it!"

"Safe travels, dear," Mom said. "Love you!"

"Love you all, too," I cried, and hung up the phone.

"Hey, Giz, I don't think you'll have to cover my costs for your wedding anymore," I said when I called her immediately following the conversation with my family.

"Why, sweetie? Did you come into some money all of a sudden? Like, did you win the lottery?"

Gizzi laughed, knowing I was part of the Lotto Ladies and what the odds were to win.

"Well, Giz, as a matter of fact, I did, we did," I said.

Silence.

"Whaaaat?"

"Yep, we Lotto Ladies won the jackpot. You are speaking to the US of A's newest multi-millionaire!"

"Why, I can't believe it, Diana! That's fantastic! Congratulations! So does that mean you're moving back to California now?"

Gizzi, I thought we had settled that issue months ago.

"No, Giz, you know I'm staying here with my family. In fact, I'm going to try to get my parents to move out so we can all be together."

"OK, sweetie, chacun a son gout," Gizzie said.

"Studying French, I see?" I laughed. I knew Gizzi was fluent in French but she hardly spoke it to me. It was funny hearing her lapse into her bilingual self.

"Well, you know, Jean-Louis has that effect on the woman he loves," Gizzi replied. "I'm really happy for you, sweetie. Maybe we can take a bit of your money and a bit of ours and invest in something really big!"

Ah, that Gizzi. Always thinking ahead. But, if anyone could sell an idea, Gizzi could.

"Well, honestly, I'm still absorbing the shock, but I'll definitely keep it in mind. One thing at a time. Right now, I have to drive us back to Vegas. I have an open house to host tomorrow."

"Oh, Diana, you're not still going to do that are you? For goodness sake, you're a millionaire! Quite possibly even a celebrity by now. You'll probably have your own reality show in two weeks. Kiss that bloody school goodbye!"

"Can't, Giz. Besides, the money doesn't hit my account for another few weeks. I have to pay the rent somehow!"

"OK, sweetie. Safe travels. We'll chat soon. We have a bachelorette party to plan!"

"Great, Giz! With any luck, it will be in Vegas!"

"Bien sur, ma Cherie!"

"Au revoir, Giz."

"Salut!"

Dear Diary,

The drive back to Vegas from the Super Duper Millions district office was the longest of my entire life. Jazzy couldn't stop talking about all the ways she was going to spend her fortune. That left plenty of time for Pamela and me to quietly reflect on our own futures. Jazzy needed no help maintaining her conversation. She was all in.

The construction on the way home extended the drive and I was exhausted by the time I hit the door to my house. Within minutes I was sound asleep. One might ask, how could I after such an eventful day? The truth is, there was no other activity I was qualified for by the time I made it home.

We knew once the evening news aired because all our cell phones were ringing constantly, asking for interviews and personal appearances. I hadn't thought past the press conference in California. As far as I was concerned, we were done. No more Jazzy and Pamela. We'd formed our group, got our millions and we were off to our own lives.

Unfortunately, the media was enthralled with our story and wouldn't leave us alone. We were three relatively normal women who had won the largest jackpot in Super Duper Millions history. Everyone wanted to meet us. It would be a whirlwind of appearances, all in the trusty company of my two Lotto Ladies companions. Will this madness never end?

Oh, and I did get a congratulatory text from Chris. Have to say, that's more than I did when his restaurant opened.

Oh, well! I'm surprised he didn't ask me for money to expand his empire.

More tomorrow!

All my heart,

Diana

Media Darlings

{ TWENTY }

"Thanks, Jimmy."

"No, thank you. Ladies and gentlemen, the Lotto Ladies – Pamela, Jazzy and Diana. We'll be right back after these messages with a beer game for your favorite pop star."

We shook hands with Jimmy Meyers, were ushered off stage and led back to the green room to gather our handbags and gift bags from the show. It was our fifth appearance of the day and all I could think to do was sleep. We had to be up again tomorrow morning at 3:30 a.m. for another morning show.

We were in New York and the time difference meant that I was now getting up earlier than I typically went to bed. But, New York is a 24 hour town, much like Vegas, and the late night shows tape early, so we were free to have a pleasant dinner before heading back to our hotel rooms.

Two more days of appearances then we would finally fly home. Each morning and late night show appearance was made on a different day so as not to compete. Morning shows, afternoon talk shows, late night shows – we were schlepped everywhere under the fine control of Angie, the ever-present Super Duper Millions press liaison, keeping us on schedule whether we liked it or not.

The good thing was all expenses were covered as we hadn't received a dime of our winnings yet. I wasn't even sure if the cost of this promotional trip would be deducted when we finally did receive our payout.

The bad things – well – I had to travel with Boopsey 1 and Boopsey 2, although we did have separate hotel rooms. And, I couldn't do any fun shopping due to lack of time and surprisingly, that constant but practical complaint – I didn't have any money. It was coming soon, but not soon enough for this trip.

"OK, ladies, let's catch a quick dinner. I just received a call that your presence is requested to do a Q&A prior to the start of tonight's performance of 'How to Succeed in Business without Really Trying' so we need to be there no later than 7. Who's up for sushi?"

I'd never been a sushi eater in my life, and I wasn't about to start now. I let the three of them go off and enjoy their raw fish while I found a nearby deli and grabbed a chicken salad and lemonade.

The unexpected Q&A went better than I thought. The crowd was fun, the actors were a blast and being on a theatrical stage was a bit unnerving but enthralling at the same time. I'd always enjoyed Broadway and stopped over in New York whenever I could on my many European business trips. Perhaps I could be a producer someday. I'll put it on my list to address when I have time to think.

The rest of the trip went well and I hoped to gather a video of all our appearances so I could make a loop and play it when I had trouble falling asleep. I didn't say much during any of the shows. Jazzy did most of the talking and when Jazzy and Pamela were together chatting about such a fun experience, you just couldn't cut in on all the giddy excitement. If anyone was going to get a reality show out of this, it would be the two of them. If I were involved at all, I would be their straight man while they got all the laughs.

Surprisingly, in spite of all the press, we never heard a peep from past members of the Lotto Ladies. Any lawyer they would have approached, except for a few media hungry ogres, would easily have seen they didn't have a case. As I had discussed with Kourtney, it had been several months since they contributed to the ticket purchase, and they willingly withdrew from the group as evidenced by their certified, notarized letters. I also suspect they would be too embarrassed to admit they dropped out and lost the opportunity to cash in, but in actuality, I wouldn't put it past the *Genesis* Girls to stir up trouble sometime in the future.

Once we were home, our promotional tour continued. We made a number of appearances on shows around the country, actually around the world, right from our own backyard. Through one of the local radio stations, we were beamed by satellite to various locales for interviews. It was fun but a little exhausting, and I had no idea who was listening. It could be a bit unnerving at times. I couldn't wait for all of this to be over so I could get back to living my nice, quiet life.

"So, Diana, what do we do now?"

I answered the phone. It was only 7 a.m. and I had hoped to sleep in at least until 10. I taught back-to-backs again today and I was still recouping from the whirlwind of appearances the Lotto Ladies had made over the course of the last couple of weeks while trying to maintain my life. I had to take off a day here or there to accommodate the promotion schedule but the school was willing to work with me. At least up to this point. They hadn't requested my resignation and I made it my priority to get my lesson plans done and attend class no matter how tired I was. Jazzy and Pamela had a harder time coping, thus the early morning call. Shouldn't they be with their husbands at such an hour? Why were they together, bugging me?

"What do you mean, Pamela? What we do now is live our lives. We now have the money to do so."

Jazzy wasn't accepting that.

"Lovey, I adore all the attention! Shouldn't we be going out to promote ourselves now that Angie has finished with us?"

"No, Jazzy, we only have to make the appearances they request. As far as I know, we're done with that bit. Besides, I don't want to go through my life making appearances as a Lotto Lady. I have other things I plan to do."

"Like what, Miss Diana? Like what? You must share! Remember, you have to include us in your plans because you need to help us manage our winnings."

Like hell I do. It was bad enough I was subjected to spending hours with these two at *The Shop at Positano*. Together, they were intolerable. Separately, Pamela was fine but Jazzy made my skin crawl. We have our payout coming in just a few days. I am not going to be held responsible for managing their money! They have to figure out how to do it themselves.

My phone pinged. Pamela sent me a photo of the two of them with sad faces, hands held in mock prayer, begging me to help them. I wasn't buying it no matter how tired I was.

"Ladies, please, you both have husbands. Sit down with them and make plans for your future. If you want to do something with each other, that's fine, but don't include me. We don't have to do anything together any more. We won. We completed our promotional tour. That's it. We can build our lives as we see fit."

"But, lovey, we've both spoken to our husbands and we all agree you're the best person to guide us. We wouldn't have anything without you. If you hadn't made those weekly trips to buy tickets and keep the group going, we would still be our poor, sad selves. Now, I'm going to be driving a Bentley! The best way I can thank you is to stay along for the ride."

Aaarrrggghhh!

"Yes, Miss Diana. It's true. My husband feels the same way. We'd be lost without you."

"Look, I'm going back to sleep. I have a very busy day ahead of me. Go off and do some shopping or something. We'll talk in a few days. And don't ever call me this early in the morning again!"

I had no intention of calling them in a few days or any days at all, but I knew they would bide their time and call me again in a day or two. In the meantime, I could get to work on my personal plans. I hadn't had a minute to really think about anything in detail at all. I just tried to keep my life as normal as possible until then. And, right now, my time needed to be spent snuggled in bed.

"So, Diana, may I interest you in a little private celebration?"

Creepy Kevin was at my classroom door, once again coming on to me. I thought he and Denora were an item. Why was he here?

"Oh, gee, Kevin, I'm so sorry," I said, trying to sound as honest and convincing as possible, even though I was lying, "but I have guests and I must really rush home. I do appreciate the offer. Perhaps you and Denora can celebrate in my stead."

Kevin came into the room, a little closer to me, a weird look on his face.

"But, Diana, it seems The Universe had plans for us to connect all along. You see, I've had this idea for an animated feature for quite some time. All I need is a bit of funding to make it happen. You could be at the ground level of the next big animation studio."

Oh, brother. Kevin was just like so many other people I'd been running into, asking me for money. And, surprisingly, they were all people I had no real connection with. My family, on the other hand, never even discussed it. They kept me grounded, allowing me to do dishes and take out the trash as always.

I couldn't stand to be in the same room as Kevin. How could he think I would be interested in working with him on a professional basis? It seems when people are passionate about their projects nothing stands in their way. Someday soon, I'll be passionate about something, but it definitely won't be founding an animation studio with Kevin.

"Look, I appreciate the opportunity but I'll have to pass. If I'm going to invest in something, I want to have a personal connection with it in some way. Animation just doesn't do it for me. Perhaps in a few years, after I'm married with children."

I thought Kevin would take the hint and bow out gracefully. Instead, he crept even closer to me.

"But, Diana, I could be your personal connection. I think we could make beautiful animation together."

He smiled a sleazy smile that I'm certain, in his mind, he thought was attractive and sexy.

I thought it was difficult to deal with life when I was broke and could barely pay my rent. Now that I had money, it seemed even worse. I should be having the time of my life, celebrating my good fortune, but instead I'm stressed out from all the leeches out there. I'd better find one of those self-help books on boundaries.

Again, I'm certain there is no country song about that. Maybe that's what I need to do with my life, write country songs about all these life situations for which there are none: compromise, boundaries. I could be the new star of country music.

I finished gathering my things, took a deep breath and headed out of the classroom, right past Kevin, rolling crate of schoolwork tagging behind me.

"I do appreciate the offer and I will add it to my list, but if you're truly serious about your film, I'd advise you to look elsewhere. I'm just not intending to fund an animation studio."

As I headed through the doorway, Kevin called after me.

"What about your co-winners? Would they be interested?"

Ah, the Boopsey Twins. My goal over the next several weeks was to disengage from them, regardless of their insidious plan to have me manage their money. I knew Kevin had amazing experience in working for the two largest animation studios in the country, on some of the largest grossing animated films of all time, but I wasn't sure he could assemble the group it would take to create a successful investment, and I didn't even know what the movie was about!

Sure, I could sic the Boopsey Twins on him, but chances were, they would drag me into every meeting or conversation, every decision or plan and the only person I wanted to see less of in my life than Jazzy was Kevin.

I just kept walking, hoping that Kevin would think I didn't hear him rather than I ignored him. Not that it mattered. I didn't want to give him one smidgen of hope.

I stopped in the teacher's workroom to check my mail slot. On my way out the door I passed Glori's office. She was sitting in her chair in the dark. What to do. What to do.

I decided to approach her. I mean, what if she was dead? She wasn't moving; she just stared out the window. I wasn't her biggest fan but it would be disrespectful to leave a dead person like that. Besides, this way, the school could clean up the mess before classes started in the morning.

"Glori?" I asked as I approached her chair from behind.

I waited a minute, trying to see if I could discern any breathing. She finally took a deep breath and turned to look at me. She had been crying. Her mascara now marked deep, black splotches on her cheeks. In all the days I'd encountered Glori, I had never seen her cry. It was a new look for her.

"Is there anything I can do?"

Glori's face hardened, her eyes turned black.

"Oh, you still have time for the little people?" she slurred.

I was taken aback. I had been doing everything I could to maintain as normal a schedule as possible at the school so that my unexpected good fortune would have little impact on the students. And, Glori, too. I didn't want to be viewed as the type of person who suddenly let the money go to my head and become a diva like Jazzy. I was just Diana after all, right?

"I'm sorry, Glori. I just thought I'd see how you're doing. You're sitting here in the dark. If you don't want to be disturbed, I understand. Just let me know."

Obviously, something bad happened today. I'm sure it had to do with her ex-husband. Surprisingly, though, I think she's somewhat sober. Is that like being only slightly drunk? Sometimes you just need to feel the pain.

"How long, exactly, do you expect to keep up this charade?" Glori asked, with a soft "a" on charade, as if she were at some early 1900's New York social event. It really wasn't like her at all.

"I'm sorry, Glori, I don't know what you mean."

Glori stood up from her chair, a little wobbly but still strong. She curved her back and reached out her arms, like a wild animal about ready to attack. I backed up a bit.

She started to breath really hard. I honestly didn't know what to do. If I approached her I feared she would scratch out my eyes. If I walked away, I would feel as if I let down another human being, in spite of the contentious working relationship we'd had.

"Do you want to talk about it?" I asked. I had to. I couldn't just let her be.

Glori stood up straight, put her arms down, and in a perfectly normal tone said, "No, you wouldn't understand," at which point she turned and sat back down in her chair.

I stood in the doorway for a minute, totally confused. She needed help but I wasn't the one who could help her. She needed a professional. I'll talk with Dean Anderson in the morning.

"OK, well, I'll be on my way. If you need anything, just give me a call."

As I walked away, I could hear Glori sobbing uncontrollably, those hurtful sobs that never truly release the pain.

I chatted with Dean Anderson in the morning. Turns out, Glori's drinking did her in. Her ex-husband's family hired a private investigator and documented her excessive alcohol consumption. They were able to get a court order to give full custody of the children to her ex as they labeled her an unfit mother. The only time she could see her kids was fully supervised visits once a month in L.A.

Unless she turned her life around, and quickly, she would never have private time again with her little ones.

Dear Diary,

Honestly. You try to do something right for other people and all you get is shit upon.

When we won the Super Duper Millions, I was convinced I needed to stay and teach through the end of the quarter for the sake of the students. Now I'm rethinking that decision and may beg off in the next week. I also wanted to maintain some sort of normalcy so as not to get swept up in the craziness of winning such a huge amount of money. I haven't even allowed myself to enjoy my winnings, trying to be so cautious after the few rough years I've had financially. Winning the jackpot was a blessing and I want to honor that gift the best way I can.

But, when I get into class, all the students keep asking for a handout. They want to know why I don't just give each of them a $1,000! As their instructor, they feel I should share the wealth. I understand their financial need, but it's still a tough call.

His Hotness seems a bit confused about how we should work together. He's been on the receiving end of substantial royalties for PodRockers, but I get the distinct impression he either feels I've become part of the capitalist energy-wasting establishment now that I have this wad of money or he'd like to be like the others and ask for some so he could get his sequels and merchandise out into the market, but is just biding his time. For the moment, I'm trying to keep it business as usual with him, as usual as it can be.

Not that I care, but even Glori has been avoiding me, ever since I found her sequestered in her office that one late night, crying. I must seem like everything she hates right now, given the situation with her ex. It's amazing all the preconceived notions and pressures that suddenly appear when your bank account grows overnight.

Having won all this money, it seems everyone wants a piece of me. I get invited to every fundraiser in town. I have VIP seats to whatever I want. And, if I don't respond or contribute, I'm looked down upon. But that's just not the case.

First of all, it's impossible to help every single person or organization. I'm sure I'm not the only wealthy individual to face this dilemma. Second, I'm still adjusting to having this huge amount of money and I'm not making any moves until I've secured my future and taken care of my family, then determined exactly what I want to do with my life. It's so rare that someone as young as I can be so blessed.

One student suggested that if I didn't want to *give* them money that I should invest in their start-up businesses. Now, that's a thought – student entrepreneurship. Of course, there's only one idea that I've seen so far that looks like it has viability, created by a student who is a true entrepreneur at heart. Alfonso has spent countless hours defining and updating his business plan. I think he'd make a great partner.

Perhaps there is some potential to becoming an investor. I love business and I love the idea of running things again, instead of being run into the ground by other people. I could be a Super Duper angel investor! If I set aside a small portion of my winnings for investment at the angel stage, and I'm really careful about my selections, I could possibly grow my bank account above and beyond its current staggering level.

Maybe I will call Alfonso and look at his business plan in more detail. He only needs $20,000. That seems like a reasonable amount for my first investment. And, it's a totally fun business, too!

More tomorrow!

All my heart,

Diana

The Buff Boys

{ TWENTY-ONE }

"Ladies and gentlemen, may I introduce to you – the Buff Boys!"

Just three months after winning the Super Duper Millions and I already had my first successful business launch, the Buff Boys Porter Service – BBPS. Alfonso came through on every detail as I anticipated he would and demand was already over the top. In just six months, I'd make back my investment ten-fold. Not bad for a former panty folder.

I hadn't expected to be in this spot so quickly, but school was getting to be a real hassle. I couldn't go anywhere without students, teachers or administrators asking me what was I going to do with all that money or if they could have some. Or, why would I still be here teaching when there's a world of freedom out there for me to explore.

I finally took their comments to heart and with such a genius of a business plan from Alfonso, took the plunge on my first angel investment. I opted to leave the classroom to take the focus off how to spend my millions and back where it belonged – on the students' education. The other department members split up my course load so everything was covered.

As for me, I was enjoying my first business venture and quite liked heading the promotional aspect of the business. This is what made my heart sing, and Alfonso was keen to listen and learn.

The Buff Boys strode shirtless down the main runway at Runway Fashion Mall, cheers and catcalls coming from the audience. These were the women I expected to take advantage of this new service at this mall and hopefully, go home and request it at their own. The plan was to franchise in a couple of years, building the Buff Boys brand nationwide.

Each Buff Boy wore a number strapped tightly to his thigh, his menu order number, so to speak. If someone wanted to reserve a particular Buff Boy, that was the number they used. It was a Japanese sushi menu come to life.

"Take a good look, ladies," I continued. "These are the men who will help you with your shopping! No more running out of hands to carry bags, or finding they're too heavy. These Buff Boys will trail behind you toting your packages throughout the mall. Shop 'til you drop, because these boys need all the weight lifting and endurance training they can get to keep those hot bods!"

I recognized this as a great idea the minute Alfonso brought it to me. I knew myself that shopping in such a huge mall was an issue. My favorite stores were spread throughout and although they had a concierge that offered a free service to store bags, you still had to get them to the concierge, then to your car or taxi. At some point, you just gave up and went home, too many bags or the weight of them too oppressive to keep shopping.

So many people came from neighboring states with empty cars and went home with shopping bags from Runway Fashion Mall, they certainly experienced this same issue. By having a Buff Boy at your side, you could shop relaxed knowing your bags were being well taken care of.

Besides, this was Las Vegas! There were ample opportunities for men to experience the company of beautiful women, but the inverse was not true. And, what activity do women like more than anything else? Shopping! So, why not combine all the sexiness of Vegas with a woman's favorite activity and you create a dream business.

Alfonso had already lined up a group of friends who were very keen to do this. They could get a good workout just carrying the shopper's bags through the mall. They were young and good looking and always ready to help a damsel in distress. Only, this time, they would get paid for it!

Start-up costs were relatively low. They needed a website, business cards, a booth at the mall with people to staff it, cell phones, licenses, some unique branding items and a bit of PR. All Buff Boys needed to be bonded and insured, and the company needed several other types of insurance for work injury, stolen bags and protection from the shopper in the event she came on a little too strong either seductively or nastily.

Otherwise, it was a pretty simple concept. Shoppers could book a Buff Boy for a minimum of four hours at $50/hr. prepaid. So, it was just $200 minimum to shop with a Buff Boy, a pretty inexpensive experience by Vegas standards. Shoppers were responsible for food and drink during that time, and a tip was highly suggested but not required.

Fees were split 60/40 between the Buff Boy and the company, so if a Buff Boy were to work a 40 hour week, with tips he'd be making at least $50,000/year. Not a bad way to put yourself through college!

Buff Boys were required to wear shirts when they were working, but they were open mesh sleeveless numbers that showed off their assets quite nicely. The shirts also had the company logo and website. They were, after all, the best advertising the company could get! They sported tight jeans with that ever-present identification number on their thighs, and nothing else but a smile!

OK, well some wore jewelry, some had tattoos and others wore cowboy boots, all indicative of their personalities. Shoppers could request a particular Buff Boy by number, or go for broke and receive a random pick. It worked for me with the Super Duper Millions so random can't be all bad!

We currently had 15 Buff Boys on staff, most of whom were booked solid through the holiday season. We planned to hire 10 more to take us through the end of the year, then maintain a staff to support demand. If we needed to hire more Buff Boys, there certainly were enough good looking men in this town to fill the roster.

Once the runway show was complete, Buff Boys posed for photos, handed out business cards and booked shopping engagements. From the moment we approached the mall, we knew this would be a win-win opportunity. They received eight percent of our revenues off the top, and we would still make a fortune in a very short period of time.

Women were gaga over the Buff Boys, a new Vegas offering sure to please many a female shopper.

"Oh, Diana, that was fabulous!" Gizzi gushed as we clinked champagne glasses, following the successful launch of BBPS. "Some of those men were magnifique! You should hook up with one or two. If I weren't engaged, I certainly would!"

"Thanks, Giz, but they're employees. I'm not about to get into trouble when I know we can all make so much money."

"Oh, please. Many singers dated their backup dancers and there weren't any repercussions. You just have to handle it the right way."

"Sorry, Giz, I'm totally excited about the Buff Boys but I have to side with Diana on this one," Helen said. "Don't play where you get paid. These guys are all great, the nicest I've ever met.

But, they're young and they're employees. Congrats, sis, but keep it clean!"

"Thanks, Helen. And I really do appreciate you all coming out to help celebrate my new venture. It's been a lot of hard work in a very short period of time, but it's also been the most rewarding thing I've done in ages."

"Oh, absolutely, sweetie," Gizzi said, finally able to have a drink without fidgeting or sniffing the air, hoping to get a whiff of someone's cigarette. Nicotine withdrawal was complete. "I don't think I've ever seen you so happy! And, you look so much better. You colored your hair, your skin has cleared up and I love your outfit! You clean up real good, kid. Just like you used to."

Leave it to Giz to remind me how low I'd gone before I had the fortune to pull myself up to immeasurable heights. At least she didn't mention anything about dieting or working out for the wedding.

"Oh, Giz, Diana has always had a good head on her shoulders, even during the down times," Helen added her two cents. "She was just smart enough to save all the brain cells for the right opportunity. Now they just look better!"

"OK, look, I'm not facing backward any more, just forward," I said, adamant that while I appreciated all I learned during my darker days, I was not going to dwell on them. "Today is a day of celebration. Let's do it!"

I looked down and saw my niece, Grace, ever-politely sipping her soda next to her Mom. Gabe and Justin opted to stay home today, knowing this was definitely a girls event.

"So, Grace, honey, what did you think of the Buff Boys?"

Grace looked at Helen, at Gizzi, at me then back at her mom before she spoke.

"They were cute but I think they need more clothes," she finally said. "We live in the desert but it gets cold here, too, even in the summer with air conditioning."

We burst out laughing! Out of the mouth of babes but Grace was so right. However, she had no idea what their official uniforms would look like. I didn't want to spoil her fun. She enjoyed offering her opinion and being part of the big girls table for the day.

"You're right, Grace. I'll work out the details with Alfonso. We can't afford for them to get sick!"

It felt so good to enjoy the company of the people I truly appreciated most in my life. The only ones missing were my parents, but this was not an event they would travel for. They hadn't even made it to my wedding with Chris. The launch of a new business venture wasn't anywhere near the top of their list. They didn't have a lot of discretionary income and they spent it wisely.

I promised them a DVD to watch with me when I made my next trip home, hopefully in a few weeks. I had more discretionary income now – heck, I had tons of it – and I planned to share. However, today was Buff Boys day and nothing else.

"Excuse me, Diana, but one of the local T.V. stations needs a sound bite or two."

Alfonso found us on the 'patio' dining area of one of the restaurants opposite the runway. After all that Lotto Ladies media blitz, I didn't think I'd ever want to see a camera again, but I jumped up from my chair and ran over to the reporter in a flash, waving my apologies back to my table. Alfonso and I worked hard to get here. We deserved the attention. And, my new cut and color looked fabulous!

I happened to glance up to the second level of the mall, just as the interview was finishing, and out of the corner of my eye, I swear I saw Chris. He was walking away, into the crowd, but I'd know that body anywhere.

Once word got out, it didn't take long for the Buff Boys to be in demand around the globe. We had requests from malls and shopping districts from large cities to tourist destinations to launch branches of their own Buff Boys Porter Service. In fact, many of the locations were willing to front the start-up costs simply because it was quickly becoming a proven concept that would return their investment in a matter of months.

I formed an investment company called Launch City Ventures. Since my focus would be on launching companies, I thought the name would evoke the community needed to actually get a new company off the ground or expand one beyond the garage. I also thought, down the road, Launch City would make a great name for a video game that taught how to build a business. At the very least it would make a great marketing tool and at best it would earn a bit of cash. I secured the domain name and put it aside for future brainstorming.

While the staff at Runway Fashion Mall kept things going, Alfonso and I looked into how to quickly set up franchisees, something we hadn't expected to do for 18-24 months. The Buff Boys Porter Service was a success and the founding group was already being contracted for personal appearances of all varieties, including the start of a Las Vegas-based reality show. I didn't want to be in front of the cameras but these guys were loving it and I expected the show to be a big success. We were a hit in every language and we planned to capitalize on it as much as possible.

In addition to the franchise opportunities, we started a Buff Boys-branded logo line of shirts and hats. Alfonso and his team also created custom carts and bags that the Buff Boys used to carry shoppers' purchases throughout the mall. The design looked like barbells and other exercise equipment which was a great reflection on the name and logo, and the Buff Boys had to fend off admirers of not only themselves but of this really cool merchandise. Men and women were attracted to the brand and we brainstormed for hours trying to come up with new ways to share it.

Things were going extremely well. I was focused, busy and happy. There was nothing that could ruin my mood.

"Hello, lovey!"

Aaarrrggghhh!

I answered my phone without looking at the caller ID, and there on my handset were the smiling faces of the ever-annoying Boopsey Twins – Jazzy and Pamela. I swear, you never saw one without the other nowadays.

While I had been working my ass off, trying to build the Buff Boys into a strong brand, Jazzy and Pamela were out having fun. Jealous? Perhaps a bit, but in the end, I would still be happier, right?

I had no idea why they were calling, although they seemed to be doing so a lot lately. I tried to avoid them like the plague when I could, for fear they would follow through on their plan to have me help manage their winnings. Hell, I was still learning to manage my own! How could I advise someone else, especially those two?

Jazzy was already well on her way to spending through her bank account. She'd ordered her Bentley which would arrive early next year and bought a penthouse condo at One Knightsbridge Place – the ultimate, premier full-service building in Summerlin. Sure, it was fabulous. Sure, I could afford it – as could she. But, I wasn't quite ready to plunk down those big bucks yet and, knowing that Jazzy would be my neighbor definitely made the place less appealing.

Between her new luxury residence and automobile, furniture, jewelry and clothing, Jazzy was already below $100 million in her bank account and was starting to freak out. It had only been a short time since we won and she had bled through a tidy sum.

Pamela did what she said she'd do – she paid off her mortgage and bought a newer home for her Mom closer to her own house. She also bought a shiny new Cadillac SUV, but that was about it. She hadn't spent another cent, not even on new clothes or jewelry and Pamela loved jewelry. She was even more conservative than I was with the money.

I was still living in my rental as I hadn't allowed myself to even consider where I wanted to live. Helen and Gabe were just up the street so some place close to them would be nice. But, I wanted a home with a view of the Strip. Whether it was a single family house or a condo, I didn't care as long as it had a terrace with a view. I still liked the family compound idea but I wasn't sure where we could find a plot of land large enough with Strip views. Plus, I didn't know how Helen and Mom and Dad would feel about the whole compound thing. So, I'm keeping my options open.

I was still cruising around town in my Ford Focus. Until I purchased another residence, any sort of upgrade in transportation would not fit with my current neighborhood and I didn't want to stand out. I'd bide my time until I was ready to make both purchases.

I did set up several trusts – one for good cash flow in my retirement even if everything else was spent and gone; trusts for my parents and my sister and even trusts for her kids. I hadn't told them anything about it yet, but I would in the near future. They were kind, far kinder than the many strangers I met who insisted that I help them financially. Helen and Gabe were content in their jobs and their kids were happy. If I gave them something, they would be grateful, but they weren't going to ask for it. Neither would my parents. But, we all knew I would do the right thing and make sure they were taken care of.

Jazzy quit *Positano* on her next shift after the trip to California. It was a little hard to hide the news given we *were* the news. Jazzy had no intention of hanging around at the store anyway. It was now beneath her. In her mind, she needed to be waited on, no longer waiting on others.

Pamela, on the other hand, requested to keep her job. It was her intent to stay with it until she could retire, but after just a couple of days, Pamela was asked to leave and now had all the time in the world. The company frowned on her involvement in the Lotto Ladies, saying it was unlawful gambling because Nevada didn't participate in the Super Duper Millions. She really wasn't given any choice and was marched out the door by security in front of the rest of the staff. Pamela was heartbroken. Certainly,

Lily had something to do with this. She was probably jealous she wasn't included in the group.

Polly took the news badly and retired immediately. She was long due to retire, but she was now so overwhelmed by her own grief of having quit the Lotto Ladies just months before our big payout that she could hardly bear to get out of bed. Coming into *Positano* just reminded her of what might have been. Luckily, she was a good saver and with her pension and Social Security, she'd be fine through her golden years. Not as fine as if she had a few extra million in the bank, but enough to cover her expenses and still have a bit of fun.

"Hello, ladies. What can I do for you?" I asked, though not really wanting to know.

"Well, Diana, we just heard about the Buff Boys and we want in!" Pamela said, massive excitement in her voice. "Since it was a great investment for you, we thought it would be a great way to invest ourselves. How much money do you need?"

The last thing I wanted was taint my lovely Buff Boys with Boopsey Twins money. I enjoyed working with Alfonso and the entire staff. I didn't want to come to a meeting and have to deal with Jazzy.

"Uh, well, we really have all the money we need right now," I said.

And, it was true to a certain extent. We were planning to expand and cash flow was good so we weren't at the point where we needed any outside investors. If the malls wanted to front the costs, that was fine. Buff Boys Porter Service was not an available investment option, particularly not to these two.

"Well, lovey, you know we need you to help manage our money," Jazzy said, words rolling off her tongue, her lips, her nose with underlying resentment. "Why weren't we brought into this business in the first place? If anyone knows about servicing a customer, it would be Pamela and me."

Oh, how I wanted to just push my hand through the phone and choke her to death.

"Ladies, please, you are responsible for keeping track of your own money. If you like, I can provide the name of one or two good financial planners here in town who can advise you how to protect those assets. The Buff Boys came up out of the blue, kind of an experiment of what I wanted to do with my own money and my own life. I lucked out. It's working. Now I have to decide what I want to do from this point forward."

"Oh, Diana," Pamela said, "you know we wouldn't trust anyone else with our money, and we know you must have other companies you want to invest in. We want in. We're your friends. You won't ignore your friends, will you?"

Honestly, you're not my friends. You just happen to be people I worked with who formed a group that won the lottery. Nothing else. There are no ties that bind here. But, maybe if I could find an investment that would keep them busy they would stay out of my hair and I could get on with my life with a smile on my face.

"Well, I'll see what I can do."

Screams from the peanut gallery.

"We knew you'd come through, lovey, we just knew it. Now, nose to the grindstone and find us a company we'll love just like Buff Boys."

Aaarrrggghhh!

Dear Diary,

I feel alive again! Having control of my business life, promoting a product I believe in, being in demand again for my business acumen – oh, how I missed this feeling! Helen was soooo right!

I know I'm very, very lucky to have been able to turn my life around in such an unusual way. I mean, c'mon – I won the Super Duper Millions! But, I had no idea mentally I would rejuvenate so quickly.

Business really is my calling, and I've always been a good judge of people. Well, at least when I've been in control of my business life, not when I've worked for others. OK, I'm not going to try to justify how well I do with other people right now. I've had my issues.

However, my drudge through the garden of get-your-life-together has taught me so many things, I'm really trying to contain my excitement as these new opportunities are exploding into success right before my eyes! Buff Boys has been such a blessing, every bit as much as winning the lottery. I'm earning a great return on my investment, I'm employing nearly 50 people, all of whom are earning a great salary, and we as a team have created so many great ways to promote the brand and expand our wallets.

I'm not sure how long Buff Boys frenzy will last. I suspect five years will be a good lifetime for the brand. Anything longer will be a blessing. So while I'm working hard on the company I'm already looking for the next best thing.

I really trust that another fun and exciting project will present itself to me when the time is right. I haven't had real fun in so long I'm making it a priority when it comes to business. It doesn't have to be comic-funny but it has to be something that puts a smile on my face when I think about it.

I really don't know what I'm going to do about Jazzy and Pamela. If I find an investment that's worthwhile, I would want to invest in it myself, but not necessarily taint it with their money. I thought once we won the jackpot, the two of them would be out of my life forever. Instead it seems we're closer than ever. Yuck!

More tomorrow!

All my heart,

Diana

The Winner Is...

{ TWENTY-TWO }

"Milan?"

"No. Tokyo?"

"No. Denver?"

"No. Miami?"

"Absolutely. Wonderland and Wonderworld?"

"Hmm...that might be interesting. Shoppers could hire the princes, but it would sex things up a bit and I don't think that fits the mood of those theme parks. We could work on a similar concept they might be willing to explore. We'll keep it on the list."

Alfonso and I were trying to narrow down the number of requests for Buff Boys franchises. We were looking at it both from a logical standpoint, but also from the perspective of which cities did we want to visit on a regular basis.

However, as we reviewed the list of possibilities, we realized adding a customized local flair to each franchise would result in even greater success. Those princes moved to the top of the list and we identified more theme parks that could be interested in the concept. Then we continued the review of inquiries.

"You know, we got a request from Sunset Mall in Troy, Michigan. It's practically right in my parents' backyard."

"Michigan? Do you really think that's a good place to expand, Diana? I mean, it's Detroit!"

"It's not Detroit, it's in the northern 'burbs. Besides, don't snub your nose at Detroit. There's a lot of money in Michigan. People just tend to be a little more subdued about it. Sunset Mall is a great place. It's like the Rodeo Drive of malls. I just think it's ironic that I've been away for so long but I still have things that bring me back to town. First, my family. Now, Buff Boys!"

Alfonso just sneered at me.

"Look, we could do something car related, maybe sexy mechanics uniforms. Rolled sleeves, open chests, Doc Martens..."

"OK, OK, you've convinced me. We'll do Sunset Mall, but it's all yours. I'll take Miami. You can travel to Detroit to do the launch. I want nothing to do with it. I don't plan to make any trips to cold climates unless it's to Sweden or Iceland. The babes there are unbelievable!"

"Well, we did get requests!"

"Sold!"

I shuffled through some more papers and looked through a number of emails. Buff Boys was Alfonso's idea so I needed to ask.

"What do you think about adding women to the team?"

"You mean in sales and marketing?"

"No."

"You mean, female Buff Boys?"

"Well, I guess, but not exactly. I've been looking through the requests and there are a number of men who would like a female companion shopper – well, perhaps a number of women as well. I guess they'd be more like stylists who could help make shopping decisions as well as plan other activities during a client's stay in Vegas."

"Sounds like some sort of adjunct concierge service. We could hire a bunch of female models and they could work either independently or in conjunction with the Buff Boys."

"Hmm…that might work. Let's table it for now but if the requests keep coming in, we'll need to address it."

"OK. It wasn't in my original business plan but we're new enough that we could react to what the market needs."

I took a deep sigh, put down my pen and paper and sat back in my chair.

"Now, what's up, boss? If you want me to update my business plan to include females, I'll get right on it. Otherwise, I think things are going pretty well for the Buff Boys. By the time this all plays out, we should have a cool few mill in our pockets, male, female or both. Not bad, I'd say."

I smiled. Alfonso was such a great guy. I was so happy I taught at MFILV or I never would have met him and had this incredible business opportunity.

"No, Buff Boys is great! It's the happiest thing to happen to me in years. What I'm worried about is what am I going to do with Jazzy and Pamela?"

Alfonso started laughing cautiously.

"You're not planning to bring them into the Buff Boys fold, are you? If so, I'd have to oust you!"

"First of all, no, I want them as far away from this business as possible. And, for your information, you can't oust me. I have a controlling interest."

"Two percent."

"I don't care if it's half a percent, it's still controlling."

"Whatever. As long as they're not involved here."

"I wouldn't do that to you – to us – but I have no idea where to send them. They're counting on me to find a good investment and while I could choose something to just keep them busy, it's still going to reflect on me, so it has to be a project that's worthwhile."

"How about DJ Daze's business?"

"Could you honestly invest in a company named Poop?"

We both chuckled.

"But, he has a good thing going, Diana."

"He does. I agree. If he was more well-known as a DJ it might help and he'll get there, but he's not there yet. I really don't have any insight into the graphic-tee market so I'm not sure how I could help him."

"Oh, and you knew about Buff Boys?"

"I know about shopping and men and I knew how Buff Boys could help facilitate a woman's shopping experience. I didn't need to know much more than that, but original designed graphic-tees are a totally different animal."

"Isn't that part of the reason for bringing you on board, to help his company grow? Since he's already established, wouldn't it be easier to get some good contacts? I mean, we've built a lot of connections through Buff Boys. Wouldn't they be able to help Poop?"

I just couldn't stop laughing.

"Look, we need to find a different company. I just can't talk about Poop anymore!"

"We could change the name."

"We could, but DJ Daze has already built the brand to a certain level and I highly doubt he'd be interested in rebranding. He seemed pretty tied to his Poop."

Alfonso tried to control his giggles. We had to look away from each other and not talk for a bit. After a deep breath, we settled down and tried to come up with another solution to the Boopsey Twins investment dilemma.

"Any other thoughts?"

"What about Cassandra's idea?" Alfonso asked. "I think she's just looking for money, not guidance."

"Oh, cos she thinks she knows everything, right?" I blurted out before I could catch myself.

I looked at Alfonso who met my gaze and we both burst out laughing. I felt like we were drunk on work. Alfonso was wise beyond his business years and he understood that his fellow student, Cassandra, had a great idea but without the right plan, advice and marketing, she'd fail miserably.

"Cassandra does have the seed of something that could be successful," I said, trying to regain my composure, "but as much as I'd like to just hand it off to the Boopsey Twins to run amok with their investment, I'll still have to be involved. It's going to require far more work than she thinks she'll need, just sourcing alone."

"You could start small. You don't have to try to implement the whole plan at once."

"This is Cassandra we're talking about."

"I know."

The two of us laughed again. At least we always seemed to be on the same page when it came to business. Alfonso might be young but he had a good head on his shoulders. I'm really glad to have him as a friend.

"I'll run it by Jazzy and Pamela and assess their interest. Regardless, on some level it has to be a business I'm interested in. And, it has to be with people I like."

Again, Alfonso let out a snorting laugh.

"You're already working with Jazzy and Pamela on this new venture, and you and I know you don't like them!"

I joined in his laughter. There was nothing I could do but laugh. He was right. I would be stuck with these two crazy ladies for a very long time, people that I didn't necessarily care to share the same air with. OK, well, Pamela wasn't so bad. But, that Jazzy was bad enough for both of them. And, the way they hung together turned my stomach. Just seeing their smiling faces on a video call ruined my day. But, at least I had the Buff Boys and Alfonso to put a smile on my face!

"Maybe I could find an investment in a foreign country far, far away so I'd never have to see them again."

"Oh, like that will work, Diana. You'll be bailing them out of jail – or worse! Best to keep your Boopsey Twins under your nose."

"As long as they're out of my hair!"

"Thank you all for being here. I really appreciate it."

"Of course, Diana. Whatever you need."

"Thanks, Helen. And thanks also for sending the kids on a play date."

"Well, you did say you had something important to speak about."

"Yes, dear, we always make time for you. You know that. There's nothing serious, is there?"

"No, Mom, but I do appreciate that you and Dad could make it. I'd rather speak with you all at the same time."

I looked around and scanned the faces of the adults in my immediate family, Helen and Gabe in front of me and Mom and Dad on the flat screen. They looked a bit anxious. I should start talking and calm their fears.

"Well, as you know, I recently came into a little money."

Everyone laughed. I felt like a stand-up comedian and I had the floor.

"So, I've decided to share some of the wealth."

No laughter. In most families, that would deserve a laugh.

"We don't expect anything from you, sis. It's your money. We have no claims on it. We just want you to spend it wisely."

"Thanks, Helen, but I've spent a lot of time working the numbers and I really want to do this."

"Really, dear, you need to think about your retirement. You're still young. That money can go fast."

"Don't worry, Daddy. I've set aside a large sum that I promised myself I won't touch. That alone will bring me a good cash flow in retirement."

"We're happy to hear that, dear."

"Thanks, Mom. Now, as my gift, I've set up trusts for each of you plus Grace and Justin in the amount of two million dollars."

Gasp! Then silence.

"That's really generous of you, Diana. You know you don't need to do this."

"I know, Gabe, but I want to. I know how difficult it was for me these last few years and I don't want anyone I love to have to go through that experience."

"Thank you, dear, but what will we do with all that money?"

"Well, Mom, at the rate you and Dad spend money, you'll never have to worry about it for the rest of your lives."

"Oh, Diana, we never worry about money. The good Lord takes care of us and our loved ones."

"I know this is all a shock to you, but once it sinks in, think about the freedom the money will give you. You could retire. Travel. Create a business doing what you love."

"But I love teaching, Diana. I couldn't think of anything else I'd rather do."

"And, we're so close to retirement, dear, that we wouldn't stop working just because we have the money. Why would we work so long to build up our retirement funds only to retire without reaping the benefits? We appreciate the gift, Diana, but we probably won't touch it for a very long time."

"That's right, kiddo. I have to agree. It's too much fun to go to work with my buddies and solve people's electrical problems. I don't know what I'd do otherwise. Your sister would never let me sit around and play video games all day."

"Oh, finally, something I said sunk in!"

Helen was laughing. So was Gabe. Mom and Dad were smiling. This was not the reaction I was expecting. I thought they'd all be thrilled and start planning for a very exciting future. Instead, they just want to keep living their lives as if nothing happened.

"Diana, you were ready for this. You've been exposed to this high class lifestyle. We're just normal people. Believe me, we're not ungrateful. On the contrary, we're thrilled that you would think to provide for us with your gifts. But I think all of us are just going to leave the money alone until we're ready, probably in 10 or 15 years!"

"Hmm…well, OK, but just know the money is there in each of your names and you can use it whenever you like."

Helen gave Gabe a stern look.

"No new car, honey?"

"No. No new car. That is retirement money. Not fun money. We are not to touch it."

Gabe looked like he wanted to say something else, but he closed his mouth and sat back, defeated. He knew Helen would divorce him if he dared to treat himself with Diana's surprise gift. He loved Helen too much to do something any more stupid than he had in the past. This marriage was for keeps, money or no money.

"Is there anything else, dear?"

"Well, Mom, actually, there is. As you know, I've often dreamed of living in a family compound."

Helen sat back in her chair, laughing.

"Oh, Diana. You haven't spoken of that for years!"

"Well, I never had the money before. I just kept it in the back of my mind for future reference, and the future is now."

"What are you talking about, Diana?"

"Oh, Daddy. Diana always wanted to buy a big piece of land…"

"To farm?"

"No, no. To build all our houses so we could live together."

"Well, who would want to do that?"

Once again, not the reaction I expected.

"I thought it would be fun to buy some land where we could each have our individual private houses but share common space like a pool, a garden, an outdoor kitchen. You know."

"Sis, that's a great idea under the right circumstances but honestly, we love our house. I expect we'll be living here for quite some time."

"Helen's right, dear. Even if we decided to move to Las Vegas, which I don't see in our immediate future, we'd probably buy a house in one of those age-restricted communities so we can be among friends."

"Yes, Diana, I'd want to be in a golf cart community. Your mother's right. If we ever did move to Las Vegas, we'd have some very specific areas we'd select. Your compound is a great idea, but maybe if there were a lot of you children and you could all live together, but with just the two of you, it sounds like so many business ideas. They're great at the conceptual stage but the execution isn't there."

Leave it to Dad to hit me with a business analogy.

I hadn't expected the reactions I received for either announcement. I guess just having money, even if you're willing to share it, does not mean it will be willingly accepted. Just like buying someone the wrong book or a scarf they hate, these generous gifts of money and the thought of us all living together don't seem to be the right fit. It's only been a short while since I've won the Super Duper Millions. I guess this is all part of the adjustment process.

Well, at least I put it out there. My family has been given their gifts, and knowing that they don't like the compound idea frees me up to buy something on my own. I really didn't have time to waste. The paparazzi discovered my little rental house and the neighbors are complaining about them camping out near the entrance gate. I can't just think of my own safety; I have to consider the safety – and privacy – of others.

"OK, well, then I'm glad we had this conversation. I need to find a new place to live, so I'll be out looking at model homes tomorrow."

"I can go with you, Diana, if you like. I'd love to see how these high end homes are decorated."

"Really? Helen, that would be awesome! Thank you for that. We could even bring the kids."

"Nope, Sunday is my day with the rug rats. You two ladies are on your own."

"That sounds lovely, dear. Just don't overspend. It's so tempting to go above your budget."

"Thanks, Mom. I'll have Helen with me so she'll be watching my check book!"

"You got that right, sis!"

"OK, just one more thing. Will you at least come out for Christmas?"

Mom and Dad looked at each other. They hated to travel during the holidays and the winter in general, but they really had no excuse this year. I could bring them to town by private jet. They wouldn't have to deal with any crowds.

"Well, OK, we'll be there."

Helen and I both lit up like little kids and started screaming and jumping up and down.

"Awesome! I'll send you a plane. Just let me know the dates."

"You mean tickets, don't you dear?"

"No, a plane. You deserve it. You're our Mom and Dad."

Ralph and Georgia smiled wide. They'd been frugal all their lives, but it didn't mean they couldn't appreciate the royal treatment.

"That's very generous of you, Diana. It will make traveling at that time of the year much easier."

"That's right, dear. Now, we must be going. It's supper time."

"OK. Enjoy! Love you!"

"Love you all, too."

Dear Diary,

I don't know how to describe it, but it's an insanely uncomfortable feeling to have so much money.

Most of the time, I don't think about it. I'm busy working with Alfonso or checking into other investment opportunities. Then, out of the blue, it hits me again. I'm worth over $100 million dollars!!!

Sometimes I'll walk into a store and estimate how much it would cost to buy every item in their inventory. Chances are, it wouldn't even dent my bank account.

For the most part, I can travel around town relatively unrecognized. I mean, aside from the paparazzi who will eventually tire of me, and my ankle weights of Jazzy and Pamela, without them hanging around, most people wouldn't have a clue who I am. And, I like that.

However, there are those who make it their business to know and seek me out. It's those folks that worry me, particularly men I date. Now that I have all this money it's hard to trust that the man is in the relationship for me and not my net worth.

For example, I met a guy that didn't recognize me at first. We were planning to go to a movie and dinner when suddenly a flashbulb went off in his head.

"You're the one from the lottery," he said, pointing at me, smiling ear to ear.

I nodded. I mean, I can't lie. I'm all over the Internet.

"Score!"

He did a fist pump into the air then started bumping his chest with his clenched fist. That was the end of that relationship. If a woman had the same reaction after she dated a wealthy man, he'd break it off before she got out of the car, so no gender bias here.

I'm grateful that I have a solid base of people that keep me grounded. Nothing like washing dishes or taking out the trash after a family gathering to keep you in line! Unfortunately, finding a good man is not any easier just because I have money. In so many ways, it's even more of a challenge.

More tomorrow!

All my heart,

Diana

Your Money or Your Life?

{ ELEVEN }

"Uh, so, like, how much money are you gonna give me?"

I finally took the plunge and set up an initial meeting with Cassandra to gauge her willingness to play nice with others. Given her opening question, the outlook wasn't very positive. If Cassandra and I didn't come to an agreement, I'd have to look for another investment for the Boopsey Twins.

"Well, Cassandra, it doesn't exactly work that way. We need to negotiate how much we're willing to invest versus how much of the company you're willing to give up."

Cassandra shook her head.

"No, no, I'm not giving up any part of my company. I know it's a winner. You can give me money if you want, like $100,000, and I'll build my company and be a big success."

{ 271 }

I had a feeling she'd respond this way. Cassandra was very passionate about her idea, and rightly so, but lacked the finesse and the skills to bring it to fruition the way she envisioned.

"Well, see Cassandra, as I said before, it doesn't exactly work that way. I do like your idea but I believe you'll need some guidance to reach the level of success you anticipate. So, I'm willing to provide 25 percent of the funding if you can show me how you'll raise the other 75 percent, along with a solid business plan."

I did like Cassandra's idea. It would take a few years to really gain momentum, but then I think it could be a solid force in fashion. People would recognize the brand and be attracted to it for years to come. However, I was dealing with Cassandra here and I had to play hardball. If it was Alfonso's idea, I would have funded the whole thing without question but Cassandra will be a pain in the ass and it was going to cost her.

This was also the company that Jazzy and Pamela would invest in through their constant desire for me to manage their money. I didn't want to deal with more frustration than I already had. If Cassandra could bring in some solid investors to provide the remaining funds – and mindshare – we could all work together to build a great brand. Otherwise, I'll continue to push back. I was in no hurry to close the deal.

Cassandra just wasn't buying it.

"This is my idea, Diana. *My* idea. Not yours."

"I understand, Cassandra, but I'm not a bank. I'm an investor. If you want a loan, go to a bank, or family or put it on your credit card. If you want an investor, then we can continue this conversation."

Cassandra could see that she was getting nowhere with me and decided to try another tack. She chewed gum constantly and burst a bubble before she spoke.

"What about the other two Super Duper Millions winners? How much are they willing to put up?"

I made the mistake of telling Cassandra that this deal involved my two amigas. Sometimes I just need to be more careful what I say so I don't have to backtrack. I wanted to have an equal share with the Boopsey Twins so the math didn't necessarily play out exactly, but it was close enough to start negotiations – if only Cassandra knew how to do so.

"I'm in control of the investment. Our total is $24,000 for a 25 percent stake in your business. Or, we could give you the full $100,000 you're requesting but we'd take complete control of the company and you can stay on as creative director."

"No, not happening. I'll build this with you or without you."

"Then, I guess it's without us. I really do wish you luck, Cassandra. It's a great idea. But, you do need some guidance to make it happen and we're there for you. On our terms."

Cassandra stood up, prepared to leave after her parting words.

"Yeah, go off and live your lush lives. I'll do this on my own. I'll build my success, not win it."

Ouch!

Even coming from a student, that comment still hurt. No, I didn't earn my balance sheet, per se, but I was making my money work for me now. Why do people have to be so cruel?

Cassandra walked out of the meeting, much as I thought she would. She needed someone like us but refused to admit it. Many people have built great businesses on their own but they ask a lot of questions and accept advice from people who can help them, doing a lot of learning with each step.

Cassandra hadn't reached the point yet where she was willing to admit she didn't have all the answers. Sure, she might find them along the way but too much time will pass and her window of opportunity will disappear.

I was frustrated but honestly, everything played out exactly as I expected. If Cassandra had agreed to my terms, I would have been shocked. She was a hard-headed woman who had the potential to be great but I wasn't sure just how high she could climb in the industry.

I called Alfonso.

"How did it go?"

"Exactly as we anticipated. I'm so glad I didn't bring Jazzy and Pamela along. It would have been a mess."

"You called that one right, Diana. So, what are you going to do now? You know they'll be bugging you for an investment."

"I think we should explore Brittnee's idea. I wasn't too keen on it at first, but it's starting to grow on me."

"I agree. Plus, she's a little older and might be easier to deal with."

"Oh, what is she, like 25 or 26?"

"Yes, she's something like that, but Cassandra is only 19. Brittnee is more mature."

"She is. But, she's also quiet and very sweet. I don't know if I want to sic the Boopsey Twins on her."

"Ah, she could handle them. I've seen her stand up for herself on several occasions."

I looked down at my phone where I just received a message from Jazzy and Pamela. It was a photo of them holding a card with a big question mark on it.

"Speak of the devil. The Boopsey Twins want to know how my meeting with Cassandra went."

"Let them down easy so they don't go ballistic!"

"Yes, I know. But, I'd like to chat with Brittnee before I tell the other two about her. Do you have a copy of her business plan with you?"

I had begun to think of Alfonso as more of a business partner on a higher level. I ran most everything past him for his opinion. He generally brought a fresh perspective to discussions and I liked how his brain operated. When I was interested in a potential investment, I'd have Alfonso take a look at the plan and give me feedback.

"Yep, got it right here."

"Great. I'll meet you at the mall tomorrow and we can look it over before I give her a call. Thanks for all your help, Alfonso."

"Any time, m'lady."

I left my frustrating meeting with Cassandra and dove into something else equally as frustrating: finding a new home. Helen was tagging along today, so at least I knew I was in for a few laughs. Or, perhaps not.

"Do you really need a house that big, Diana? I mean, who's going to clean it?"

Helen sounded exactly like Mom as she and I pulled up in front of the first luxury home stop of Project: Diana's Digs, to check out the model homes. When I was younger and we were both still in Michigan, we used to look at model homes for fun, although at a much lower price point – something we could actually afford. Mom and Dad sometimes went along, too. Then we'd stop for dinner and compare notes, all in fun.

Helen was always fascinated by the decorations and we often had a huge discussion about floor plans. I was certain today would have a much different level of debrief with the pressure I now had to find a place to live. Any one of these homes would potentially become mine, future cleaning lady and all. Now, where was my checklist?

"Relax, Helen. I'll just hire a staff!"

Helen smiled but she realized that might be a true statement. However, these were only semi-custom homes which meant I still wasn't at the top of the housing market for my net worth just yet. I'd explore those possibilities when I grow my investments by another hundred million or so.

The saleswoman greeted us as soon as we entered, her sky high lipstick, stilettos and tight clothing all tell-tale signs that we were in a luxury community. I suspect the majority of buyers at this level are men and the saleswomen do all they can to attract their attention.

She did exactly what I'd seen sales people in other high-end industries do: she gave us a quick up and down, then focused on our shoes. I guess if the shoes aren't on her approved list, she didn't consider us a viable prospect. I'd driven up in my Ford Focus so I'm sure she expected us to simply be tire kickers.

"Welcome to Lone Mountain Hills. Are you looking for the two of you?"

Helen smirked. She would never live in a place where the likes of this woman got a commission from the sale.

"No, I'm looking for myself. My sister is here to offer guidance."

Quickly, her eyes focused on Helen's shoes. Her face immediately changed, feeling this would be a waste of her time.

"What is your budget?" she asked me.

I hated that question. I hated it nearly as much as the income question on surveys. It was really no one's business. When I saw something that said "Home" to me, I'd buy it.

"I really don't have one."

The saleswoman knew the code. When the customer doesn't have a budget that means they can't afford anything at all. They're just checking out the furnishings for the next decorator's sale. However, in this case she would be wrong.

She handed me a set of floor plans and a price list, which started at $550,000, then pointed to a door.

"You can access the models through that exit. Let me know if you have any questions."

Helen and I scurried out of the sales office as quickly as we could. We couldn't stand to be around such pretentious people, especially since I was worth one hundred times more than her in a heartbeat.

We toured the three models – one single story and two two-stories – and took our time. Helen and I loved to sit and chat in different parts of the houses and backyards, envisioning what it would be like to live in each one. Most people would think we were crazy but to us it was amusing and informative.

I finally realized it was nearly closing time. I expected the saleswoman to come and kick us out at some point; surely there were security cameras recording our every move and possibly our every comment. But, she left us alone and we headed back through the office to my car.

On our way out, the sales lady stopped us.

"See anything you like?" she asked, with a smile on her face.

I knew that smile. I'd been made.

"Honestly, I'm not sure. I've just begun to look. I'll be in touch if I'm interested."

I turned to walk away. Helen felt very uncomfortable in these situations. I wasn't keen on them but they were now part of my life and I had to learn to deal with them.

"Thanks for stopping by," she called after us. "Don't hesitate to contact me if you have any questions."

I knew I should probably be using a realtor, but I wanted to fly under the radar for a bit. Unfortunately, I appeared on everyone's radar at some point. I'll relent and find a realtor that I feel could do a good job for me. The last one I encountered was Rosa who Chris used when he and I were looking at luxury properties when we first moved to town. I'd never go back to that woman who introduced my husband to slut wife. Hopefully, my new realtor wouldn't know either of them.

As we drove out of the community, Helen looked concerned.

"What's wrong?"

"Do you think it will be safe enough?"

"Sure, why not? It's gated."

"Your current place is gated and everyone gets in there."

"I know, but this community will have a guard 24/7. No one will be able to just slip in."

"I don't know, sis. If you only had a million or two, I'd say it'll be fine. But you are a Super Duper Millions winner. And I think you're going to be traveling a bit now that you have the freedom and money to do so. You don't want to come home from a fun trip only to find your place robbed."

Cindi R. Maciolek

Helen was right. She was thinking way ahead of me. I was just looking for a place to hang my hat but security was critical and I hadn't even put it on my checklist, if nothing more than to keep Jazzy and Pamela at bay.

"What do you suggest?"

"I hate to say it, but you might want to consider a full-service condo."

A condo? I was shocked! Helen loved living in her home so much I hadn't anticipated she'd even suggest a condo. Chris and I had looked at some luxury units and the feeling of a single family home was still something I coveted but I had to keep my options open. I would probably be traveling and the security would be a definite plus. I'd also have a better chance of getting a place with a Strip view than many of these single family homes I planned to visit, and a view was tops on my list.

"Well, let's keep an eye on security levels as we look. Maybe if I find a good realtor, she can suggest communities that have strong security. I mean, there are a lot of wealthy people in this town. They must live somewhere!"

Helen nodded, a little relieved that I was taking her advice.

"Sounds like a plan. What's for dinner?"

Dear Diary,

I'm so stressed!!!

I had no idea how difficult it would be to both find a realtor and a place to live.

I checked out some properties online and contacted the listing agents. Both the homes and the agents left a lot to be desired. I guess the old adage holds true: money doesn't buy taste. Or manners.

My personal checklist consisted of things like Strip views, a gourmet kitchen, fabulous walk-in closet, a great home office, a great media and sound system throughout and security. Sure, there were other items I needed to consider but some of the houses available for sale were so over the top I couldn't imagine living there.

I don't feel I need such things as a cigar room, a wine cellar and a theater that seats 30! Maybe I'll grow into that as time goes on and I'm surrounded by other wealthy people who also have such amenities in their homes, but I was simply looking for a larger floor plan that felt intimate. I know it exists. I'd seen such places when Chris and I were house hunting.

In order to get a house in a community that offers both security and Strip views, I'll have far more house than I need in addition to all the stuff I don't want. I may just have to remodel. I'm sure the realtor will tell me to enjoy and leave the rooms as they are because they'll be good for resale. Who knows?

I suspect a condo would have more of a simplistic floor plan, although the penthouse Jazzy bought does have a spa and his and hers beauty salons along with an artist's loft. This is my adopted home town. There has to be a casa for me somewhere out there! I refuse to live near Jazzy, even if that community does check off everything on my list.

In the meantime, I'm working off my stress at the gym and starting to shape up very nicely. Gizzi's wedding will be here before we know it, and I want to look my best – and be settled into my new digs by then.

Having money is wonderful – truly a blessing – but it does come with its own issues. It's all so fresh. I'm sure I'll adjust. I have to. I'm never going back to the way my life was when I first moved to town. This is the new me and it's only the beginning of a beautiful future.

More tomorrow!

All my heart,

Diana

Quel Charme

{ TWENTY-FOUR }

"Dogs?"

Jazzy's face scrunched up with an expression somewhere between insulted and confused.

"Yes, dogs. Well, and other animals, too. What do you think?"

"No, what do *you* think, Diana? You're the one managing our money."

"How many times do I have to tell you…"

Pamela looked at me with her puppy dog eyes. I wasn't managing their money but I was leading by example – hopefully – and looking for a viable investment opportunity for them.

"Seriously, lovey. You invest your own money in something sexy like the Buff Boys and you throw a second-rate business our way that has to do with dogs! You're keeping all the good ones to yourself. It's not fair. We're equal partners in this. We want your top-tier stuff."

I hated hearing the word 'partners' drop out of Jazzy's mouth. It made my skin crawl! We were investing equal amounts in the business but I was hesitant to use the P word. I'd rather call us investors-in-common.

I looked at Jazzy who stroked the diamond tennis necklace around her throat, one of many gifts to herself since winning the Super Duper Millions, including the Bentley, the condo, and, well, you know.

"Jazzy, not every business opportunity will have the panache of a Buff Boys. That's a once in a lifetime idea. I was just testing the waters and it was successful. I lucked out! But, believe me, my money is invested in this new business as well, so why would I give you a losing proposition?"

Pamela smiled and looked at Jazzy, her independent mind surfacing for a moment.

"Diana's right, Jazzy. She's too smart to throw her money away. That's why we want her to help us find the right investments. We have to trust her. Let's try this one and see how you feel in a few months."

"Actually, more like a year or so. Most businesses don't return quite as quickly as Buff Boys has."

Jazzy snorted.

"OK, fine. A year. I love doggies, Jazzy. I think it could be a lot of fun. Let's hear her out."

Pamela was doing her best to sell her friend on the idea.

"Well, I do love doggies, too, so, OK, I'll listen."

Jazzy sat back in her chair, legs crossed, arms folded in front of her. She might say she's listening but her body language indicated otherwise. Didn't matter. Pamela was obviously open to the idea and if I couldn't convince Jazzy, perhaps Pamela could.

"OK, so the idea is to create a line of high end accessories – initially charms – for animal lovers, starting with dogs. We'll focus on the more exotic breeds as well as the ones with the highest numbers at the shelters. High net worth individuals like unusual things so the exotic breeds are a natural, and a lot of celebrities adopt shelter dogs so if they like our jewelry that will be instant publicity. We'll also do a men's line as there are limited options for men when it comes to tasteful, high-quality expressions of their love for their pets."

"So, you mean we could do charms and cuff links and brace- lets and rings and such?" Pamela asked.

"Precisely."

"And, could we do some other things like custom pieces, may- be even platinum charms with sapphire embellishment?"

"Sure, I don't see why not. We have to keep in mind, this is Brittnee's idea and she'll be running the show. We'll only be there to advise and to provide funding. Her first launch will be women's charms, but we certainly can suggest these options and others."

I could see Pamela and Brittnee will get along just fine, much the same way Alfonso and I do. Jazzy, on the other hand, was going to be a handful.

"Tell me, lovey, if we have all these ideas, why should we give them to Brittnee? Why can't we just start our own business?"

"Well, that would be unethical so we can't. Besides, our ca- pacity as advisors provides the perfect forum to suggest ways for her to expand her business. We don't want to be locked into just one business, like Brittnee's. As investors, we want to find people with great ideas who can grow their companies and we can get a sizeable return. Brittnee's idea is one in a long line of future investments. It's much more palatable to me to have multiple in- vestments going rather than launching a single entity. Of course, if you prefer, you can manage your own money."

Pamela couldn't jump out of her seat fast enough.

"No, no, Miss Diana. We want you to manage our money. We decided that long ago. Whatever you say, right Jazzy? Whatever Diana says, we do."

Jazzy let out a big sigh that somehow still reflected her fake British accent. How she was able to do that, I had no idea.

"Well, can we at least sex it up a bit? I mean, this is Vegas. Can we bring in some hot male celebrities and have them model the men's line for us – shirtless?"

Jazzy let out one of her snorting laughs. She really was quite full of herself.

"Anything is open to discussion, but as CEO, Brittnee will have the final say. We're only taking a 30 percent stake in her company."

"Sex sells!"

"So do good business practices."

"But they're not as much fun."

I now feared what Jazzy might actually do once her money was invested in a company, given her last statement, but there was only one way to find out.

"OK, well, it sounds like you guys are on board. I'll set up a meeting with Brittnee to finalize the arrangements. I'm pretty sure she'll agree as we've already had a preliminary discussion. I'll let you know when and where. In the meantime, here's all her contact information."

"Oh, Miss Diana, thank you so much. I knew we could count on you! Wait till I tell my husband we're investing in a business for animals. He'll like that a lot."

I looked at Jazzy. I don't think she's fully on-board, but if she could have a sample of everything Brittnee creates in platinum, loaded with diamonds, she'd tell the world. Might not be such a bad thing. Jazzy was part of our target market, at least from a net worth perspective. Her diva selfishness might actually lead to a whole custom design division. I'll have to keep an open mind.

Oh, there I go again – too much *The Secret*, not enough country music. I need some practical advice about dealing with Jazzy and *Keep an Open Mind* is not the title of any country song I've ever heard. But, I'm sure there's one titled, *Back off, bitch!*

I called Brittnee and gave her a breakdown of my discussion with the Boopsey Twins and by the time we met, she had already updated her business plan and worked out a launch calendar.

She was a female Alfonso. I could never imagine being blessed with two such wonderful people in my life. In this regard, money can buy happiness. Now, if only it can help me find a man...

Brittnee also built into her plan an automatic one percent charitable donation to animal rescue and welfare organizations. That percentage could always be adjusted but she wanted to make sure she addressed it right from the start. George, her instructor at MFILV, really fought her on it. He said a company needed to be successful first; then it could look at giving back. Brittnee disagrees and wants to prove him wrong by incorporating the charitable component from the beginning.

Brittnee and I sat down to chat before Jazzy and Pamela arrived to go over the key points of the business plan. I hadn't read the update so I was anxious to hear about Brittnee's changes. When we spoke on the phone she seemed fine but now I was feeling an odd vibe from her. I really hope she's not backing out.

"Is something wrong, Brittnee?" I asked, almost afraid to hear her answer.

She shuffled some papers then looked me straight in the eye.

"May I be perfectly honest with you?"

Oh, boy, nothing good ever follows that question.

"Of course. Always."

Brittnee took a deep breath, sat up straight and smiled.

"It's about the Boopsey Twins."

Oy! I'll have to think quickly. They'll be here in a few minutes. How do I explain that Brittnee no longer wants their money?

"What about them?"

"Well, I know you're not going to be happy..."

OK, here it comes...

"But I have to say, I like them!"

"You what?"

I couldn't believe what I was hearing! Brittnee actually likes the Boopsey Twins? So much for my thinking she had a good head on her shoulders.

"I like them. They're actually a lot of fun. They're lively and crazy and creative. And, funny! You know, when the three of you were doing your press tour after winning the Super Duper Millions, they were actually trending on all the social media sites. I don't want you to take this the wrong way, Diana, but in comparison, you're boring. You're like the Mom who wants to control everything, keeping her teenagers as little kids. Jazzy and Pamela are free spirits. I'm really looking forward to working with them."

Wow! Definitely not what I expected. I don't even know how to respond to that.

"And, I've decided I'd like the three of you to increase your investment, if you're willing, to 40 percent. I can see working with JP, things will move swiftly with all the energy they bring."

"JP?"

"Jazzy and Pamela. Honestly, I have a business to build. I don't have syllables to waste! Besides, #JP is much easier."

Brittnee was being serious, and quite proud of herself, having the courage to tell me everything up front. I needed a beer – now!

"Wow! That's quite a lot for me to absorb, Brittnee, but it is your company and we're here to advise you. So, if that's what you want, it lies within the realm of reason."

"See, there you go. Using concepts instead of telling me how you really feel. I know you're shocked, but I know you'll do what's best for the company and you'll see I'm making the right moves. Oh, and there's more."

Great.

"I've decided to use JP as spokespersons. They're so unpredictable, they'll be totally viral in no time. That's what I need for my business. You could still help with all the traditional marketing stuff but JP will make this company a success. That's why I want to have you increase your stake. We have a lot of growing to do."

Is she calling me old? I have just a few years on her. Alfonso hasn't ever called me old, at least not that I'm aware of. I'll have to discuss this with him.

I looked at Brittnee and she had the confidence and passion of a CEO, someone who was content in her own skin, knowing she was doing the right thing. I was envious – but proud.

"If you think you can control Jazzy, then you're making the right decision."

Brittnee sighed.

"Diana, it's not about control. It's all about finding what makes a person tick and allowing them to follow that passion! Jazzy likes attention. She likes the finer things in life. She wants to be heard. And, honestly, she has a lot of great ideas."

"You've been in touch with her?"

"Yes, JP and I have had a couple of discussions. I used their input to update my plan."

"You took Jazzy's advice?"

"Oh, Diana, don't be such a freak. I think she's smart enough not to ruin her investment. She knows the potential return even at the low end, but with her hyping the business we could easily reach the higher spectrum of our plan."

"I just don't want you to lose focus, Brittnee."

"And I don't want to lose opportunity."

Just then, JP walked in, smiles and hugs all around. I didn't understand this whole dynamic, but my exposure was limited so I was willing to let it ride for a bit. I'm not typically a gambler but hey, this is Vegas, baby!

Dear Diary,

I'm still in shock!

For a couple of years now I've viewed the Boopsey Twins as the bane of my existence, the darkness in an otherwise happy life. They make my skin crawl!

But, I stuck with them even after five others dropped out of our Lotto Ladies group. And, thankfully, in due course, we won. I hoped that would be the end of it, but they're now more entrenched in my life than ever.

Alfonso never really interacted with them but he supports my feelings. I thought Brittnee was the same but quite the contrary – she likes them! She actually likes them! Has hell frozen over?

I'm concerned about Brittnee losing focus but I have to just let it go and concentrate on my own opportunities with Alfonso. We have so many good things happening, I want to keep that momentum going. And, with the Boopsey Twins out of my hair – hopefully – I can get a lot more accomplished.

There's always a reason someone comes into your life. Were the Boopsey Twins the reason I won the Super Duper Millions? Would I not have this financial freedom if they hadn't continued to push me to stay with the Lotto Ladies?

Was I meant to teach at MFILV so I could meet Alfonso and Brittnee – and even His Hotness – and build such exciting businesses with them? Teaching didn't do a damn thing for me so there had to be some other reason I was there and now I have these really cool people in my life – although I do worry a bit about Brittnee, particularly after her recent revelation.

I'm not sure why Chris and I crossed paths, but going through this transition the last few years has taught me a lot. Perhaps, he was meant to get me to Las Vegas, to my new starting point.

Do you think he ever thinks of me? Will I ever find someone I pine for more than him? I sure hope so. Aside from His Hotness, it's been slim pickin's in this town and there's nuthin' happenin' with Gray!

More tomorrow!

All my heart,

Diana

The Vegan Las Vegas

{ TWENTY-FIVE }

After an exhaustive home search and much thought and consternation, I finally bought a penthouse condo – something Chris might have liked but, surprisingly, I love. I don't know why I even consider his opinion, but he's always there in the back of my mind, particularly as I make these major changes in my life. Your dream home is supposed to be occupied by you and the love of your life. Since Chris filled that position at one point – and no one has even come close since he vacated it – he's the only face I can place in my dreams.

I was really keen on the whole family compound thing, but once my family shot down that idea, I had no choice but to fend for myself. I actually liked where I lived but because of my recent fame, I was running into issues, making it nearly impossible to stay put. So, I accepted the fact that purchasing a new place was my only option.

My issues all started when Jazzy and Pamela somehow found out where I lived and stopped by often. I cringed every time my doorbell rang. I tried to ignore it but when I didn't answer the door, they would send me text messages and photos of them standing outside, somehow indicating that they knew I was home. They must have planted some sort of GPS monitor on my cell phone. Wherever I go, there they are.

Maybe the Boopsey Twins visits were what led the paparazzi to my rental. After all, Jazzy was such a sucker for attention she would talk to any of those stalkers, giving out information that should be kept confidential. One time, she actually posed in front of my house! Even the fact that I lived in a gated community didn't matter. Jazzy and Pamela just waited until someone who belonged there opened the gate and drove right in. Same with the paps.

After weeks of the paparazzi hanging around my rental house, the neighbors began to complain to the HOA and the police. It's crazy to think that a photo of me taking out my recycling or driving to the store would be of interest to anyone. I lead a pretty boring life, which some of them figured out and went on to more lucrative game. The landlord wasn't too keen on the pap situation, nor the HOA, and gently suggested I find a place of my own now that I had enough money to buy the entire neighborhood.

Helen and I had a blast looking at model homes, but I had to rein in the fun and get down to business. These homes were beautiful but so extravagant, it was difficult for me to accept that I could afford any of them.

I wanted luxury, but it didn't need to be completely over the top. I hadn't initially considered buying a condo but once I started analyzing my future, a condo seemed to be the most practical. I'd probably be traveling a lot and I didn't want to worry about upkeep on a house, or security or managing a staff. With the condo, I could just close my door and be on my way. But, I had to find the right one.

I hadn't been paying much attention to the condo market in town, or even the housing market quite frankly. Until recently, I didn't have the funds to purchase anything so I didn't waste my time dreaming of my perfect home. Now that I could afford anything I wanted, it was critical for me to find something I'd be happy in for quite some time. Plus, a well-secured condo could thwart future intrusions from the paparazzi, which was definitely for the best.

I finally found a realtor I liked who specialized in luxury condos – no, not Rosa – and started exploring my options. I did go back to the condo Chris and I looked at a few years ago, but it just didn't feel like home. Maybe the whole divorce situation left a bad taste in my mouth and influenced my opinion of the place. Plus, it was further away from my family and I wanted to remain within a short drive of Helen and my parents' future home in the local age-restricted neighborhood.

After doing some research online, I discovered a new luxury condo development in the northwest part of town, not far from where I was currently living and within a few minutes' drive from my preferred location. I'd seen the buildings going up but I thought it was either an office complex or apartments. I didn't realize that this was one of the most unique places in the world in which to live.

The Vegan Las Vegas was being built on a plot of land that was intended to be developed prior to the drop in the economy. It now had a new developer with a great emphasis on energy efficiency, which I loved! The name itself reflected an earth-friendly lifestyle which appealed to me. Even His Hotness couldn't complain about this one.

In addition, the area surrounding *The Vegan* was to house a collection of retail, restaurants and other businesses operating with an eco-friendly mindset. Everything in the area would be within walking distance, building a strong sense of community and the charming effect of a small town downtown. It's the first of its kind community in the country – perhaps, in the world!

In spite of the large size of the condos – each unit was between 3,000 and 5,000 square feet – they were the model of energy efficiency. The buildings were powered by solar panels, designed into the most unique locations to provide the best solar exposure. They all had tankless hot water heaters among numerous other environmentally-conscious upgrades. And every private garage had an outlet for that all-important electric car.

Each unit had beautiful terraces and the purchase price included a pre-planted container garden of vegetables and herbs of your choosing – mint for your mojitos, anyone? If you didn't want to maintain the garden yourself, the HOA would do so, including picking the ripe goodies and delivering them to your door.

The Vegan consisted of seven mid-rise buildings, interconnected with a common walkway and a central building that housed the concierge, mail boxes, juice bar and other communal rooms. This particular penthouse included all my must-haves: strip views, a private elevator to my unit and multi-layer security. I couldn't even consider anything else.

Though the architecture was a nod to mid-century modern, the design of the community also boasted a number of references to old Vegas, including very hot Elvis impersonators manning the juice bar. *Vegan Las Vegas*, anyone?

A penthouse wasn't exactly on my list when I began looking, but once I stepped foot inside this particular unit, my heart leapt! I just felt at home. I could have all the privacy I wanted, but I also had plenty of room to entertain. I didn't think the $3.5 million dollar price tag was outrageous for my dream home. Sure, it would cost at least another $500,000 to furnish and outfit it, but it was perfect.

I'd move in around the first of November, which would make everyone in my current neighborhood very happy. Holiday dinners would be at my house this year and Santa would have a new tree to visit.

I could only imagine how cool it would be to sit on my terrace and watch the fireworks on the Strip on New Year's Eve.

"Jazzy, don't spend any more money!"

Jazzy and Pamela made one of their unexpected visits to my rental house. When I opened the door, they came in and made themselves at home, something I detested. They seemed to think we were friends, no, maybe more like family. I would never treat my friends this way. At one point we were colleagues but now we are simply joined together by the unlikely circumstance that we won the largest Super Duper Millions jackpot in history.

As they sat on the sofa, Jazzy recapped everything she purchased that week. She and her husband were still hunting for items to furnish their new super luxurious condo, that over-the-top multi-million dollar mansion in the clouds. She also had added a number of gems to her wardrobe, all of the finest quality and far more extravagant than any woman should wear with blue jeans and ballet flats. Oh, and she ordered a second Bentley for her husband.

Jazzy was out of control. She seemed to be going through her winnings like water. Jazzy was even less disciplined than I was when I was making good money as a marketing consultant years ago. I spent large quantities, but I did occasionally buy on sale. Who doesn't like a bargain?

But, Jazzy was another story. It seems as if she dreamed for years of this ultra-glamorous lifestyle and now that she won the Super Duper Millions, she intended to live it. Unfortunately, it doesn't matter how much money you have. It can be gone in a much shorter timeframe than you anticipate. So many lottery winners went broke or even filed for bankruptcy within just a few years of winning. We were so very blessed with this outrageous good fortune that it was important that we respect what the money could do for us.

Why I cared about Jazzy and how she spent her money, I don't know, but I felt compelled to at least give her some food for thought.

"Why can't I spend my money? You are!"

"Yes, that's true. But I'm not wasting it on clothing and cars. In fact, I didn't spend a dime until I set aside money for my family and a large chunk for retirement, none of which I will touch. And, my new home cost significantly less than yours.

"If you want to take a nice trip, do it, but if you keep spending at this rate, you're going to run out of money before you know it. One hundred million dollars…"

"One hundred and twenty million."

"Fine, one hundred and twenty million dollars may seem like a lot, but without any more coming in, if you don't control your spending, the money will rush out of your bank account like a swift moving stream. You need to preserve as much as you can and make the money you have work for you!"

Pamela was listening intently. She had been very careful with what she spent so far as well, taking my advice, meeting with a lawyer and setting up a trust as well as retirement accounts for herself and her husband. Aside from the homes and the new car, which she desperately needed, Pamela hadn't spent a dime.

The paps didn't seem to know where she lived – the two of them were always hanging out at my place! – so, she could stay where she was for the time being. She might eventually want to move, but she was taking it slow. Luckily, she looked up to me as an example, and not to Jazzy, regardless of their friendship.

"Then maybe we should just put your name on our accounts and have you handle the money," said Pamela.

They'd brought up this notion in the past, and I wasn't about to get suckered into it. I had enough trouble keeping my own life straight. *I* was still adjusting to this immense good fortune. *I* had trouble controlling *myself*. I, too, wanted to buy those wonderful designer duds I used to wear. But I'd been through such a hard time financially over the last few years that I didn't want to ever experience that again, especially when I'd been given such an amazing second chance.

I wanted people to admire me for what I'd done with my winnings. I wanted to set an example for people everywhere that you can get a second chance. I wanted to feel good about my life and what I was doing with it. I wanted to help people achieve their dreams!

There were certain messages I wanted to express through my life's work: You can do great things with your life; you can make this world a better place; and, once you finally figure out what you want to do with your life, you can be successful and happy. I wasn't quite there yet, but I was definitely on my way. What I didn't need was to be bogged down by the Boopsey Twins. Their involvement with Brittnee should take them out of my hair for several hours a day – I hoped – but I had a hard time envisioning that those Lotto Ladies cords would ever be fully severed.

"No! I've told you a hundred times. I'm happy to offer some guidance. Well, ok, I'm not really happy about that, but I will not take over your money management."

When Jazzy and Pamela got together, they were like two rescue pups that you just had to take home and nurture. Those big puppy dog eyes, those pleading faces. I was waiting for one of them to touch my hand and put her head down, waiting for me to scratch it. Or, nudge a ball into my hand in the hopes I'd throw it. I could just see them run around for hours, chasing this little ball, happy as two-year-olds.

"Look, I'm willing to help you do some initial angel investments, but that's it. The rest of the money you have to manage on your own. We're starting out with Brittnee's company and if I see anything else that I think might interest you, I'll let you know."

"But, we'll make money on that, right?"

"Hopefully, but not for a while and not a hundred million dollars. Not all businesses are successful. Some make it. Some don't. We'll see what happens. In the meantime, you need to put a padlock on your spending!"

Pamela looked to Jazzy, then back to me.

"OK, Diana, enough lecturing. Now, can we go out for some ice cream?"

"Well, do my ears deceive me?"

"Very funny, sweetie. I've been busy. How are you?"

I hadn't heard from Gizzie in forever and it was nice to have a real conversation with my best friend.

"Things are going pretty well over here. You saw my messages about Brittnee and the Boopsey Twins."

Gizzi started to laugh, almost uncontrollably!

"I didn't think it was that funny. In fact, it's almost scary! Someone actually likes Jazzy and Pamela!"

Gizzi finally composed herself.

"No, no, it's not that. It's just that Brittnee and the Boopsey Twins sounds like a great 80's girls' band!"

Now I was rolling on the floor laughing! If my investment didn't pay off – which I was pretty certain it would – I might steal the name and create a band of my own. Eighty's nostalgia was hot now. It could be a success!

"I'll put it on my list for future projects. In the meantime, the three of them are getting along splendidly and we're all very excited to finalize some designs. I just want to be a thousand miles away the first time JP goes on one of the talk shows. I'm afraid of what might come out of their mouths."

"Oh, don't be such a worry wart, Diana. Loosen up a little bit. You have money again. Have some fun! Those gals are crazy and in this day and age, crazy is good! At least you're working on something interesting. I'm still stuck dealing with semiconductors."

"Crazy is good. Certifiably insane, maybe not so good."

Gizzi gave a little chuckle.

"It's good to have you back, sweetie. I've missed you!"

"I've missed me, too. I'll be better in a year or so."

"Can't wait! And, I'm amazed at how many great ideas the students have developed. Who knew there was such a treasure trove of viable businesses in Las Vegas."

"Honestly, I had no idea myself. This has all been such a Godsend, but I'm suspecting other student entrepreneurs around the country are just waiting to find their angel investor. I'll have to look into it when I have more time. So, where did you visit this trip?"

"Oh, I've been all over Asia. We even did a stretch of the U.S., taking in a number of conferences. There are so many this time of year, it's hard to pick and choose. I'm sure you remember the fall grind. Your amusing messages keep me going, At some point I'll leave high tech and move into something fun and purposeful."

Hmm…aside from Gizzi's intention to stay home and start a business once she had children, she never mentioned leaving her job. Either she's planning to get preggers very quickly or she reached her goals in the industry and is ready to pursue something new. I'm pretty sure she's not preggers now. Not with the wedding just a few weeks away.

Regardless, now was not the time to broach the subject. She already had too much on her plate, but I still wanted to open that door to a future partnership with my best friend and her hubby.

"We'll have to find a really cool project to work on together, Giz. Maybe in the New Year we can chat about it. You need to get past your wedding and honeymoon."

"Oh, Diana, you have no idea how much work is required, how many decisions we need to make on a daily basis! I'm exhausted! Colin has been an absolute dream, but as we get closer to the wedding, we realize just how much we want our personal stamp to be on everything. We don't want the night to be over and wish for a redo."

Wow! I couldn't believe Gizzi was worried about how fantastic her wedding weekend would be! But, I understood where she was coming from. That's why I decorated the house Chris and I lived in when we moved to Vegas. Sure, I could have paid a designer, but I loved searching for all the little details. However, having done that once, I wasn't so keen to do it again. I'd want some involvement, but I didn't need to research every last doorknob.

A wedding was different, however. Surely, Gizzi and Jean-Louis were to be married only once in their lifetimes – you could just see they were soul mates. Having regrets over a misplaced flower or not enough appetizers or the wrong tablecloths or whatever – so many details went into a wedding, particularly one of this magnitude – it was important to have unique touches that personalized it. When you walk in, you want to instantly know that this is Gizzi and JL's wedding, not some exquisite but generic event.

"Giz, I'm sure you're being too hard on yourself. You were excited about working with Colin and from what I've seen of his work, he takes personalizing an event very seriously. So, I'm sure he's processed everything the two of you have said and determined a way to make it special for you and your guests."

I could hear Gizzi let out a big sigh.

"You're right. I've over thinking the whole thing. Colin is wonderful! Everything is on schedule. And, honestly, I don't have a second more to put into the event. I'm excited for our wedding day but I'm also excited to move on and just be a happily married couple."

"With children."

"Bien sur, ma Cherie!"

"Well, let me know if I can help in any way."

"Thanks, sweetie. When do you go for your fitting?"

"Tomorrow."

"I knew you hadn't gone already or I would have heard from you. I know the dresses are in a bit early, but that just takes one more worry away."

"Anything you want to share about the dresses?"

"Nope. I want you to have your moment. Call me after your fitting. I'm sure I'll be on a plane somewhere but I really want to hear your opinion."

"No hints? You bridezilla, you!"

"That's me! Ask anyone around me. They'll totally agree."

Gizzi was so level-headed, I'd find it hard for her to be an obnoxious bride. But, pressure can do strange things to people.

"I highly doubt that Giz! But, I have to say, I am quite excited to see my dress. It's the most special thing I'll have worn in a long time."

I could hear Gizzi start to cry. See, she's such a softie.

"You're the best, Diana. I wish I was there so we could hug it out. I miss spending time with you. It seems like all of a sudden, we grew up. We're no longer the carefree single ladies we once were. I miss that."

"I miss that, too, Giz. But just because we're older doesn't mean we can't have new and exciting experiences together! You're getting married now, and in due time, I'll find the right man for me. Then we can plan ways to share our future."

"Oh, you mean like comparing hip replacement stories and getting our first bifocals?"

I burst out laughing! Leave it to Gizzi to jump 40 years ahead, not just one or two.

"Girlfriend, you need a drink and some sleep. It was good talking to you. I'll let you know how my fitting goes."

I could hear the seal break as Gizzi twisted the cap off some minibar liqueur.

"Take care, sweetie. I'll be in touch."

Dear Diary,

I'm still a bit consumed with Brittnee's comment that I'm boring. Boring! Me, boring? I've never thought of myself as boring. I've always been the one who went against the grain, moved across the country, then again to Vegas. I took the fun road of travel and independent consulting rather than finding a job I could stay in for 30 years.

Of course, I had a number of missteps along the way, starting with my marriage to Chris. But, boring? Maybe she means restrained. I mean, I am opinionated – or at least I was before I worked in retail. Hmm...maybe that stint in retail muffled my voice to the point I wasn't deemed exciting any more.

I am older – and a bit wiser now – and totally against filling my life with drama. I recoil at the thought of it. I've worked so hard to bring a happy balance into my personal life that I just don't have the energy for drama. But, maybe without the drama, I'm boring!

Is it too much to ask for relationships where everyone either gets along or is at least respectful of the other person's ideas? Sure, I could have blown a gasket when Brittnee told me she liked the Boopsey Twins and wanted to use them as spokespersons, but I admired her ingenuity and wanted to allow her to either make her own mistakes or pursue something that I certainly didn't see.

There's so much yelling and screaming I could have done with Glori, Lily, Alyssa, Holly, The Bitch, The Witch, Lysette and even Chris, but in my opinion, it doesn't get me anywhere. I'd rather channel that rage into positive moments like building my businesses.

If that makes me boring, so be it. I'd rather be boring and happy than dramatic and sad. Those aren't trending on social media, but they are a perfect country song…

More tomorrow!

All my heart,

Diana

La Belle Concierge

{ TWENTY-SIX }

"La Belle Concierge. How can we help you today?"

Alfonso and I tracked our Buff Boys Porter Service booking requests and were surprised to see the large number asking for female shoppers! While the Buff Boys were doing hot business – and I do mean H-O-T!!! – we were losing out on a substantial amount of income because we only employed men. Females weren't even on our radar when we launched BBPS, but the demand was so great, we couldn't ignore it.

The people who booked our Buff Boys, including women, men, couples and groups, were extremely satisfied with the service. The Buff Boys themselves were making nearly as much in tips as they did in salary. It was such a fresh component to the Las Vegas shopping experience that it triggered other latent needs, female shopping assistants being one of them.

We termed them shopping assistants because people were looking for more than a stylist, and they certainly weren't Girls to complement the boys of Buff Boys. Clients sometimes wanted a friend; other times, a substitute spouse; some men requested the skills of their executive assistants when it came to purchasing gifts for their family while on business trips to Las Vegas. The requests were all over the map.

We jumped on the project and began to define the key aspects of the business rather quickly. Then came the interviews. Finding Buff Boys was a bit easier than Les Belles. The boys needed to look great and be kind and respectful. That was about it. The women needed to be knowledgeable in fashion for men, women and children as well as be able to respond to whatever requests the clients made. If they spoke multiple languages, that was a plus. From a physical standpoint, we wanted statuesque – nothing shy of 5'10", the taller the better. That made them stand out in the very crowded Runway Fashion Mall. After numerous rounds of interviews, we had La Belle Douzaine.

Uniforms were simple. They were meant to look like sexy secretaries. They wore form fitting button front blouses, sleeves rolled below the elbow, black or nude hose, black shoes of a respectable height – they would be on their feet for hours – and a pencil skirt in the color of the season. The current hot color was deep violet, providing an instant fashion connection with anyone who saw them.

Atop their skirts were woven belts in black and white that read, La Belle Concierge. Around their necks they sported beautifully designed custom painted silk scarves with the LBC logo. Their hair was worn in a loose chignon, twist or bun, held together with combs resembling black pencils. They constantly carried tablets with the company name on the cover pointing outward, both a useful device for helping their clients as well as a great marketing tool.

Alfonso and I wanted to offer the same type of number identification system that we did with the Buff Boys so people could reserve their favorites, but I didn't feel comfortable placing a number on their thighs. Women are objectified enough and we were aiming for classy sexy – as Jazzy reminded me, sex sells – and we'd already classed things up with the French name. Still, we needed a unique identifier for each belle.

After careful thought and numerous discussions, we designed simple upper arm cuffs with large crystal numbers for the Belles to wear over their sleeves. The blingy numbers were large enough to be seen from a distance and crystals are available in so many different colors, the Belles could wear their favorite or match their skirts. It was a perfectly Vegas solution!

Naming the Belles was a bit of a challenge. I had concerns about calling our offering a concierge service because the mall already employed a concierge to assist mall patrons. However, it was a service that did not contribute to the bottom line.

So many people were viewing the Belles as personal assistants, they were being asked to book shows and make dinner reservations as well as shipping purchases back home. Once we realized we needed to add other services to the shopping mix, we were, indeed, a competing concierge service.

We approached Runway Fashion Mall who, surprisingly, was more than grateful to turn over their desk to us. La Belle Concierge would be an income generator for them as they got a cut of the business, while still keeping the hordes of shoppers happy. We would need to man the desk, so to speak, with an LBC model for those who weren't using our services, but we made more than enough money from paying clients that it was a way to attract new customers. We began to book numerous clients on the spot, either LBC, BBPS or some combination of both.

LBC had so many unsolicited requests for their services, we opted not to do a launch. Plus, we were handling the concierge desk for the mall so we already had a captive audience. It was a risk, yes, but we opted to offer LBC as an adjunct to our existing business to see how strong demand really was. We wove LBC into the BBPS website and moved the Buff Boys kiosk next to the concierge desk. The interplay was fantastic, and once again, we were profitable from the start.

What we hadn't planned on was the interest in LBC branded merchandise. The scarves, the belts and even the crystal cuffs were such a hit we had a hard time outfitting the staff! Women ordered the cuffs in their favorite colors with their lucky numbers – how Vegas! – and our coffers were spilling over with merchandise orders. We opted not to sell the skirts or the combs, but between BBPS and LBC, we had a lot of happy customers.

Overall, I was still in a bit of shock. It had only been a few short months since we won the Super Duper Millions, only a few weeks since the Buff Boys launch and already I had two successful companies under my belt and a third – Brittnee's Quel Charme – coming online shortly. Oh, yeah, and we were franchising BBPS!

We had no time to celebrate. There was too much work to do!

"Welcome back, Miss MacKenzie. How nice to see you again. Would you like some champagne?"

Well, wasn't that a twist in treatment. The last time I was here, Jolie barely tolerated my low-life presence, only because she was being paid a handsome sum for her troubles, regardless of my own financial stature. The snottiness was gone. She was actually pleasant, the way I would want to be treated. OK, well, maybe some of that snottiness was still there.

Besides, she should be nice to everyone, especially in this town. One never knows who just won a big jackpot! It's a bit like Silicon Valley. It's hard to tell the winners from the losers since the winners were all just regular people until their sudden success.

I could see that look in her eye, that look of recognition. It wasn't because I was her customer several months ago. No. She saw me somewhere – on TV, online, in the paper or a magazine. I'm not sure where. I don't know if it had to do with the Super Duper Millions or the Buff Boys. Either way, this was going to be a different visit than last time.

"No, thank you. Is my dress ready?"

"Absolutely! And your shoes are here as well, Miss MacKenzie. Please, follow me."

Jolie took me to the largest fitting room in the salon, closed the curtain behind me and turned to proffer the most gorgeous silver crystal encrusted Coco Bennett pumps I had ever seen.

"Wow!" was all I could muster.

Jolie smiled, that look that sales people have when they know they snagged a sale. This was already paid for, but when the client is happy, everyone is happy.

"Aren't they exquisite?" Jolie asked.

I took one in my hand. It was a little heavier than I thought, but with all those crystals, it should be!

"I've never seen anything like them. I can't wait to see the dress!"

Again, Jolie had that sneaky smile on her face. She turned and unzipped a white garment bag to reveal the most beautiful tangerine silk satin tea length dress I had ever seen. I was speechless.

"Fabulous, isn't it? Carolina Wu designed them just for the wedding. The lace along the bottom is the same as the bride's, identifying you as the maid of honor."

Carolina Wu? I'm going to be wearing a custom gown designed by Carolina Wu? I nearly fainted.

"Sit, please," Jolie said as she helped me into a chair and began to put on my Coco Bennetts.

I took off my wrap dress, exposing my newly toned body. Even Jolie was impressed.

"My, we have done some work since our last visit."

Bitch. At least she didn't disappoint.

She held the bridesmaid dress down for me to step into, pulled it up, zipped it and turned me around to look. It was a perfect fit! Not a single thing needed to be done. I'd never had such an incredible clothing experience in my life! How did Ms. Wu know I'd been working out and my measurements would be smaller than what Jolie took in the spring?

The silk satin was soft as a baby's bottom but had the body to hold up to a full day of festivities. And the color was magnificent! I'd always been able to wear colors in the orange family, something hard for many people, but this seemed like it could go with any skin tone and hair color. The dress with the sparkling shoes was princess-worthy.

"Here, these are the earrings you'll wear," Jolie said as she handed me the crystal drops. Knowing how much this wedding cost, I half-expected them to be diamonds but even I knew how cost-conscious Gizzi was. Still, they sparkled like diamonds and lit up my face in the most fabulous way.

Jolie had a seamstress step in, just to make sure everything fit properly. She tugged and pulled and lifted, then smiled.

"Everything fits perfectly, madame. You look beautiful."

I blushed and smiled. I did look beautiful. I'd never looked so beautiful in my life. I was happy for Gizzi but seeing this change in me from just a few months ago, the significance was startling. One day, I'll be married again, in the right way to the right man. But, after the way Jolie treated me on my first visit, I'm not sure I'd use her in the future.

"Could we take a picture, please? I want to send it to Gizzi."

Jolie could not restrain herself from rolling her eyes. Certainly, she'd been trained better than that.

"Fine, Miss MacKenzie. Then we'll take everything off so it's not spoiled before the big day. Then, you're free to go. We'll ship the dress, shoes, earrings and petticoat to San Jose. Everything will be taken care of. That's the way Mr. Bailey wants it."

"Yes, I know Mr. Bailey has this all organized. Thank you for your time, Jolie."

Jolie had the seamstress take a photo with my cell phone. It was too beneath her to do it herself. I'd send it to Giz once I got home. Surely, she'd want to see how I looked. Unless Colin had cameras hidden somewhere, how else would Gizzi know?

I took off my princess outfit, put on my own dress and shoes and walked out of the salon on a cloud. This was going to be one awesome wedding!

Dear Diary,

I had no idea how exquisite the bridesmaid dresses would be for Gizzi's wedding. After trying on my gown, I was floored! I'd worn a lot of designer clothing before, but this was custom designed by one of the most amazing designers ever! I wonder if Carolina Wu designed Gizzi's gown, too. I could only imagine how beautiful it will be after seeing my dress.

Even though the dress arrived a couple of weeks earlier than anticipated, I was ready. I'd been working out regularly, through all those tough financial times, and once I had a bit more money in my pocket, I moved up to private training sessions three times a week. I have to admit, I look HOT! I am toned. I am ready. I'm in fighting shape for Gizzi's wedding. Gone is the *Positano* poundage. I'm back to my svelte California self.

I'll definitely keep up my routine right up to the wedding – well, and probably afterwards. I'm sure I'll run into a lot of people from my Silicon Valley days and, just like attending a high school reunion, you always want to look better than the last time they saw you. Especially, now that I'm a known lottery winner, people will expect that I've put some portion of my money to making sure I keep my youthful figure.

I was a bit surprised that the dress fit so amazingly well. I'd been a bit flabbier when Jolie took my initial measurements, but perhaps Gizzi planted a bug in Ms. Wu's ear about my determination to shape up before the wedding, so she tailored the dress down from the numbers Jolie originally provided to Colin.

I'm sure Jolie laughed when I told her I planned to lose weight before the wedding. I suspect a lot of people say that and they don't. However, in spite of my tight financial situation months ago, I stuck it out and now I look amazing. Yay!!!

I'm also shocked at the high level of access Gizzi has, not only through her good fortune and Jean-Louis's money, but I'm sure through Colin Bailey's connections as well. Not everyone in the world has custom designed bridesmaid dresses by Carolina Wu. But, Gizzi does, and I've always known she was special.

Oy! All this from trying on a dress!

More tomorrow!

All the best,

Diana

Team Brittnee

{ TWENTY-SEVEN }

"You look like shit!"

"Right back atcha, sistah!"

I'd been exhausted time and time again over the last several years, trying all sorts of things in order to make enough money to pay my bills. Now that my bank account was secure and I had money to my name, I got even less sleep! Either I was working, working, working or, when I finally decided to go to bed, my brain was racing a mile a minute.

I kept a notepad on my nightstand and woke up constantly with ideas that I had to jot down. If I didn't, I'd surely forget them by the time morning came and they were too good to ignore. Besides, if I didn't respect that I'd been given the ideas from the ever present Universe, I'd be considered an ungrateful bitch and my ideas would be deposited with someone else who would appreciate and act upon them. It might seem like a farfetched idea, but I really believed it deep down inside.

Alfonso was experiencing a similar fate. He was equally exhausted from hiring, training and outfitting the staff, managing the two companies – BBPS and LBC – on a daily basis while attempting to complete his college degree. He initially thought he'd be one of the Buff Boys, hauling client packages around the mall, looking hot and buff as ever.

However, the business took off so quickly, Alfonso had little time to enjoy the practical calm of spending time with just one client. Instead, he was harried trying to keep everything on schedule, again, something we thought would be much easier but reality has proven us wrong. In the end, he'll have a bigger payoff but for the time being, sleep sounded really good.

As we became more experienced with BBPS and LBC, we discovered that shopping clients seldom relinquished their charges at the appointed times. If someone reserved a Buff Boy for four hours and the shopper was accomplishing more than anticipated, our Buff Boy would stay with the client for two or three additional hours, all paid for, of course. This behavior caused a scheduling problem as the next appointment was anxious to get going. Everyone was happy with the extra hours except for the client waiting in the wings. There was shopping to be done!

We lucked out that most clients, at least at this point in time, were willing to take the luck of the draw and didn't necessarily reserve by menu number. So, we hired additional Buff Boys to help with those overlaps, as well as to assist shoppers without reservations. It was one of those good problems to have – our business was more successful than we could have imagined. Luckily, there is no shortage of good looking men in Las Vegas, willing to do simple manual labor for a great income.

The Belles had similar situations. Shoppers waited until the end of their reservation time to request additional services such as shipping purchases, buying show tickets, making restaurant recommendations and so on. They were invariably late for their next appointments, so as difficult as it was to find those statuesque beauties with fashion and administrative skills, we needed to pad our staff.

Women of our preferred height in this town were often show-girls or dancers or happily married and not working. Las Vegas was a big town but the demand for specific types of employees made for slim pickings, especially for a startup such as LBC. Aside from importing some Icelandic beauties, our other option was to lower the height requirement in order to fully staff our business.

Although we were a startup, people were interested in work-ing for us. We offered a clean, safe environment that didn't in-volve hawking food or drinks. There was a chance to build a rapport with the client without the craziness of a restaurant or a casino. Another plus? There's no smoking in the mall.

Alfonso and I were keen to offer health and retirement bene-fits as well. Once we saw how quickly demand built, we wanted to be able to give back to our staff. When employees are happy, they stick around. Dad would be proud that we added these ben-efits so early in our business.

This was all good information to have so we could share our experiences with our franchisees. We opted to launch six loca-tions after the start of the New Year and each franchise came as a package of BBPS and LBC. We saw how well the two worked together that we couldn't imagine separating them.

Our initial franchise locations were Beverly Hills, Miami, Washington, DC, Chicago, Dallas and Detroit. Alfonso was keen to launch a franchise in Iceland and there really was no way I could stop him. He was just too excited about it for me to tell him no.

We also developed a licensing division for theme parks. We would license the concept and the parks would design costumes and provide services appropriate for their location. We, in turn, would do quarterly training for the first year and receive a royal-ty payment based on total sales. We expected the theme park di-vision would be a multi-million dollar business within two years.

"So, have you had a chance to review the org plan?"

I gave Alfonso a look I reserved for my sister when I was little and they tried to wake me early on a Saturday morning. It became known as, The Look, and to this day, not one family member will chance it. They fear for their lives and refuse to wake me before noon – ever!

"I took a glance but I've been trying to finalize the contracts for the franchises and make sure we've covered all the main theme parks in the country."

"In the world."

"Yes, well, some of them do have locations outside of the country, so they will be included automatically. I'm not pursuing any others. Isn't a theme park mostly an American phenomenon?"

I wasn't sure, and frankly, I didn't care. I'd never worked so hard in my entire life. We needed to staff up outside of the Boys and the Belles. We needed to create a corporate environment somewhere, and that included leasing office space for at least Alfonso's company, if not my own. Word got out that I'm investing in student entrepreneurs and now I'm being bombarded with business plans from around the country. I love working from home – in spite of my current living situation – but a corporate office is probably more practical.

I'll need to employ an executive assistant, a business development director and a marketing director, at the very least. As we launch these new locations – as well as new businesses such as Brittnee's – I'll need someone to keep things under control while I'm out of town. With my condo, I could lock the door and not worry. I wanted the same comfort level with my Launch City Ventures staff except I wanted activity in my absence, not the lack thereof.

Alfonso grabbed a soda and sat down on his recliner. I knew if he didn't speak quickly he would be sound asleep, so I continued the conversation.

"Have you had any good interviews?"

Alfonso quickly blinked his eyes open and sat up straight.

Cindi R. Maciolek

"Yes, well, I'm starting to get some good resumes. I think we need people who have supervisory experience in restaurants, retail or cocktailing. They're out there, but most people aren't job hunting during the holidays."

"Oh, yeah. I forgot."

I'm not sure how I could have forgotten. Every time I went to the mall I could hear Christmas music – and it was only late October! It had been playing for so long I lost track of time. I think they started with Christmas in July and just kept going.

"I suspect we have a lot of competition for applicants, particularly in retail. Everyone is trying to staff up for the holidays."

Alfonso looked at me rather seriously.

"Diana, I know things are going well, but these next couple of months will really prove the validity of my idea. If we have any major screw-ups, we'll lose our franchisees and there goes our exit strategy."

Alfonso was referring to our forecast Buff Boys lifecycle. We anticipated it had a shelf life of a good five years. We planned to build it and promote it like crazy for the first three years, then sell it and take our money and run. If things go as planned – and believe me, our current reality far exceeds what Alfonso's initial plan estimated – we'd have a multi-million dollar return on our investment. Then, we'd take a portion of that and reinvest in another company and put the rest of our profits in safe investments, just in case we ever ran into a string of bad luck or found a great opportunity to purchase a company and we needed cash on hand.

Alfonso and I were not partners in Launch City, but I could see that we would follow the same investment strategy and would probably do multiple joint ventures. We talked about it a lot. However, at this time, I couldn't even focus. I needed some sleep. As if BBPS and LBC and Quel Charme weren't enough to tackle right now, I would be moving shortly and I wanted to do it right. Hopefully, once I get settled at *The Vegan Las Vegas* and Gizzi and Jean-Louis are happily married, I won't feel so exhausted. Sure,

I have moments of high energy, but the pace was starting to get to me.

I heard an odd noise. I looked across the room. Alfonso was snoring. I packed up my briefcase and headed out to my car, hoping I didn't do the same thing on the way home.

The next day, I stopped at Brittnee's house to see how things were going. I hadn't heard from her or Jazzy and Pamela in a few days and I was starting to get worried. One quick look and I could see why they were so quiet. They were busy!

"How's it going?" I asked as I approached the workroom Brittnee set up in her garage. The weather was still nice outside so the solution would work for now, but once November hit, she'd probably have to move things inside.

"Oh, lovey, there you are! We've missed you! We have so much good news!"

Good news. That's what I like to hear.

"Yes, Miss Diana, we've been doing teaser shots and videos on all the social media sites and we're already gaining a large following of animal lovers, and they don't even know what our products will be!"

Well, gosh and golly, who knew that Pamela would become a social media expert? I always viewed her as a quiet housewife who worked in high-end retail but spent her off time cleaning and shopping. Sexist, I know, but she just had that quiet personality. Aside from her friendship with Jazzy, she was a positive influence in my life and always brought a smile to my face.

Brittnee finished her phone call, a big smile on her face, and joined the conversation.

"You're gonna love it, Diana! I just closed another deal! It's amazing what a seed of an idea, mixed with great teamwork, can become. This company has struck a nerve in the animal communities and we haven't even launched it yet! Two big deals plus a slew of followers. I can't even comprehend everything that's been happening! See, I told you that JP was the right choice!"

Wow! Brittnee was full steam ahead. She and the Boopsey Twins were hard at work designing the first series of charms and selecting styles of bracelets and, surprisingly, everyone was happy! I was relieved, although cautious about my emotions. If things fell apart, all fingers would point to Ms. MacKenzie.

Brittnee was working the phones and locked in two deals that I hadn't anticipated. The first was with the Kennel Club of America, KCA, to do charms for the Best in Show each year, initially going back 10 years and every year going forward for at least the next 10. They would build backward based on customer demand.

People could buy the entire bracelet with the current charms, or buy the bracelet separately and add charms as they liked. Twenty-five percent of all sales would go to the KCA. The bracelets would sell at a premium so Brittnee's profit margins would remain intact.

The second deal was with Breeder Downs to do a commemorative charm bracelet for winners of the Breeder Downs Championship, following the same time span as the KCA. And hopefully, by the end of the year, she would lock in the same deal for the Churchill Cup. The donation for these bracelets would be to race horse welfare and retirement organizations.

Brittnee put a lot of thought into the look for these race horse bracelets. I mean, dogs look different but a race horse is a race horse, right? At least as far as the detail on a small charm. So, each one will have the year and the racing team colors to distinguish the winners. Very clever on her part, I must say.

Pamela helped Brittnee make some connections regarding sourcing. As a jewelry lover – more so at the manufacturing level than the retail level Jazzy enjoyed – Pamela had a surprising number of contacts in her cell phone.

I may have underestimated the Boopsey Twins' contributions. It almost seemed as if the Universe brought everyone together as it should be. Fingers crossed, it would continue on this track. If Jazzy got out of line one bit and ruined this amazing business, I'd have to deal with her severely. However, I was so excited about Brittnee's progress that I felt a bit left out. She relied on JP for input and looked to me only for financial guidance.

My cell phone chirped, indicating a message from Jazzy and Pamela had arrived. I was standing right beside them, so I wasn't sure what warranted a text message. It simply said:

For you!

The attached photo was of a beautifully gift wrapped small box. I had no idea what it could be and I was a bit fearful to find out, but the Boopsey Twins – and Brittnee – couldn't wait to show me.

"Open it," Pamela said as she handed me the real box, smiling like a Cheshire cat.

I looked at all three of their faces and each was beaming more than the one before. I lifted the lid from the box and inside was a bracelet with the company logo charm, one that we had discussed could stand alone or to brand our bracelets alongside the customers' charms. It was beautiful!

Pamela held up her wrist whereupon Jazzy and Brittnee did the same. Pamela approached me and attached my charm bracelet to my wrist. I choked back the tears.

"These are the first samples and we liked them so much we had four made, just for us," Brittnee said tearing up. "It just makes everything real, you know? I felt it would keep us focused and it was a relatively inexpensive treat."

"Besides," Pamela said, "Without you, we wouldn't have this opportunity. We're a team!"

Jazzy's bracelet caught my eye. It had a bit of sparkle to it. Jazzy snort laughed.

"Oh, lovey, you know I have to bling things up a bit!"

We all laughed. I was touched they included me in their inner circle. I was, after all, the one that pulled this team together, but

I wasn't much of a joiner and I finally felt as if I were reaching a new level on the inside.

Maybe I needed this experience in order to help me find the right personal relationship. Sharing and teamwork are all important to a lasting marriage. Just as the students taught me in the classroom, this team was teaching me about life.

Dear Diary,

I'm so happy for Gizzi.

Although Gizzi and Jean-Louis's wedding will be way over-the-top, the whole process has really been quite traditional. This is the way a wedding is supposed to be, a joining of two people, of two families, not the drive-thru ceremony Chris and I had. Sure, that works for a lot of people but it just never felt right to me. I want my family and friends to be there when I take my vows. I want them to love my husband as much as I do.

It's so crazy to realize that I could love a man like Chris when no one in my family ever even met him. How could I have married him when my parents weren't there to give our union a blessing? I was really head strong back then. Chalk it up to immaturity on my part. I've grown so much since then. I now see where I'd gone wrong, even though a part of me still loves that bastard.

I was caught up in all the intensity of Silicon Valley. I'd never made so much money in my life! I watched what other people did and I followed their examples, never thinking twice whether or not that decision was right for me. It got me into a heap of trouble and I paid for it for a long time.

Now that I think I'm in better control of my life, I've been blessed with financial abundance. I've been reading that things come to you as you're ready for them. Maybe now is the time for love instead of empty hope, for happiness instead of tears, for truth and responsibility instead of acting someone else's life script.

No country music tonight with my beer – I've been listening to Delilah!

More tomorrow!

All my heart,

Diana

Moving Day

{ TWENTY-EIGHT }

"So, what do you think, Diana?"

Blake, the interior designer for my new home at *The Vegan Las Vegas* led me into my finished condo for the first time. I was overcome with so many emotions I didn't quite know how to respond.

My choice of *The VLV* penthouse had more to do with location and price than its main selling point of eco-friendly everything. However, now that I'm here, I'm sold! Uh, I guess for a second time.

The whole process of furnishing my condo was well-orchestrated through the developer. Once my contract was signed, Blake and his staff were at my disposal to create the home of my dreams, all within their parameters. *The Vegan Las Vegas* was a certified Platinum community, the most prestigious honorific a commercial development could have. The developers chose to continue the vision on every level throughout each unit. To the maximum level possible, furnishings within the confines of *The Vegan* would be environmentally friendly.

Blake was an expert in sustainable living, an encyclopedia of design options, something I worried about, particularly at the luxury level until I met him. I wanted my new home to have a comfortable level of luxury – one that looked gorgeous but the sofa could be slept on and the dog or the kids – ones I didn't currently have – could jump on, no problem. I also worried that my unit, although beautifully designed and well planned, would be a mass of white, off-white and tan. I couldn't live with that, and it was something I hadn't thought of when I initially purchased my condo.

But, Blake to the rescue! From the high-end energy efficient appliances to the sustainable bamboo flooring and even the super-comfy sofa covered with recycled upholstery remnants, everything was luxurious to the max. I had no idea the large quantity of options available at every price level.

I still had some furnishings from Chris's house, but I realized they no longer fit, in so many ways. Chris owned a modern Mediterranean home whereas this was a more mid-century contemporary look. I'd also had the bed, sofa, dining table, desk and everything else for several years. Looking at them reminded me of sad times and hard times. I didn't want to bring that energy into my new place. I'd been blessed with a fresh start and I wanted to feel it on every level. Aside from a few art pieces I loved loved loved, I parted ways with everything else.

But, oh, what wonderful beauty now surrounded me in my new home! Just as Gizzi was grateful to have Colin planning her wedding, Blake filled that spot for me in furnishing my condo. Sure, I could have spent hours online and in stores, searching for the perfect everything like I did when I decorated Chris's house, but maybe that was my downfall. I took focus off my business and put it solely onto my personal life. You manifest what you think about, and back then, I manifested an incredibly gorgeous home – for Chris!

Now, having embraced those hard-learned lessons, I realized my focus should be on my new business ventures and the people who are important to me in my life. The material things are just icing on the cake. I put my complete trust in Blake and his staff who delivered above and beyond anything I could have ever imagined.

"It's positively breathtaking, Blake! You've created an absolute sanctuary that's perfect for relaxation but also for entertaining."

"Thank you, Diana. I hope it reflects your personal taste everywhere you look."

"Absolutely! It's hard for me to imagine that with just a few meetings and approval of specific items or special requests that you could create all this!"

I swept my hand around the open floor plan. There was not a nook or cranny that did not convey my taste. Yet, Blake left space for me to add personal touches of my choosing, long after he departed.

"I'm absolutely amazed that this is all eco-friendly."

"Oh, trust me, Diana. If it wasn't, we wouldn't offer it. People have a misconception that eco-friendly means ugly or boring or unlivable. Quite the contrary. When you work with the earth, more opportunities are presented to you."

I couldn't agree more. If I wasn't a convert before selecting *The Vegan Las Vegas*, I was now. I didn't know why everyone in the world wouldn't want to live in a place like this.

Blake took me on a tour of my new place and pointed out the variety of fun stuff I now got to enjoy on a daily basis: the counters made from recycled beer bottles; LED lighting throughout; no VOC paint in all the wonderful colors I requested; organic cotton high thread count sheets; natural latex-topped mattresses; reclaimed wood and metal for accent pieces – the list went on and on.

I also cherished the small workout facility adjacent to my master bedroom suite. I could use the one in the club house, but I much preferred the privacy of my own unit whenever possible.

Nothing eco-friendly about the equipment from what I knew, but it fit within Blake's allowances so I now had my own personal gym.

Once the tour of the interior was complete, Blake led me to the terrace which had the most stunning views of the Strip along with my container garden. Leaf lettuce and a variety of herbs were already planted. I could make additional choices with the gardener in a few days, after which he would adjust my selections on a seasonal basis.

"I can't wait to see the lights tonight," I said. "Why don't you bring your husband over and I'll invite a couple of friends for champagne?"

"Oh, Diana, that would be lovely but we have tickets to a show tonight. Could we possibly do it another night this week?"

"I'm in town for a bit, so just let me know what works for you. It will be great to finally meet Michael after all I've heard about him."

"And, he, you," Blake responded with a sneaky smile.

"So, seriously Blake. We live in the desert. I know it's cooler now, but how big will my electric bill be next summer? This place is 5,000 square feet."

"Oh, don't worry Diana. Your electric bill should run about $50 a month or less, depending on how often you charge your car."

I was shocked. It seemed everything in this place ran on electricity, including the elevator that entered directly into my unit. I was still cruising around in my Ford Focus, but started researching an electric car to purchase. I was totally sold on living the lifestyle here at *The VLV* and an electric car clearly fit that picture.

Besides, I mostly just drove around town. There was no reason for me to own a gasoline-powered vehicle. Charging stations were being built in Las Vegas and along the interstates, just like gas stations, so even a trip across the country with an electric vehicle was easier than ever. But, as many wonderful benefits that there were living in *The VLV*, I still couldn't get over the small price of my summer electric bill! I know it's only my first day here, but I want everyone to know they can live this way!

"I can't believe that, Blake! All this luxury and I'm basically getting my electricity for free."

Blake smiled.

"Yes, Diana, once you understand all that eco-friendly living has to offer, you'll be spreading the word. I didn't fully understand everything until I began to work in the industry. Now, I couldn't imagine doing anything else."

"Well, I certainly hope you stick around. I'm sure there's a ton of stuff I could learn from you."

"Vegas is my home base, but I go where the work is. I like to think of it as traveling the country to do set design in movies. Michael thinks I'm crazy but I lead a life quite like an actor or a director. I stay in a town until my work is complete, then come back to Vegas for respite."

We looked at each other and laughed. Vegas – respite! Hah!

"Well, I really must go, Diana. Michael and I want to head downtown to dinner before the show. It's our date night and we adhere to it strictly."

"Good for you, Blake! It's great that you've found that special someone and that you respect the relationship."

I must have had a sad look on my face as I spoke because Blake gave me a big hug.

"Don't worry, Diana. You'll find someone special to share this home with. I feel it. You're a unique woman but there's a man out there who can keep up with you. Promise me you won't settle."

I smiled. It was like listening to Helen, Gizzi and Mom wrapped into one.

"I promise, Blake. Now, go have some fun and check back in a few days. I think this place is a bit big so I may go dog hunting soon. At least I know I'll get unconditional love from someone!"

Blake looked at me sternly.

"You'll do no shelter shopping without me, girlfriend. Promise?"

I chuckled. I could see I had a new friend in Blake.

"Promise."

"Well, I must go, doll. Enjoy bonding with your new casa!"

Blake gave me a hug as he waited for the elevator to arrive.

"Thanks, Blake, for everything. I couldn't have done it without you."

"My pleasure, madam," Blake said as he skillfully backed into the elevator, bowing before me then disappearing as the doors closed.

I looked around my now empty condo, empty except for me. I was excited but wondered if I bought too much space. If I didn't have the money and if this unit didn't have such amazing views, I probably would have purchased something smaller. But, I wanted this to be my home for a very long time, to share with my future husband and our family.

Tonight, I'd unpack a bit, then toast to my new place with Helen and her tribe. Aside from that, as beautiful as this place was, it did seem vacuous. The condo was about four times the size of my rental house, and for the first time in a lifetime, I couldn't look out the window and see my neighbor's house. There were no paparazzi and not even Jazzy and Pamela waiting outside my door. I was on top of the world, but as the saying goes, it's lonely at the top. Still, I felt an inner peace that I'd never felt before, and as lonely as I was at the moment, I knew it wouldn't last forever.

I turned my attention to the few boxes that arrived before me. There wasn't too much for me to move in, mostly clothes, shoes, books, my office stuff and some paintings, most of which Blake and his staff skillfully unpacked and displayed in the most artistic and welcoming way.

Other than the few things I brought with me, everything was new! It was such a different feeling than getting your first apartment out of college when you can only afford the least expensive of everything. Sure, those items were new – well, at least some of them were – but much of it was hand-me-downs, including the furniture. I moved to California right after graduation but I still received used items from my new friends in order to furnish my first place.

This – well, this was completely different. The overwhelming, uplifting atmosphere was a feeling that I wish everyone could experience, just once. It took a long time for me to get here, but I finally did. And, the best part of it all? I'm being kind to the earth – in Vegas! While I'd been aware and concerned for the environment all my life, I wasn't particularly driven by that regarding my new home purchase. However, now that I see how beautifully one can live and still be earth friendly, I feel it's part of my mission in life to let people know.

Blake was efficient down to every last detail. All video, music and wi-fi were functioning at full speed. I didn't need to make a single call or spend an entire day waiting for someone from the cable company. Life was good. I turned up the tunes and danced around my condo, bonding as Blake would say, celebrating this special day.

When I got hungry, I didn't even have to go grocery shopping. Blake had truly thought of everything, and my fridge was filled with organic fruits, vegetables, drinks and some prepared dinners from the local restaurants for me to microwave once I finally came down from this high and realized I needed some nourishment.

One of the coolest aspects of *The VLV* is that nearly every homeowner lived here full time, unusual for a luxury condo in this town. It also meant there was a steady stream of customers for the local businesses. I already eyed my favorites – an organic grocery store, two clothing designers who specialized in eco-friendly clothing – Hmm…The Bod would do well here – a coffee shop that utilized organic free trade beans, jewelry made from local stones by regional artisans, an art gallery that utilized reusable resources, restaurants and cafes with farm to table menus, an earth friendly dry cleaners – the list was endless. There was also a weekly farmers market and *The VLV* concierge was well versed in nearby products and activities that reflected a healthy earth slant.

Helen, Gabe and the kids had just a few minutes to come and toast to my new home, between school and their guitar and dance lessons, and frankly, I needed to get to the mall to check on BBPS and LBC. No champagne for this crowd!

"Wow! This place is just the like hotels on the Strip. I didn't even have to park my own car."

"That's right, Gabe, but I do have extra remotes for my underground garage, so if you want to just park there and come up in the elevator, you can do that."

"No way! I like the look on their faces when the valets have to drive a normal car, not some luxury vehicle."

"Kids! Come here!"

Helen was trying to keep Justin and Grace under control. They were running everywhere, exploring my new home.

"This is just too awesome, Aunti Di," Justin said.

"For sure! I've already scouted out where I'm going to stay for sleepovers," said Grace.

"You can't just invite yourself over, kids. Aunti Di needs to offer an invitation," Helen reprimanded her children.

"It's OK, Helen, really. I'd love to have the kids stay as often as they like. We're just a few minutes down the road from you. And, this house is kid and dog friendly. I made sure of that!"

Helen seemed a bit relieved but waited to hear something fall or break as the kids continued to explore.

I grabbed a bottle of sparkling cider from the fridge so we could all join in the toast, pulled five champagne flutes from the glass fronted doors that Blake designated as my crystal cabinet, poured the cider and passed the glasses all around. Helen lifted her glass, and we all followed suit.

"Sis, here's to years of love and happiness in your new home. May you have the blessings of a husband and children –"

"And a dog," Grace chimed in.

"And a dog to keep you company in this beautiful space. Wait – you're not getting a dog, are you?"

"I plan to. Blake and I are going shelter shopping soon."

"But who will take care of it when you're out of town?"

Helen gave me a look that said, 'Don't be relying on me to do this. I have enough on my plate and I don't want my kids to get used to having a dog.'

"Well, if you can't manage, I'm sure Blake and Michael would pamper the little one. Or, one of my other friends. I'll figure it out."

"Can we just get back to the toast, Mom? I have a guitar lesson." said Justin.

"OK, OK, so, here's to an amazing new life in this amazing new place –"

"And may you host Thanksgiving dinner this year," added Gabe.

We all laughed. This is what I really wanted for my new place. I hoped to remember this moment forever.

Helen raised her glass and with tears streaming down her cheeks, said, "Cheers!"

We clinked glasses, sipped our cider and immediately fell into a group hug, tears falling all around. I could have all the money in the world but nothing beat the love of family.

"Hey, sweetie!"

"Hey, Giz! How's it going?"

Gizzi let out a deep sigh.

"The truth? I'm exhausted! However, I couldn't be happier!"

"That's exactly how I thought you'd be so close to the wedding. Everything in order for the big weekend?"

"You mean the bachelorette party?"

We both laughed.

"Well, sure, but I was more interested in the wedding!"

"OK, fine. Everything is right on target. We've gone a bit over budget, but it's exactly as we want it to be."

It's hard for me to imagine going over budget on a million dollar plus wedding, even given my current bloated financial status, but I guess if you want something a certain way, it's going to cost you no matter how much you're already spending.

"And, may I say, you look fabulous!"

I smiled. I had sent the photo of me in my bridesmaid's dress to Giz a couple of days ago and hadn't heard back. She knew I was gearing up for the move so out of respect, I guess she didn't want to bother me other than to wish me luck. Either that, or she's horrendously busy. Now that I'm all moved in, we could have a good chat.

"Thanks, Giz. I really worked hard to get in shape for your wedding."

"I'm sure not only for me but for the countless single men in attendance."

"Well, OK, that, too. And the dress is extraordinary! But, my biggest question is, how did you know to have my dress made smaller?"

"Oh, sweetie, I saw you at the engagement party and you just didn't look like yourself. I knew you'd pick up your feet and knock off those extra pounds. You weren't getting the free meals anymore at *Positano*, so I figured that would help, too. I just told Colin to subtract a couple of sizes from your current measurements and make the gown like that. If it didn't fit, you'd still have six weeks to hit your goal."

That Gizzi, always on top of things. She knows me better than I know myself sometimes, and it's good to have a friend who has your back like she does.

"Besides, once you knew who designed the dresses, you'd make every effort to get your single lady body back!"

"I must admit, you'll have the best looking bridal party north of Hollywood!"

Gizzi roared!

"Oh, sweetie, don't even go there! Suddenly, we're not only the darlings of Silicon Valley, every entertainment show is interested in interviewing us. And, since they somehow know we're best friends, it makes an even bigger story. I never expected anyone would be interested except for family and friends. Thankfully, you're right, the photos will look amazing! You'll be immortalized forever in your rock star shape!"

If ever I wanted to participate in some worldwide event – outside of a product launch – it was for Gizzi and Jean-Louis's wedding, only because I know how down to earth they both are and to them, this whole experience is like an E-ticket!

"So, how do you like your new house?"

"I'm in love!"

"Wait! Did I miss something? With whom?"

"With my house! I can't believe how happy I am here. I hope you'll have a chance to at least visit while you're in town for the bachelorette party. I know everything is on the Strip, but if you could sneak away for just a few hours, you could see for yourself."

"I hope so, sweetie, but Colin schedules everything like we're in the military. Even though we'll have some down time, it will be relaxing at the pool or something like that, and I really do want to focus on all my bridesmaids. This is our special weekend."

"I understand, Giz, no worries. Once you get back from your honeymoon, maybe you can come down for a quick weekend. There are plenty of guest rooms."

"Sounds like a plan, sweetie! I'd rather be able to spend time with just you while I'm in your new digs, not have to worry about everything else that's going on. Understand?"

"Of course! You only get married once. I'll be living here for a long time. This is your special moment. Enjoy!"

"Thanks, sweetie, but do send me lots of pics!"

"You bet!"

"OK, I've gotta go, Diana. We'll chat soon, and we'll see each other in just a couple of weeks!"

"Bye, Giz. See you soon!"

Dear Diary,

It's hard for me to imagine that just one year ago I was still working at *Positano*, dealing with the drama and job hunting. What a difference 12 months can make!

And, I've been so busy since we won the Super Duper Millions, I can hardly remember what life was like back then. It's almost as if that were the dream and this is reality. Well, it is, of course, but it's just such a 180 from where I was, it's really hard to fathom.

In just 12 months, I've gone from begging my sister for leftovers to buying a luxurious penthouse, starting four businesses and making a ton of friends I never had in all the time I've lived in Las Vegas. I'm also financially set for life, as are all the members of my immediate family.

There's a calmness that comes with knowing you have financial security. Suze Orman often said that, but I couldn't believe it until I experienced it myself. I always seemed to be on edge, even when I was making big bucks in Silicon Valley. Now, I have real money and I'm doing a pretty good job managing it. Of course, it's only been a few months since we won, but I feel confident that I've set everything up in such a way that I won't ever have to worry about my finances again.

I'm a different person now, but I'm me. I feel like I'm the real me, that this person was hiding inside me all along but I never really connected with her or let her out to play. I'm crazy busy. I'm exhausted. But, I'm super happy! Finding the right man to share all this joy with is the only thing missing from my life. Oh, and perhaps a couple of kids and a dog.

His Hotness is still in the picture, although we're not really dating or anything. We occasionally text each other but I think he is going through a bit of shock himself. It's not just the people who suddenly come into money that change; people around them go through an adjustment process as well.

It's hard to believe that in many ways, I owe what I have to the Boopsey Twins, who kept me on track when I wanted to quit the Lotto Ladies and quit them, too. Now, they're still annoying but given their rapport with Brittnee, I think we're coming to an understanding about our friendship as well. I'm sure they always felt it was there. I was the doubting Thomas.

After all my crazy experiences the last 12 months, I can only imagine what the next year will bring!

More tomorrow!

All my heart,

Diana

The Tell-All

{ TWENTY-NINE }

Those bitches!

First of all, I'm the one who came up with the name, Lotto Ladies. No, I didn't trademark it. I didn't think I had to. Now those stupid *Genesis* Girls have written a tell-all book about all eight original members of the Lotto Ladies and how the three of them along with Polly and Lynn were left out in the cold, having stepped away mere months before we hit the big one. I can't imagine that they would think they could reap the rewards of the jackpot without contributing a dime. They left willingly – to my knowledge – and they knew the agreement and abided by it.

Naturally, the book paints them in the best light and shines extreme darkness on the three of us who stuck it out to actually win. I didn't know they could think in complete sentences, let alone pen an entire book in such a short period of time.

Much as I hated to give the *Genesis* Girls a penny of my money after what they'd done, I unfortunately had to purchase a copy of their book, just so I could see what we were in for. I wanted to be prepared for off-putting questions the next time we launched a company. Certainly, any smart-minded journalist would be all over this book.

I'm not sure where or how they got their information, but a lot of it was pretty accurate. I know Helen and Gabe and Mom and Dad wouldn't have spoken to anyone, not knowingly. It's possible those sneaky bitches might have posed as innocent fans and weaseled info out of my closest confidantes.

They made me out to be a real bitch, starting, leading and controlling the Lotto Ladies, presenting them with a contract they willingly signed but supposedly they are now claiming they hadn't reviewed with a lawyer. Didn't matter. No contributions, no winnings. As the old saying goes – no tickee, no washee.

They dared to disclose things about myself that while true were not items I wanted to see in print. I had to relive my horrible working relationship with The Bitch, my hatred of Lily, my tolerance for Jazzy and my overall despair at having to work retail considering I had a college degree and tons of business experience.

It's one thing to share those thoughts in my diary, or among family and friends, or even blurting them out on the sales floor out of desperation, but the *Genesis* Girls never would have put those words in writing if they hadn't lost out on the jackpot. It was their own fault they withdrew from the Lotto Ladies. No one forced them out…at least I'm pretty sure no one did. I wouldn't put anything past Jazzy. Now they were looking for their 15 minutes of fame and a reasonable book advance.

Sure, this tell-all might attract attention for a week or so, but honestly who cares? I mean, we're yesterday's news. There are so many more important and interesting things going on in this world, or even the world of celebrity, that we are nothing but a flash of the past.

Lost in thought over the insanity of the whole thing, I didn't hear my phone buzz. I looked down to see a text from Jazzy and Pamela:

They're making a movie!

And the attached image was a photo of the two of them holding signs that said, "Who will play me?"

A movie! Holy crap! Who the hell would fund a movie about us? Aside from our business dealings, we've led pretty quiet lives since winning the Super Duper Millions, although Jazzy did take every opportunity to speak to the press. However, she didn't really divulge too much personal information about me. Again, not that I was aware of.

I'd like to think the fervor would die a slow death, but looking online I noticed one of the nightly entertainment shows was already planning a week-long look into the book, followed most certainly by another week once the movie was ready to air. At least it won't be in the theaters. I'd dread thinking of my likeness splashed across such a big screen. Unfortunately, it will probably live forever on the Internet.

This book – and movie – couldn't come at a worse time. Gizzi's wedding was just around the corner. She doesn't need this mess surrounding her maid of honor.

I looked down to see another text from the Boopsey Twins:
Should we write our own book?

I honestly hadn't thought about that, but what better way to counter this situation than with a tell-all book of our own. Or, we could focus on the good that we're doing with the money, helping start-up businesses which employ people and keep the economy going. We could explore the dangers of having so much money at once and how to handle it. Sure, the television show that started this whole thing a few years ago kind of addresses those issues but not enough people watched the show to keep it on the schedule. Our own book and movie could be an excellent PR move – and we could fund it ourselves!

Of course, none of us knows anything about the entertainment business, but neither do the *Genesis* Girls. What I do know is that we'll have to hire a publicist – something I had put off but now see it as a necessity. I'll also have to do a bit of snooping to see who took on the *Genesis* Girls as clients and how they managed to snag two such big deals in such a short period of time.

Oh, and I wonder who wrote their book. The three of them weren't talented in that way. There had to be a ghost writer. Maybe they weren't even behind the idea in the first place but someone had already done research and approached them to finish the deal.

It's a shame how many haters are out there. Just when you think you've finally left all that bad stuff behind you, it comes to the surface, more syrupy and darker than ever. I'm not proud of what I went through but I am proud that I survived to live another successful day.

I realized I had over 240 emails and numerous phone messages and texts regarding the *Genesis* Girls book. This was not going to be a happy day. I had no comment and I needed to guide the Boopsey Twins to remain silent as well. Pamela would cooperate but Jazzy was always the loose cannon. It was impossible to tell what tack she might take. If I was getting calls and messages, so were both of them. We needed to act as a team or this would become a huge mess.

I sent a message to Jazzy and Pamela:

My house. NOW!

I received a text back sooner than expected.

We're outside your elevator.

And so it goes, my life with the Boopsey Twins. In spite of the fact JP was spending a ton of time with Brittnee, helping to define her business, they still managed to stalk me, even at my new secured condo. We weren't joined at the hip, but at times I felt as if we had Siamese bank accounts.

I thought multiple layers of security would keep the Boopsey Twins from unexpected visits, but they were seen in my company so much, security was a little lax with them. Of course, I still had to authorize their elevator ride to my unit, but the fact that they made it into the lobby without a problem meant that I had to do some talking to the head of security.

Jazzy and Pamela took a seat on my sofa and I served us all some lemonade.

"Look, I'm not happy about this whole book thing from the *Genesis* Girls," I said. "They must have rushed the book out to get the holiday sales. This is going to be a headache for a while. I think we need to hire a publicist and that we all share the cost. We should be able to get someone for about $120,000 a year, which will be about $40,000 each."

"But, lovey, you just told me to quit spending money," Jazzy admonished.

"I realize that, but this isn't a new car. This is a cost of doing business, so to speak. We've been pretty quiet about our situation, at least since that initial press tour that the lottery commission required of us. I'm not much for sharing personal news, but we do have a number of business issues to deal with, and while each business launch and promotion will have its own marketing budget, situations like the *Genesis* Girls will require someone to do crisis management for us, as well as look for new opportunities for us as a whole."

"But, I don't think responding to the items in their book is a smart thing, Diana," said Pamela.

"You're right, but taking a pro-active approach, we could have our own project in the media prior to the launch of their TV movie. I have some ideas and I think it's the way to go.

"If we had planned to move to some exotic island and disappear for the rest of our lives, it would be different. I would say to ignore the book and go about your business. But we're being given an opportunity to shine here and to make the *Genesis* Girls look like sore losers."

"Which they are, lovey. They have a lot of nerve publishing that book. I told them they'd have nothing to do with us once they withdrew from the group, so now they're trying to get their money in other ways. Although, as the actual Lotto Ladies, shouldn't we get a cut of their earnings?"

"Jazzy, we just want to ignore what they're doing, so to speak, and launch our own initiative."

"Ooh, like the first punch!"

"Well, actually, they threw the first punch."

"So, this is a counterattack."

"I'd say it's more a strategic response on our part. Anyway, I wanted to make sure that neither of you speak to anyone about the book. I don't want to see quotes or hear comments on the news or entertainment shows. If we're asked, we just ignore the question or pass it on to our publicist. We have to operate as a team. Got it?"

The two rescue pups nodded their heads in unison, but I knew Jazzy would be impossible to control. She was keen on seeing this movie be a success because that would give her greater notoriety.

The Boopsey Twins left, agreeing to behave but it wasn't two hours later Jazzy was quoted online as saying she'd love to see Rita Ora play her in the movie. Oh well. I might as well dream, too. Who will play me? Blake Lively?

"Hey, sis. What's up?"

I answered my cell phone, but there was no sound on the other end of the call. Hmm…maybe Helen butt dialed me by mistake. I hung up. The phone rang again.

"Helen? Is that you? Is everything OK?"

Suddenly, all I could hear were major sobs coming from the caller.

"Helen, what's wrong? Where are you? I'll come to you."

Through gasps and sobs, Helen managed to give me her location.'

"Lone…Mountain…Hospital..ER."

"Stay put. I'm on my way."

I had no idea what happened, but the hospital was just a short drive up the road. I was really concerned because Helen was always a rock. Nothing rattled her. That's what made her such a great Mom and a great teacher.

But today, she was upset – uncontrollable! Did something happen to Mom or Dad? Gabe? Justin or Grace? Her? I was shaking as I drove. I had no idea what the problem was, but I was really concerned.

I parked my car and flew into the ER. I didn't see her anywhere, so I checked at the desk to see if they had moved her to a room, which they had. They scanned my driver's license, gave me a visitor's badge then led me back to see her.

Helen was sitting on the edge of the hospital bed with Justin who was hooked up to all the monitors his little body could hold. She saw me and ran into my arms.

"What happened?" I asked, holding Helen tight while Justin gave me the thumbs up, looking a little worse for wear.

"Thanks for coming, Diana. I couldn't reach Gabe. He's on a roof somewhere and he's not allowed to take his cell phone with him so he doesn't get distracted and cause an accident."

"Where's Grace?"

"I had her go home with one of her friends. I didn't know how long I'd be here and she has homework to do."

I can't believe Helen is thinking about homework at a time like this – although, I still wasn't sure what exactly this time was.

"Mom's really freaking out," Justin said. "I keep telling her I'm OK, but she won't listen. She just keeps crying. I've never seen her cry so hard before."

Helen stepped back and smiled, wiping tears and snot from her face.

"I'm sorry, Diana. I'm normally not like this."

That's for sure. You're freaking me out!

"It all happened so fast. Justin was running –" she turned to give Justin a stern look – "not walking to my classroom, when he tripped on his own feet, fell down and broke his leg. They're checking to make sure everything else is OK, that he doesn't have a concussion or broken nose or anything."

"They're going to give me a walking cast, Aunti Di! I'll be the coolest kid in my class."

"Well, Justin, I'm glad you're feeling that way. You'll probably have it for a few weeks, so don't get too excited."

I was somewhat relieved that it seemed to be just a broken bone, not that there wasn't anything to worry about. My biggest worry was for Helen who seemed to be really out of sorts.

I gave Helen a sisterly hug, helped to dry her tears, then asked, "What's really bothering you, sis?"

Helen got choked up, but she was able to respond.

"It's all been so much, Diana. First you got married, moved here and got divorced. Then we moved here and found new jobs and a new house. You won the lottery and became famous. Now the *Genesis* Girls book is out. And, the holidays will be here in a few weeks. It's too much! I need a break. I miss Mom and Dad so much. I wish they would come out for the holidays but you know that's never going to happen even though they said they would. And, now my baby boy has a broken leg."

Oy! Helen was keeping more inside than I ever expected. As the oldest sister, I looked up to her to lead the charge, but this was one time I needed to give her a break. I wasn't sure what I could do about Mom and Dad, and I was sad that she already heard about the tell-all, but I could be present for her right now, until she was able to get her wits about her again.

"Look. Just relax. I know a lot has happened. I've having trouble figuring it all out for myself. But, right now you need to think of Justin. The doctor is going to take care of him and release him. We'll go back to your place in my car. I'll make dinner and get the two of you into bed then Gabe and I can drive over to get your car. I'll sleep on the sofa tonight and stay with you tomorrow until you feel you can handle things on your own again, OK?"

Helen looked up at me with her big brown eyes. I can only imagine how cute she was as a baby. A lot like Grace, I suppose.

"You'd do that for me, for us? You don't have some important business stuff that needs to be taken care of?"

"Helen, don't ever think that. Family comes first – always. I'm here for you."

Helen smiled and gave me a big hug. Justin smiled, too.

"Say, Aunti Di. Instead of cooking, can we have pizza?"

I laughed. Pizza is always such a calming food group.

"Absolutely! As long as I'm the first to sign your cast."

"I'll loan you my Sharpie," the doctor said as he came into the room.

He was quite the hottie. Then, I noticed the wedding ring. All the good ones are taken!

"OK, let's get you cleaned up and on your way, buddy! And, no more running in the school halls, promise?"

Justin looked up at his Mom then the doctor.

"Did she pay you to say that to me?"

Dear Diary,

No matter what I do with my life, it seems I'll always have Chris on my radar.

In today's paper, I noticed an interview with him and slut wife. *Christopheles* is doing so well in Las Vegas, they've decided to go international and open two more locations, one in Athens and the other in his home town of Stockholm.

Considering the costs involved with this expansion, I'm surprised he hasn't contacted me to invest in his business. Maybe he finally backed down and accepted money from his family. Or, perhaps, slut wife has more of a stash of cash than I imagined and she's funding at least part of it.

Sorry, Chris, but I still haven't eaten at your restaurant. Tempted to check it out, yes. Actually gone there. No. Not on the off chance you or slut wife will be there. What a Kodak moment that would be.

I did receive a fun call today. Due to my work with the student entrepreneurs here in Las Vegas, I've been invited to speak at a student entrepreneurs club at a university in Detroit. Who knew my projects here would attract interest back home?

It will be great to see Mom and Dad, but I think to make this trip totally worthwhile for the club members, I should bring Alfonso and Brittnee along. They are proof that student ideas are worth backing if you find the right partner and are willing to work with your investors. I think their perspective and experience could have a big impact on the students. Plus, we might actually find some new businesses to consider for investment.

That's it. It's settled. Alfonso and Brittnee will join me in Detroit. After the meeting, we'll drive to Mexican Town just under the Ambassador Bridge and lunch at *Xochimilco*. I love their food and crave it all the time! I think this will be a good trip all around.

More tomorrow!

All my heart,

Diana

Destination Detroit

{ THIRTY }

"My route to success, at least financially, was a little unorthodox, but I discovered along the way who I really am. I couldn't do anything else but what I'm doing now. I love it and I'm good at it. You have to find a way to make your dream happen. Does that answer your question?"

After the student shook her head, "Yes," the club president took the mic.

"Are there any more questions?" he asked.

The president pointed to a guy in the center of the room, dressed rather smartly with a smart-ass grin on his face. I could tell what was coming.

"Yes, I have a question. What is your response to the Lotto Ladies book?"

Alfonso and Brittnee looked at me, knowing I was the only one who could answer and unsure of exactly what that answer might be.

"I feel, in business as in life, there are multiple sides to every story. People choose to make money in either positive or negative ways. I feel, as a co-winner of the Super Duper Millions, that the three of us are doing great things with our winnings. That's where I prefer to put my focus."

Smarty pants wasn't happy with my answer.

"But, is the information true?"

"In every bit of fiction there is some truth, and in every bit of truth there is some fiction," I responded.

He could tell I wasn't taking the bait and no one else dared to ask the question. They were smart. They all had business plans in their back pockets and they were hoping they could at least get them in front of me to consider funding their ideas. The rest of the club understood that you don't bite the hand that feeds you and you don't piss off your future investor.

Uncomfortably, the club president once again took control of the mic.

"Well, that should wrap things up. We'd like to thank Diana, Alfonso and Brittnee for spending their valuable time with us today, teaching us how to support student entrepreneurship. Your examples and guidance will be valuable as we plan our initiative for next year. Perhaps someone in this room has an idea that you will find worthy of your investment."

A big Woot! Woot! came from the audience.

I smiled. Once you have money and a bit of success, everyone wants to do business with you.

"Actually, until I was blessed with this good fortune and I met Alfonso and Brittnee, the thought of investing in student businesses never crossed my mind as a viable enterprise. Now, I see how lucrative this can be. You're young. You're in the thick of things. You're part of the key demographic for every advertiser out there. You know what you want and you aim to get it. Not every business is successful, but you learn your lessons and move on. It's an exciting place to be."

"If I may add," Alfonso piped in, "if it wasn't for Diana, I'm not sure that we would have gotten BBPS or LBC off the ground. There's a window of perfect opportunity for a business and I felt this holiday season was it. Thanks to Diana's commitment, investment and guidance, we've been successful. She's a great partner and I highly recommend you at least pitch her with your ideas because if she sees potential, she'll be on your side in a second."

I half-smiled, half-laughed.

"Thanks, Alfonso. You've been a great partner as well."

"Well, don't leave me out of this mutual admiration society," Brittnee said. "I have to agree with everything that Alfonso said about working with Diana. In my case, my business needed a larger investment and she brought on her two Lotto Ladies partners. We now have a really strong team and we expect to hit market sometime next year. Unfortunately, I can't share the details right now, but keep an eye on social media outlets for updates on Diana's business ventures. She's sure to be all over it when my business launches."

"Well, at least Jazzy and Pamela will be," I added.

We all laughed. We didn't want to disclose how precarious that whole relationship was but at least we understood the dynamics of it all.

"But seriously," Brittnee continued, "Diana has this innate ability to look at a plan and know if the business is worth pursuing. So, an investment from Diana should be worth pursuing as well!"

"OK, then," the club president snuck in. "I'm sure we could go on talking forever, but we must break as this room has another group moving in for a lunch meeting. I'd like to thank you all for attending and again, our thanks to our guests. Their contact information is available on our club website, for members only, so please do not share with your friends without consulting me first. Have a great afternoon."

"How do you think it went?" Alfonso asked once we were back in the car.

"I thought it went pretty well. We have a stack of business plans to review, so who knows what will come of it. It's just a nice way to give back to my home town."

"Do you really want to open businesses in Detroit?" Brittnee asked.

Brittnee was bundled up from head to toe to stave off the late fall chill. I had been invited to speak to a multi-university student entrepreneur club in Detroit and wanted to bring my two best examples of student entrepreneurs, Brittnee and Alfonso. I couldn't guarantee that we'd have success with every student business we launched, but Alfonso's was off to a roaring start and Brittnee's would prove itself sometime next year.

Brittnee was clearly a desert rat, having grown up in Las Vegas. Although I was Detroit born and raised, my blood was as thin as hers. I pulled my collar close around my neck and waited for the car heater to warm up. It was two weeks before Thanksgiving and three weeks before Gizzi's wedding in California. Alfonso and I were crazy busy with the Buff Boys and LBC, but I really felt compelled to do this visit, so I accepted. I was covering the travel – first class – so it didn't take much to convince Alfonso and Brittnee to join me.

We could have traveled the Jazzy way – by private jet – but I opted for first class commercial, something I quite enjoyed during my Silicon Valley days. Maybe I'll fly private the next time. That's an expense I could well afford but had never experienced.

I had reserved a rental car for the rest of my stay in town, time I would spend with my parents, but for today, I hired a town car with a driver. I may have grown up here but I still didn't know my way around town all that well. This way, we didn't have to worry about getting lost and I could give my full attention to my business partners. We used cars in other cities for press tours all the time in high tech, so it just seemed logical.

Cindi R. Maciolek

"Well, I hadn't really thought about funding any Detroit-based businesses, but the city does have a lot to offer and we will be starting a Buff Boys franchise here shortly. I'll be spending time in town so I might as well consider other money-making options. And, just because we met the students in Detroit does not mean they want to stay here. So many businesses today are portable but if we could keep the companies local, that would be best."

"I told you – Reykjavik over Detroit any day," said Alfonso.

Brittnee and I laughed. She was now in my inner circle and the three of us often shared inside jokes.

"Just keep an eye out the window. There's some amazing stuff in this town."

"All I see are boarded up buildings with an occasional strip mall and a gas station," said Alfonso.

"Look harder!"

"Where are we going anyway?" Brittnee asked.

"We're actually going to my favorite Mexican restaurant in the entire world – *Xochimilco*. It's in Mexican Town near the base of the Ambassador Bridge."

Both Alfonso and Brittnee looked at me like I'd gone crazy.

"You mean to tell me, your favorite Mexican restaurant is in Detroit? How is that possible?" Alfonso asked.

"You know, I've traveled all over the world and lived on the West Coast for some time now, but I still crave the chicken and cheese enchiladas at *Xochi's*."

Alfonso rolled his eyes and smiled.

"Sure, Diana, sure."

Brittnee had her nose pressed against the car window, looking outside like a little kid visiting the city for the first time – which she was.

"What's an Ambassador Bridge?" she asked.

"It's the bridge that connects the United States to Canada."

Both she and Alfonso sat upright and looked at me, shocked.

"You mean we're that close to Canada?" Brittnee asked.

"Sure, you'll see. Detroit is on this side of the river and Windsor, Ontario is on the other. We used to go there all the time when I lived here. It's the only place where you have to travel south to get to Canada. Very cool."

"Wow! Do you think we'd have time to visit?"

"Sorry, no. We'll have lunch, then the driver will drop us at the airport so you can catch your flight back to Las Vegas and I can pick up my rental car. Maybe next time. You have to bring your passports anyway. It is a foreign country!"

We laughed and Brittnee returned her attention to what lie outside the car rather than the conversation inside. All of a sudden, she gasped and pointed out the window.

"What is that?" she asked.

I took a peek through the window beside her. There, in all its glory stood the abandoned Michigan Central Station.

"It's gorgeous!"

Brittnee's full attention was on the amazing building outside her window. She was so enthralled, Alfonso slid to her side of the car to take a look.

"That is really cool! You'd never see anything like that in Vegas," he said.

Well, you might see some sort of facsimile, but this was the real thing.

I took a long look out the window as well. I had driven by MCS a couple of times on visits during my high tech days. I loved *Xochi's* and sometimes we took a different route to the restaurant. I remember being floored the first time I laid eyes on this amazing Beaux Arts building that had been abandoned since the late 1980's. It needed a ton of work to be useful once again and although many plans had been proposed, it still sat empty.

My heart connected with MCS in a way like no other building I'd ever seen. I immediately had a vision for it and vowed that, should I ever have enough money, I'd make MCS the center of an industry other than automotive. I'd honestly forgotten about it, but now, it was as if the building was calling to me.

Even with all my millions, I wasn't sure I had enough to make it happen. And, I still wanted to be smart with my money and not invest it all in one project. What am I saying? I'm getting way ahead of myself. I'll put the idea in the research file in my brain and keep my focus where it needs to be – on my existing projects.

"It is an amazing building, isn't it? It was actually designed by the same team that designed Grand Central Station in New York City. Unfortunately, while Grand Central Station had Jackie Kennedy to fight for its preservation, MCS has had no one to rescue it from ruin. So, it sits, waiting."

Brittnee turned to me and asked, "Waiting for what?"

I smiled.

"Waiting for the same things you are, and all the students we saw today – the right business partners, ideas, plans, opportunity. I've always loved that building. It's utterly amazing."

Alfonso looked at me. He saw that look in my eye. I shook it off and realized the car had come to a stop. We were in the parking lot at *Xochi's*. MCS would have to wait for a later date.

"Maybe you should do something about it, Diana," Alfonso said as we got out of the car. "You have the right combination of experience and creativity…"

"And money. Or, at least business partners," Brittnee chimed in.

"That's right, Britt. Diana, I'm sure your mind is already going a mile a minute. Of course, it would mean coming to Detroit pretty often to keep the project on track!"

The three of us smiled as we rushed from the warmth of the car to the heat of the restaurant.

"Look, it is a beautiful building and I could think of a few different things I would do with it, but I don't even know if it's available."

"We could check," Brittnee said.

"No, I'm not doing anything right now. It's been vacant for decades. Nothing needs to happen overnight or will happen overnight. We need to make sure Buff Boys and LBC have a strong holiday season and Brittnee, your business needs to get off the ground and start earning some money. Oh, and I have Gizzi's upcoming wedding and the *Genesis* Girls to deal with."

"And the Boopsey Twins," Alfonso added.

We'd had such a nice morning and my phone had been quiet all day, I'd almost forgotten about the two of them. And, as if on cue, I received a message that asked,

What do you think?

Attached was a photo of Jazzy and Pamela in beautifully well-tailored suits to emphasize their desire to be involved in future business ventures. I admired their interest but the suit doesn't make the person. It takes a lot of energy to keep them in check. We need mutual investments but I want us to take them on slowly, so we can make the right decisions and give each business the attention it deserves. I had always wished Jazzy and Pamela would go away. Now, I was wondering just how much money they'd be willing to invest.

I looked up from my phone as we were seated at our table.

"Let's not worry about any of that now," I said. "I'm starved!"

After the most amazing lunch I'd had in forever, the driver hopped on the freeway and took us directly to the airport. I wished Alfonso and Brittnee good flights home, then got into the shuttle that would take me to my rental car. I enjoyed their company immensely but I had a lot of thinking to do, and I was about to finally hug my parents for the first time in a long time.

I passed Sunset Mall on the way to my old neighborhood, making a mental note to check in and see that everything was on track for a mid-January launch. Every one of our potential franchisees was eager to get started, but introducing the brand just days before the holidays made no sense. I wasn't keen on being here in the cold and snow, but maybe I'd luck out and they'd have a mild winter. Hah! I just jinxed myself.

I pulled into the driveway of the house where I grew up and my emotions overtook me. So much had happened since I graduated from college, packed my bags and took that leap of faith to move to California and start working in high tech.

Now, here I was, in my 30's, having survived one of the worst personal and financial ordeals of anyone's life. In fact, not just surviving but blossoming! I had no indication this was how my life would turn out. None of us do. But, seeing my childhood home again brought everything to the surface. I sat there for a few moments, regaining my composure.

Moments later, Mom and Dad came running out the front door to greet me. I was so grateful to be able to spend time with them, but this trip was short. I headed home tomorrow. I didn't have much free time until after Gizzi's wedding. I planned to savor every second of my time with my parents.

"Oh, honey, we're so glad you're here!" said Mom.

She looked a bit older, though no worse for wear. Video calls are great but there's nothing like a Mom hug to make your day.

"Yes, dear, it's so good to see you," Dad said.

We went inside, out from the chill. Dad grabbed my overnight bag and led me up the stairs, directly back to my old room which coincidentally, hadn't changed a stitch since I moved out. So many memories! Who was the person who lived here?

"There you go, honey. Come on down when you're ready and we'll have some coffee."

"Thanks, Dad."

I quickly hung up my coat, kicked off my boots and put on some warm slippers from college. Oy! If Mom and Dad are ever to move to Las Vegas, I definitely need to come back here and clean out this place. I'm sure Helen needs to do the same with her room. Hmm…maybe that's a good reason to come back for the holidays. Oh, yes, aside from the fact that Helen had a complete meltdown and really needs to get here pronto!

I made my way back down the stairs, anxious not to waste a single minute of my stay, knowing Mom and Dad went to bed early. I had an early flight in the morning, too, so I really had just a few hours to get caught up and make some plans. I decided to jump right into it.

"So, have you guys thought about retiring and moving to Las Vegas to be with your kids and grandkids?"

Mom and Dad looked at each other and smiled.

"We have, dear. Everyday. Your father and I have spent hours discussing our future, especially after your generous gift. It really got us to thinking."

"That's right, Diana. Georgia and I have had a lot of discussions about our finances and work. We both met with our human resources departments. I'll be eligible to retire in eight months and Georgia is already eligible."

I smiled the biggest smile I had in a long time.

"Now, just because we're eligible doesn't mean we'll take advantage of it, but it seems our friends are jumping on the early retirement bandwagon and we'll be all alone here in Michigan in short order."

"And, as we get older, the thought of dealing with the winters doesn't appeal to us. You know, most of our friends move to Florida, but since you kids are in Vegas, it makes more sense to go there."

"That's right, Georgia. And, don't forget, Joanie and Mark are buying into one of those retirement communities just down the road from Helen and Diana."

This was the best news I'd heard in years. I got up and started jumping up and down.

"Now, Diana, we haven't officially made any decisions as to when. We still need to clean and pack and sell this place, plus purchase a place in Vegas."

"Oh, don't worry about any of that. You guys can come out any time and we can go house hunting. Just say the word and I'll buy it. As for cleaning this place, I was thinking I'd fly everyone here for the Christmas holidays and maybe Helen and I can help you out – at least with our old rooms! Plus, I'll be making periodic trips here to check on a business I'm starting at Sunset Mall."

"Now, Diana, you've done enough already. We don't want you to pay for the new home. We own this home outright so we'll use the proceeds to purchase a new one over there."

"Nonsense. Besides, you have to buy it when you see it."

Dad seemed to be getting a little annoyed with me.

"Diana, dear. We spoke with our accountant."

Well, that was some major progress. I never thought they'd accept the fact that they had this money.

"We plan to invest your gift in some high dividend securities and some very safe investments. Then, we'll live off the interest and dividends, along with our pensions and other retirement savings. We don't expect to need more than about $40,000 a year to live. Even if we withdrew that amount from the principal of the trust every year, which I would never do, we'd have more than enough to last us our lifetimes. We can't have you buy the house, too. What will we do with the leftover money in our trusts when we die?"

Oh, how I hated when they started to talk like that. I know families should have these discussions. I just liked to keep things happy.

"You can do whatever you want. Give it to charity if you like. But, you never know what the future will bring. Don't worry about it. Let me do this for you."

Ralph and Georgia looked at each other, then to me.

"Fine. Sleep on it. We can talk about it some other time. If you want, I can buy the new house and you can pay me back when this house sells."

Mom and Dad both looked relieved when I made that comment.

"That would be great, dear. You know we like to pay our own way."

"Yes, I know. But I also want you to enjoy life. You can now have or do anything you want. So, accept that!"

But nothing else mattered to me. I heard what I wanted to hear. Mom and Dad would be moving to Vegas about a year down the road, after they were both eligible for retirement. That was music to my ears. I couldn't wait to tell Helen. I would, however, keep the Christmas trip a surprise, at least until Thanksgiving.

Dear Diary,

Is Gizzi crazy?

Now, I recognize my life has changed a bit in the last few months, and Gizzi, in the heat of her engagement moment, selected the first date available with her wedding planner. However, if someone looked at the calendar, they would have realized it was in the midst of the holiday season!

Now, technically, the bachelorette party takes place the weekend before Thanksgiving – the weekend before Thanksgiving!!! – so the holiday season doesn't officially begin until a few days following. However, as far as I'm concerned, it doesn't matter.

Would it have been that different if they waited until January to marry? Of course, they couldn't file joint tax returns for another 12 months, but the strain on everyone at this time of year is enormous already and I'm certain the two of them are not thinking in terms of tax returns.

I'm excited, sure I am, about Gizzi and Jean-Louis tying the knot, but between my commitments to her as maid of honor, the family stuff I have to deal with, along with my involvement in four budding businesses, I'm just a little busy. It's hard enough to launch one business at a time, let alone four.

I know, I know – friendship is far more powerful and important than business – but when I'm exhausted I can't think of anything else but complaining. At least I get to do so in the beautiful confines of my new abode – where I'm still unpacking!

Everything will get done as planned. I'll eventually get some sleep. Once the wedding is over, I'll have some mindshare freed up to think about something new – like MCS?

To those who say 'sleep is overrated' or 'I'll sleep when I'm dead' I have just one thing to say: I'm tired!!!

More tomorrow!

All my heart,

Diana

The Bachelorette Party

{ THIRTY-ONE }

"C'mere, hot stuff."

Abigail Winthrop slithered over to the stage from our V.I.P table to stuff some of her inheritance into the, um, dong strap of the dancer she'd been flirting with since the start of the show.

Over the last few months, Gizzi faced a tough decision. One of her cousins had dropped out of the bridal party, claiming she was too shy to have her photo plastered over the Internet for years to come. After much deliberation and consultation, Gizzi turned to an old sorority sister of hers to fill her cousin's shoes.

There was nothing shy about Abigail, her assets pushing the upper limits of her bustier, an E-cup on a 32 inch bust. We all waited for them to reach a new high and share their freedom with the gaggle of, shall I say gentlemen, who accompanied their women at the adjoining table. I had no idea Gizzi even had people in her circle who had paid to enhance their personal portfolios in such a way. Most of us would have put that money into a long term bond.

In fact, although many of the women in the room had fistfuls of dollars to do their weenie stuffing, including the other five at the V.I.P. table, Abigail proffered tens, twenties and even hundreds from her handbag – and this was our fourth stop of the night.

Gizzi gave me a look that said, "What have I done?" as Abigail was dragged on stage with the men of *Cowboy Carnivale* – one of the many male reviews Colin had booked for us to visit on our bachelorette weekend.

However, I could guarantee Colin had not investigated Abigail's past DUIs, citations for disorderly conduct and tickets for public nudity. Abigail was a wild child, an heir to a hair care fortune whose Daddy overlooked every little indiscretion his daughter had – public or private – because his baby girl was his little princess and money could fix anything. And, it usually did – particularly her hair. It looked gorgeous!

Looks-wise, Abigail was tall, thin and beautiful – certainly a requirement for those all-important wedding photos and one who could wear the now-vacated bridesmaid's gown. Gizzi put a lot of thought into who she would share her special day with, at least regarding the bridal party – the reception would be a mash-up of relatives and industry insiders – but males ran deep in both Gizzi and JL's families so there were limited choices when it came to a female replacement. Gizzi had to turn outside the family to complete her bridal party roster.

Abigail drank more than any of us who were sipping – sipping – our champagne, trying to drink at a pace that would last the whole weekend. Abigail, however, was already the center of attention – not Gizzi, the bride – and I expected it would continue that way for the entire 48 hours we were together, save for the lap dance Abigail paid for Gizzi to enjoy by Cowboy Joe – which she didn't. Not that he wasn't good, he was fantastic! It just wasn't Gizzi's style. She'd rather be shoe shopping. I had only one thought: Abigail was perfect for Pierre.

"Ohhhh, ooohh, mfgmh."

Abigail held an ice pack to her head as we sat in the living room of one of the luxury villas at *Positano*, hoping to alleviate the pain only too much liquor can cause. One would think she would be immune to hangovers, given the amount of alcohol she imbibed on a regular basis. The only other explanation for her pain would be the amount of deposits she made in dong straps over the course of the evening. Only an unemployed heiress could appreciate the lethal combination of free-flowing champagne and a bottomless bank account.

I hated the fact that we were staying at the *Positano*, but they did have the best villas in town and Colin Bailey was always about the best. He even sent a limo to fetch me for the bachelorette weekend so I could experience the same as the other bridesmaids. He booked the largest of the villas for us – 10 bedrooms, his and hers beauty salons, a private pool, a massage room, an exercise room, a theater/game room and a chef's kitchen which was already utilized by a private chef to serve us the most amazing breakfast I had ever had.

Generally, celebrities and their entourages or politicians with security detail stayed in this particular unit, but Colin plunked down his black American Express and we had the run of the place for two days.

Colin planned out the weekend to the minute and we were well into hour 16. Once everyone arrived and checked in, our luggage was left with the butler who unpacked and steamed all our clothing. Each one of us had our own room and bathroom, a little less prom night and a little more homecoming weekend.

While our rooms were readied, we enjoyed a pre-dinner cocktail, compliments of the hotel. Ain't that a rush! Former employee treated to complimentary beverages in luxury villa! No one else here could appreciate the irony of the situation more than I.

We dressed for the evening which – given there were seven adult women took two hours – then headed to the best French restaurant in town, on property – *Henri's*. The Provençal menu provided some good sustenance for our evening's exploits, which most likely would go well into the wee hours of the morning.

Everywhere we went, we were accompanied by a V.I.P host and a luxury ride to be assured we would be welcomed like royalty, and in one short evening we managed to take in four separate male revues, all of which I knew existed but never patronized. I was as much a tourist on this little expedition as everyone else, save the host. I now understood why so many bachelorette parties came to Vegas. It was one big brawling hunk of manliness.

Abigail needed to be corralled from *Cowboy Carnivale*, our last stop of the night before heading back to the villa for pizza and beer. We had one more show scheduled, but opted out as we were getting, well, tired. The nightclub scene was only truly beginning when we left, but we were no longer youngsters and it's amazing how quickly you can tell your age when you're partying at 3 a.m.

"OK, ladies. If you'd like to shower and wear just your complimentary robes, we'll head over to the spa for an afternoon of relaxation and healthy eating to combat the damage we did last night."

Just what we needed, a host with a wry sense of humor. I wonder how many times he'd used that same description to a private party – bachelor, bachelorette, birthday, reunion – they all came here. And his emphasis on the word complimentary drove me nuts. This hotel gave nothing away. OK, perhaps those initial cocktails. Other than that, this was all compliments of the soon-to-be Mr. and Mrs. Ricard.

Abigail waved a hundred dollar bill above her head to get the host's attention.

"Waiter, do you have something for a hangover?"

He grabbed the bill from her hand, quickly pocketed it and said, "Why, yes. I'll order a drip immediately."

Within moments, a woman dressed in a sexy nurse's outfit arrived with a vitamin drip for the heiress. Twenty minutes later, Abigail's hangover was history and she ran up the stairs to shower for our spa day.

Tonight would just be a fun night – dinner, a Cirque show then a bit of clubbing. Given our age, as much as we wanted to maintain a high level of energy to celebrate these last vestiges of singledom for our esteemed friend, our bodies called it quits far sooner than our minds. We're not old; we're just not as young as we used to be.

I was a bit stressed as tonight would be our bonding night when we all toasted the bride at dinner. This was my trial run for the wedding and although I knew no one else this weekend, I knew Gizzi and that's all that mattered. As the maid of honor, I'd be the first to toast and while I always appreciated a good glass of champagne, I made sure none passed these lips until I was done with my moment in the spotlight. I adored Gizzi and I could never do anything to jeopardize that friendship.

We had a private dining room at *Cakes*, the nickname the chef gave his wife when he realized she would answer to it instead of babycakes, saving him two whole syllables of time and effort. The Asian/Brazilian fusion restaurant had an interesting menu but all this rich food could be saved for someone else. I wasn't much of a foodie. Give me a good broasted chicken or some tasty enchiladas and I'm a happy camper. I was just grateful Colin hadn't booked us into *Christopheles*, the hottest new restaurant on the Strip. I'm sure Gizzi, my dear, dear friend had insisted on an alternative.

I stood up, steadied myself, cleared my throat and looked the bride straight in the eye.

"Giz, in just two short weeks, you'll be married to the man of your dreams, although your life together has already begun."

"Toast!" Abigail said as she raised her glass and guzzled the champagne.

Ignoring Abigail, I continued with my tribute.

"Who knew, when we first met so many years ago, that our lives would turn out as they have. We've shared so many ups and downs –"

Abigail pounded the table.

"Truth or dare. Truth or dare."

The host held her hands to prevent her from interrupting again, at least with her table pounding. Unless he put a gag on her, she was sure to spew again. She initially fought back but our host was a honking hunk of muscle and Abigail was no match.

"I've always admired you. I've counted on you to keep me in line and to open my mind to the truth. I've cherished every second of you as my friend. Now, I wish you a lifetime of happiness with your husband, your soulmate, Jean-Louis."

Gizzi and I started crying and she jumped up and gave me a big hug. The other bridesmaids raised their glasses in toast and drank up. Abigail broke loose from the host and contributed to the moment.

"Oh, quit being so sappy, for chrissake. This is a bachelorette party. Why aren't we reliving all those party days from Gizzi's past, her sexual exploits, her crazy moments she'd like to forget but we want to capture on video for posterity."

"Wow, big words coming from little Abigail," Tally, one of Gizzi's cousins, piped up. "Gizzi doesn't have any of those memories. She's not like you, Abby. Now, quit trying to spoil the weekend, not only for us but most of all, for Gizzi."

Abigail flushed from head to toe. No one ever told her off. She was always the leader of the pack, the center of attention. Abigail didn't quite know how to respond but it appeared she and Tally had a bit of history. She opened her mouth but nothing came out. She sat back in her chair, trying to assess the situation and respond accordingly. She finally regained her composure.

"Look, this is Vegas. I'm here to party. I wasn't one of Gizzi's first picks like all of you were. If we're not going to have fun, I'll find my own crowd and catch you back at the villa."

Whereupon, Abigail grabbed her clutch and stepped gently out of the dining room, gingerly steadying herself on her stilettos, pulling her bodycon dress low and tight over her bosom. The host obliged her by ordering a separate car and host. The *Positano* couldn't risk pissing off Colin Bailey by having anything happen to one of his guests, regardless of the situation. We wouldn't see Abigail the rest of the night. It would be Sunday afternoon before she rolled into the cabana at the pool to finish out her bachelorette weekend with her fellow bridesmaids.

Gizzi took the whole situation in stride. Certainly, as a CEO she has her detractors, but as a woman she has a limited circle of friends and relies mostly on her family. You could see she felt that inviting Abigail into the bridal party was a bad reflection on her even though no one can control how another person acts. Gizzi and Abigail met regularly for lunch since college and Gizzi had hoped Abigail had given up her partying ways from their college days. Instead, it appears, she got worse.

The rest of us were grateful Abigail found her way out of the dining room and into whatever sleaze and trash she could collude with for the night. We were all pretty conservative and while we knew we were in Vegas for Gizzi's bachelorette party, none of us expected to become fodder for a female version of *The Hangover*. We'd honestly rather sit around and tell stories in the privacy of the villa than deal with the noise, smells and meat market of the clubs.

"What have I done, Diana?" Gizzi asked me after she watched Abigail storm out. "She's one of my bridesmaids. The wedding is in just two weeks."

I put my arm around her shoulder and gave her a squeeze.

"Gizzi, it will be fine. She'll grab all the attention she can, for sure, but she's smart enough to know that it's your day. If she screws things up for you it will reflect badly on the family name.

I know her Daddy has been able to keep things covered up till now, but he will have no control over this. If she wants to keep her bank account, she'll behave herself."

Gizzi looked at me, totally not believing a word I said. I didn't believe it either, but it was the best I could do.

"Oh, Gizzi, we'll keep her under control, don't you worry," said Tally, and the other bridesmaids shook their heads in agreement, followed by a group hug, sans moi. I guess that's what I should have said and the attitude I should have taken, but once again, even at my best friend's bachelorette party, I was an outsider. This was *The Bod* all over again.

We finished dinner, enjoying crazy toast after crazy toast. Then our host politely gathered us in the limo and carted us to the Cirque show, which we all quite enjoyed. To appease Colin, we managed an hour at one nightclub before we decided to head back to the villa, partly because we were tired, partly because we felt on display.

After our thousand dollar bottle service in the roped-off V.I.P. section of the club, we began to feel extremely uncomfortable. People approach the ropes then walked away.

"Why are they staring at us?" Tally asked.

I looked at our current slate of onlookers then totally understood.

"They're looking for the celebrities that usually inhabit this space. So, they come, they stare, they realize they don't recognize a soul and go about their evening before the next crowd appears."

"Oh, thank goodness," Gizzi said, heaving a sigh of relief. "I thought they might actually know me and post photos of me on their social media pages. That's the last thing I need."

I laughed.

"What's so funny?"

"I just hope JL and his friends have the same attitude. I think once he and Pierre get together, they might revert to their childhood mentalities and cause a bit of a ruckus."

Gizzi snort laughed at me.

"Well, even if they do, they're in a very small town in France. I can't imagine they'd get into that much trouble. We're in Vegas. We have a whole world of hurt we can get into here."

Jean-Louis's sister smiled. She claimed she didn't speak very good English but she sure seemed to understand everything that was going on. She's probably going to report back to Maman et Papa when this weekend concludes.

"C'mon, let's get back to the villa where we can have some privacy," Tally said.

Hmm…for someone who has a moderate income and plays a secondary role to maid of honor, Tally certainly wants to take control. Either I have to step up my game – for a wedding! – or just let it slide off my back. I'll be friends with Gizzi forever. If Tally wants to grab a bit of the spotlight, let her.

We stayed in a 10 bedroom villa but the majority of the time we slept on the sectional in the living room, after a night of activity followed by pizza and beer, enough to put us into a carb coma. One by one, in the wee hours of the morning, we'd slowly make our way up to our rooms, only to be summoned downstairs by our host early the next morning for our scheduled activity.

Sunday was a laid-back day, swimming, sunning and relaxing by the pool. Vegas was experiencing a rather warm autumn and while the pool was typically closed by this time of year, we were able to enjoy it in all its glory.

Long about early afternoon, just an hour or so before we needed to pack up and turn into pumpkins signaling the end of our weekend fun, Abigail came sauntering back into view, carrying her stilettos and wearing the same dress she'd worn the night before. She plopped her heels in the cabana, whipped off her dress and jumped in wearing nothing more than her thong. If she wasn't part of our little group, I'd be laughing my ass off, but this was just one more concern for Gizzi.

"I think we're done here," I said.

All the bridesmaids put on their robes and gathered their belongings, intending to go the villa and grab lunch before the flight home, leaving Abigail to fend for herself.

"You go ahead. I'll stay here," Gizzi said.

We were all a little shocked, but Gizzi was our leader and she was not about to leave one of her flock behind. We plopped our weary butts on the chaise longues and waited until Abigail finished her swim.

Dear Diary,

Gizzi is such a class act.

In spite of the rude way Abigail acted during our bachelorette weekend, Gizzi stood by her, as a good friend would, and made sure she remained part of the group. I hated the way Abigail behaved but Gizzi must have seen her party in the past and knew she'd come around. Gizzi is such a pillar of strength. I'm positive I would not have been so forgiving to a friend who needed to capture the spotlight.

But, I'm not Gizzi and that's why I respect her so much. I'm sure Abigail is receiving a Gizzi smackdown as we speak, hoping she'll take her advice to heart and turn her life around. Abigail is so privileged, she should be doing something wonderful with her life but at least until now, she's only been a party girl. That won't get her a husband and kids, nor happiness as her good looks – and great hair – fade. We all have decisions to make in life and I guarantee you, they hurt!

One decision I'm facing right now is who to take to Gizzi's wedding. I'm wealthy, successful and look better than ever, but the short answer is I'm going alone. I went through my list of potential plus ones and there's really no one that's the right fit.

Alfonso wouldn't be appropriate, nor anyone from the BBPS team. His Hotness would be fine to take along, but I'm not sure I'm prepared for his reaction to such excess materialism which I'm sure will be quite evident at this wedding. Kevin would gladly come along but I want to stay as far away from him as I can. Tom and Gabe are still friends but I haven't really spoken to Tom since we broke up so it would be extremely awkward if I invited him. I don't want to give him the wrong impression. So, that's it! That's the short list and I don't want any of them to accompany me.

I want to fully enjoy myself during the wedding. I should know some attendees, although they're probably all coming with dates – or spouses! I could hang with Gizzi's family. And, there's always Pierre...

More tomorrow!

All my heart,

Diana

A New Start

{ THIRTY-TWO }

"How's this, Aunti Di?"

Justin was keen on getting it right. He and his sister were busy, sitting in front of the television, slicing cranberries in half for pie. Cranberry pies were a family tradition and we needed a ton of sliced berries for the dozen or so pies we would bake in the next several hours. We couldn't eat all of the ones we would make today, but we'd pass them around as gifts to friends and store a couple unbaked in the freezer for the holidays.

This was my first Thanksgiving in my new condo and I was loving it. I convinced the family to spend Thanksgiving Eve in my place, and it was honestly the most fun I'd had in forever, including the bachelorette weekend. Sorry, Giz! We ordered pizza and stayed up late playing board games and watching movies. It was the kind of housewarming this place needed and I was happy to share it with my sister and her gang.

We were awakened by Helen making chocolate chip pancakes, something I hadn't had since I was a teenager living at home. She was such a culinary artiste; she even made her own whipped crème! We scarfed down the pancakes, then plunked ourselves in front of the big screen in the great room to watch the numerous parades.

Then it was time to start thinking about dinner. I was the turkey queen, as I deemed myself, so I began the prep for the largest Tom I had ever cooked. I can't imagine how many hours it will need in the oven. Perhaps I should have started this last night. With any luck, we'd be eating by Christmas. Helen focused on the side dishes and appetizers and the kids cut cranberries in preparation for their first lesson in making pie. Gabe supervised.

Helen and I were technically alone in the kitchen although without doors – or walls – anyone in the condo could hear our discussion, so I wanted to use this time to surprise her with the holiday trip. She'd been a bit more subdued the last couple of weeks, and I could see her internal pain as she watched Justin hobble around in his cast. This wasn't like her and I wanted to help fix her – if just for a bit. I missed my sister and the strength she provided the family, her love, her humor and her wisdom. To my surprise, she started asking questions as soon as we were working in earnest.

"So, how was the trip home? We haven't really talked since you went to Detroit, everything's been so crazy for both of us."

That it had. That was one of the reasons I was so happy to have us spend Thanksgiving together.

"I know you had open house last year, but since I moved into my new place, I thought it would be nice to host it this year. I'm old enough now that we could alternate if you like."

Helen stopped for a minute to look at me. It was as if for the first time she really saw me as an adult and not just her little sister.

"You know, I'd like that. I'm sure Gabe and the kids would enjoy it, too. I know you're not married now, but hopefully when you are we'll be able to keep up this new tradition. I have to say,

I quite liked having us all spend the night here. It was almost like going on a mini-vacation, which we could all use."

Ah, the intro I needed.

"Speaking of which…I had a long talk with Mom and Dad."

"I know. I spoke with both of them after your visit, but I never truly got any details other than they're considering moving here sometime next year."

I smiled so wide I couldn't help myself. Helen laughed.

"You're such a kid."

"What? That I'm happy my Mommy and my Daddy are going to be down the street once again? I miss them!"

"I miss them, too. Honestly, if you hadn't won the Super Duper Millions, I'm not sure they'd make the move. We really owe it to you. Now the kids will get to spend more time with their grandparents. I'm not sure when we can go back for a visit. Maybe over spring break or next summer. I have to check the kids' competition schedules."

"Well… how does Christmas sound?"

"How does Christmas sound for what?"

"For a trip back to Detroit, silly! Mom and Dad won't come out here in the winter even though they said they would, you're off for two weeks, I'm in a position where I can do my work anywhere. As long as Gabe can take the time off, let's do it! I'll hire a private jet and we can leave and come back whenever we like."

I thought Helen would collapse on the floor, as if the weight of everything these last few months had lifted unexpectedly and she was thrown off-balance. I grabbed for her arm to steady her. Gabe noticed and jumped up to help.

"What's going on?"

Helen looked at Gabe with wonderment.

"Can you get some time off over the holidays?"

"Uh, sure, I think so. I have some vacation time coming and most of the guys like to work during that time because they'll get time and a half or double time for some of the days. Why?"

Helen turned to look at me and smiled. Gabe looked, too, then looked back at his wife.

"Because Santa is buying us a trip to Detroit for Christmas!"

Gabe's face lit up. He picked up Helen and started spinning her around, then grabbed me with an arm and hugged me tight. The kids came running – well, Justin was hobbling – and we did a group hug. They certainly heard what Helen said and it appeared they couldn't be happier.

"That's the best gift ever, Aunti Di," gushed Grace.

"I'll get to see all my old friends, I can't believe it!" said Justin.

"I really do appreciate this, sis. I can't tell you how much it means to me. I know you gave us a financial gift but I want to save that for retirement, and the fact that we can all be together as a family this year is really special."

"Great! I'm so glad you feel that way! Just let me know by Monday when you'd like to travel and I'll get it scheduled. I'll also book a couple of rental cars and perhaps a hotel?"

"No way!" Justin shouted. "I'm staying with Grammy and Pappy. You can stay in a hotel if you want, but I'm staying with them if I have to sleep on the couch."

Grace nodded her head.

"It will be like Christmas camping! We can dig out some sleeping bags and pillows and sleep on the floor in the family room."

"There will be no sleeping on the floor," Helen piped in. "Grammy and Pappy have enough room for us all to sleep. As long as they're up to it, we'll stay with them. If they want us to stay in a hotel, we'll do that. We can't just invite ourselves to stay with them. But, it would be a lot of fun!"

I hadn't seen Helen so perky in so long. I had no idea she missed Mom and Dad that much. Or, was it Detroit and her friends? I now gave her a reason to look forward to the holidays. She didn't have to be the Mom and hold the open house like she did last year. We'd all be helping our Mom to do so as was her tradition in our childhood home. I was looking forward to it, too, but first I had to get through Thanksgiving.

"Everything smells really good, Aunti Di," Justin said as he hobbled down the hallway from the guest room after taking a shower. "I could eat now!"

"You could eat all day and all night," said Grace.

Ah, sibling love.

"It does smell good, though, I agree. Can we help with anything?"

Wow! It was so nice to have such little helpers. I'd never held an open house, and the last official dinner I hosted was Thanksgiving with Chris a few years ago. This was a totally different feeling.

The phone buzzed. It was security.

"Ms. MacKenzie? This is Gordon from security. I have Alfonso and Brittnee here to see you."

"Oh, thank you, Gordon. You can send them up. Have a good Thanksgiving."

"You, too, ma'am."

A few minutes later, Helen and Gabe emerged from their guest room, all showered and looking fine. Then, the elevator doors opened and Alfonso and Brittnee arrived bearing gifts – pumpkin pie and green bean casserole.

"Happy Thanksgiving!"

Hugs and air kisses all around, I could feel this was going to be a fun night.

Helen took the casserole while I grabbed the pie and placed it on the counter.

"What can I get you to drink?" Gabe politely asked.

I thought that was so sweet of him to jump in like that. That's when I knew everyone felt at home.

"What do you need, Diana?" Brittnee asked.

I looked around. For once, everything was on schedule. We had just a few minutes before we would eat. Gabe brought out a selection of beers, wines and champagnes and we each selected our poison. Alfonso cleared his throat. He was going to toast! I was so excited that I didn't have to make the toast. I was the toast-ee! I loved it!

"I just want to say how much I – well, we all, I'm sure – appreciate everything you've done for us these last few months, Diana. You've really affected each of us on such a personal level. You've shown us that dreams can come true and it is possible to find the right people to hang with and to work with. And, inviting Brittnee and me here when we have no family in town is really kind of you."

"Here, here," Brittnee said. "And, may I add, I agree with everything that Alfonso said, that I'm really grateful to be spending time with my new family this year, and…how incomplete this moment is without Jazzy and Pamela."

We all burst out laughing! I loved all the sentiments but I had to admit, Brittnee's comments were a hoot and half, that love/hate relationship with #JP ever present.

Gabe saved the day as he raised his glass.

"Cheers! And Happy Thanksgiving!"

"Happy Thanksgiving!"

I paused for a second to savor the moment, realizing just how much this contrasted with that first Thanksgiving I spent in Las Vegas where the only person in the room I knew was Chris. Now, I know and love everyone in this room. These are my peeps. These are the ones I want to keep in my life forever. The only one missing is Gizzi, but it's so close to her wedding she couldn't tear herself away. Even if she wasn't getting married, she'd probably still spend the holidays with her family. I was always the one invited to her house for special occasions because I was alone.

We had the most magnificent evening, everyone relaxed and having a good time. It was kind of like a housewarming as well as Thanksgiving dinner since this was really the first time I entertained in my new place.

Dinner was followed by more movies and board games. We all laughed so hard my ribs hurt! In spite of the fact that tomorrow we had to be at the mall by 6 a.m. for those early morning shoppers, we didn't get to sleep until after midnight. Helen and her family stayed the night once again but Alfonso and Brittnee headed home before we turned into pumpkins.

In spite of my hectic schedule, I felt it was time to consider what I wanted to buy myself for Christmas. Every year since I was a child, I would always buy something that I could attribute to the holiday, something I knew no one else would get for me, something no one else would even know I would want, even if it was just a book or a tube of lipstick. I had a little bit more petty cash this year so my list of possibilities grew exponentially. Surprisingly, the selection was so important to me that I did manage to find time to think about my gift whenever and wherever I could. And then it hit me.

Now that I was getting settled into *The VLV*, it was time to buy a new car. My fun little Ford Focus had served me well, but it was time to pass it on to someone else and indulge in something fun to park in my garage. I researched extensively for an eco-friendly vehicle that would make me happy. I knew I wouldn't feel comfortable bringing a gas guzzling car onto the property, and while my Focus got excellent gas mileage, it was time to move on up.

Porsche was always my dream car. I coveted that sleek, smooth design from the time I was a teenager, always checking out the new models and hoping that one day I could own one again. When I worked in high tech I drove a used Porsche for a short time but I eventually traded it for a new BMW. I couldn't afford a new Porsche at the time – but now, I could buy a dozen if I wanted to! I hate to sound like Jazzy, but a Porsche actually sounded like a pretty cool Christmas present to myself.

While conducting my research, I discovered the company offered a hybrid in the most luscious amethyst metallic. That was it. I was sold! Unfortunately, the local dealer didn't have one in stock but would work his magic as best he could to get me one before Santa made a visit.

I even found a gorgeous purple leather tote and purple and leopard crystal sunglasses to complete the look. OK, fine. Jazzy isn't the only one to take a diva attitude. Besides, I had to allow myself a little bit of accessorizing, n'est-ce pas?

The purple Porsche hybrid was rare, to be sure, but I was at a rare point in my life and the car would complete my list of treats for the year, perfect for a homeowner at *The Vegan Las Vegas*. Even after I purchased the car, I still had play money in my account, but I wanted to keep a bit in the kitty in the event I decided I needed to jet off to Bali or buy a Warhol. I highly doubted either happening, but the cush in my account made me feel good.

On top of everything else on my plate, I managed to finish reading the *Genesis* Girls book and studied the week-long expose on the syndicated entertainment program. I should have waited until after Gizzi's wedding before I allowed myself to dive into this, but I wanted to be prepared, not only for any questions or comments during the wedding, but also to get my mind rolling on how the three of us Lotto Ladies should respond.

Even though the information appeared to be accurate, the authors spun it in such a way that it almost read like a fiction novel. I reference 'the authors' because I'm not convinced the *Genesis* Girls are capable of putting two words together, let alone penning an entire book.

The *Genesis* Girls admitted to changing names and some of the details so as not to face any legal action. But, the contents of the book didn't bug me. No, my biggest issue was trying to figure out who was behind all of this. The *Genesis* Girls were not intelligent enough to concoct this whole ruse on their own, nor were they skilled enough to implement it even if they had. Having worked with them, I find it difficult to believe they could they have penned the book, hired a publicist, landed an agent and a publisher and manipulated their way to their 15 minutes of fame.

These ladies had obviously been coached on many levels, in addition to having a support team most celebrities would envy. They also had the financial backing to make all this happen, and it didn't come from hawking skin care. Their legal team alone would cost well into five figures if not more. A hater had obviously agreed to protect them if they went along with their dastardly plan. Someone wanted to see Jazzy, Pamela and me suffer but no one was giving up information. I suspect they were forced to sign confidentiality agreements.

I was still trying to determine if we had a case against them, but Kourtney said we were better off just letting this blow over. At some point, probably when the movie airs, the criminal masterminds behind this whole thing will be exposed. And, when they are, I suspect I won't be surprised who it is, but it will still hurt.

And, the book is hurting me in other ways. I really thought I'd disappear into the normalcy of life after our initial press tour when we won Super Duper Millions, but now we're forced to hire a publicist and manage our reputation and opportunities. In the end, probably not a bad idea, but not something I had hoped to be doing. Then again, I also thought my time with the Boopsey Twins was long over and we all know how that's going.

Dear Diary,

I can't believe it's here – Gizzi and Jean-Louis's wedding!

First, we waited for months for him to ask her to marry him. Then we had to wait like the entire year for the wedding – and now it's here!

We had the rehearsal dinner tonight and it was as exquisite as expected. Colin Bailey closed down *La Poisson* in downtown San Jose, right across from the *Moore Hotel*. I'm not a big seafood fan, but they did have chicken on the menu and my lemon chicken was fantastique!

Over 100 people attended the dinner, which was far more than I anticipated, but since the wedding reception would have so many industry folk the bride and groom wanted to host something special for family and friends, remembering to include all those out-of-towners. San Jose has good eats but it's not like Vegas where you can get nearly anything you want at any hour, so including them was very thoughtful.

Gizzi and Jean-Louis are so in love and so loving toward each other. I'm really happy they made it work. I guess when it's right, it's right, and you make time to be together.

We all have to be up at the crack of dawn tomorrow, so we were back in our rooms by 9 p.m. I'm not sure I'll fall asleep at a respectable hour – I'm too excited! This is like the night before Christmas – only better!!!

I was relieved that Abigail behaved herself tonight. She was almost gracious. Maybe she got her meds adjusted. One more day and we can all breathe a sigh of relief, although there still is that Pierre issue…

Gizzi confided in me months ago that she and her soon-to-be hubby will spend an extended honeymoon in France. Considering both of their schedules, I'm sure it won't be so much a vacation as simply a different environment to pull out the laptop and cell phone to conduct business. Neither of them could leave their jobs for very long and still be effective. We're not talking royals or celebrities here. These are real, hard-working people who love what they do in a position that offers little down time.

This will be the first time Gizzi will meet all of JL's extended family and tour the vineyards and the country homes they own. And, I'm sure, guzzle a gallon of Ricard champagne daily.

Ah, tres magnifique!

More tomorrow!

All my heart,

Diana

Gizzi Gets Hitched

{ THIRTY-THREE }

"Morning, Giselle."

"Morning, cheri. Sleep well?"

"Yes. And, you?"

"It's not the same without you next to me."

"Gizzi!"

"Diana! What kind of trick are you trying to pull on my wedding day? I thought you were Jean-Louis."

"I got that. I never call you anything but Gizzi but now that you'll be Mrs. Ricard, I thought maybe I should start calling you Giselle like he does. You know, it's kind of like switching from Kate Middleton to Duchess Catherine."

Gizzi let out a deep, heavy sigh.

"Look, sweetie, I'm not a duchess. I'm not even royalty. I'm just Gizzi, your friend. And, we can keep it that way if you stop calling me Giselle!"

"Well, OK, if you insist. But, you are Silicon Valley royalty. At least for today!"

"Diana, sweetie, I love you, but do me a favor. Go back to bed and wake up on the right side."

"Will do, Giz. I can't wait to see you! I'm so excited I hardly slept last night!"

"Sorry to hear that. I slept like a log."

"Good for you! Do you think it has anything to do with sleeping in your old bedroom?"

Gizzi had a tough time deciding where she wanted to spend the night before her nuptials. She could stay at the *Moore Hotel* with the rest of us, but she traveled so much, she really didn't want to wake up in a hotel room on her wedding day. She might forget why she was there and start rehearsing a presentation.

She also felt a bit weird about staying in her own house. It was her last night as a free woman, but for some reason, being alone didn't seem right either. Sure, I could stay with her, but some of the other bridesmaids might want to join in and that could become uncomfortable – or we could imbibe a little too much alcohol and look and feel terrible the next day.

So, Gizzi did a very beautiful thing and decided to stay with her parents. She was older and successful enough that Daddy wasn't exactly giving her away, but it was probably a very long time since the three of them were able to spend quality time together, and the night before her wedding seemed like the best gift she could give to them.

"Honestly, I think it was the shots of tequila we all did just before lights out."

"You had tequila with your parents? How cool is that! I could never do that with my parents. They'd simply sit me down and try to have a birds and bees talk. No alcohol. Maybe a root beer!"

Gizzi laughed but I could hear a faint knock on the door through the phone.

"I'll be right there, Mom!" Gizzi said.

"Sorry, sweetie. Gotta go. Mom and Dad want me to have a big breakfast since I probably won't have a bite to eat for several hours. Can't have me passing out just before we take our vows now, can we?"

"I don't know. That would make for a pretty good YouTube moment!"

"Oh, Diana, I'm so glad you're my maid of honor. You keep it real for me! See you soon, sweetie."

"Yep! See you in a couple of hours. Have fun!"

Breakfast arrived shortly after I got off the phone with Gizzi, provided as part of Colin Bailey's exquisite treatment of both bridal party and guests. I ate, showered and donned nothing more than my personalized tangerine silk robe and slippers. I grabbed my clutch and room key and headed down the elevator to the luxury buses – one for the men and one for the women – that would take the bridesmaids and ushers to the wedding.

It was a bit strange – Tally, Abigail and the others – together once again. The last time this group gathered privately was at the bachelorette weekend which had such an odd vibe. I was too happy to let anything bring me down right at the moment, and one look at the six of us and I couldn't help but laugh. Proudly wearing our monogrammed robes and matching slippers, we looked like a bunch of overgrown kids heading to spa camp – or princess convicts going to a very minimum security prison.

We arrived in the parking lot of St. Anne's Church, a full three hours before the service. The twelve of us were led into the grade school for our primping, windows covered to keep out prying eyes, ushers at one end of the hall, bridesmaids at the other. I had no idea where Gizzi and JL were getting ready, but they had to be somewhere nearby. The back of the church was too small for a bride to dress, but perhaps the groom. Colin must have a secret space reserved just for them.

The school became a hive of activity as we were surrounded by a bevy of stylists. We each had our own little prep station with a stylist who did hair, makeup and clothing. I couldn't imagine the cost of this team alone!

But, once we were dressed, stilettoed and sprayed with a signature scent created just for the wedding, I felt like a princess. One look in the mirror and I glowed like I never had before, even at my own ceremony. All that hard work at the gym and with the personal trainer paid off. I was toned and sculpted and I looked the best I ever had! Of course, the bronzing paired with the tangerine silk satin tea-length gown might have played a role.

Today was truly a very special day, particularly for Gizzi and Jean-Louis, but I hoped all this pomp and circumstance signaled a turning point in my personal life as well. Unfortunately, I had but one thought on my mind: How to keep away from Pierre.

That thought quickly disappeared when before our very eyes, the most stunning of all women appeared. There was no taking your eyes off the bride. Gizzi looked absolutely radiant! She was always beautiful and well-dressed, but her fashionably classic custom Carolina Wu gown fit her to a tee, showing off her best assets while allowing for easy movement. The lace trim on the bottom of my dress was the exact same as hers, identifying me as the maid of honor and signifying we were friends for life.

I ran up to give her a big hug, but the closer I got, so did the multitude of stylists. We might be friends, but we weren't allowed to touch! So much time and effort was put in to make us look good, we'd have to wait until the wee hours of the wedding to actually show our affection. So, we simply clasped gloved hand to gloved hand and smiled, tears welling up in our eyes. Today was Gizzi's day and she owned it!

We would go straight to the church for the ceremony. The pastor, Fr. Bell, did not allow photos of the happy couple before they were actually married. He thought those photos were a sham, that the only way to convey the true message of marriage was to take photos of an actual married couple. So, the big group shots would have to wait until after the "I do's." Or, in this case, perhaps the "Oui's."

Once the bridesmaid director was given the signal, we lined up, received our bouquets and the six of us were quietly led to the church, ready to walk the aisle. *Pachelbel's Canon* played in the background. As we slowly made our way to the altar, I searched for JL and Pierre, but I couldn't find them. I stepped to the left as I was instructed in rehearsal and took my position. Once I was in place, JL and Pierre stepped out from the side entrance and took their places, Pierre up on the first step behind JL as I was to Gizzi; Jean-Louis, in all his French splendor, at the foot of the altar in wait for his bride.

As the last to enter the church, the doors were closed behind me to build excitement for the bride's entrance. *Here Comes the Bride* began to play, the doors opened, revealing Gizzi and her dad, glowing in the softness of the church light. I took a quick glance at JL whose heart I think actually skipped a beat when he saw her. Ah, true love!

"Who giveth this woman to this man in holy matrimony?" Fr. Bell asked.

"Her mother and I do," Gizzi's dad answered.

Mr. Boudrot then gave Gizzi's hand to Jean-Louis, kissed his daughter gently on the cheek, shook JL's hand then made his way to the pew to sit next to his wife.

When Gizzi arrived at the altar, I took her bouquet and gloves, straightened her veil and gown and exchanged a quick smile. Once back at my perch, I noticed the church was packed to capacity. Looking out on this crowd, the pastor would be wise to pass the collection basket. Given the combined net worth of the attendees, the parish could cover their annual operating expenses in one fell swoop.

Otherwise, there was very little to indicate such a high profile wedding was taking place. Fr. Bell was very strict. No amount of money would sway him from altering the very special way they decorated the church for the Advent season. No decorative touches were allowed. No lights hanging from the century-old ceiling. No flower petals on the runner. No boxed trees lining the aisle. Only flowers at the altar and ribbons on the pews along with a white runner were acceptable. The flash would have to wait for the reception.

As expected, Fr. Antoine, the priest from Jean-Louis's home town, joined Fr. Bell to marry the happy couple. The bride and groom took traditional vows in both English and French – so cute to hear Gizzi agree to love her man in her paternal tongue – and exchange rings blessed by the two priests. There was none of that, "I promise to make you laugh forever" crap, just the simple vows that people have taken forever, including Gizzi's favorite word of today, "asunder."

And, just like that, Gizzi and Jean-Louis were hitched!

After Mass, we spent nearly two hours taking formal photos before we headed back to the *Moore Hotel* for the reception. The church had the most magnificent garden where more informal photos were shot. I still wasn't allowed to hug Gizzi for fear we would damage her gown in any way. We were both frustrated but those important photos would live on forever and we accepted the fact that we'd have the rest of our lives to share affection.

Back at the hotel, we were ushered into a meeting room to undergo a mini-primping prior to the reception. Not only would our faces be touched up, our clothing would get a quick steaming as well to get out all the wrinkles. Upon Colin's cue, we lined up to lead the happy couple into the reception.

And what a glorious reception it was! While the city was dressed up for Christmas, the ballroom was dressed for wedded bliss – splendid, elegant, orange!

Gizzi and Jean-Louis were the wedding of the year in Silicon Valley. Not only were they two of the most powerful leaders in town, they were both gorgeous! Either could easily be deemed the sexiest CEO of the year. Details about the day would be in high demand worldwide, so as a precaution, all attendees were asked to leave their cell phones at home to avoid photo and video leaks of the event.

The wedding was large but elegant and sophisticated. It had to be large – everyone wanted in – accommodating almost 1,000 guests. The only way to avoid such an extravagance would have been to have just a small, private ceremony with family members only. Instead, Gizzi and JL decided this would truly be a moment to remember.

This was the type of wedding where you didn't bring a gift. You were just expected to show up and help the happy couple celebrate. Both had far more money than many in attendance and each had a well-supplied household they were merging, so the invitations were very direct – no gifts, just bring yourself and your good wishes.

Colin Bailey outdid himself with his impressive design for the reception. As a nod to the state of high tech, so symbolic of the region and the industry where the bride and groom each got their start, guests felt like they were walking into a cloud when they entered the ballroom.

Known for his extravagant floral arrangements, Colin enhanced the cloud theme by adding abstract floral laptops, tablets, cell phones, silicon wafers and circuit boards, all done so discretely, you had to really study them to determine the image. For Jean-Louis, there were French country murals "painted" by plant materials and 10-foot high champagne bottles made of flowers. The only other time I'd seen such amazing detail was at the Rose Parade.

But, one can't forget this was a wedding.

After the seemingly endless receiving line, we were treated to a plated dinner of our choice of filet mignon, lobster or my favorite – chicken – followed by the traditional best man and maid of honor toasts. This was the part I dreaded most yet meant the most to me. Pierre would go first, then me and that would be it. So many weddings today left an open mic and toasts went on for hours. This happy couple wanted everyone to enjoy their evening thus limiting the toasts to just two.

Pierre stood up, took the microphone and smiled sneakily at Jean-Louis. I had no idea just what words would spew from his mouth and as he chose to toast in French, neither did most of those in attendance. JL laughed along with Pierre and Gizzi rolled her eyes as he spoke, just adding to the beauty of the moment. Pierre raised his glass, said, "Salut!" and we toasted to whatever words Pierre shared with the happy couple.

Now it was my turn. My toast at the bachelorette weekend was just for us girls. This had to be something more meaningful to the two of them. I spent hours trying to write the perfect toast but I left my notes in my hotel room. There was nothing I could do. I took a deep breath and spoke from the heart.

"Gizzi, Jean-Louis. Today is a very special day for each and everyone one of us, and it's not because of this amazing and elegant wedding. No, today we are joined with the two of you as one, joined as family and friends, all here to celebrate the love that surrounds us. We're here because we bear witness to true love. There is no better feeling in the world than the love that reaches to the depths of your very being, that feeling of calm oneness, of contentment. True love is almost impossible to find, and yet you did. You've shown all of us that we should never give up, that keeping our hearts open can lead to amazing happiness. There's no need to wish you a long and happy marriage. It is yours. No doubt in my mind. But, I thank you, for sharing with us that elusive gem of true love and for allowing us to give the love right back. Oh, and may you have a houseful of kids because I definitely want to be an Aunti!"

We laughed and cheered the bride and groom. Gizzi practically snorted her champagne and once I sat down, we touched shoulders, still banned from any normal physical affection until later in the evening.

After dinner, the bride and groom made their way to the dance floor for their customary first dance. They could have chosen any song they wanted because they didn't have just a band – they had an entire orchestra! And, when the orchestra took a break, a DJ filled in. The music was non-stop for hours.

Toward the end of the reception, the DJ grabbed the mic for that auspicious moment that all single women dread at a wedding – the bouquet toss.

"Gather 'round, single ladies. It's time for our lovely bride to throw the bouquet."

The DJ went around the dance floor, looking for single women of all ages. I was a bit reluctant to join the crowd at first, having been married in the past, but as Gizzi made her way to the front of the stage, we locked eyes and I was certain the bouquet was coming my way. At least, I thought it was until I saw her acknowledge JL's sister in a similar way, and then she looked at Abigail! I took my place to Gizzi's left and down a bit, surrounded by a gaggle of stilettoed techno-glam; JL's sister was to Gizzi's right; Abigail stood front and center. I didn't realize just how many unattached women attended the wedding!

"OK, Mrs. Ricard. On the count of three, give it your best shot."

Gizzi took a quick look behind her, to her right and her left, to decide where she wanted to toss her incredibly gorgeous bouquet of tangerine roses.

"Are you ready, Giselle?" the DJ asked.

Gizzi shook her head.

"All right ladies. Are *you* ready?"

A big "Yes" came from the crowd on the floor. Honestly, I thought they stopped doing this sort of thing. I wonder who began the tradition to have us all here begging to be the one to catch the bouquet, identifying us as the next woman to get married.

"On the count of three. One. Two. Three!"

The drumming contributed to the intensity of the moment, but even though I was excited, I was also a bit blasé. I mean, honestly. I'd already been married. I still hoped for a wonderful man but catching the bouquet was not going to make one moment of difference in my life.

Then, as if in a dream, the sea of Silicon Valley socialites parted as the bouquet landed gently in my arms. It was mine! I could see Abigail skulk off while JL's sister had enough champagne that she didn't really care. I'm not sure they even toss the bouquet in French weddings.

"Well, it looks like our maid of honor, Diana, is the lucky lady tonight. Anyone you want to drop a hint to, Diana?"

I was laughing and shaking my head "No," as Gizzi ran up to give me a big hug. A hug! We were finally allowed to hug!!!

"You're next, sweetie! I know you are."

"Well, I don't know about that, Giz, but I will cherish this regardless!"

Jean-Louis came up and gave me a quick hug and a kiss on the cheek. It was now his turn to throw the garter. A momentary look of shock came across Gizzi's face as she knew what JL had planned. The wedding belonged to the bride but the garter toss was all groom.

Someone brought a chair to the center of the dance floor and Gizzi took her seat. I missed all this silly fun at my wedding; there's not much room for bouquet and garter tossing at the drive-thru wedding chapel.

"Single men. This is your chance. You, too, can find the love of your life. Have Jean-Louis show you how!"

The floor was soon crowded with far more single men than there were women for the bouquet toss. I was amazed at how well some of these former programmers now CEO's cleaned up once they had a bit of extra money at their disposal.

The band began to play a strip tease and Jean-Louis started to prance around his bride, swinging his hips in untold contortions. This was a very private moment for them being played out in front of family, friends and business associates. When Gizzi lifted her gown, several men in the crowd responded as if they'd never seen a woman's thigh before. And, I'm certain, they hadn't. At least not in person.

Jean-Louis was surprisingly agile as in one fell swoop he dropped down to his knees, bit the garter off Gizzi's leg, pulled it down and over her foot, then sprung back up. It was obvious they had practiced this move privately several times to get it right.

The garter was red, white and blue, symbolizing the colors of the flags of both home countries – the U.S. and France. Once Gizzi had given up her garter to JL's adept moves, she stepped aside to let her husband have his moment in the spotlight.

"Come on up here, Mr. Ricard. Turn around and look at that ocean of optimistic men, single men who hope beyond hope to find a woman half as lovely as Giselle. Spot the man you want to pass that hope to. When you're ready, we'll do it on the count of three."

Jean-Louis played along, picking out different men and joking with them. He finally took a deep breath, a quick look to heaven, then turned around.

"All right. We're ready. On three. One. Two. Three!"

The garter went nearly straight up. On its descent, who would run from the sideline to catch it but Pierre! He wasn't even in the crowd. This, too, must have been planned.

"Well, look at that. The best man and the maid of honor are the lucky ones tonight. Diana, if you could join Pierre up here for a photo."

Ugh. My night was going just fine. I'd avoided Pierre as much as possible, only spending time with him when I absolutely had to. I looked amazing today for those all-important photos, but the last one I ever expected to have taken was Pierre and me with bouquet and garter in hand.

I stepped up to the stage. Pierre held out his hand, helped me up and planted a wet one on my face. Naturally, that's the shot the photographer took. It's always about the action shots.

"Here they are, ladies and gentlemen. Perhaps our next happy couple?"

I quietly shook my head no and exited the stage as quickly as possible, heading right for the bar. I did catch the bouquet.

Maybe that was a sign from the Universe that it's time to step up my game and find my man. I could accept that. I was in a much better place now than ever. But, I would never spend my life with that disgusting imbecile. There has to be a country song about how to survive the bouquet toss. I'll mention it to the DJ for his next set.

I took my glass of champagne and perched myself near a wall as far away from the dance floor as I could. I was never a wall flower, and given my current successful life state, there was no reason for me to hide, but I needed a quiet moment to collect my thoughts before I checked in with Gizzi to see if she needed my help with anything. Not that she would. She had Colin Bailey and his staff to handle everything, but sometimes things are a bit personal and you just want your best friend at your side.

I noticed Tarek, his wife, Krissie, and Jonathan and Emanuel with their dates, coming straight at me, drinks in hand. I knew it was inevitable that I would wind up talking to my former clients at some point during the wedding, but at least I was in a much stronger position than at our last encounter. I didn't need them anymore. Still, it was not a conversation I was looking forward to.

"Well, well, well. I suspected you'd show your face here. I know how tight you and Gizzi are."

Tarek must have been appointed spokesperson for the group, but I was surprised he was being so snotty. Must be the alcohol.

"Yes, Gizzi's my best friend. I couldn't think of a better place to be right now."

I nervously spun the ribbon of Gizzi's freshly-caught bouquet in my fingers. I had no reason to be nervous. I never was around these guys. I was one of *them*! They always welcomed me into their group with open arms, laughing and joking and doing great work together. Or, at least we had in the past.

Now I'm off doing my own thing as a Super Duper Millions winner and they're at new start-ups. Funny, they never contacted me to consult with them even though their companies launched months before I won the jackpot. Regardless, now I had as much money in my account as they did, well, probably significantly more. I had no idea why Tarek would be so rude to me; the others remained silent.

"The last time we met was at *Isabella's*."

Tarek paused for effect, to make sure I knew that he knew I worked at *Isabella's* without blatantly calling me out on it. I had to be the laughing stock of the industry thanks to his wife, but Tarek was the only one to tell me to my face.

"My, how things have changed."

"Yes, yes they have. Circumstances have certainly improved, for both of us."

Tarek, clearing his throat replied, "The only difference is we worked for our millions."

Tarek and the group lifted their champagne glasses in a mock toast, turned and walked away.

That comment from Tarek was so unfair. I, too, worked for my millions. I'd like to see him spend week after week dealing with Jazzy! He'd have none of it. If he had to go my route to financial freedom, he would have dropped out long ago. That was a tougher life lesson than being gifted with founder's shares.

I sniffed the fragrant roses in Gizzi's bouquet, a bit in shock, trying to ignore the ingratiating comments from Tarek, instead filling my mind with memories of this happy day, of dreams fulfilled for Gizzi, of the essence of true love. But it was hard to suppress my anger at people who I believed at one point in my life respected me.

I thought Tarek was a friend of sorts. I thought they all were. A client friend, but never someone who would say such mean things to me. We worked together for years until they dropped me like a hot potato for the chance to work with the Martin Heller agency when the economy was in the tank. How fickle people can be.

Just because they made their money through an IPO and I won mine in the lottery doesn't make it any less valuable. I'm doing great things with my newly found funds. I'm proving that

I am worth every single penny I have – and then some! I could never imagine going to them and being as smarmy as they were. It just goes to show you. Money really brings out people's true colors, good or bad.

Just when I was feeling great about myself and my life. Just when I was starting to get my groove back. Just when it seemed like the darkness of the past was finally vanquished forever, Tarek and his buddies had to be cruel, and they had to wait till nearly the end of the wedding to do it. When can I quit reliving my painful past and just focus on a happy future?

I took a deep breath and tried to gather my thoughts. Honestly, it didn't matter what anyone else said or thought. I finally felt comfortable in my own skin. I'd had the best year of my life! I'm financially free. I've started four successful businesses. I've made some great friends. I look better than ever. The only thing missing is someone special to share it with. I know that time will come, too. I've read that you'll find your soul mate when you quit looking. He'll just suddenly be there.

"Diana?"

The man's voice behind me sounded somewhat familiar, but with all the noise from the crowd and the music, I just couldn't be sure. I spun around to face an outstretched hand.

"May I have this dance?"

Acknowledgments

Everything I write is a labor of love, and I truly appreciate all the support of family and friends as I create and edit these books.

I also want to acknowledge the people who inspired me to create the characters that I have in this series. Although they are compilations with much fabrication, the types of feelings and experiences they have are recognizable to the average reader. Searching for love, happiness and success are key components to life and I hope I can offer that journey through my books.

Jake has been an absolute Godsend with his skill and knowledge to finalize the covers and create elegant interiors. Thank you, Jake, and I look forward to your help on many future books.

And, to my readers, your support is so very greatly appreciated. Thank you for coming on this journey with me, to give voice to these stories.

About the Author

Cindi R. Maciolek is entering the fiction world with the release of her first fiction novels, part of **The Diana Diaries** series. The first three books in the series complete the initial story arc, with more books in the series to follow.

Divatiel: Reflections of a bird's companion, is a loving tribute to her fine feathered companion. Through the book, she reaches out to bird and animal lovers about the loving place pets have in our lives and the lessons they teach us.

Poetry and lyrics are a mainstay in Cindi's writing life. She loves to tell a story through rhyme. Her collection of poems published under the title, **Java Jems: 5 Minute Inspirations for Busy People**, both in book form and audio CD/mp3.

Cindi's first foray into the publishing world was the release of **The Basics of Buying Art**. It sold out its printing and is currently unavailable pending an update.

Cindi was a contributing writer to *Luxury Las Vegas Magazine* and *The Robb Report* for many years. She's also had articles published by *Delta Sky Magazine*, the *Old Farmer's Almanac* and syndicated by *The New York Times*.

Cindi was born and raised in Detroit, Michigan, an MSU Spartan for life – Go Green! She worked in high tech marketing and public relations in Silicon Valley and currently resides in Las Vegas, Nevada.

Her travels have taken her to 23 countries in North America, Europe and Asia and most of the United States.

Keep up-to-date with Cindi on her website at www.cindimaciolek.com. Book club questions are also available.

www.ingramcontent.com/pod-product-compliance
Lightning Source LLC
Chambersburg PA
CBHW060142260626
47160CB00001B/82